Freedom of the Waves

A NOVEL

PETER L WARD

ILLUSTRATED BY STEVE CRISP

Order this book online at www.trafford.com
or email orders@trafford.com

Most Trafford titles are also available at major online book retailers.

Printed in the United States of America.

ISBN: 978-1-4669-0946-5 (sc)
ISBN: 978-1-4669-0945-8 (hc)
ISBN: 978-1-4669-0947-2 (e)

Library of Congress Control Number: 2012906335

Trafford rev. 09/12/2012

 www.trafford.com

North America & international
toll-free: 1 888 232 4444 (USA & Canada)
phone: 250 383 6864 ✦ fax: 812 355 4082

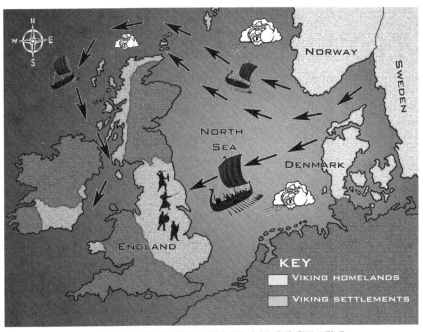

VIKING INVASION OF BRITAIN

About the Author

Peter Ward took his Degree at the University of London (Joint Hons. Botany and Zoology.) He is a former Chief Producer with BBC Education but also produced/directed for prestigious BBC Radio 4, Current Affairs.

He was commissioned by CUP (Cambridge University Press) to write the children's book *The Adventures of Charles Darwin* ISBN 978-0-521- 31074-1. This was re-issued in 2009 and has been translated into several languages, including Japanese and Portuguese.

Peter lives in the beautiful Sussex Weald with his rescued Patterdale Terrier, Pickle. He keeps up a lifetime interest in the Natural World and Conservation matters.

Currently, he sings in two local choirs and composes short vocal pieces for performance.

He has two daughters and two grandsons.

Freedom of the Waves

A Novel

Peter L Ward

Illustrated by Steve Crisp

The first story, *Vimp the Viking's Epic Journey,* has been adapted
into the Musical:

'The Viking's Song – a quest for Freedom'
by
Michael Fields and Peter Ward.

Premiered Joseph Rowntree Theatre, York, UK, February 2012
27th Annual Jorvik Vikings Festival.
Presented by York Archaeological Trust.
www.jorvik-vikingcentre.co.uk

Information: www.peter-ward.net

Reviews

With captivating full-page illustrations and dozens of chapters that all detail epic adventure, this book is ideal for imaginative readers who are young or young at heart. Fans of Norse mythology or those new to it will be delighted by the presence of deities and monsters from ancient times without feeling lost or overwhelmed. The author's pace and language is easy to understand for all readers, with more experienced readers hungrily devouring the texts and the younger audience enjoying every page of the journey. Each story of the trilogy leaves the reader ready to start the next immediately, and once the story has concluded, there is a strong resolution despite a chance for more adventures on the horizon. This trilogy deserves a spot among the other beloved young adult fantasy classics.
The US Review of Books

Vimp the Viking's Epic Voyage
'. . . the first novel in a rollicking Viking Trilogy. Mixing elements of Norse mythology, adventure, cheeky humor, romance and magic, this page-turning read follows a young band of Viking tweens as they try to escape a destiny of violence . . . 'With rich and compelling black and white drawings by Steve Crisp, the books offers an engaging introduction to Viking History . . . adventure with heroic kid appeal.'
blueink REVUE

'Peter L Ward has the makings of a great story here, and Steve Crisp's illustrations nicely complement Ward's book, bringing some of the characters and battles vividly to life.'
Foreword Reviews

'. . . at the heart of this epic voyage is an exciting story about bravery and the many forms it can take, including the choice not to fight. It's also the first book of in a trilogy, so there's time for characters to grow and explore their new surroundings . . . a strong start to what looks like a good series.'
Foreword Reviews

'The next few days of the absconders' lives are filled with a steady stream of demons, serpents, killer fogs, a poisoness purple haze and one angry sea god, all of which keep the pace scooting along and the suspense quotient up in the red zone . . . A flashy adventure tale that's sure to make young readers laugh.'
Kirkus Reviews

Freya and the Fenris-Wolf
'An action-packed plot works well to move the story forward . . . Shifting points of view will keep the readers engaged and invested in a number of storylines . . . Familiarity with Norse mythology or Saxon culture is unnecessary, due to Ward's gift for lively exposition.'
Kirkus Reviews

Ward sustains a consistent authorial voice here; there are big ideas on the table, including the replacement of mythology with Christianity. Various themes are explored without weighting down the story. Characters are well-developed, and settings are described with visual flair . . . . Readers who have come this far will want to read the final volume to see how things end.'
Foreword Reviews

Eric and the Mystical Bear
'. . . the story becomes a high seas adventure to rival Homer's *Odyssey*. The gang encounters sea witches, hostile Norsemen, duelling giants and treacherous mermaids as every chapter brings

a new adventure and a certain brush with death. Both the novel and the trilogy come to a satisfying and complete conclusion, sure to captivate any child with an interest in mythology. Lush settings and exciting adventures make for a read kids will love.'
Kirkus Reviews

'The final volume resolves nicely. The undersea escape itself is a thriller with unexpected twists. Steve Crisp provides great illustrations that capture the grandiosity of the gods as well as the humble domestic moments of village life . . . Amid all the myths and legends there's a sadness running through the story. Loss of home and family are deeply felt . . . Ward is to be commended for creating a series that had improved with each volume, one built around a strong moral center . . . The book serves as a golden-rule message for young readers to absorb.'
Foreword Reviews

Dedicated to Jack Chandler and Louis Dennis.

Also the children of
Mottingham Primary School, Bromley, UK,
1991 - 2000

Contents

PART 1

Vimp
the Viking's
Epic Voyage

CHAPTER 1

How Vimp Got His Name

The quiet waters of the sea lapped lazily at weed stranded on the shore. Across the bay, only the merest ripple disturbed the surface. But beyond, a formidable range of mountains frowned down from craggy summits. Eagles patrolled steep slopes, snatched suddenly upwards by air currents rising from meadows far below.

There was hardly a breath of wind on the cool air. A tall young Viking stood arms folded, fair hair falling over his shoulders. Vimp gazed across the estuary trying to imagine the Gods glowering down.

It seemed this morning that all was at peace. Yet in the middle of the night Thor, God of Thunder, had woken from his restless slumbers. White lightning crackled over his mountaintop kingdom, dazzling the rocky cliffs. Thor's mighty voice boomed out. He smote his anvil with the colossal hammer forged in his furnace. The blow thundered across the night sky.

Vimp had spent the night trembling in the shared straw bed on the floor of his family's hut. He was anxious about the God's bad mood. Perhaps Thor had been insulted by another God? He was known to have a prickly temper. If that was so, humans too would have to be on guard. These included the simple villagers living in the fishing hamlets on the estuary.

Tucked under animal skins with his younger brothers, Vimp had lain awake for hours. His brothers never stirred, sleeping soundly through the storm in the mountains across the bay. Vimp felt sure that the great Thor was sending a message that something awful would befall the innocent Viking folk.

Tossing and turning, Vimp detected a slender shaft of dawn light through the narrow gap between curtain and outer wall. As the sun crept over the mountain peaks, he finally dozed off, knowing that he had important work to do in the morning.

His head felt fuzzy when he awoke. To his relief, the morning passed without incident. Thor was saving the thunder for his rival Gods. In the Viking settlement by the sea, people went peacefully about their work. Young boys herded their cows to day pastures whilst shepherds kept a wary eye out for wolves prowling behind boulders. Village mothers with children fed hens squawking and clucking around the safety of the huts. It had been a perfectly ordinary morning. Now, staring out over the bay, Vimp's thoughts went to the boat he and his friends were building. It was starting to take shape and would soon be completed. The young apprentices were proud of their achievement. It was to be the funeral ship of the Old Chieftain.

A call went up from the forest beyond the pastures. A hunting horn? There it was again. Short, sharp, and plaintive. Evidence that the Chief and his huntsmen were back from the chase. They had roamed the forest for days and the villagers eagerly looked forward to the game they would bring home. The people expected to celebrate, and mouths watered at the prospect of fresh meat.

Harald Strongaxe had led his hunters into the forest. He was the new Chieftain of the Viking settlement. His father, the old Chieftain, had grown frail and would soon die. The old Chief's grave illness was a reason why Vimp and his ship-building friends were so determined to finish their vessel. The brand new ship was destined never to sail, for it had been designed to be his funeral boat. After his death, the body would be placed in it and buried under a high mound outside the village.

The hunting horn sounded a third time. Nearer this time. Children broke off from simple games and scampered over to the trees. Some of them had not seen their fathers for a week. Vimp turned to see riders emerge from the forest. Burly, bearded men rode their horses across the marshy meadow.

Harald Strongaxe struggled with his steed as the children ran towards him. Older villagers ran up, having cast aside their tools or nets. They saw the long faces of the Chieftain and his men. The crowd quietened when they saw the hunters had returned empty handed. Harald faced them with his piercing blue eyes.

'No deer!' he shouted. 'We hunted high and low.'

He gestured towards a net of dead hares dangling from the side of an old mare. 'A few overgrown rabbits to show for our efforts. What's happened to the forest? The deer have deserted the trees for the higher ground. We searched the slopes, but never a sign.'

A low moan of disappointment swept through the villagers. They turned to trudge back to work. Harald Strongaxe had let them down. He gathered his reins and rode towards the huts on the outskirts of the settlement. With a curse, he hurled his hunting horn high into the air.

'It's useless. There's a curse cast upon it.'

The horn landed on the village rubbish tip, narrowly missing a starving dog searching for fish heads and bones. A large woman ran up to the Chief. She had a pinned shawl around her shoulders and gesticulated with round, red arms.

'You've done your best, Harald. So have all the men. Ride over to the communal hut. We'll serve you a hot supper. We've got fish entrails for soup. And cod on the boil, fresh caught this morning.'

Harald and his men glanced at each other uneasily. They did not want to appear ungrateful now that they had let down the villagers.

5

'If you prefer,' the woman went on, 'there's mackerel grilled on charcoal.'

Harald tried to hide his disappointment. He had hoped to bring a change to the villagers' boring diet of fish. That was the whole point of going off to the forest. With no venison, fish remained the only choice. A huntsman rode up alongside Harald's horse and whispered to the Chieftain.

'My wife's always going on about fish. Says it's good for the brain. But where's the sense in that? Fish are so stupid they don't have brains like us. If they did, we'd never catch them!'

Harald agreed. Reluctantly, he turned back to his men and ordered them to follow him. Standing at the back of the crowd, Vimp sympathised with the hunters, but he was secretly glad that no deer had been killed. To him, they looked such noble creatures. They were better left to roam the forest glades in freedom. He wandered back towards the huts, where his attention was drawn to the dog that had been struck by the Chieftain's hunting horn. It was a mangy looking cur, long legged with coarse brown hair. No-one owned it so it skulked around the huts seeking scraps.

The rubbish dump was set at the outskirts of the village and positioned so the wind carried its stench out to sea. As Vimp approached, the dog slid behind a rotting mound of vegetables. Vimp gulped as he took in his first breath of bad air but summoned up courage, working his way through the garbage. It was not long before he detected what he was seeking. Chieftain Harald's discarded hunting horn lay where it had landed. The young Viking bent down, picking off the remains of dead fish and extracting a small slug trying to slime down the blow hole.

Vimp had always wanted to play a musical instrument but his parents insisted on giving him mock weapons for his birthdays. He was too old for wooden swords and not interested in fighting. As the Chieftain had thrown away the horn Vimp thought he would take it home and try it out.

He stepped cautiously over the muck and angered a cloud of flies that buzzed around his head. He was only too glad to get away. Tucking the hunting horn into his leather belt, Vimp headed for the huts. Smoke drifted from small fires where cooking stones were being heated for supper. He watched an old woman struggle up to her fire with a heavy cauldron of water. She hooked it over a tripod made of sticks. It did not strike Vimp to help her. The woman was strong and fit, and like any other male Viking he considered cooking was women's work.

'Hey, Vimp!'

A cheery voice called from the shade of the nearest hut. He recognised it at once. It was his friend Lief, sitting on an outside lavatory.

'I'm trying to think up a new Viking legend,' he said casually. 'The old ones have been around for such a long time. Sitting here is where I get all my ideas.'

His expression turned serious. 'Can you help me? I'm stuck. I need a word that rhymes with *hnelfatalf,* but nothing springs to mind.'

Vimp shook his head.

'It's no use asking me. I'm no poet. I'm an apprentice shipbuilder. We leave reading and writing to you.'

Lief pulled a long face and stood up from the bench.

'I've been ordered to work on your funeral ship. The poor old Chief's on his last legs and the Head Family's worried he'll die before you can finish it. Imagine me handling a mallet.'

Vimp grinned.

'We'll give you a saw,' he said, wickedly. 'Except you'll cut off your hand. Then we shan't have to suffer any more of your poetry.'

It was bit unkind and he did not really mean it. Lief opened the wicker gate and joined his friend.

'I heard something really strange but didn't know whether to believe it. My older brother, who's fought in Saxon England, told me about the last raid. Said it was a complete disaster. His crew were out at sea and ready to row up a creek as the tide turned. All of a sudden, on the far bank, there was a burst of flame. It was a piled beacon of sticks and branches. The boat entered the creek and approached a Saxon village. Ripe for plunder. They expected a good haul of treasure from the monastery up on the hill.'

Vimp frowned. The idea of raids did not impress him.

'So what happened?' he asked, dreading a tale of savagery.

'Well, you know what my brother Thorvald's like. Always exaggerating. He said when they landed the village was deserted. Not even a cat or dog was left in the place. As for the people, they'd already fled with half their belongings.'

Vimp frowned. He had heard rumours of the trip.

'When Thorvald's crew jumped off the boat,' Lief continued, 'they spotted fresh hoof prints and cart tracks heading for the forest. But they didn't follow as they feared a Saxon ambush. They're fierce fighters.'

'Yes,' Vimp said. 'I remember. They were the raiding party that returned with almost no loot. The Chieftain was furious. Before they left Saxon England they torched the village.'

Lief nodded. He bent down to pick up a slate by the side of the path. It might come in useful for writing his next poem.

'Thorvald helped set fire to the first hut,' he said. 'Pure revenge. But you can't blame the Saxons for fleeing. What would you do to save your family? The big puzzle is how they knew our crew was about to strike.'

To Vimp the answer was obvious.

'You said they lit a beacon. That was their warning signal.'

His friend agreed.

'Exactly! But our raiders discovered one Saxon who was too old to escape. He was hiding under a hay stack. They dragged him out and he said his fellow villagers had got wind of the boat as it stole along the coast. Said the lookout on the shore could *smell* the sweat of the men rowing! So they set light to the beacon to raise the alarm. The villagers got out quick.'

The two boys looked at each other, wriggled their noses, and sniffed. Vimp pulled a face and grinned.

'It can't be true. Saxon stories. They don't like us. Surely we don't smell that bad?'

Vimp bade his friend good-bye and went on his way. He fingered the hunting horn as he trudged home. It was still attached to its strap so he slung it over his shoulder. He recognised his own hut by the pile of logs stacked outside. Pushing aside the heavy leather curtain, he entered his simple home. His mother, Eggtooth the Unlovely, looked up from her low stool by the fire.

Vimp remembered the horn he had rescued from the rubbish dump. He put it to his lips, took a deep breath, and blew hard. The sound he produced was dreadful. His mother, imagining that Vimp was choking, threw herself through the heavy curtain and thumped his back. She beat him so hard he begged for mercy.

'What's that horrible noise?' she complained. Then she spotted the horn lying on the floor.

'Get rid of that thing. If there's anything I can't stand, it's music. No son of mine will ever become a musician. Our family would never live down the shame!'

She grabbed Vimp by the ear and hurled him through the curtain. He rolled over, ending up at the feet of his friend. The young poet laughed.

'You're weird, Vimp. I'll never make you out. You're different!'

Vimp glanced up unhappily.

'Thanks! Friends like you I don't need.'

He picked himself up then ducked as the horn sailed close over his head.

'I told you to take that disgusting thing with you,' his mother shouted. 'Don't come back until supper's ready. Salted cod, followed by boiled haddock for dessert.'

Eggtooth turned back to her curtain.

'Don't be late!' she shouted over her shoulder.

Vimp shot his friend an embarrassed glance. He retrieved the horn and cast an eye over it for damage.

'I'll find out how to play this if it kills me,' he promised.

After his fish supper, Vimp struggled into bed alongside his brothers – a thin pile of flea-ridden straw on the dirt floor. There were no goodnight stories. His mother was in a rotten mood. She even refused to tell Viking tales to frighten the younger boys to sleep.

Vimp was very unhappy with his name. He had heard that when he was younger he had a perfectly ordinary Viking name, but now had no idea what it was. For as long as he could remember his parents had called him Vimp. It was his father, Eggbreath's, idea. One of the very few ideas Eggbreath had ever had.

'As far as I'm concerned,' Eggbreath told his wife, 'he's a complete vimp! He's never rude to people and I've even heard words like 'please' and 'thank you.' He's a disgrace to our race.'

'Vimp?' she mused with a toothless grin. 'You've got it in one, my husband. Vimp's a perfect name for the boy. Let us call him Vimp the Viking. Our own son, who only last week helped a wounded warrior off a raiding boat. He carried half his loot back to his hut and didn't have the sense to take any for himself or his family.'

Eggbreath the Unpleasant tossed back his brutish head and drained his bowl of beer. He was one of the village's foremost warriors; a Norse legend in his lifetime. The most celebrated Viking poet of the day had composed a heroic ode in his honour:

Eggbreath, oh dreaded Eggbreath, how greatly you are feared,
Your enemies run before you once they've smelled your beard.
Eggbreath, oh dreaded Eggbreath, your name the very word,
Makes Anglo-Saxons shiver
And very, very scared!

His especially fine poem had won first prize at the Annual Goathland Festival, later to be passed down Viking generations.

Parents frightened their children to bed with the awesome threat:

'If you don't go to bed this minute, old Eggbreath will steal in when it's dark and <u>breathe</u> on you!'

The great warrior had defeated his fellow competitors in the *All-Viking Bad Breath Championships,* five years running. Even battle-hardened teenagers trembled at the thought of being breathed on by Eggbreath in the small hours of the night. But it was all threat. After a dozen or so bowls of his wife's gruesome beer he slumped to the floor, snored, and slept for two days. Eggbreath was not capable of frightening a baby! His wife surveyed her brood in the dull glow of the dying embers of the fire. She was proud of them, knowing they would turn out to be proper Vikings. They were likely to grow up every bit as horrible as their parents. Eggtooth had done her best to raise an unhealthy brood of disgracefully behaved boys. And it filled her hard heart with joy!

She captured a large flea from her arm and examined it closely between her fingers. Her expression darkened.

'I don't know what will become of that Vimp. Only the other day, he said he wanted to travel to Saxon England to become a Christian monk. And went on about learning to read and write!'

She crushed the flea between finger and thumb.

'Sometimes I think that boy wants his head examining,' she grumbled. 'Vimp's a great worry to us, my husband.'

CHAPTER 2

The Maid in the Forest

Next morning, Vimp woke to sounds of shouting and banging outside the hut. He blinked sleepily in the growing light of dawn. His brother, Eggenuff, turned over, grunted and clasped his hands to his ears.

Vimp crawled out from under the bearskin and peeped outside. Small groups of men hurried to the shore, where a large boat was tied to a jetty. On board, a broad-shouldered man stood by the mast shouting orders. The sailors struggled up the gangplank carrying heavy loads on their shoulders.

Quickly pulling on his coarse leather sandals, Vimp slipped outside. He stumbled upon the horn lying on the spot where his mother had hurled it. Almost without thinking, he picked it up and snaked between the huts. The boat was due to sail on the morning tide. If any of the crew were missing the captain might order a search of the village. Boys of Vimp's age could be grabbed and dragged on board. They often ended up getting killed or wounded on overseas raids.

Clear of the village, Vimp stumbled towards the forest through the low-lying mist. He kept his head down, dodging behind cows grazing in the wet grass. They turned their heads as the young Viking made for the safety of the trees.

Vimp knew some of the secret places of the forest. Looking back to make sure he had not been followed, he ran lightly along a winding path until he reached a hidden glade. Here, he laid up for a few hours. The sounds of the village faded as he became aware of a sweeter sound drifting through the forest. It seemed to call him and he stepped into the grassy glade, surrounded by dark trees. Vimp had heard such thoughts in his dreams and believed it might be called 'music'. As his mother had forbidden her family to play or sing music, it was hard to know exactly what it was really meant to sound like.

Vimp took a few more steps onto the grass, his feet soaked with morning dew. He felt sure that the enchanting sound came from beyond a small bush with white blossoms. Dropping onto all fours, he crawled forward to discover a girl of about his own age sitting on an old tree stump. She swung her legs and wore a long, blue dress supported by straps. Flaxen hair tumbled over her shoulders and on one bare arm she displayed a gold bangle.

The young Viking knelt down, entranced by the beauty of the maiden, who sang a bewitching melody. As he watched, a flock of finches swooped across the glade and gathered round her feet. He was startled when a ring dove flew down to perch on his shoulder. This attracted the girl's attention, and she stopped singing, startled to see an intruder in her secret part of the forest.

'Who are you?' she asked. 'Why are you here?'

The dove took off from Vimp's shoulder and alighted on the girl's outstretched arm. He struggled to his feet as she stared at him with pale blue eyes. He was embarrassed, hardly knowing what to say.

'I'm sorry,' he stuttered. 'I've . . . run from the village. The raiding boat sails on the next tide and I don't want to be on it. I didn't mean to disturb you but couldn't help hearing you singing.'

Vimp looked down at his feet, shyly, and fingered the cow horn. The girl rose from the stump where she had been sitting.

'Give it to me.'

She spoke calmly and Vimp did as asked. He handed her the horn which she put it to her lips. Then she took in a breath and the sound she made was deep and beautiful. The Viking boy stood rooted to the spot. Suddenly, she stopped.

'I asked who you are. Haven't I seen you in the village? You must have a name.'

Vimp was ashamed of the unkind nickname his parents had given him.

'They call me Vimp,' he mumbled. 'Son of Eggbreath the Unpleasant and Eggtooth the Unlovely.'

His face flushed with embarrassment but the girl smiled. It gave him confidence.

'My name is Freya. I come to the forest to be with my wild creatures.' As she spoke, a shy deer with tiny antlers slipped into the glade. 'They're attracted to the sound of your horn,' Freya told him. 'It's a lovely instrument. I could call up wolves if I wanted to.'

Vimp shuddered, suspecting dark shadows slinking through the trees.

'Do not be afraid, son of the warrior Eggbreath,' she said. 'You are safe with me here. No wild creature will harm you.'

Vimp kept a wary eye on the shadows.

'I don't think I'm afraid. How could I be when I hear such wonderful music?'

He looked into the sweet face of the maiden. He'd seen her in the village, but only at a distance. It was her name that most puzzled him.

'Freya,' he said. 'Where have I heard your name before? Is it somewhere in a tale? Or maybe in a legend my grandmother used to recite?'

The girl did not answer. Vimp looked into her pale blue eyes and knew he was already under her gentle spell.

CHAPTER 3

Freya's Wild Idea

Vimp was back at work as one of a group of apprentices – young carpenters learning their trade. They were building the old Chieftain's funeral boat. The former Chieftain of the village had been seriously ill for weeks. Rolf, Slayer of Serpents, had lost the will to live. Getting the vessel ready in time for his funeral was almost impossible.It had to be finished before the old man passed away. Older village shipwrights repairing nearby long boats shouted rude comments.

'You wouldn't catch me going to sea with that bunch building it,' said one. 'It would fill up with water and sink before you could say "fish paste"!'

His bearded friends laughed, pouring scorn upon the young apprentices. Ulf Blacktooth, a fearsome looking ruffian, folded his arms across his broad chest and let out a beery belch.

'It's a good thing it's never going to sea. That useless tub will turn over the moment the first big wave hit it. Except,' he added, 'it'll never happen.'

The youngsters took no notice and hammered away to drown out the insults. Vimp turned to his friend Lief, newly recruited to the job, who was trying to chip out a groove with a sharp chisel. He was hopeless.

'Let me do that for you, Lief,' he suggested.

The young poet looked up gratefully.

'I'm no good with my hands,' he agreed, then sighed and mopped beads of sweat from his brow.

Vimp felt sorry for Lief. The sun was dipping fast over the bay, and the supervisor got ready to tell the boys to pack up. The two friends were joined by Bjorne Strawhead, a lad whose family had lived in the village for generations. Bjorne was a buoyant character who never let things get him down.

'I really wanted to answer back, just now,' he told the others. 'Those oafs stop work every afternoon to have a go at us. They're so stupid. What's the point of telling you that a boat isn't seaworthy when it's never meant to sail?'

It was a fair point. It seemed such a waste – all those trees cut down from the forest, not to mention the young shipwrights' efforts.

'D'you know what I've heard?' Bjorn went on. 'They'll lay his body in this boat and slaughter his best horse to lie with him. A waste of a good horse. Then they'll bury the Chief's helmet and his weapons. All in this funeral boat to be covered with earth. If I ever make it to village chieftain they don't bury my cow horn in *my* funeral boat.'

Lief could not help laughing.

'Your chances of receiving a big Viking burial are about the same as me being made the Bard of Skagernak.'

Bjorn and Vimp laughed. Vimp had no intention of becoming a fighter and secretly hoped he'd spend the rest of his life building boats. Wishing his apprentice friends a safe night he trudged home. When he reached the family hut he pushed open the entrance curtain. His eyes stung in the cooking smoke, and through the gloom he could just about make out his brothers' grimy faces. They looked up hungrily as Eggtooth stirred a pot containing the evening meal.

'There you are, at last,' she croaked. 'Where've you been all this time?'

She dredged her spoon slowly through her foul stew. Vimp stood at the hut entrance. His mother peered up at him through the tangled locks of her greasy hair. Smiling a toothless grin, she instructed one of her brood to fetch the wooden platters.

'There's a change of menu tonight,' she said. 'Just for once it's not fish. Your little brothers came back with a couple of warty toads. It's not often we get our hands on such fancy food!'

Vimp looked on in horror as his mother dished out the slimy remains of unfortunate amphibians. The jellied remains of an eye floated in olive green gravy.

'Take this knife,' she ordered the boys, 'and divide the toad skin between you. There's plenty of juice. Leave the flesh for your father. It'll be like his birthday. He loves his dish of toad!'

Vimp felt sick. He pulled back the curtain and stepped outside.

'My family likes disgusting food,' he muttered. 'What's wrong with fruits, and nuts and berries from the forest? They're delicious if you know which ones to pick.'

He threaded his way past tightly packed huts to the stream that flowed out to the cove. As he drew nearer to the shoreline, Vimp was aware of a slight figure on the path some way ahead of him. Almost at once, he sensed who it was and increased his pace. Freya turned and ran towards him. She was as pleased to see him as he was to see her.

'I knew you'd come,' she cried breathlessly. 'My grandmother says I possess a sixth sense. I'd love to know what it means.'

The young Vikings picked their way along the banks of the running stream, following it to the point where it flowed into the sea. Freya darted onto the muddy beach and danced in the shallow water. She turned and called to Vimp to join her. Together, they ran along the edge of the shore, splashing in the tiny waves. The old Chieftain's granddaughter skipped back to the sand where her foot marks filled with water. Vimp tossed his long hair in the breeze and followed.

Heading for a bold outcrop of rocks, Freya leapt to the top like a mountain goat. She sat and gazed over the wide waters of the bay. Vimp joined her. A trading ship lowering its rust red sail approached the harbour, using the light wind. Freya brushed away strands of hair blowing across her face and delved into a bag hanging at her side. She pulled out two apples.

'I've had an idea,' she said and bit into her apple. 'Since I tried to make music on your old cow horn I've been thinking that we should start a . . . "

She glanced at Vimp nervously.

'Well,' she went on, 'I suppose we could call it a *band*. Like a band of brothers, except we'd invite our friends. Of course, I hardly know any boys. I certainly wouldn't want my brothers to join. But a few of my girl friends might want to join. Some of them like singing. So I think they're musical.'

Vimp sat tight on the exposed rock and followed the course of the trading boat as its crew pulled for the shore. The young Viking pondered over his friend's strange suggestion.

'I expect most of my shipwright mates can dig out an old cow horn knocking somewhere around their huts. But I don't know if they'd be interested. They're a bit rough. You should hear their language when they bash their thumbs with a hammer. I don't think your friends would like them. They're too posh!'

Freya turned on Vimp. A flash of anger sparked in her eyes.

'We don't think like that. Just because I'm a member of the Chieftain's family doesn't make me better than you!'

She picked up a pebble and tossed it into the waves lapping at the foot of the rock. Vimp blushed.

'Of course you're better than I am,' he said humbly. 'Everyone in our village knows his own place. Our family's way down the order. You're lucky, because you're the top family and your father's Harald Strongaxe, our new High Chieftain. I'm not fit to step into his footprints in the mud!'

Freya sprang from her sitting place. She lifted her tanned face to the sun setting over the headland.

'How can you say that? All that stuff's out of date!'

The sinking sun sent a rippled reflection over the shimmering sea. Freya remained on her feet.

'You don't really know my friends so you can't speak for them. Anyway, my best friend Emma is our family slave. She's Saxon and was captured on one of my father's raids on the English coast. In her own country, she belonged to an important family. Now, she has to do all the dirty jobs around our hut. But that doesn't change who she is. She's kind to my grandfather.'

Freya dropped her eyes and looked thoughtful.

'I expect you know he's dying.'

The young Vikings sat in silence. Then Freya rose slowly and grasped Vimp by the hand. She helped him to his feet.

'We must go. My parents will kill me!'

Picking her way down the rock she jumped onto the beach.

'The tide's turned. Think about what I told you. I just *know* that young people are musical. You should hear my Emma sing. In Saxon England, she played a stringed instrument. We'll soon have a brilliant band, and everyone in the village will come and listen to us!'

Vimp was not so sure, unable to imagine his family showing even the slightest interest. In fact, he feared Eggbreath would say performing music was 'wimpish'.

'Go back and talk to your friends,' Freya told him. 'I'll ask around mine. We've got to do something to liven things up in this village. We can arrange concerts and dances!'

Vimp and Freya found their way home in the gathering darkness with hardly a word between them. The young boy had the feeling that Freya was somebody special. Even so, he dreaded putting her wild idea to his rough shipbuilding friends.

CHAPTER 4

Concert at the Thing

The boys took a lot of persuading. The notion of learning to play music did not go down well, but Lief sparked their interest by cleverly pointing out they'd be meeting girls. Suddenly it seemed like a good idea, even better than kicking an inflated pig's bladder around the village.

At last, the building of the boat was completed. Even the hard taskmaster Tharg Thugfellow had to admit he was pleased with the result.

'You lads have earned a few days off,' he told the apprentices. 'Go and enjoy yourselves. Make the most of it, because it'll soon be time to learn how to fight. If you think boat-building's hard work, then just wait until you're told to report for warrior training!'

The boys tried hard not to think about it. They simply did not want to kill people, not even Anglo-Saxons.

Next morning they met at the boat. After giving it a few, final admiring glances, they went off to the forest to meet Freya and her friends. One or two passers-by enquired where they were heading, but Vimp told them they were off hunting. As none of the boys carried weapons it did not sound very convincing.

Once they had reached the trees the apprentices filed along a single track. Thord Bony Knees felt uneasy. Never in his life had he ventured so deep into the wood.

'It's spooky,' he whispered to the lad in front. 'Gives me the creeps.'

The group ploughed on, beginning to lose faith in Vimp's sense of direction. Suddenly, sweet sounds filled the air. He signalled to the party to halt.

The unnerving sounds swirled around the boys' heads, a gentle piping echoing amongst the trees. The party moved forward, unable to resist the summons. As they wound through the wood, the path led to a sunny space deep in the heart of the forest, where flowers sparkled amongst the grasses.

On the far side of the glade, a small group of girls sat in a circle with Freya directing from the front. The boys stood awestruck. When she had finished, Freya turned to welcome them.

'Join us.'

Some of the girls giggled but made room for the uneasy ship-wrights to sit with them. The first music lesson began but the sound they made was awful. However, they stuck to their task as it was a matter of pride. After three more days' hard work, the boys showed signs of progress. Her instruction was successful mainly because she employed her magical powers. Before long, she had nearly all the boys playing like angels.

'You're so good!' Freya told them. 'Well done for working so hard. I've got news. We're going to give a concert.'

The boys were shocked. They had not expected to play in public. Freya told them they'd be playing in a concert at The Thing, the outdoor meeting place in the village. This was where Viking people gathered to discuss village matters and speak their minds. Lief designed public notices in Viking runes and pinned them up on the huts:

Music at the Thing
Freya's Cowhorn Band
Frigg's Day before sunset

Vimp had not the heart to remind Lief that almost no one could read. Frig's Day arrived. Late in the afternoon, shadows grew longer as the sun set over the tops of the trees. Freya assembled her band on the mound of earth known as The Thing. The youngsters were nervous when they glanced down at the audience of expectant faces. It seemed that most of the village had come along, but it was difficult to know if they had come to listen to the music or out of curiosity. Vimp spotted his own family near the back of the crowd. The vulgar Eggtooth scowled and husband Eggbreath swayed drunkenly with two small, scruffy boys perched on his shoulders.

In contrast, the gracious Freya stepped forward, smiled to the gathered people, and signalled to her band to take up their instruments. As Freya raised her arms, they took in deep breaths and placed the cow horns to their lips. The concert began in the last rays of the setting sun, and the sounds they made silenced the crowd's chatter. For a moment or two, the young musicians held the audience spellbound. But the magic did not last long.

The first rotten cabbage missed Big Eric's nose. But only just. It was tossed from the back where a rowdy bunch of pig's bladder kickers had collected. Lief was the next target. He staggered and lost his balance as a large lump of cow dung struck him in the eye. Then a clump of rotten swedes sent Ingrid and Astrid tumbling. Vimp manfully carried on through the attack doing his best to follow Freya's increasingly panicky directions. But he had to duck as a sheep bone hit him on the ear.

The startled musicians wavered under a salvo of apples and rotten eggs. It was the best entertainment the villagers had enjoyed in years. Better than the All-Norseland Belching Championship when the winner's burps echoed back across the bay. Vimp stepped forward and grabbed Freya by the hand.

'Run!' he yelled. 'We can't stay here!'

The band broke up in panic as a volley of turnips felled the front row of horn players. Vimp and Freya fled for the safety of the dying old Chieftain's hut. They threw themselves inside to find Freya's grandmother sitting on a stool, weeping. She was being comforted by Emma, the family's English slave. The old lady looked up. Her body shook as tears trickled down her cheeks.

'Freya, my child,' she sobbed, 'your grandfather's breathed his last. He passed away earlier this evening.'

The bereaved wife of the old Chieftain dabbed her failing eyes as her granddaughter struggled to take in the sad news.

Chapter 5

Warrior Training

Shifting the stains of rotten vegetables, bad eggs, and cow dung from his clothes and skin was just about the nastiest thing Vimp had ever done. He and Lief stood up to their knees in the chilly waters of a stream.

'I'm so cross,' Lief said, 'that I feel a strong poem coming on. I've been trying to think of words that rhyme with "filthy", "stinking", "louts", "ignorant", and "obnoxious", and I'm having particular difficulty with the last word. When it's complete, I'll read my poem out loud at the next meeting at The Thing. I'm so disgusted with the behaviour of the people of our village. No wonder Vikings have such a bad name!'

Vimp tipped icy water over his head. Inside he was fuming. What should have been entertainment had been ruined. The wreckers had planned to spoil things from the start. He did not look forward to going home to the sneers of his family. But curiously, they did not try anything on. They were embarrassed by his display of true musical talent that they didn't know how to handle it. So the family chose to pretend it had never happened.

Next morning, Vimp woke up early and scrambled out of bed. It was the first day of Warrior Training and the boys had been ordered to report to the village Weapons Centre. The encampment was shrouded in grey mist. As Vimp wound his way between the huts he became aware of other figures heading

in the same direction, huddled against the damp and cold. The shipwright apprentices met up in twos and threes, but no one spoke as they feared the grim day ahead. And they were correct. Outside the Weapons Centre stood the most feared warrior of all. The boys trembled at the gigantic figure of Olaf Skullcrusher, a legend in his own lifetime. Olaf towered over the motley crew, his dark eyes blazing through the visor of his war helmet.

In one gnarled fist, he gripped an iron sword. In the other, he grasped a mighty wooden club whose name was known to all the villagers. This was 'Nutcracker' and Olaf boasted that more than two hundred enemies had fallen to its ferocious swing. This was curious, as he could not count. And he generally forgot to mention that most of his victims were peaceful farmers who had only been trying to protect themselves.

Olaf had a particular hatred of the Saxon English peoples on the other side of the sea. He had plundered many a coastal village and regularly returned to the Land of the Vikings burdened with treasure. He surveyed the miserable bunch of apprentices cringing at his feet.

'You're late!' he thundered, raising his bushy eyebrows.

This was not true. If anything, the boys were early.

'That means no lunch break,' he continued. 'If there's anything I can't abide it's lazy varmints who can't get out of bed on time. No lunch, I say!'

He thrust his sword into its massive sheath and grabbed a chicken leg from a bag tied round his middle. To the horror of the watching boys he devoured it whole, bones and all.

'Now!' he said, spitting odd bits of chicken over the front row of recruits and wiping his greasy hand on his orange beard. 'Follow me and I'll learn you your first lesson.'

Lief thought of correcting Olaf's language then thought better of it.

The warrior turned and marched across the fields to the edge of the sea. A tied up raider boat, long and sleek, rose and fell on the swell of waves lapping at the jetty.

'Jump aboard, now. Look lively!'

Olaf whirled the club over his head and the unhappy boys took the hint. The giant stepped on the deck, causing the boat to dip dangerously to one side. It steadied as he made his way to the mast.

'Get up on the starboard side,' he ordered. 'Face the water and be ready to jump. Wait for the count. Last one off's a sissy!'

The anxious apprentices clambered up on the gunwales of the boat as Olaf moved over to the port side to balance it up.

'Well?' he said, glaring at his trainee warriors. 'You heard what I said. On the count of . . . '

He paused and looked puzzled.

' . . . whatever comes after two. Swim to that rock beyond the boat. Go right round it and come back. Ready?'

Near panic broke out amongst the apprentices.

'I can't swim!' Eric Bignose wailed. 'I'll drown and my mum will be ever so cross!'

The giant's eyes rolled in disbelief in their deep, bony sockets.

'Can't swim, did I hear?' he mocked. 'Now's your chance. What's the use of a Viking raider who can't jump off his boat when it approaches an enemy beach? He won't have his mummy with him then, will he?'

He started the count.

'One . . . '

He paused, straining.

'Er . . . two . . . '

Another pause, this time longer.

'Er . . . '

Olaf removed his tight-fitting helmet to give his brain more space to work in, but no inspiration came. After a few more agonising seconds, he cancelled the swimming activity.

'Forget it,' he snapped and ordered the boys off the boat. 'See that pile of logs at the end of the jetty? Grab as many as you can. Run over to the boat and pile the whole lot on board. Neatly now. Go!'

It took the rest of the morning to load the warship, which began to float lower in the water. Like the other lads, Vimp and Lief were in a state of near collapse. Their arms ached with the effort of carrying the logs and their legs felt as if they were made of lead.

'I can't move,' Vimp moaned. 'I'm finished. I'm going to die.'

Lief could hardly speak.

'What's the point of this?' he croaked desperately. 'The ship's nearly sinking under the weight of these heavy logs!'

To his dismay, Olaf overheard.

'What's the point?' the old thug repeated, jabbing his finger into Lief's chest. 'Point one . . . don't ask questions. Point two . . . do what I tell you. Now you've managed to get the logs on board I want 'em all off again – smartish. Jump to it and no slacking!'

The boys groaned and reckoned to have words with Lief, later. Olaf bullied them back to work and when the logs were back in a pile, on land, he gave them a short break.

'You've completed your first important lesson,' he announced. 'When you carried the logs on board it was like stowing goods stolen on your first raid. And when you took them off again, that was like arriving home with the stuff and presenting it to your village. Get it?'

With little strength left in their exhausted bodies, the unfortunate apprentices were ordered through a new series of manoeuvres. Running twenty times round the village was one of the milder activities. But setting fire to a ruined hut proved very dangerous. Sparks shot out from the burning thatch and lodged in one of the lad's tangled hair.

Worst of all was the final exercise of the day. Olaf called it 'Splitting the Turnip'. The trainee warriors were nearly on bended knees when he led them to a field where turnips had been dug up. These were fixed onto the tops of wooden stakes driven into the ground at an angle.

'I want you to imagine,' Olaf bellowed, 'that this is your first sight of the enemy. You've got to believe them turnips on sticks are the heads of stupid Saxons. It's your duty to destroy them!'

He handed round a set of heavy wooden clubs.

'When I shout "Charge" I want you running at them turnips, screaming blue murder. Give 'em a good thumping and bash their brains in.'

Lief turned to Vimp with his hand covering his mouth.

'Turnips don't have brains,' he whispered.

His friend shook his head wearily.

'I know. But the Saxon English might have. Olaf's trying to train us to be killers. It's revolting!'

A small party of village onlookers gathered at the far end of the field to watch the spectacle. Turnip-bashing was huge entertainment and they cheered the boys on as they attacked and pulverised the defenceless vegetables. Olaf permitted himself his first happy moment of the day.

'Good lads! That's more like it. I'll make warriors of you, yet.'

When they'd finished demolishing the vegetables, he called in his turnip-bespattered crew and told them what he wanted them to do next morning.

'First thing,' he announced, 'you've got sword and dagger control. Followed by how to handle an axe. After lunch . . . thieving, nicking and pilfering. Off you go, now. On the count of . . . er . . . one . . . two . . . er . . . "

Sweat began to run from below his helmet.

'Clear off! And don't be late tomorrow morning. Here at first light.'

The down-hearted troupe of apprentices trudged home. Despite their exhaustion they seethed with anger.

'I'm chucking it in,' Bjorne Strawhead announced as soon as it was safe. 'Who wants to learn how to kill other people?'

Lief and Vimp agreed with him. Before they reached the outer huts of the settlement, everyone was in favour of deserting.

'We could run away,' Vimp suggested. 'Into the forest. They'd never find us and we'd survive'

There was a murmur of approval.

'Let's have a show of hands.'

Everyone agreed. They had suffered enough of Olaf's bullying and killer training. Vimp sensed rebellion in their minds.

'We'll meet at mid-night,' he said stepping forward as leader. 'Make yourselves up a bag of food that'll keep you going for at least three days and nights. Don't let anyone see you escape. Make for the remains of the old hut we set fire to, this morning. From there, we'll take the path to the nearest trees.'

His friends grunted their assent.

'Just one more thing,' Vimp went on. 'Try and find your cow horns. We're going to need them. It gets really dark in the forest. If we lose each other, we can make calls until we join up again.'

The boys shook each other by the hand and set off for their homes. The die was cast.

As the daylight failed, Vimp was startled by a sudden shadow flickering across his path. It belonged to Freya who'd been patiently waiting for him. She called his name.

'Vimp, I have terrible news,' Freya said. 'My grandfather's funeral has been arranged for next Odin's Day. The body will be wrapped in his Old Chieftain's robes and placed on the boat you built. Thiar, his famous old war horse, will be slaughtered and laid with him . . . "

Freya choked on her own words and Vimp saw she was close to tears.

'I know,' she said. 'Slaughtering a horse sounds awful, but it's Viking tradition. Your grandfather's spirit will need Thiar when it enters Valhalla.'

Freya wiped away tears swelling in her soft eyes.

'Far worse,' she said. 'At a Chieftain's funeral it's also traditional to sacrifice a human slave whose body is placed on the boat. Vimp . . . '

Her voice faltered.

'I can't believe it.'

Freya fought hard to control herself.

'They've selected my dearest friend, Emma.'

Vimp froze to the spot. He'd heard rumours of such things but hadn't really believed them.

'Emma?' he gulped. 'But that's wicked. What's the point?'

Freya fought back tears as she looked him in the eye.

'Emma and I have made our own decision,' she said haltingly. 'I've come to say good-bye, Vimp. We're leaving tonight. You and I . . . we shall never see each other again.'

She felt for his hand and gripped it tightly.

'We're running away,' she continued. 'Fleeing the village. It's our only hope. Three of the band girls want to come with us. They're really upset about Emma. Slave or no slave. We're all going together. Leaving our families forever.'

Freya slipped her hand out of his grip, but Vimp took her arm. His mind was working fast.

'Listen to me,' he said. 'If you think I'd let you and the other girls go and live in the forest all by yourselves, you're wrong. You're not safe, even with your powers. My friends have also decided to leave the village tonight. We don't want to be forced into becoming warriors, so we've decided to find a new life. Peace, not war. You girls can join us.'

The young Vikings walked out across the marsh in the gathering gloom. They were aware that they were about to make the biggest decision of their lives. Drawing near to the sea edge, Vimp spotted the sombre silhouette of the funeral boat against the faint light of the horizon. He stopped in his tracks. An incredible thought blazed through his mind. Before he could speak, Freya took his hand and gave him a nervous smile.

'I know what you're thinking. Our freedom lies not in the forest but a long way from here.'

She gazed at the darkening sea.

'Across the waves to another land. Together we'll travel to a new country and find people who wish to live in peace.'

A slight puff of wind ruffled Vimp's hair. He stood in silence over-awed by Freya's words.

'To another land,' he said wistfully. 'We're of the same mind. You're a very special person, Freya.'

CHAPTER 6

Girls on Board

A half moon rose over the Viking settlement and cast its silvery light on the thatched roofs as the warriors and their families slept. Only the occasional sharp bark of a village dog and the rattling of its chain disturbed the night silence. Vimp lay awake, determined not to drift off to sleep. He listened to the gentle snores of his brothers under the huge bearskin. Low grumblings and vulgar snorts sounded from behind a hanging curtain, where his mother and father slept.

Vimp slipped out from under the bearskin without disturbing the other children. He crawled to the hut entrance and stuck his head out of the doorway. The closest huts cast sombre shadows in the moonlight. Even so, he was able to make out the untidy pile of firewood stacked against his own dwelling. Reaching behind, he pulled out a leather bag tied with a cord. After supper, he had filled it with lumps of left over bread, apples, cheese, and salted bacon wrapped in a cloth. It was all Vimp could get his hands on in the little time he had to plan his escape. He lifted a branch of firewood to find the old cow horn and slung the strap over his shoulder. His worst fear was that he would disturb a guard dog.

Without a sound, he headed for the remains of the burned out hut. Despite the poor light, Vimp detected a slight movement ahead of him. Dropping onto his tummy, he lay still as a shadowy figure emerged from behind a water barrel.

'It must be one of the gang,' he thought.

The figure disappeared, so Vimp crawled forward. He reached the fence, swung his legs over, and dropped into a field. So far so good. No alarm had been raised. Moments later, he reached the charred embers of the burned out hut and was relieved to find the others had got there before him. His apprentice friends crouched low clutching onto their precious bundles. A shrill whisper penetrated the cold night air.

'Who's that?'

Vimp stopped still.

'It's me,' he answered nervously. 'Vimp! Who's that?'

'You're late,' Bjorne Strawhead scolded. 'We've been waiting for ages. Everybody's here except Long Legs Peder and Cunning Cnute. We reckon they got scared when they went home.'

Vimp recalled that Cnute had lost a brother in a fishing boat accident and was afraid of the sea. He hoped desperately that he and Peder wouldn't give away the plan. His heart skipped a beat. If Peder and Cnute had betrayed their friends, an ambush party might already be lying in wait. The escapers would be in for a terrible beating so he was keen to move on.

'Let's go,' he advised. 'But keep a sharp lookout.'

In the dark, the boys found it difficult picking their way over the wet ground. But keeping to the raised track proved nearly impossible. Two of the boys plunged into the marsh and sank up to their wastes to be hauled out by their companions.

Chilled and cheerless, the gang arrived at the funeral boat. Its stark silhouette stood out like a dark monster in the pale moonlight. Eric strode round to examine the tight wooden wedges holding the boat in place. The tide was up and soft waves lapped at the beach, only a short distance away. He had given some thought as to how to launch the boat, using logs as rollers and slipping them under the keel as they pushed. The side-supporting wedges would need to be knocked away. It was a tricky operation at the best of times. Tonight they had to work in near silence.

Eric organised the boys to do different jobs and whispered the order to start.

'Keep the noise down,' he insisted, loosening the wedges, 'else you'll wake the whole village.'

The newly built boat shuddered. Two burly apprentices carrying a heavy roller log between them struggled to the prow and shoved it underneath. They took care to make sure their fingers did not get crushed. A second pair of boys staggered up with the next roller.

'Push!'

Eric organised his workers on the sides and rear of the boat as it lurched forward onto the first roller.

'Stick the next one in,' he commanded. 'Be ready with the others.'

Inch by inch, the boat rolled down the sloping shore to the water's edge. Pairs of boys shoved extra logs under the vessel and soon its curved prow entered the water. Vimp, one of the pushers, strained every muscle to shift the boat forward. A worrying thought flashed through his mind.

'This boat was never meant to go to sea. Is it seaworthy?'

There was no reply but it was too late to worry now. With a great deal of muscle, the young apprentices achieved their first aim. The funeral boat slid into the water and Eric ordered some of the lads to hang onto its sides. They clung on to prevent it from floating away. Lief came running up with two thick ropes trailing behind.

'I found these on the shore,' he panted. 'We can tie the boat up and stop it drifting.'

Eric agreed and assumed command.

'You lot,' he said to the pushers as they stopped to admire their achievement, 'there's no time to waste. Get in and sit by the oars.'

The boys splashed alongside and helped each other up. Soaked to the skin, Vimp tumbled into the shallow bottom of the boat and felt around for the nearest oar. He was angry that Eric had taken cover, but had to give him credit. Perhaps it was luck, but so far everything had gone their way and the boys were nearly ready to sail. It was at that moment that Vimp recalled something important.

Freya and the others. Where were they?

He got up from his rowing position and stepped onto the side. A small party of girls ran up out of the darkness, each clutching a heavy bag. Freya realised Eric had taken command.

'Don't leave without us,' she said breathlessly. 'We want to come with you. Help us aboard!'

Vimp did not need to imagine the expression on Eric's face. By the terse tone of his voice he knew the big Viking was not in business for extra passengers.

'Girls?' Eric exploded. 'What in Valhalla are they doing here? We'll have the whole village after us. Get back to your huts. We're about to sail.'

The apprentices not yet on board were just as surprised as Eric. They pushed the girls aside and scrambled over the sides.

'Vimp said we could come,' Freya insisted. 'Please, Eric, give us a hand up. We can't go back now.'

The self-appointed commander sensed the young male crew was on his side and ordered the girls to stand off. Vimp confronted him.

'They're coming with us, Eric,' he said grimly. 'I made a promise. There was no time to tell the lads. Emma the slave girl's been selected for sacrifice. She must escape!'

He leant forward and offered a hand to Freya. Eric grabbed Vimp by the arm and shoved him aside.

'You should have said,' he complained. 'It's too late to change plans. Crew, get ready!'

The last two boys still in the water gave the boat a final push before they were hauled aboard. In the distance, a dog barked and set off its noisy neighbour.

'Hurry up!' Eric urged. 'The whole village will be here any moment. Obey my orders. It's now or never!'

The next thing he knew, he was flat on his back with Lief the poet sitting astride him.

'Quick, Vimp!' Lief shouted. 'Get those girls on board!'

Eric struggled to free himself. Now every dog worth its salt barked its head off. In no time, torches flared and men shouted. Vimp got hold of Bjorne Strawhead and thrust him up against the ship's side.

'Let them get on!' he commanded. 'There's no way we're leaving them in the water.'

Bjorne responded meekly and offered Freya his arm, bundling her into the boat. Then he turned to help the next female passenger as Vimp leapt back into the sea to lift little Emma on board. In no time, all four girls had been hauled over the sides, soaked to the skin. Vimp grabbed onto Bjorne's outstretched arm and swung himself up.

'Row, lads!' he shouted. 'For your lives!'

A bobbing line of flaming torches headed for the beach. Eric wrestled with Lief and threw him off. The poet offered no resistance.

'Sorry, Eric,' he panted. 'You were great – honest! We'll take responsibility for the girls. Take hold of the tiller and set a course. That's what you're best at.'

He glanced anxiously at the ragged line of flares racing towards them. The shouting increased.

'Go!' Lief yelled. 'They'll never catch us in the darkness!'

CHAPTER 7

Freya Weaves
Her Magic

The young Vikings fled their village as storm clouds obscured the moon. If there'd been time to think, a few might have felt scared as they'd never ventured to sea. No one knew how to navigate. It hadn't even crossed their minds. All that mattered was that they had made their escape.

Vimp was worried about getting caught. Glancing back at the shoreline, he could see the villagers' faces in the flickering torchlight. But the angry mob stopped at the waterside and made no attempt to pursue. Mysteriously, the raiding boats remained tied up at their moorings. Freya slipped alongside her friend as Lief stood at the mast, clapping his hands and shouting instructions at the rowers.

'They're afraid to come after us,' Freya whispered. 'They've found out we've stolen my grandfather's funeral boat. They'll say we've offended the gods and must be punished.'

She felt for Vimp's arm.

'If we've done wrong,' she said, 'I must take the responsibility.'

Vimp gazed at the crowd growing smaller at each powerful pull of the oars. He wondered if his own family were there. Something tugged at his heart. Suddenly, the village did not seem so awful.

49

Beyond the protection of the far headland, the boat began to rock on the rising swell. None of the rowers knew where they were going. The buffeting of the waves strengthened by the minute.

'Don't be afraid,' Freya cried. 'Remember my powers. Trust me and we'll reach the place we seek. The gods have selected us for a special mission.'

A strong gust of wind struck the boat. Vimp grabbed for the side as the vessel tipped, threatening to throw him overboard. One or two of the rowers slid from their wooden benches. They scrambled up again as Lief clawed onto the mast.

'Keep rowing!' he yelled above the howling wind. 'Stick to the rhythm.'

It was work for grown men. Vimp clambered alongside Bjorne, struggling with his oar.

'I'll give you a hand,' he offered.

Cold spray lashed his face, soaking his jerkin. Vimp sensed panic all around him. The girls huddled at the bottom of the boat where icy water slopped over them.

As the moon appeared briefly in a gap in the angry clouds, Vimp was able to take in the situation. The funeral ship was in danger of being tossed around like a cork battling against the waves. He caught a fleeting glimpse of Eric wrestling with the side rudder, determined not to stray off course. Vimp's heart went out to him. Brave Eric, strong as an ox, refused to give in to the sea. His determination gave Vimp new strength to encourage his rowers.

'Fight!' he shouted. 'Give it all you've got.'

His words were lost in the howling gale but the apprentices responded. With Bjorne steady again, Vimp crawled forward to help another rower who'd tumbled from his bench. Fresh blood trickled from a wound on the boy's chin. Vimp wrestled the oar from his grasp and plunged it back into the churning sea.

51

A jagged streak of lightning ripped out of the clouds. It crackled into the water and was followed by an ear-splitting thunderclap. The boat rose onto the crest of a big wave before pitching down the other side. The fearful rowers fought for their lives. They had no time to be frightened. Putting their backs into the work they pulled hard as the next wave crashed into the boat, threatening to plunge it to the bottom. Then Vimp saw something that convinced him he was losing his mind. High on the raised prow of the vessel, the ghostly form of a young maiden appeared. She was clothed in pale green. Her slim outline glowed in the darkness. Other maidens joined her to dance on the waves, twisting and twirling in the teeth of the gale. The ship filled with an ethereal green light. To Vimp, it seemed these extraordinary figures were mocking the efforts of his oarsmen.

A second crackle of lightning fizzed over the sea's raging surface. Vimp was dismayed to find his oarsmen had ceased rowing. From the startled expressions on their frozen faces he worked out they'd seen something dreadful. Following the direction of their glazed eyes, he turned to see the gigantic bearded face of an old man rising from the waves. Sea water streamed from his skull and trailing wisps of beard swirled in the turbulent waters. He spoke in a tumultuous voice, drowning out the whine of the wind.

'Who are you who dare set out upon my ocean?' he cried. 'You have seen my daughters dance about your vessel. Once you see the wave maidens, your end is near. No one survives such a sight!'

He reached out with hands the size of the ship. Claw-like fingers closed over the mast.

'With these hands,' he thundered, 'I shall carry you to the depths of my kingdom!'

Freya sprang to her feet and thrust her face into the wind. A golden light shone on her and she held aloft her musical horn.

'I know who you are, old man,' she cried. 'You are Aegir, God of the Oceans. Your wife is Ran. Her net traps innocent sailors, smashing their boats against jagged rocks. Move aside, Aegir. Let us pass!'

The ancient ruler of the oceans threw his head back and roared with laughter.

'Who are you, mighty mouse, who dares defy me? I shall crush your boat until it is no more than splinters upon the surface of my ocean.'

Freya raised the horn to her lips, faced into the wind, and blew. The waves subsided and the Sea God found himself at a loss to speak.

'I am Freya,' the girl told him. 'You must respect my name and powers. When I blow once more upon this horn, my music will drain your strength.'

Freya blew. The eyrie sound carried across the waves. Aegir raised his hands above his head, let out an unhappy groan, and sank slowly beneath the waves. The waters churned and bubbled. Abandoning the moon, dark storm clouds permitted its magical light to dance once more upon the sea. Freya's golden glow dimmed as she stepped down to be with her friends.

Only the poet, Lief, had witnessed all that had taken place between the young Viking girl and the God of the Sea. One by one, the boys picked up their oars and rediscovered their rhythm. The boat pressed forward. Soaked and starving, the crew rowed into the night.

Chapter 8

Breakfast at Sea

Scarlet rays of the rising sun lit up the morning sky. The funeral ship rocked gently on the sea, touched by a light breeze. Hardly a soul on board was awake. Most of the young rowers sat collapsed over their oars. Freya and her friends slept at the stern of the boat, huddled up for warmth. Before he fell into a heavy sleep Eric had headed the boat up wind and lashed the rudder. With the sail tightly furled, it made little progress.

Only Vimp lay awake. He clamped his arms round his chest and shivered in the morning air. Hunger gnawed at his stomach and made him think of his food bundle. But his mouth was dry and salty from sea spray. Reaching for his bag, he pulled out strips of bacon spirited from his hut. Heavily salted pork was the last thing he needed. His parched throat craved for cool, fresh water. To his dismay, Vimp discovered he had forgotten to bring a leather bottle. He dug deeper into the bag to find an apple. Crunching into its flesh, he allowed the juice to spill over his leathery tongue.

Other members of the crew began to stir. Stretching their cramped arms and legs, the boy rowers discovered all sorts of aches and pains. Vimp struggled to stand up whilst Bjorne, on the bench in front, flexed his shoulders.

'I'm starving,' he grumbled, 'but I forgot bring any food. Who'll give me have some of theirs?'

The other rowers pretended not to hear and ferreted around in their own bundles. Eric, awake at the prospect of food, bit ravenously into a chicken leg.

'Sorry, Bjorne,' he said, his mouth full. 'Can't help you. You should have brought your own stuff. You'll have to do without breakfast.'

The unkind remark stung Bjorne who had rowed into the teeth of the storm. He made a grab for the chicken leg.

'Give me that!'

Eric punched him and Bjorne slipped, landing on top of Emma. She rolled over and accidentally poked Ingrid in the eye. Ingrid woke up and lashed out at the nearest person. It was Eric. The tall helmsman lost his balance and tumbled over the side.

'Man overboard!'

Lief grabbed a rope and threw it to Eric, struggling in the water. Vimp rushed to help. Together, they hauled him alongside and got him on board. Eric spouted water like a stranded fish. Freya stepped up to take charge.

'For goodness' sake,' she cried, 'stop quarrelling, you boys! Emma and I will take charge of the food. Pass your bundles down so we can see what you've got. We'll divide it into daily rations.'

The hungry rowers protested. Freya's scheme failed to impress those who had brought the largest bundles.

'It's not fair!'

'No one's having my stuff!'

'*I'm* not sharing!'

'Do as you're told,' Freya cried. 'Anyone who doesn't want to can get off.'

The oarsmen mumbled with resentment. Vimp and Lief stood up for the two girls.

'Freya's right!' Vimp cried. 'If you don't like it, jump overboard and swim home. We're in this together. Either you're with us, or you're not!'

Lief backed him up.

'Freya's talking sense,' he argued. 'The only way we'll survive is to share things. Leave the girls to sort it out.'

There were grumbles from the more rebellious rowers at the front, but Freya won the day. Food bundles of all sizes were reluctantly passed down. Vimp turned his attention to Eric, who lay on his back, soaking, and gasping for air.

'I've got a spare jerkin that's dry enough. Ask around the other lads to see who's got a spare pair of trousers.'

Eric dripped his way forward. Meanwhile, Freya organised the girls to provide equal amounts of food for the crew's first breakfast. It was not much of a meal. The bread had been soaked during the storm. And the raw, uncooked swedes were uneatable. As the unhappy rowers sat munching their breakfasts, they were learning life on the waves was hard. Lief wondered how long Vimp intended staying out at sea. He sat next to him and asked where the boat was heading.

'I'm beginning to wish we'd never set out,' Vimp told him. 'We've been so stupid. Getting upset because the village hated our music and chucked rotten food at us. Then we chickened out of warrior training. D'you know, my dad was right about me. I *am* a wimp. Trouble is, I've fooled our mates into coming along with us.'

Vimp stared glumly at the flat, featureless sea which stretched to the horizon in every direction.

'D'you think we should go back?' he went on. 'Turn round and go home? We should never have taken this funeral boat. Harald Strongaxe and the Elders must be furious.'

Lief swallowed a piece of soggy bread.

'You're not the only one who thinks about things. There's no way we can return to our bad old ways. Anyhow,' he added, 'there's a big argument to stop us going back.'

Vimp looked at him with interest.

'Young Emma,' Lief said. 'We must keep going for her sake. If we turn round, now, she'll be sacrificed at the funeral.'

Vimp shivered at the thought of the fate awaiting Freya's friend.

'You're right!' he said firmly. 'We'll carry on. But the big question is *where*? That's the bit no one's worked out.'

He looked up at a wispy cloud crossing the early morning sun. Lief moved closer.

'We'll sail to Saxon England,' he whispered. 'Mind you, if we ever get there we'll have to get the Saxons on side. They're unlikely to give us a friendly welcome.'

Vimp agreed.

'It won't be easy. But you're right. Saxon England is the only place to go!'

Chapter 9

Pirate Attack!

Eric Bignose stood gripping the tiller with the rowers pulling hard. The funeral boat cut through the waves like a knife. Vimp held up his hand and felt a breeze. He ordered the great rust-coloured sail to be raised. In no time, it billowed out in the wind, halving the work of the young oarsmen. The boys found their rhythm, putting the Viking coast far behind them.

Freya and two of the girls slipped between them, offering refreshing sips of water. Ingrid, however, squatted next to Bjorne as he battled the rising waves with his heavy oar. She admired his efforts. Bjorne was determined to prove that he was up for it.

One thing puzzled Vimp, who had been watching as Freya organised the food collection. She seemed to be managing the rationing very cleverly. There was always enough to fill the hungry crew's stomachs. Lief, who commanded the oarsmen from his vantage point at the mast, had also been keeping an eye on Freya. He gave the boys a brief break and had an urgent word with Vimp.

'I don't understand. It's miraculous. Freya's food store never seems to run out.'

His friend gave him a funny look.

'Steady on, Lief. You're telling me that Freya's a miracle worker? Only gods and goddesses do that sort of thing. In legends.'

Lief looked at his friend quizzically. He rose slowly to his feet and signalled to the crew it was time to get back to work.

'Come on, lads,' he urged. 'One more big effort. We need to row 'til sundown.'

With few complaints, the boys lifted the oars and lowered them into the sea. The boat soon picked up speed. At the helm, Eric kept an eye on the movement of the sun, knowing if it stayed on the port bow he would be steering the correct course.

'We need to head South West. With any luck that'll take us to the coastline of the Saxon English.'

As he settled down to his work, a shrill shout went up from one of the girls.

'Over there!' she cried. 'Look . . . a sail!'

It was Emma who gave the warning. She pointed to a craft on the horizon. Vimp joined her. The alien boat bore down fast from the south. In an instant, Vimp worked out it was not pursuing them from the village. Either it was a trading boat or a raider. Whichever, Vimp was not going to allow it come close. He yelled at Eric to swing the tiller and run with the wind. Lief urged the rowers to redouble their efforts.

'It's coming after us,' Emma cried. 'It doesn't look friendly.'

Vimp pretended not to be bothered.

'If it's a raider,' he argued, 'it'll leave us alone once it sees we've got nothing to offer.'

The newcomer gained fast. Lief realised there was no point trying to outrun it, so ordered his rowers to rest their oars.

'That's a large vessel,' he shouted to Vimp. 'We can't win.'

The proud prow of the oncoming Viking longboat creamed through the waves, powered by rough-looking sailors. Their hard eyes glared under metal helmets. Emma shivered as she made out the dragon head arching over the oncoming bows. A row of shields formed a wall along the near side. To his dismay, Vimp spotted warriors crouching behind their defences. This was no merchant ship. It pulled up close with the captain standing at its head. He was built like an ox with a red beard that ruffled in the wind.

'A bunch of kids?' he laughed. 'Just out of your cradles by the look of things. Where are you bound?'

His crew hooted at their leader's insult. He puffed out his mighty chest.

'Where've you come from in your toy boat? Won't your mummies worry about you?'

He leered back at his rough crew who enjoyed his coarse humour. He was not finished yet.

'These are the High Seas, little ones. Me and my companions have met some very nasty people who sail on 'em!'

Vimp's anger rose but before he could respond he was thrust aside by Lief. The young poet's heart thumped yet he was determined to sound cool.

'We're from Thardnorsk. We're not fighters. There's no booty to hand over. Can you advise us, please? We're bound for Saxon England. Is this the right direction? You may have visited their lands on your travels?'

The warrior captain pulled a dagger out of his belt and pointed it at Lief. His menacing eyes blazed like hot coals.

'*Can you advise us?*' he mocked, turning to his grinning crew. 'The young gentleman, shipmates, requests the benefit of our . . . advice!'

He broke off suddenly as his evil gaze fell upon Emma and the other girls. His scarred face lit up.

'I see you have young ladies with you. Very interesting! Did I hear the gentleman say he has no booty to hand over?'

The grisly crew leered over the tops of their battle shields. A rumble of laughter rippled through their ranks.

'D'you know who I am?' the captain said. 'Have you any idea whose precious time you're wasting?'

Lief tried hard to show he was not frightened.

'No,' he replied, lamely. 'I don't think we do.'

The captain cursed in contempt and puffed out his chest.

'I am Foulbeard, Brute of the Waves. All those who sail fear my name.'

The cruel mouth twisted into a grin.

'There are those who call us *pirates*,' he continued. 'Except me and my crew prefer to call ourselves *Gentlemen of the Waves*. We spend our time searching for young maidens in need of rescue. Being gentlemen, we always return the poor creatures to their anxious parents!'

He guffawed and spat into the sea.

'Now, my pretty boys, you may not have any treasure or fine cloth tucked away. But no problem. Me and my lads will be happy to settle for them young dames. You'll not object if and invite the ladies to come and join us? We'll treat 'em with the greatest respect!'

A menacing growl rumbled through the pirate crew. Foulbeard laughed and spat again. He turned to the girls.

'Make yourselves ready, my beauties. Ready to hop on board. Why are you mixing with boys when there's *real* men to look after you?'

Vimp stepped up alongside his friend, blood pumping through his veins.

'If you think,' he retorted, 'we're going to hand over the girls you'll have a fight on your hands. We're not scared of you, Foulbeard.'

He spat into the water.

'If you take my advice you'll clear off whilst you have the chance!'

A vulgar explosion of laughter rocked the pirate ship, but the cruel smile on Foulbeard's face faded. He snapped a short order to his men to move up alongside. As the pirates pulled at their oars, Freya stepped up to stand shoulder to shoulder with the boys.

'Stop, Foulbeard Brute of the Waves!' she commanded. 'Pull away at once or I, Freya, will make you regret every disrespectful word you have uttered!'

The bullish pirate captain gawped at Freya. He bowed low.

'So, the little lady speaks! She's ordering the nasty pirate captain to row away empty handed.'

His ingratiating smile darkened to a scowl.

'Foulbeard, Brute of the Waves, is about to teach you true pirate manners.

Boarding party . . . ready with your weapons!'

They were the last words Foulbeard ever spoke on the high seas. Freya, hair blowing in the wind, raised her slender arms. Slowly, she lowered them, palms outwards. Her eyes flashed as she spoke into the waves. The water beyond the boats seethed and boiled. The pirates froze at their oars. Foulbeard, clinging onto the dragon-prow, cried out. He gazed in awe as a dreadful spectacle broke through through the surface.

'Iormungandr, Serpent of the World,' cried Freya, 'arise from the unfathomable depths of your ocean floor. Show no mercy to these mortals who bring evil into other men's lives. Carry them to your dark lair. And there, let them perish!'

Foulbeard's jaw dropped. He stared helplessly as the thrashing serpentine tail of an enormous beast beat on the waves. The pirates cried out and covered their eyes as a writhing knot of reptilian coils churned the sea into angry foam. A monstrous, scaly head exploded through the surface on the far side of Foulbeard's boat. It reared up to fix the crew with its wicked red eyes. The serpent hissed and flicked its forked tongue. Its powerful tail curled around the longship, lifting it high in the air. Pirates clung on for dear life as shields, oars and helmets tumbled into the swirling waters.

Vimp watched in horror as the sea reptile opened its jaws and bared its fangs. The pirate boat, locked helplessly in the coils of the monster's tail, turned upside down. The dragon prow broke off, plunging beneath the surface as the men fell to horrible watery deaths.

The furious serpent glowered at its awful deed, breathing a cloud of purple mist from its flaring nostrils. Freya, in command of the event, cried out to her crew.

'Cover your faces! Do not breathe in the venom of Iormungandr!'

Engulfed in the ever-tightening coils, the pirate ship disappeared without a trace. Iormungandr, Serpent of the World, flicked out its tongue for the desperate men still on the surface. Gradually, the waters calmed and the deadly cloud of venom dispersed on the wind. One by one, the white-faced boys and girls dared to uncover their eyes. Up at the mast, the frail figure of Freya hung limp and exhausted.

It was some time before Lief recovered his senses. In a shaky voice he asked his crew to pick up their oars. No one spoke. Slowly, the boat got underway. Eric, reliable as ever, set course and took charge of the tiller.

Shocked by what he had witnessed, Vimp sat on his bench trying to fathom out the meaning of the extraordinary incident. He knew of sagas his grandparents had told and passed down the generations. Of the time Earth would come to an end. A time when Viking gods would destroy everything they had created. That was when the legendary Serpent of the World would emerge from its gloomy oceanic den. It was said that when this happened the waters of the Earth would engulf all known lands. What had Freya done? Had she unleashed powers even she did not fully understand?

Vimp stared unseeingly at the great expanse of grey water. He shuddered to think of his friend's ability to control or call up the Gods. Who was she? Could it be that she was a goddess, herself? Perhaps half human and half god? His eyes cleared. Vimp was astonished to find his strange companion hiding her face in the long locks of her hair. She wept as Saxon Emma slipped an arm around her slender shoulders. Emma spoke words of comfort to the Viking girl who had rescued her from death.

CHAPTER 10

Dolphin Antics

Half a day's hard rowing helped the young oarsmen push memories of drowning pirates to the backs of their minds. They headed south west, but even when they took a break for a cold supper they avoided talking about the nightmarish happening. Most rested on their oars and gazed silently out to sea as the red orb of the sun set over the horizon.

'Surely,' thought Vimp, 'by tomorrow we must find the land of the English. I don't want to spend one more horrible night on this boat.'

The crew settled down to its second night at sea. Spirits were low, especially amongst the shivering girls. They slept fitfully on hard wooden planks at the bottom of the boat, covered only by damp jerkins. As for the rowers, they were so exhausted they collapsed into fretful slumber. Some cried out in their sleep, disturbed by dreams. Horrendous serpents spewing fumes of poison. Bearded giants rising from the deep and threatening to pull their boat under the waves. Brave Eric pounded the air with his fists to fend off a savage pirate who attacked him with an axe.

At last, darkness gave way to light and the first faint rays of the sun peeped over the horizon. The unhappy crew sat sullen and rebellious. Resentful eyes accused Vimp of taking the escapers on a perilous journey leading nowhere.

Ulrik, the boy handling the first oar in the bows, stood up and confronted his leader.

'We want to turn round! It's crazy carrying on like this. You'll get us all killed.'

The others murmured in mutinous agreement. Another lad, two oars in front, rose unsteadily to his feet.

'Ulrik's right,' he shouted shaking his fist. 'You're useless, Vimp. We should go home and take our punishment.'

Sharp as ever, Lief the Poet was equal to the situation. He understood the crew and came out with a reasonable suggestion.

'Just one more morning's effort, lads!' he said, raising his voice over the grumbles. 'We'll make this the last day of sailing from home. If we don't find the English shore by the time the sun's high in the sky, we'll head back.'

The reluctant crew discussed the matter and agreed to give it one more go. Freya and the girls organised breakfast whilst Emma went round with fresh water. But even on the calmest of seas the rowers pulled with no will. Their hearts were not in their work and Lief struggled to keep the boys together.

Gazing idly over the starboard side, Emma spotted a disturbance in the water. Was it another fearsome creature about to attack? Her fears were put to rest as two dark, streamlined shapes leapt from the water. Others followed. At the crest of the jumps, their rounded backs arched before dropping back into the waves. Emma recognised these creatures from tales told at village fires.

'Look ahead!' she called out. 'Dolphins!'

The graceful creatures disappeared beneath the surface. It was Ingrid, on the opposite side of the boat, who first spotted them again.

'Three of them!' she cried. 'Playing . . . '

The dolphins dived under the boat, inventing their own game. The rowers on Emma's side craned their necks.

'My side again!'

Ingrid could not contain her excitement. One large dolphin skimmed over the surface then turned to avoid the flailing oars. Raising its smooth head from the water, it fixed Ingrid with a friendly eye.

'Is it smiling at me?' she wondered.

All of a sudden, it spouted air from its blow hole. Then, sucking in a noisy breath, it splashed its flat tail down on the surface. The dolphin dived, spray hitting Ingrid full in the face.

'It's gone!' she laughed and wiped her stinging eyes.

'Look out your side, Emma.'

Bjorne, meanwhile, suffered problems with his rowing as two younger dolphins frolicked around the tip of his oar. They soared over it as it dipped into the sea. When it emerged again, the youngsters dived under. It was a hazardous game, throwing Bjorne off his stroke. He raised the oar, but accidently struck the head of the nearest dolphin.

Bjorne tumbled off his bench. Everyone laughed except Emma, who had spotted the sea youngster on its side. It wallowed in the water, half conscious. She leapt to her feet.

'Stop! Everyone stop rowing!'

From his place at the mast, Lief backed up her order and the rowers tilted their oars. Two adult dolphins streaked up to the stricken youngster and prodded it with their snouts. It flipped over on its back, lifted up and down on the boat's bow wave. One of the adults dived beneath it and attempted to turn it onto its stomach. It failed and the stricken youngster began to drift.

'If it stays like that,' Lief cried, 'it won't be able to breathe. It'll drown!'

Without a thought for his safety, brave Bjorne scrambled up and hurled himself over the side. Disappearing under a wave, he surfaced to strike out for the drowning dolphin. Seizing a flipper, Bjorne wrestled the animal over as Vimp jumped into the water beside him.

'Grab the back fin,' Bjorne spluttered. 'Keep it upright!'

Salt blinding his eyes, Vimp felt for the rubbery fin and gripped it for dear life. Bjorne swam round to the head of the young dolphin. He slipped his hands under its jaw and supported the head above the surface. The dolphin shuddered. Then a cloud of water vapour and air exploded from its lungs and shot out of the breathing hole. Almost at once, Bjorne sensed life returning to the injured animal. It sucked in a deep breath of life-giving sea air.

One of the parents slipped alongside Vimp and nosed under its child. The other parent came alongside to help push the youngster away from the boat. Spluttering and treading water, the two boys strained to see the parents swim away with their young one. A crew member shouted from above their heads.

'Catch!'

A coil of rope spun through the air and hit the sea between them. The intrepid rescuers grabbed hold to be hauled back on board.

CHAPTER 11

Fogbound

Eric Bignose struggled to hold a steady course. He screwed up his eyes and peered ahead but did not believe what he was seeing. The horizon had disappeared. He was hoping to be first to see the Saxon coastline but what loomed before him was not land. Whatever it was billowed towards the boat, in shapeless white fingers. The young helmsman shouted a warning to Vimp, who had taken a turn at an oar. Vimp glanced over his shoulder. His jaw dropped as he found himself staring at a wall of dense fog.

'Steer to starboard' he yelled, scrambling back to the tiller to be with Eric. 'Tell the lads to pull hard, Lief. We can outrun it!'

Vimp sensed panic sweeping through the rowers, even though they were unable to see the mist rolling towards them. They sensed the light was changing. It dulled as the air chilled and the first wraiths of wet vapour wrapped around the mast top.

In no time, the confused crew found themselves surrounded by an impenetrable white curtain. Ingrid and Astrid cried out in alarm as the fog blotted out the blue sky. Even Eric sounded anxious.

'Which direction?' he shouted. 'Tell me which way to steer.'

No one had an answer but stared hopelessly into the white-out, threatening to envelop and imprison the boat.

'We could sail round in circles,' Vimp whispered. 'And not know it. Perhaps we should stop rowing and let the boat drift. Except I've heard these sea fogs can last for days. We might end up way off course.'

It was a scary prospect. Even Freya seemed nonplussed. For once, she seemed powerless to summon her mystical gifts. The white silence was broken by Bjorne. He had spotted a disturbance in the water beneath his raised oar.

'What's that under the boat?' he cried. 'I can't make it out. Hold on . . . two of them!'

A sleek, dark shape broke the surface, swiftly followed by a second, arched and streamlined. They lifted their smooth heads and nose-dived beneath the waves. Bjorne laughed. His first thought was that the fearsome serpent had returned to menace the crew. But two sets of interested eyes and smiling mouths gave the game away.

'It's the dolphins,' he cried.

The crew sat tight, unable to respond. It seemed as if they had resigned themselves to their fate. Bjorne, however, sensed something unusual was happening. Close enough to be seen through the fog, the dolphin pair swam strictly in line. The leader spun off from the front, then sped round to the back to join in again. On the opposite side of the boat, a similar dolphin pair played the same tricks. Astrid watched with open eyes, forgetting for a fleeting moment the danger she faced.

'I know what they're doing,' she cried. 'Follow the leader!'

The dolphins swam just out of range of the oars. Freya, suddenly alive, ran the length of the boat dodging between the rowers. She stood at the prow, almost invisible to Eric. Then she turned round, her thin figure ghostlike in the wet mist. Her face lit up.

'We're saved,' she called. 'Don't you see, Astrid? The dolphins are telling us something. It's not follow the leader. They're telling *us* to follow *them*!'

Ahead of the bows, both lines of dolphins joined with three leaders in single file. They seemed to have set their own course.

'Row!' shrieked Freya. 'Follow the dolphins!'

Lief resumed control of the crew and called out his rhythm beats. The Viking boat glided forward. One or two of the younger dolphins sped by, missing the oars by a whisker. But their judgement was perfect. It seemed that they wanted to swim as close as possible to their new friends.

Despite heading blindly through the fog blanket, the boat made good progress.

'We're getting somewhere,' Vimp thought. 'But where are the dolphins leading us – and why?'

Eric, leaning on his tiller, was first to see the fog thinning and spotted brief patches of grey sea beyond. Pallid traces of sunlight penetrated the remains of the fog bank. Little by little, the sea began to appear blue, again.

'The fog's dispersing,' Eric shouted. 'Clear water ahead!'

The crew could hardly believe their luck and sent up a hearty cheer. They took a well-earned rowing break and the girls went round with food to celebrate. Freya's rations never grew any smaller. Everyone relaxed in the sun whilst Lief, standing at the mast and stretching his arms, gazed around. A knotted clump of seaweed bobbed past on the port side, its curled strands caught around something that looked solid. He looked harder. The object bobbed on the gentle waves. It was pitted and deep brown. The bow wave turned it over in the water.

'A log?' Lief wondered. 'Part of a tree trunk, with seaweed caught in its branches?'

He had an inspired thought.

'A floating log – part of a tree – can mean only one thing.'

He thought about calling Vimp over.

'Just how far from land would a log float?' he pondered.

A seagull wheeled overhead. It circled the boat, homed in, and thrust out its white wings. The young poet marvelled at the gull's precision as it braked in the wind to land on the top of the mast. He glanced up at its yellow beak as the gull gave out a raucous cry which the young travellers recognised. It was a reminder of their homeland where greedy gulls were seen searching for fishy scraps amongst the garbage. Unaware it had become the centre of attention, the gull opened its beak and called again. Lief felt certain that its sudden appearance was a welcome sign. He summoned Vimp over.

'That gull. We may be close to land. It might even be the Saxon coastline.'

He pointed to the log as it drifted away on the port bow.

'See?' he said. 'That could only come from land.'

Lief was interrupted by Eric.

'Land ahead! We've done it, boys!'

Freya shot him a dark look and he corrected himself.

'And girls.'

The boat rolled as the crew leapt to their feet. They turned to see where Eric was pointing. Vimp steadied himself and peered into the distance.

'Is he right?' he asked. 'Or are we just imagining things?'

On the horizon was a dark, purplish line. Had they succeeded? The desperate runaways who had dared sail across the sea had found what they sought. Their mission was nearing its end. By their own brave efforts, they had journeyed to a new land. Vimp's mind raced back to the dolphins, the wild creatures of the waves who had guided the Viking voyagers to their target. He glanced over the side but their friends from the sea had slipped away. Task completed, the dolphins rocketed towards a tempting shoal of herrings!

CHAPTER 12

Safe Landing

The sun was already sinking as the Viking vessel headed for the shore. Vimp organised the crew to roll up the great sail so the boat's last lap was left to the efforts of the rowers. He was not the only person to smell land scents borne on the light offshore breeze. Astrid too had been sniffing the air. There was just a suggestion of plant fragrance; pine with a mixture of summer flowers.

Vimp stood with Eric to examine the coastline getting clearer, by the minute. Low cliffs stood stern and solid, protecting the land from the battering of winter storms. Stretching towards them, Eric spotted lines of jagged rocks. They projected into the water spelling danger to approaching vessels. Small waves burst over their crests raising spray that frothed on the incoming tide.

'Keep away from those rocks,' advised Vimp. 'They'll rip a hole in the hull.'

He need not have worried because Eric was ahead of the game. He had worked out the most suitable spot to beach the boat.

'Over there!' he pointed. 'The sandy bay between two headlands. I don't see any rocks.'

With a skilful touch on the tiller, Eric eased the boat towards his target.

'Steady, boys!'

Lief read Eric's mind. The bay looked safe as the shore sloped gently down to the tide mark. It was a near perfect spot to land.

'When I say raise oars,' he told the rowers, 'do so immediately. We don't want any of them snapping.'

A straggling line of moist seaweed stretched along the top of the shore.

'We're in luck,' said Eric, who understood its meaning. 'We're going in on the tide. The boat will ride high up the shore. That'll save us pulling and pushing.'

Vimp ordered the four nearest rowers to ship their oars.

'Get ready to jump in. We're approaching the shallows.'

Lief shouted his final order and the remainder of the rowers rested, leaning on the oars to keep them high out of the water.

'Now!' Vimp shouted. 'After me.'

Leading by example, he heaved himself over the side and dropped into the sea. Misjudging the depth, he shuddered as cold water rose to his ribs. He heard the splashes of the other lads. The moment they found their feet, they grasped onto the side of the boat and dragged it through the water. It was much harder than they had imagined. They felt it judder when it grated on the sand and slid to a stop.

'Sling the anchor over!'

Lief knew they could progress no further, so he made sure the vessel remained where it rested. Soaked through, Vimp splashed through the light waves and hurled himself onto dry sand. It clung to his wet clothing. He dived onto his belly and beat both feet on the beach. Quite unashamed, he wept. Vimp was joined by a few of the other lads. They danced around like happy five-year-olds, scuffing sand into each other's faces. Still on board, Lief kept calm telling the rest of the rowers to stow their oars.

'Ready to step off, one at a time. Give the girls a hand!'

The front pair of oarsmen helped them into the chilly water that came up to their knees. The girls struggled across to Vimp in the soft sand. He looked up and grinned.

'Welcome to Saxon England.'

Emma ran up to him, eyes shining.

'This is my land,' she laughed. 'It's *me* who should be welcoming *you!*'

Emma was thrilled to be back on her own soil. It was something she had dreamt about during her capture. She never thought she would never get the chance to see her home again. Yet here she was, carried by a boat crewed by the sons and daughters of Vikings. Emma's friends gathered round and gave her big bear hugs.

'It's great just to run around,' Bjorne cried, taking off for the cliffs at the far end of the bay. The others raced and cart-wheeled over the beach. Vimp let them enjoy themselves for a short time before getting back to the pressing business of survival. Once the antics had died down he outlined the plan for the remainder of the day.

'We're fairly certain this is Saxon England. You've all done brilliantly. Eric especially!'

The crew applauded the successful helmsman.

'We'll need to get all our stuff off the boat. Lief's in charge of that.'

Vimp pulled two pieces of flint out of his pocket.

'We must light a fire.'

His suggestion went down well. Lief's mouth watered at the thought of hot food.

'I'll lead the fishing party,' he offered.

Back home, Lief had been a keen fisherman. Some of the lads volunteered to help.

'I need people to spend the night on the boat,' Vimp continued. 'The rest can make a camp in the dunes. Take it in turns for guard duty. We don't know if there are Saxons around these parts. If there are, they're not likely to make us welcome. They may even think we're a raiding party.'

He eyes rested on Bjorne.

'You're in charge of camp arrangements. Select a good spot then carry stuff up from the boat. Choose your own team.'

Bjorne glowed inwardly. Ever since the baby dolphin rescue, his reputation amongst the crew had blossomed. He had earned his place as a member of Vimp's circle of trusted friends.

Freya stepped forward.

'The girls should collect firewood,' she said. 'We've spotted driftwood on the beach and bits and pieces up in the dunes. There's a forest nearby.'

Vimp recalled Freya's love of woodland. It seemed a sensible suggestion but he was surprised when Eric stepped forward.

'If you're going into the forest,' he said, 'I'm coming with you. Girls shouldn't walk alone in dangerous places.'

Freya shrugged her shoulders.

'We'll be fine. Don't worry about us. I'll take my musical horn along. That'll keep us safe.'

Eric looked cross and glanced at Astrid.

'No!' he said gruffly. 'Girls need protection. Even Freya. So I'm coming with you.' Freya saw he was stung and tried to ease his pain.

'Of course you can come with us, Big Eric,' she said. 'You can carry all the heavy stuff back!'

The girls agreed. Astrid was especially happy.

'Fine!' laughed Vimp. 'Agreed. We can't hang about. Let's get set up by sundown.'

The Viking party split into groups and got down to their tasks. But as they worked they failed to spot hidden watchers behind large boulders upon the far cliffs.

Freya led her party up the sand dunes topped with spiky grass tussocks. They relaxed to the feel of loose sand running between their toes. Astrid lingered at the back of the foraging party with Eric. They said nothing but were clearly pleased to be in each other's company. She gave him her hand.

Whilst Bjorne saw to the setting up of the camp, Vimp needed words with Lief. They wandered off down the beach.

'We've been lucky, so far,' he said. 'Maybe we've landed on an uninhabited stretch of coast. As we pulled nearer the shore I looked for signs of smoke. But I spotted nothing.'

Lief wasn't so certain. His finger traced over his chin.

'Maybe it's *too* quiet,' he suggested. 'I was speaking to Emma. She said Vikings have a terrible reputation with the Saxon English. They used to fight the raiders but, nowadays, they're more likely to run off and hide. Who knows? They may even be watching us now. My fear is that they'll keep an eye on us until they work out what to do next.'

He kicked carelessly at a stray strand of seaweed.

'What would you do in their place? Allow us settle in? Or attack when we least expect it? *We* know we're not here to harm the Saxons, but do *they* know that?'

His mind flashed back to the incident with the pirates and the awesome sea serpent.

'Finding land seems like the best thing that's happened to us so far. But maybe our problems are only just beginning.'

He bent to pick up a large shell and pondered its scalloped shape.

'I'll tell you my secret worry. Promise to keep it to yourself. We've got enough tools on the boat to cut down trees and put up shelters, but we don't have weapons. If the Saxons find out they'll know we're defenceless.'

The two Viking friends continued down the beach. Not another word was spoken before they trudged back to the landing party.

CHAPTER 13

Anglo Saxons

Freya breathed in the freedom of the forest where leaves of late summer were turning gold. Her firewood collecting party soon found a track crossing other paths trodden by hunters and trappers.

Emma wandered ahead in a trance, delighted to return to her native land. At the back of her mind, there seemed to be some previous, faint memory of this place. Ingrid Applecheeks, for her part, enjoyed the peace and tranquillity. The woodland birds fell silent as soft evening sunlight filtered through the treetops.

Without thinking, the three girls plunged deeper into the wood whilst Eric and Astrid trailed behind. Their secret dreams had come true and they treasured this precious moment. Reaching a cross-junction of tracks they continued on, unaware that the other girls had turned left. It was not long before Astrid realised that she and Eric had separated from their friends.

'Where's Freya?' she asked. 'And Ingrid and Emma. D'you think they went down the other path?'

Eric, his head in the clouds, was not sure.

'I'll call them,' he suggested.

Before he could do so a piercing scream echoed through the wood. It was a girl's voice, stopping them in their tracks.

'That's Ingrid,' Eric cried. 'She's in trouble. They're on the other path.'

A dog barked, followed by sounds of men's voices. They were not far away.

Eric turned and raced back to the junction. Then he dived down the other track. He was confronted by a gang of rough men tussling with the girls who fought back like cats. Ingrid clung onto one fellow, scratching his cheeks with her nails. He yelped in pain. Pinned against a large oak, Freya drummed her fists against the stout ribs of an enraged Saxon. An excited hound snapping around her feet.

Eric sprang forward. He started on Freya's captor, swinging his clenched fist into the fellow's face. The blow split the Saxon's nose. Then he turned his attention to the hunter trying to make off with Ingrid. The man drew a knife from his belt and held its point against her throat. He leered horribly and shouted something incomprehensible. Eric, who spoke only Norse, swiftly got the message.

'No!' he shouted in his own language. 'Don't do it!'

The man pricked his knife into Ingrid's soft skin. The young Viking hesitated, not knowing what to do next. In that instant, three men sprang from their hiding place in the forest. Brandishing murderous daggers they grabbed Eric who lashed out as they closed in. Astrid screamed, begging Eric to give up. He raised his hands and submitted. The Saxons pulled leather thongs from their belts and trussed up his wrists. Eric, along with the girls he had volunteered to protect, would make prize prisoners. The leader, a scar-faced villain, ordered his men to drag the captives through the forest.

Back on the beach, Vimp kept an anxious eye on the evening shadows.

'It's ages since the girls set out,' he said to Lief. 'They should be back by now.'

Lief agreed.

'It's getting late. But I don't see how they can come to harm with Big Eric.'

He tried to sound more cheerful.

'They'll soon be back.'

Lief was wrong. Volunteers were chosen to venture into the forest in the fading light, although Vimp and a few others remained behind to guard the boat. It was nearly dark when the unhappy searchers returned without news of their missing friends.

'We'll try again at first light,' Vimp said grimly. 'I guess they've holed up somewhere for the night. They're bound to turn up.'

But he could not be sure. Darkness had fallen by the time Eric and the captive girls had been dragged to the Saxon settlement. A cluster of squat wooden huts, surrounded by a stout fence of stakes, had been erected in an open part of the forest. The prisoners were pushed through the outer gate into the light of a brightly burning fire. Surprised villagers jumped to their feet at the sudden appearance of the young Vikings. They seethed with hostility.

A lean, elderly man in a belted tunic and loose-fitting trousers stepped forward. He spoke to the leaders of the hunting party, demanding an explanation. When he was satisfied, three of the captors seized the girls and marched them over to a nearby hut. They shoved them into its gloomy interior where they were forced to squat on the floor. To the girls' relief, the men left them to set up guard duty outside.

Poor Eric, trussed up like a helpless chicken, was powerless to help. He was set upon by two sturdy henchmen and forced to kneel before the village Elder. The Chieftain's eyes blazed.

'You evil young Viking!' he shouted. 'We know why you are here.'

The men hauled Eric back on his feet and roped him to a vertical post set in the ground. People cursed or spat at him as they passed whilst the duty guards outside the girls' hut kept watch.

As the long night drew on, Eric's chief concern was for Astrid and her friends. He felt so guilty letting them wander deep into the forest and hung his head in shame. Freya and her friends spent a worrying night fearing for Eric's safety. Moments before dawn, the curtain was thrown across the entrance and two new guards strode in with flaming torches. They ungagged their captives and freed their wrists. A third guard entered with a steaming bowl of lumpy porridge, wooden platters and spoons. He scooped it out and thrust it in their faces.

'Eat!' he commanded and turned to cover the entrance.

Emma flexed her stiff wrists, rubbing them to restore the flow of blood. As she spooned the first mouthful she became aware of one guard staring at her. She turned her face away but, to her annoyance, he grabbed a lighted torch from his companion and stepped closer. It was more than Emma could bear.

'Go away!' she cried in her native tongue. 'Leave me alone.'

The young man bent down and held the torch close to her face.

'I think I know you. You're one of our people. Your name is Emma.'

The captive girl could hardly believe her ears. She looked at him suspiciously in the flickering light.

'How do you know my name? What do you want?'

The other guards were astonished to discover Emma spoke their language. The one with the torch spoke urgently.

'Emma. Don't you know me?'

He handed the torch to his companion and knelt by her side.

'My mother is your mother's sister. She moved away from your parents' village to live here with my father. She's sleeping close by.'

His expression softened.

'Years later,' he continued, 'she wanted to visit her old village. The one where you lived. That's when she took me and my brothers to meet you. Her own close family. It was the first time we'd ever left our forest.'

Ingrid and Freya moved over to be with Emma. Although they didn't speak Saxon English, they sensed they should show support to their friend. Emma's mind raced as she recalled the past meeting with her Saxon relatives. She saw the young guard was smiling.

'Are you Edwin?' she asked disbelievingly. 'Edwin, my cousin?'

He nodded and took her arm.

She translated the extraordinary news for her Viking friends then turned to Edwin.

'The next year we travelled to see *you*. We must have come to this village. I *knew* I'd been here before!'

Edwin seized the opportunity to speak to the other guards.

'Run and wake my mother at once. Ask our Chieftain to come as well. He won't like it, but tell him it matters.'

It was not long before the whole forest settlement was awake and buzzing with the puzzling news that a young Saxon girl had been captured. Villagers flocked to the hut and crowded outside. They stepped back respectfully when their Chieftain arrived.

'I understand you claim to be a Saxon girl,' he said. 'I find this difficult to believe. Why are you with these Viking raiders?'

Emma cleared her throat and spoke.

'I was captured many months ago. My village isn't far from here. Edwin is my cousin. These Vikings are my friends. They saved my life. I owe them everything. Please believe me.'

The Saxon Chieftain asked further questions but when Edwin's mother identified her lost niece, he accepted something unusual was afoot.

'I believe you,' he told her, solemnly. 'I shall give orders for your companions' release.'

Emma fell at his feet and he placed his hand gently upon her head. Big Eric was released from the stake. He was ungagged and fed food by the girls although his wrists stayed tied. Despite his trust in Emma the Chieftain remained cautious.

'I hope this isn't a trap,' he went on. 'We need to see this boat on the beach. Our village has been plundered before. As Chief, I shall never let this happen again to my people.'

To be on the safe side, he had already sent runners to nearby settlements to request men and weapons. He did not tell his captive Vikings he expected an army of Saxon warriors to arrive before sunrise.

CHAPTER 14

When to Attack?

Chieftain Alfred was a wise man. He had lived a long time under the dark shadow of Viking raids. Before he was made chieftain, he had grown sick of fellow Saxons fleeing from approaching long ships. Now that he was in charge, he had made plans with fellow-chieftains of villages along the coast. They had agreed the next time raiders threatened they would have men ready to take up the sword and fight.

Alfred sent fast runners bearing flaming torches to warn nearby villagers that a new gang of Vikings had landed. In the middle of the night, farmers and craftsmen left their beds, armed themselves, and hurried back with the runners. By dawn, Saxon fighters streamed into the Chieftain's village. They lit fires and tucked into hearty breakfasts prepared by the women who knew these brave men were willing to die for their families.

The moment Emma discovered what was happening she begged her cousin Edwin to listen to her extraordinary story. At first Edwin refused, as he wanted to fight, but with Freya and Ingrid's support, Emma persuaded him to go to Alfred. He found the Chieftain talking to his army leaders, discussing tactics and agreeing plans. Alfred had no time to waste on a youngster like Edwin.

'Go away, boy.' he snapped. 'I'm busy. Practice sword fighting if you want to make yourself useful in today's battle.'

'You must hear me,' Edwin pleaded. 'There's no battle to fight. The Vikings on the beach are Emma's friends. They're young like me and have no weapons. She told me they escaped from their own land and wish to settle here. They come in peace.'

'Nonsense!' one fierce looking fellow exploded. 'There's no such thing as a peaceful Viking. The only good Vikings are dead ones!'

His companions agreed but Edwin insisted they listened.

'It'll be like slaughtering lambs. Is that how Saxon warriors fight?'

Chieftain Alfred considered what the young Saxon had to say then put an idea to his army leaders.

'We have Viking captives in our village. It's true they're young. Four of them are girls. The other's a young fellow who looks as though he's never handled a battleaxe in his life.'

He paced up and down before the glowing embers of the fire.

'I'll make a proposal,' he continued. 'We'll keep our captives hostage whilst we find out what's happening on the shore. The Saxon girl and one other Viking girl will come with us. She speaks their language. If she's leading us into a trap she must be made to understand that her friends will be put to the sword. The Saxon girl will lose her life too.'

Edwin turned pale at the thought of his own people killing Emma. The leaders grumbled their agreement to go along with their Chieftain's plan.

'Meanwhile,' Alfred told them, 'prepare for battle. Tell your men to be ready for my signal to strike for the shore.'

At the rising of the sun, the gathered Saxon army moved out. They slipped silently down narrow forest paths, determined to do their duty. Weapons hung from their belts. The more timid volunteers worried about the forthcoming fight, fearing they would never see their families again. But most of the younger men were eager to get to grips with the Vikings. If they survived the encounter they might be greeted like heroes.

Emma, accompanied by Freya and Edwin, was ordered to stay close to Chieftain Alfred and warned not to try anything on. Her life, and those of her friends, dangled by a thin thread. The rag bag army of Saxon farmers and craftsmen reached the edge of the forest. Before them lay an open area of rolling sand with wild grasses. Beyond lay the foothills of the high dunes. Alfred sent scouts ahead to spy on the Vikings' movements. Edwin, Freya, and Emma watched from the trees as men darted forward. Every now and then they crouched behind spiky clumps of grass.

There was no Viking response so they continued onto the dunes and began to climb. Nearing the top, they dropped onto their stomachs to peer over the crests. They took in the activity on the shore as their leader signalled to the main army to advance. Three rows of Saxon warriors lined up in the dunes waiting for Alfred's command to go over the top.

The three youngsters, sticking close to the Chieftain, ploughed through the sand to the peak of the highest dune. They edged forward to hide behind a convenient clump of marram grass.

The scene they witnessed on the shoreline swept their breath away. The young Vikings had gathered around their beached boat. Bjorne Strawhead had climbed to the top of the mast and was telling his companions to look out to sea. With their backs to the dunes, they presented a perfect target for the Saxons to launch their attack. Alfred rose to give the signal, but Emma tugged his sleeve. She begged him not to strike and pointed to a second Viking vessel, out in the bay, rowing slowly in on the tide.

In the increasing dawn light, Alfred saw it was crewed by doughty Viking warriors. Had Emma had tricked him? He shook her off and drew his battle sword. Far better to finish off the young Vikings, on shore, before the support troops landed.

100

A shout went up from the approaching boat. The shore Vikings answered back and the shouting developed into an argument between the two crews. Alfred hesitated, unsure of what was going on. Emma took instant command of the situation.

'Wait! I can hear what they're saying. That's an enemy boat. They've come to capture our friends. They'll kill them.'

She sank to her knees before the Saxon Leader.

'Please,' she begged, 'you've got to help the friends who rescued me.'

CHAPTER 15

The Magic of Music

Down on the shore, Vimp and Lief stood side by side, dismayed by the approach of the hostile raiding boat. Their hearts sank as they recognised the figure of a burly warrior perched on the advancing prow.

'Ahoy!' he shouted across the waves. 'Don't look so pleased to see us. We've come to take you home!'

The two boys were horrified. Vimp's heart missed a beat.

'I don't believe it,' he said. 'It's Olaf Skullcrusher. How could he have found us?'

The old barbarian wielded his legendary club.

'See this, you varmints? I've brought old Nutcracker with me.'

He whirled the deadly weapon around over his helmet.

'Nutcracker's looking for cowardly skulls to split. He doesn't forgive runaways. And he can't stand boat thieves.'

Olaf grinned through the matted bush of red massive beard. Half his yellowed teeth were missing.

'We're here to save your skins,' he went on. 'If you come back and take your punishment like proper men, Chief Strongaxe might find it in his heart to forgive you. Of course, if you want to tough it out, old Nutcracker's happy to do his work!'

Olaf wildly brandished his club and nearly toppled out.

Out of sight and on top of the dunes, Emma translated Olaf's threat into Saxon for Chieftain Alfred. The Saxon army ached to get into action. She looked back to the beach to see Lief stride into the water. He raised his fist and shook it at Olaf.

'Go home, warmonger!' he cried. 'You're not wanted here. You give Vikings a bad name!'

Vimp splashed alongside to join in.

'That's right!' he shouted. 'Turn your boat round, Olaf Skullcrusher, and clear off! You woke us up with your horrible smell!'

The veteran trainer of Viking warriors could not believe his ears. He turned to his Chieftain, at the rear of the boat. Harald Strongaxe looked as though he was about to explode. Skullcrusher cleared his throat and bellowed forth once more.

'One last chance,' he told the boys. 'I'm going to order you, on the count of three, to step into the boat you stole and get ready to sail. You're to follow us back.' Olaf dropped his heavy club on the deck and began the count.

'One . . . two . . . er . . . er . . . "

He fought furiously to remember the next number in the sequence.

'It's the number that comes between two and four,' Lief laughed. 'You've been wearing that tight helmet too much!'

The boys on the beach jumped up and down and jeered.

'Twenty-seven,' called Bjorne Strawhead.

And from the back, 'Two hundred and twelve!'

Lief and Vimp collapsed. A great cheer of support rose up behind them. Olaf was pushed aside and Vimp's father, Eggbeard, called across the short gap between the two vessels.

'Listen here, Vimp, my son. Me and your old mum just want you to come home. We miss you. There's no one for us to tease any more. Your mother takes it out on me all the time. It's more than a man can bear. Mind you, she sends her regards and says there's a lovely meal waiting the moment you return.'

Vimp fixed his father in the eye.

'My mother couldn't cook a lovely meal to save her life. Or yours!'

Eggbeard looked at him plaintively.

'That's not fair. I captured an enormous rat in my bed a few nights ago. So I skinned it and handed it over. She popped it into her stewing pot and said, 'That'll do nicely for our Vimp when he returns to his senses. When he comes back to the full embrace of his warm and loving family'.'

Vimp shook his head and laughed.

'My mother doesn't know words like that. This is a put-up job. If we come back with you, we'll be skinned alive – like your rat!'

Further off, at the lookout posted high on the dunes, Emma continued to translate the extraordinary Viking conversation for the Saxon Chief. Alfred held back his men as the arguments on the beach raged. Eggberk, a respected traveller in foreign lands, rose to his feet in the Viking raider and addressed the hostile youngsters.

'Boys, you don't know what you're missing. We've got some great trips lined up for next year. There's a fellow called Eric the Red who's looking for sailors to go back to Greenland. Six months at sea, lots of fresh air, and as much fish as you can catch. He says Greenland's a stunning place. Good hunting. You might make your fortune in the fur trade. Much better than this useless Saxon dump you've sailed to!'

Vimp and Lief pretended not to listen.

'Then,' Eggbert went on, 'there's the inland river cruise through Russia to the Black Sea. You can take in the scenery on the way. Fantastic views and a chance to get your hands on the natives' jewellery and come back as rich men. Of course, if it's a sun tan you're after, there's the mid-summer trip to the Med. We plundered a vineyard there last time. Got as drunk as lords. Had to stay an extra week to get rid of our hangovers!'

Lief held up his hand.

'You people don't understand, do you? No one here wants to be a warrior. We don't think killing people's smart. Leave us alone!'

Eggberk shook his head, unable to think of any more to say. He was pushed aside by Olaf Skullcrusher whose temper was at fever pitch.

'Right! You've had it!' he bellowed, shaking his bony fist. 'Don't say we didn't give you a chance. We've come here to bring you lot back whether you like it or not.'

Skullcrusher turned to his crew and snapped out an order. A rumble of agreement broke out as his men gathered swords and axes. They were itching to leap over the sides of the long boat and tackle the easiest opponents they would ever face.

All of a sudden, Freya sprang out of her hiding place high in the dunes and dashed down to the beach. Even Emma was caught off guard as her friend ran towards the boat. Freya vaulted over the side and stood before the mast. Looking wildly around, she raised her arms and addressed her companions.

'There's only one way to teach these barbarians. Jump on board and find your cow horns. You've each got one. Hurry now!'

The young crew bustled around turning the boat upside down in the frantic search.

The raiders in the big war vessel stared at her bemused. Freya organised her band into sections and instructed them to tune up. The air filled with deep, breathy sounds. It was more than Olaf Skullcrusher and his men could take. The warriors trembled at the very thought of music and jammed their helmets hard down over their ears. After a final set of instructions, Freya raised her hands. The sounds they made were pure harmony, drifting over the sea and over the dunes. A delight to the musical ear, but for the unmusical Viking crew it was pain beyond description.

Olaf Skullcrusher, the least musical of all Vikings, fell down on his hands and knees and pleaded for the music to cease. His rowers cried out, hurled their weapons over the side, and snatched up the oars. Olaf struggled to his feet and shouted rowing instructions. The raiding boat lurched forward, gathered speed, and turned for the North. The desperate men pulled on their oars as the music they so hated faded into the distance. They scythed through the water, never having rowed at such speed in all their years of plunder. In no time, the war vessel had dipped over the horizon.

The magical music continued until Freya signalled for her friends to cease playing. The only sound remaining was the breaking of light waves on the shore. The musicians stood still, quietly pondering their private thoughts. A radiant Freya smiled and lowered her arms.

A burst of spontaneous applause sounded from the Saxon dunes. The young Vikings looked up to discover a ragged line of armed men standing against the skyline. But they offered no threat. When the applause died, the men drew their weapons from their belts and dropped them to the sand. Then they ran down the dunes.

Emma spurted ahead followed by cousin Edwin. The young Viking crew jumped off their boat. Emma dashed into Freya's arms and the Saxon defenders straggled onto the beach. No one knew what to do next. But there was an unspoken understanding between Saxons and Vikings. They no longer regarded each other as enemies.

Emma invited Vimp to meet Chieftain Alfred. The wise Saxon stepped forward and offered his hand in greeting. A loud cheer went up from his men. Vimp turned, clenched his fist, and instructed his friends to respond. There were happy faces all round.

It was a curious return to the forest settlement. Saxons and Vikings walked side by side communicating by hand gestures and smiles. Once back at the settlement, brave Eric, Astrid, and Ingrid were set free from their bonds. They greeted Emma and Freya, hugging and plying them with a hundred questions. Chief Alfred ordered a celebratory feast, after which he gave permission for the Viking adventurers to settle in the village.

Two evenings later, heads swimming with memories of the events following their extraordinary sea escape, a small party of young people strolled barefoot along the shore. Astrid lagged behind with Eric. Ingrid and Bjorne peered into a rock pool and laughed at their reflections as Emma, Freya, Vimp, and Lief talked quietly about their new situation. The Land of Vikings seemed a long way over the sea.

'Maybe one day we'll return. But we'll sail back to the old village on our own terms,' Vimp said. 'For now, Saxon England is where I want to be.'

He turned to Freya who had left the group and stood looking out to sea. Wisps of hair brushed her cheeks in the light onshore breeze. She took another step forward, hesitated, then continued slowly to the sea's edge. Vimp wanted to follow her but found himself rooted to the spot. His muscles seemed locked. Freya had almost reached the nearest waves lapping the shore. He attempted to call her but no sound came. He was unable to move his lips.

The high-born Viking girl stepped into the swirling water and turned to face her friends. As she did so, her skin glowed in the reddening rays of the declining sun.

The shore party of young Vikings stood frozen. Dancing flames licked over Freya's frail shoulders then darted down her arms to her fingertips. She raised her hands to the sky, a pale light shimmering through her now translucent body. The last of the flames dropped into the water to suffer instant extinction. A golden glow emanated from the water where Freya had stood.

Little by little, the petrified watchers emerged from their trance to scour the shore for evidence of their friend. But they found no trace. Emma stood by Vimp's side, gripped his arm and rested her head on his shoulder.

'Freya could not stay. She wasn't really one of us. She possessed powers that even she didn't fully understand. One day we may meet Freya again. Perhaps when the time comes for her to be a goddess.'

The Viking boy shivered in the chill of the evening breeze. He bowed his head. The English maid whose life he and Freya had saved accompanied him along the shore.

'I think we should return to the village,' Emma suggested. 'You will need to learn our Saxon ways and settle.'

As the young heroes left the beach, a beautiful white gull appeared in the sky. Lost in their own thoughts, they had no idea of its presence as it circled high above their heads. It swooped down and dipped past the friends as if to say good-bye.

Finally, the gull turned from the shore and headed out. It had no choice. The fragile bird obeyed the summons of Viking Gods.

PART 2

Freya
and the
Fenris-Wolf

The Gull Heads Out

The white gull sped low over the swelling sea. It kept to a straight course as the sun sank below the horizon. Darkness fell over waters dividing Saxon land from the Viking shore. The bird dropped almost to the surface, spray showering its drowsy head.

Dull eastern light crept over the sea. It fell on a line of distant cliffs. The bird circled and settled clumsily on a narrow ledge. Tucking its head under the curve of one wing it slept.

Time passed. The morning sun rose over the sea warming the cliffs' colony of herring gulls. They pecked and argued at untidy nests. An adult, grey wings flecked with black, swept past the intruder's ledge.

'Gag – ag – ag!'

A cry of aggression.

'Gag – ag –ag!'

Sweeping upwards on a rising air current the herring gull soared to the cliff top, looped, drifted and plunged down, leading with its cruel, yellow bill. A second gull joined it.

'Kyow! Kyow!'

They had spotted something new and unwelcome nestling upon a narrow surface.

The sharp alarm alerted other gulls who gathered to circle over the white gull's sleeping place. The colony rose as one, dipping and rising as the confused gull peered sleepily from its shelter.

One bold assailant sped like a missile towards the ledge. At the last moment it broke off the attack, wheeled away, and swept down to the waves pounding at the base of the cliffs.

Cringing on the ledge, the new arrival kept its head down as another young herring gull showed off in front of its elders.

'Go away!' it yelled. 'You don't belong here.'

Turning into the wind it wheeled round once more.

'This is your last chance!'

The aggressor skimmed past the ledge.

'Alien! You're not one of us.'

The small gull shrank back. There was no escape. It feared it would be torn to pieces by the tormenting cliff dwellers. A wheeling squadron of gulls assembled for attack.

Suddenly, the menacing flock parted, panicked and scattered. Two enormous birds plunged through its midst – formidable white-tailed eagles. Their fierce, yellow eyes scanned the rock face. They spotted the cowering bundle of feathers frozen on its risky ledge. Sweeping past, they rose slowly on their tattered wings and returned.

'Listen! You must follow. Do not delay. Your enemies will return. We offer your only chance.'

The white gull fluffed up its feathers and obeyed. It stepped nervously onto the edge of its shelter and launched off. The eagles flew on ahead but circled back to encourage the youngster to keep up. Faint calls of angry herring gulls echoed from the skies but not one was bold enough to challenge the giant birds. Heading north, the close flight of three birds stuck to the coastline. The weary gull began to flag behind its powerful escorts.

'I can't keep up,' it cried. 'I can't go on!'

The gull faltered, losing its way. One of the white-tailed eagles turned back and flew alongside.

'Keep going,' it hissed. 'It's a long journey ahead. We're under the strictest orders.'

The white gull felt faint, hardly able to take in what the big bird had told it.

'But I'm starving,' it pleaded. 'I haven't eaten for ages.'

The magnificent sea eagle, curved bill glinting in the morning sunlight, circled over the choppy sea. Its sharp eyes spotted a shoal of shining mackerel, feeding close to the surface. The fish darted through the water, pursuing smaller prey. They were unaware of the danger above their silvery heads. The eagle plunged down, thrusting out its cruel talons and hit the sea. It snatched a tasty mackerel. Its victim wriggled and writhed in the eagle's iron grip. But there was no escape as the masterful bird beat its wings to regain height.

The second eagle closed in on the small white gull.

'Follow me!'

The gull, too feeble not to do as it was told, tucked in behind. The leader flew on, seeking a small island off the coast.

'Look!' it called back. 'You can eat there.'

The white gull spotted the eagle's partner swooping onto the island, far below. The lifeless body of the mackerel hung in its talons. Gaining in confidence, the young gull followed it down to the rocks. The eagle hopped clumsily away, leaving the dead mackerel on a slab. It invited the gull to feed.

'Rest a while,' the first eagle spoke above the crash of the breakers. 'Nothing can attack you here. You're under our protection. Eat swiftly. Our masters will not forgive us if we fail.'

As it pecked at the mackerel, it was hard for the small gull to understand what was happening. Somewhere, deep in the recesses of its tired memory, it suspected it had set out from a far coastline. It sensed it had not always been a gull and might have existed in another life form. For the present it accepted its fate, not knowing if the white tailed eagles were friend or foe.

Perched on a clump of sea wrack, the first eagle presented a formidable sight. Its strong talons clung to slippery weed as waves broke over. Its yellow eyes fixed on the bony remains of the mackerel.

'Finish quickly,' it snapped. 'The gods will be angry if we're late.'

The gull gobbled down the last twist of fish entrails as the second sea eagle landed in the strengthening wind. It seemed edgy and anxious to take off as soon as possible.

'Hurry!' it insisted. 'We must arrive before sunset. The gods insist.'

Something strange flashed through the white gull's brain. That word again – gods. She had heard the term before. In another life?

'Now!' commanded the eagle, 'you've had enough.'

The three birds lifted into the wind to continue their northern course. Heading towards clouds billowing in from the west, they became small dots in the grey sky.

CHAPTER 2

Asgard

It had been an uneventful day for the god Heimdal, out on his bridge. The other gods led lives of luxury inside their splendid palaces; eating and drinking to bursting. They lolled around on fur-covered couches by roaring fires, attended by servants. It seemed they had little better to do.

Patrolling the bridge in shining white armour, Heimdal sat on his golden-maned steed. He had been appointed Watchman on the rainbow bridge joining Earth and the Viking Heaven. The God of Light considered this responsibility a high honour. Named Bifrost, the rainbow bridge sparkled in a dazzling array of colours. Heimdal was the right God for the job. He needed almost no sleep. This helped him to on patrol all night. His sight and hearing were legendary. Even in pitch dark, Heimdal's eyesight penetrated a hundred leagues. It was rumoured he could hear wool growing on a sheep's back. Nothing that made sound, or moved, escaped the attention of the rainbow's guard. From his high watching place, Heimdal peered into the lower world of men, giants, and dwarfs. It was his task to deter any bold adventurer who dared challenge Asgard, home of the Viking gods. When Asgard was threatened, Heimdal raised his trumpet to sound the alarm. Not that the foolish humans below offered any threat. Rather, it was the menacing giants over which Heimdal had to keep a watchful eye. They were not to be trusted and loved to pick fights.

Heimdal took his duty to signal danger to Asgard seriously, and enjoyed the loneliness of his house on the bridge. Heimdal of the golden teeth and handsome looks gazed solemnly at fleeting wisps of cloud floating across the rainbow. Little had happened all day. Suddenly, he heard a voice, mean and menacing.

'I know what you're thinking, Heimdal my friend.'

It was a sly, disturbing voice that Heimdal recognised immediately. He turned to confront the god he hated most of all.

'Loki!'

He spat out the word.

'Why are you here, on my bridge? Is not your Great Hall satisfactory to you?'

The trickster Loki smiled at him through the narrow slits of his eyes.

'You make me so welcome, Watchman. I imagined you might be glad of a little company. Even companionship as humble as mine. I understand, of course, there are fairer goddesses whose company you would prefer.'

Heimdal fought to control his anger. The trickster God made him feel uncomfortable.

'I was perfectly content until a moment ago,' he said. 'I observed the stone mason, below, construct his great wall. A mighty task. Soon, he will finish the defences of Asgard and no enemy will be able to attack. Not even the formidable army of Frost Giants. But this stone mason is a giant, himself. Did we not make him a promise when he offered to improve our fortress?'

He peered over the edge of the rainbow to view the massive fortification the giant built. It had taken him only a few months. Now the towering wall nearly surrounded Asgard. The giant had cut every single slab of stone by hand.

At first, he worked slowly, dragging each heavy boulder from the quarry. It seemed the building would take ages. But the stone mason asked if he could fetch his horse, a fine black stallion, to help him. The gods agreed so the pace of constructing the wall increased. It seemed the stone mason would finish his task on time.

Cunning Loki studied the final efforts of the giant's work.

'Heimdal, my friend, I know what you're thinking. You blame me for what is about to befall. Yet, it is unwise to underestimate Loki. Am I not the most devious and mischievous of all gods? Have you ever known me lose in an argument?'

Heimdal flashed his gold teeth.

'You're too sure of yourself. It was you who agreed to the stone mason's ridiculous demands. First, that he would take the goddess Freyja to be his wife. Second, that we shall hand him the sun and the moon. Very soon he will claim his rewards.'

Heimdal's blood ran hot.

'You know how Freyja feels about this extraordinary arrangement. She spends her days weeping. How can she possibly give up her godhood to be spirited away by a vulgar giant? And what shall we do without the sun and the moon? The Gods will stumble around in the blackness and freeze.'

The guardian of the bridge flashed an angry glance at Loki.

'It was you who persuaded the Gods to agree to the stone mason's outrageous demands. You told them he could never build his fortress in the little time you gave him. *But you were wrong.* In only a few hours, this mighty task will be complete. He will have met your demand and gentle Freyja will be handed over to him. Darkness will descend for ever over Asgard.'

Loki twisted his foxy face into a smile. He pointed to the sweating giant toiling below. The final boulders were being lifted in place.

'I shall visit the simpleton,' he said. 'You know giants, Heimdal. All brawn and no brain. It is a simple matter of outwitting him. Do you see Svadilfari, the finest stallion imaginable? How his black coat shines in the golden evening sun. Without the pulling strength of that horse, the giant is lost.'

With that Loki disappeared. Heimdal glanced down to the foot of the rainbow bridge. The giant took up the reins of his magnificent horse and led it away to the stone quarry for the final time. One more heavy load and construction would be complete. Then he would earn his reward.

The sun sank lower in the reddening sky as the mason and horse toiled up the stony path. They carried the final pieces of rock to complete the fortress of the gods. Suddenly, from behind a small scrubby bush, a young white mare stepped out. She pranced before Svadilfari, stretching up on her hind legs and pawing her fore-hooves in the air. She whinnied and cantered around, driving the young stallion mad with desire. All his life, the great stallion had dreamt of a mare with whom he could raise the finest race of horses. The mason jerked at his reins, but despite his enormous strength he failed to control the enraged beast. The leather snapped like flimsy strands of wool, allowing the mighty stallion to break free. He galloped up the steep slope. The mare threw down her challenge and Svadilfari snorted, flared nostrils steaming. He kicked his master to the ground who lay gasping in the dust.

The giant's hopes had been dashed. Without the aid of his great horse, he could not complete his work in time. He beat his fists into the flattened surface of the path. The stallion dashed up the valley side in pursuit of the mare. Slowly, the unfortunate giant builder rose to his feet and let out a mighty roar. Holding his heavy, sun-burned head in his hands he struggled forward, bent and beaten, shaking dust from his matted hair.

Cunning Loki had triumphed. From his lofty perch up on the rainbow, Heimdal felt a pang of sorrow for the builder of Asgard's magnificent fortress. The giant had only just failed complete his work but had run out of time as he had lost his horse.

Heimdal felt the swift breath of wind at his shoulder. For a fleeting moment Loki appeared, grinned, and disappeared to start trouble in some other part of the kingdom of the gods.

CHAPTER 3

The Hall of
Dead Warriors

The mighty Odin was in a foul mood. He had clashed with his goddess wife, Frigg, whom he suspected of taking a secret lover. He had been informed of Frigg's faithlessness by his two dark ravens, Hugin and Munin. The two birds were sent out each day to find and bring back news to Asgard. Odin, their master and Allfather of the gods, needed to hear about the behaviour of his fellow gods, as well as the activities of mortals and giants. By keeping ahead of the news he could act swiftly and strike his enemies.

Odin sat brooding in a watchtower high in one of his three palaces. He gazed out at the skies, refusing to join the lavish feast prepared in the greatest palace of all. This was Valhalla, a colossal building, erected amongst trees whose golden leaves danced in the light breeze. Its massive walls had been constructed from the spears of dead warriors, and the great golden roof of battle shields glinted in the light of the sun. Beneath, burned fires whose smoke curled up and passed out through holes cut in the roof. Valhalla, the Hall of the Slain, was breathtaking in size. Arranged around its sidewalls were five hundred and forty doors. Each one was so wide that eight hundred warriors, standing abreast could pass through each one. Odin turned moodily from his thoughts as his trusted slave entered his watchtower. The slave bowed low.

125

'Great Master, your companions, the lesser gods, request your divine presence at this afternoon's battle, before the feast. New warriors have arrived from Midgard, the place of men. All were slain in war and now come here to regain their lives. It is rumoured that there are mighty fighters amongst them. Olaf Bloodsword and Sigurd the Slayer managed to kill each other in the fiercest of battles. Now they pay you homage. Once restored to life, they promise to fight again for your entertainment and the amusement of the gods. This afternoon's show will be unsurpassed in ferocity and valour. No quarter will be asked or given. Both warriors are determined to prove, once and for all, which of them is bravest. I beseech, you, my Lord, honour your fellow gods and join them in the Great Hall.'

The slave dared not raise his eyes to those of the Allfather. His master stroked his beard and rose slowly from his seat.

'You are right, Prael. An amusement would be welcome. Also, I await news from my ravens. They should have returned by now. You know I never attend a fight without them.'

The slave shuffled his feet.

'I understand, Master, that Hugin and Munin have flown on a special mission. As far as the mortal lands of Midgard. The ravens are expected back before nightfall.'

Odin pinned a wolf fur around his powerful shoulders.

'Escort me to Valhalla,' he commanded. 'I do not wish it to be said that Allfather Odin is out to spoil the party.'

The scene that greeted Odin was repeated each day in Valhalla. The Gods assembled to view mass battles by brave Viking warriors who had lost their lives on Earth. To die on the field of war was the highest honour a Viking could attain. Only cowards died normal deaths. It was a soldier's dearest wish that he would be visited before a battle by Freya, Goddess of the Valkyries. She would select him to die, no matter how skilfully he fought. Freya and her superwomen promised to bring the slain to Valhalla, where they would live to fight forever.

127

Each day, the old warriors met in the great Hall of Spears and battled, yet again, to the death. They wished each other well, knowing at the end that their broken bodies would be mended. Following that they would sit down together at long wooden tables and eat and drink as much as they could consume. The delighted gods would applaud them and return next day for a renewal of the fighting.

Today was different, however. Former Chiefs Olaf Bloodsword and Sigurd the Slayer had been sworn enemies on Earth. Each had led Viking raiding parties onto the other's territory, clashing many times, and their bodies bore the scars of deep wounds.

Odin, greatest of the gods, strode into the hall. Hundreds of Viking warriors stood in ranks around the walls. For once, they had not brought their armour with them. Like the spectating gods who lounged on wooden couches covered in thick bearskins, they looked forward to a magnificent contest between two brave men. Odin stood before the two rivals and surveyed their weapons – mighty swords, swinging axes, and heavy shields.

'You are welcome, legendary Vikings,' he told the contestants. 'Today you will fight to the death just as you did in Midgard. Step forward, put on your helmets. Shake hands.'

The two old warriors obeyed the god and looked each other in the eye through narrow visors. Neither flinched. They shook hands grimly and chose their first weapon – the axe. Thrusting forward their shields, they rushed at each other yelling blood-curdling oaths. Olaf feinted in one direction before lurching back and striking Sigurd on his unprotected shoulder. The blade sliced through to the bone, but Sigurd seemed not to notice. He lunged at Olaf, who managed to parry the blow with the centre of his shield. The onlooking warriors cheered. This was their day off and they were enjoying the spectacle.

For the next three hours, the Viking chiefs aimed deadly blows at each other. They swapped axe for sword and blood began to flow. Olaf was unfortunate. His sandal slipped in a pool of his opponent's blood and he lost his footing. In an instant, his assailant towered over him. Olaf was helpless and desperately attempted to get his shield in the way of Sigurd's raised sword. But he was too late. The deadly weapon sliced clean through his bulging neck. His severed head, matted with the blood of both warriors, rolled under a table.

The gods and old soldiers rose to their feet to cheer the victor.

'Magnificent!'

'Such a cut!'

'In one blow!'

The winner staggered back, breathing heavily, runnels of sweat streaming down his rough face and mingling with his beard. He raised the sword above his head and accepted the tribute offered to him. The god Odin had never witnessed such a ferocious contest.

'Bring Sigurd to my table,' he commanded. 'He shall eat as my honoured guest.'

Yet, as Sigurd proudly took his seat, a miracle took place. Olaf Bloodsword heaved himself slowly up from the floor, his head restored to its rightful place and saluted the victor.

'You fought fair and well, Sigurd,' he admitted, struggling for breath. He straightened up. 'I salute you!'

The vast gathering of old soldiers cheered loudly and the hall rang to their shouts. Two of them stepped forward to escort Olaf to a table where other soldiers had gathered.

'Come and eat,' they said. 'We are proud to have you join us!'

Olaf, flushed, was pleased with himself. He tucked into a deserved meal of roast venison, boar, and swan. Flagons of ale were consumed as immortal gods and eternal warriors drank toasts, looking forward to future contests between more heroes.

Out on his bridge of rainbow colours, Heimdal the Watchman patrolled alone. The light slipped away as two small, dark shapes approached through the clouds. Hugin and Munin, the ravens of the Allfather, had returned. They alighted near to where Heimdal stood and hopped awkwardly over to him.

'Look well, Keeper of the Bridge,' Munin croaked. 'Before nightfall, the two sea eagles will arrive bearing their hostage. It is a small white gull. Nothing to look at but do not ignore it. We must report to our Master and warn him of the event. He has been expecting this for some time. This afternoon's fight was only the warm-up to the evening's entertainment. We would not wish to be that gull for all the gold in Asgard!'

CHAPTER 4

Freya's Appearance

The white gull gained strength after its brief meal of mackerel. Its eagle escorts flew on, ever higher. They headed into thick clouds forcing the gull to fly blind in damp greyness. The trailing eagle flew up alongside.

'Keep going, little one! We shall soon be through this cold mist. Our journey is nearly complete.'

In a flash, the yellowing rays of the evening sun dazzled the gull's eyes. It blinked but struggled on, adjusting to the new light. Below lay a world of puffing white clouds stretching in all directions.

'Look ahead!'

The gull peered forward. It was flying towards a gigantic tree, whose twisted branches clambered into the sky. As the three birds approached, the small outline of a golden cockerel appeared on the very highest bough. Its duty like that of the God, Heimdal, was to give warning of danger. But the cockerel did not crow.

'We fly to Bifrost,' the leading eagle called.

At that moment, far beneath the branches, the shimmering rainbow of the trembling bridge appeared. Heimdal, astride his golden-maned steed, looked up and signalled the fliers to continue. The gull looked so tiny in the sky with an eagle escort on each side. He could not help feel sorry for it, knowing what lay ahead. He wondered how a small bird could cause such offence to the gods. Surely they were too powerful to be bothered by a creature so fragile?

The eagle escorts began the final glide to their destination. As the gull descended it saw that they headed for a colossal wooden building, glinting red and gold in the evening sun. Open, gilded doors appeared immediately in front of them. The eagles swooped in, beating back their wings to slow their approach. They flew over the crowded heads of warriors. Talons outstretched, the powerful birds touched down on the stone floor at the feet of the great god Odin. He sat there, his two ravens perched upon his broad shoulders.

'You are welcome, brave travellers. I see you have completed your task and brought with you the gull the Gods wish to question.'

Odin rose and gestured to a side table where strips of raw meat had been prepared for the sea eagles.

'Feast now, then rest. You must be weary after your long flight.'

The two birds abandoned the gull and hopped awkwardly over to the place where their reward had been laid. Odin pulled himself to his full height and spoke to the assembly of old warriors. The gods and goddesses lounged on comfortable couches. 'Before you stands a small bird. You may imagine we immortals have no place for this earthly gull in the Hall of the Slain.'

The crowd jostled to catch sight of the bird that had landed in their midst.

'Do not be fooled, my friends,' Odin continued. 'There is more to this gull than meets your godly eyes. I call upon Loki to use his magic to reveal the true identity of this unwelcome guest.'

A buzz of interest ran through the watchers. Loki the Trickster stepped forward, ingratiating and sly. An unpleasant smile of self-importance crept over his foxy features as he turned to address the throng.

'The Allfather is right. With powers specially granted me, I can disclose the true nature of this imposter bird that dares to fly to Asgard.'

From its humble place on the floor the gull began to tremble.

'This is no bird,' Loki proclaimed. 'The wretched, feathered creature has flown here in disguise. It brings danger to the Kingdom of the Gods.'

He stepped closer.

'Reveal yourself!' he commanded. 'Let the Gods know your true identity.'

A blinding light startled the silenced watchers. In place of the tiny gull stood a beautiful young maiden. Her long hair was as golden as the bangle on her wrist. The girl stood still in a pale blue dress. The crowd gasped at the extraordinary transformation. Disbelief swept the hall as Loki raised his thin arms and demanded silence.

'You see, before you, a mortal from the place we call Midgard. A stripling of a girl and daughter of a minor Chieftain. Yet she had ideas above her position. She imagined she possessed powers not normally granted to mortals.'

Loki looked around sensing he had his audience in his grip. It pleased him and he turned to the Allfather.

'Great Odin, examine this young mortal. Ask her to explain the tricks she played upon the Earth.'

Loki smiled wickedly.

'I bow to your great wisdom, my Lord, and leave her to your judgement. However, if I may be so bold, I suggest we show her no mercy.'

He turned to his audience once more.

'The Gods will be filled with anger when they learn of her earthly deeds.'

Loki bowed low.

'By your leave, great Odin.'

The trickster walked over to the seat reserved for him at the high table. His moment of glory gave him satisfaction. Loki signalled to a hall servant, who filled his empty bowl with mead.

Odin ordered his ravens to fly from his shoulders. They waddled over to the spot where the two sea eagles binged. There were plenty of scraps left over. The god raised his right arm and called for silence. Immediately, the vast room grew quiet. He ignored the timid young maiden standing before him.

'I call the giantess, Ran,' he said. 'She has made a long journey to be with us. Ran comes from the oceans she rules with her husband, Aegir.'

Pushing her way through the mass of warriors, an extraordinary figure appeared. She stood far taller than the tallest man. Bedraggled locks of matted hair fell untidily about her face. Seawater dripped from her soaked clothing and ran over the floor as she made her way through the ranks. She stank of fish and salt. Glistening strands of brown seaweed dripped from her shoulders. Odin stepped forward to greet her.

'You are welcome, Ran. I see you have brought your net with you.'

The giantess grinned toothily and sensed a slight shudder pass through her audience.

'There may be some here,' she began, 'whom I have ensnared in my net and carried down to my underwater palace. Brave souls, no doubt, but always at risk when they set out upon my waters. After all is it not I, Ran, who makes the seas boil and churn?'

Odin nodded and drew her attention to the stricken maiden.

'We understand, Ran, that it was this mortal who humiliated your husband? The foolish child made him feel weak and powerless in his own ocean.'

The dripping giantess looked down on the girl. She removed a piece of seaweed attached to her shoulder.

'Is this the offender?' she said. 'She looks small. Can this be the mortal who dared challenge the great Aegir?'

The girl's heart quickened. When she had taken the form of a gull she seemed to have no memory. Now, pictures of past events flooded her mind. She *had* been human, before. It was in another time and she recalled how she had stood upon the deck of a seagoing boat and defied the Sea God, risen from the depths. It came back to her in a flash. She raised her face and glanced up to Ran. Suddenly, her fears vanished.

'I am Freya,' she cried in a strong voice, causing the warriors and Gods to crane forward. 'It is true. I challenged the great god Aegir. He appeared from the depths and would have snapped our boat with his gigantic hands. He meant to drown us all.'

In her mind, she conjured up images of her companions. Vimp, Lief the Poet, Big Eric, her Saxon friend Emma and two Viking friends, Ingrid and Astrid. They had set out on a mission, daring to cross the waters without seeking the Sea God's permission. She felt all eyes on her, hostile and accusing. Odin smiled grimly as she stood her ground.

'You have much explaining to do, Freya. You are accused of angering a God. Worse than that, you made him feel foolish in the eyes of your mortal companions.'

The girl's spirit rose and she took a step forward.

'What would you do in such circumstances?' she challenged. 'I did what I thought best.'

A busy murmur of interest spread around the Great Hall. Odin glowered at her from under his bushy eyebrows.

'Did you not command the God to return to his watery kingdom beneath the waves?' he asked. 'This was no mortal act. You summoned up powers not granted to mortals. With these you insulted Aegir.'

An audible gasp echoed round the assembly.

'No mortal,' Odin continued, 'has the right to challenge a God. Humans are not blessed with our gifts. They obey what we demand of them. Tell us, Freya, daughter of Harald Strongaxe, what is so special about you?'

The giantess Ran grasped the rough handle of the human net in her watery hands. She looked forward to punishing her next victim.

Chapter 5

Freya's Fate

To Freya, the trial seemed to go on forever. Ran, the sea-soaked giantess, ranted and raved. At one point, a slippery eel slithered out of the wet folds of her garments. It slid across the floor, under a table, and between godly boots. The watchers were greatly amused. This was definitely the sort of thing they had come to see and hear. As for Ran, she was so angry she could hardly contain herself.

'It is not I who should be here,' she shouted. 'It is my husband, Aegir. But since this mortal made him feel foolish he has refused to come out of his deep cavern. He has not eaten for days.'

Freya knew she was losing the battle. The calm she had adopted quickly began to evaporate. She felt the hostile gaze of the crowd before her. They seemed to go along with Ran, realising Freya had meddled with powers she did not fully understand.

'I found I could talk to wild creatures in the forest,' she tried to explain. 'Was that my fault? It meant I made friends with birds and deer. I have no idea where this magic came from. It was inside me.'

The gods were not sympathetic.

'You pretended to be a goddess on Earth,' Odin accused. 'What you did to Aegir is unforgivable. It mattered not that your companions would drown. They were mortals and of no importance. Once you had triumphed over Aegir who did you plan to take on next?'

Freya shook her head in despair. Odin surveyed the gods on the nearest high table.

'Would you contest Thor, God of Thunder?'

Thor shot Freya a dark look. Loki arose from his place and stalked to the middle of the hall.

'Permit *me*, Allfather,' he said, 'to answer your question. 'The maid did not stop with Aegir. The gods will know I have three children. Some call them monsters. I confess they have not turned out as I expected. My daughter, Hel, resides in the place of the dead who were not slaughtered in battle. And Fenrir, who takes the form of a wolf, is fierce and uncontrollable. He has been chained and banished from our company. Then there is Iormungandr, a serpent so menacing that he has had to be cast into the seas of Midgard.'

Gods and warriors alike knew the reputations of Loki's dreadful offspring.

'This impudent maiden,' he pointed at Freya, 'dared to call upon Iormungandr, Serpent of the World. She raised him from his watery lair and caused him to destroy a boatload of Viking warriors returning from their conquests.'

The onlookers shook their heads in astonishment. Calling Iormungandr from the black depths of the ocean was the most dangerous act imaginable. They all knew that the world would end, and the universe destroyed, when the serpent rose from its cavernous lair. Freya tried one last time to defend herself. She stepped onto a wooden bench and flung herself at the mercy of the deities seated nearby.

'My friends and I were upon the open sea,' she cried. 'We had escaped from our village as my friend, Emma, was to be sacrificed at the funeral of the Old Chieftain. The boat that attacked us was not manned by brave warriors but evil pirates. After they ran us down and discovered girls on board, we were threatened with capture.'

She stood up on her toes to plead with her sympathetic listeners.

'We could not allow this to happen. What would have been our fate? These men were not honourable. Where my mystical powers come from I do not know. Nor do I understand. I stood up and called to the Serpent of the World to come to our aid.'

The gods remained impassive, unimpressed by her explanation.

'Iormungandr rescued us. The Serpent destroyed the boat. He breathed poisonous fumes on the pirates who suffered watery graves.'

Freya suddenly felt very small. Her previous boldness deserted her. She hung her head in shame.

'I am very sorry,' she said meekly. 'I apologise to the Gods.'

With that she stepped down, covering her face in her face in her hands. The earthly maiden sobbed uncontrollably. The gods remained unmoved.

Thor, God of War, rose from his table and addressed the gathering.

'We have given the maid the chance to explain herself,' he growled. 'We have heard all we need to hear. She exceeded her powers and played at being a Goddess without authority.'

He cleared his throat and turned back to the angry audience.

'I call for her death,' he demanded. 'Spare no mercy. This mortal must be cast from the highest turret in Asgard and her body dashed upon the rocks.'

The whole throng rose as one.

'Death to the maiden!' they cried. 'Let her flesh and broken bones be pecked by crows!'

Freya fell sobbing to the stone floor. Not one God had spoken in her defence. There was deathly silence. The audience waited for the Allfather to complete the trial. To their surprise, a beautiful Goddess stood up gracefully from her place at the high table and took the floor. This was Freyja, Goddess of Love and Beauty. Vikings prayed to her for those they held dear. She travelled great distances in a chariot pulled by her favourite cats, whilst swallows and cuckoos circled around her head. The Viking people held these birds in honour, such was their respect for the Love Goddess. Yet Freyja had known unhappiness. Her husband, whom she adored, often deserted her when going on long journeys. She rose to quell the anger of the Gods and warriors pressed into the Great Hall.

'This maiden from Midgard,' she declared quietly, 'has taken my name. She has no one here to speak for her, so this duty I undertake. She has told us of gifts bestowed upon her. Who else could have granted these but the Gods themselves?'

The well loved goddess appealed to the other deities.

'The maid has never used these powers for her own purposes,' she said. 'Quite the opposite. She used them to save the lives of friends and companions. What could be more honourable than that?'

Freyja lifted her gentle face to the audience.

'Let the maid live. Do not destroy a person so precious. Does she look to you as if she could cause harm? Return her to Midgard. Let her become mortal once more. We can remove her powers to ensure they are never used again.'

She sensed her audience was being won over.

'Let her live!' she demanded.

The assembled ranks of battle-scarred warriors and privileged Gods rose to their feet.

'Let her live!'

Mortal Freya, a crumpled heap on the stone floor, slowly raised her small frame. She turned her tear-stained face towards the goddess her family had told her about. The Goddess of Love smiled and stretched to take her trembling hand. Odin, Allfather of the Gods, rose to pronounce his final decree.

141

'The Goddess has spoken,' he said. 'She has our respect and speaks with compassion and wisdom. No good will be served by destroying this young mortal. I strip her of her mystical powers so she may never call on them again.'

The audience murmured their agreement. Odin turned to the young mortal.

'Go now, maid,' he commanded. 'Return to your human state. Tell no one of your time here in Asgard. This is a secret you must guard all your life.'

The girl looked up, gratefully, and smiled through her tears.

'Loki,' the Allfather called 'you are the great traveller. Take this child back to Midgard and find her a place where she may continue her life.'

Sneaky Loki smiled

'At your command, Great Father,' he replied. 'Come,' he turned to the maid. 'Make haste. You may spend one night here, at Asgard, to rest. Then you begin your return journey in the morning.'

Lost for words, Freya expressed her gratitude to the Love Goddess after whom she had been named. Then she followed Loki out of the Great Hall, but did not see the cunning smile on his face.

Cђдрҁ∈ʀ   6

Anglo-Saxons

A small gathering of young people stood still upon the Northumbrian shore. Six were Vikings but one, Emma, was English. They did not speak but gazed out over the cold sea, each individual lost in silent thought.

So much had happened. Only days before, together with other friends from their village, they had stolen a boat and deserted their Viking homeland. The boys had defied their elders and refused to train as warriors. They had no wish to plunder homes of innocent people across the waters. Escape was the only answer. They took the boat they had spent months building.

However, it was the girls who had most reason to flee. Although most were safe in their Viking village, one was in peril of her life. This was English slave girl, Emma, captured on a cross-sea raid. But over the months she made new friends. One especially – Freya, daughter of the Chieftain, a privileged member of the first family.

The high-born Viking girl and English slave became close companions and shared many secrets. It was Freya's friendship that made Emma's harsh life more bearable. However, the close bond between them had been threatened. Freya's grandfather, the old Chieftain of the Viking settlement, died. His death was to be honoured in the traditional way. The craft the boys constructed would act as his funeral boat and buried under a large mound. The old chieftain's body was to be placed inside the boat, along with his war helmet and weapons. His faithful horse was to be slaughtered and laid alongside him. Far worse, a human sacrifice had to be made. To satisfy the gods, and to ensure the old Chieftain would make his way in the new world, a young person must be killed. That body too would be placed in the boat for burial. It was Emma the English slave who had been selected for sacrifice.

With the boys in rebellion against fighting and killing, and Freya and her friends horrified to discover Emma's undeserved fate, the young villagers planned a perilous escape in the middle of the night. They took over the recently built funeral ship and dragged Emma off with them. Then set out across the sea with little knowledge of sailing or navigation, yet they had survived awesome adventures.

First, there was the angering of Aegir, the great sea god. Raging with indignation against youngsters who had not sought his permission to sail upon his seas, he had risen from the depths to terrorise the stricken crew. But it was Freya, daughter of the Viking Chief, who confronted the infuriated God and quelled him with powers she hardly knew she possessed. As the journey progressed, Freya's mysterious gifts rescued the crew from marauding pirates. She had summoned Iormungandr the World Serpent, lurking in the blackest depths of the ocean, to destroy the pirate craft and its villainous crew. Freya's powers were as much a mystery to her as anyone else. She had no idea how she had come by them. It was as though the Gods, themselves, had bestowed them upon her. Eventually the exhausted crew, with Eric Bignose at the helm, had sailed across the sea to land on a lonely Northumbrian beach.

But their troubles were only beginning. A small Saxon army of farmers and carpenters was on the alert, keeping a sharp lookout for Viking invaders. They were not to know the young escapers were harmless and unarmed. For them, every Viking was a violent Viking. Once more, it was Freya's magical powers and quick

thinking that saved the day. And because Saxon slave girl Emma was with them, she was able to explain to her fellow countrymen that the young Vikings had saved her life. And that they wanted to settle peacefully. At first suspicious, the Anglo-Saxon leaders finally granted permission for the foreign visitors to stay.

Vimp, Eric, Lief the Poet, Astrid, Ingrid, Bjorne Strawhead, and rescued Emma stood still on the sands as tiny waves lapped up the beach. Freya had stepped into the water and they thought nothing of it. Yet, in a trace, her mortal body glowed. Small flames darted about her shoulders and tumbled into the sea. Freya's form became translucent and she began to disappear. In seconds, nothing was left of her. Vimp, rooted to the spot, could not move a muscle to aid her. The ethereal Freya vanished from his vision whilst, above his head, a small white gull dipped its wings in farewell, circled the group once. It flew on a straight course to its eastern homeland, across the sea.

Freya's time on Earth was over. Now, in the form of a sea bird, she would begin her journey to godhood and make her way to Asgard. The white gull had no choice but obey the command of her powerful Masters.

After several minutes gazing, uncomprehendingly, at the empty ocean, the small party on the beach turned back to their new village home. Vimp broke the painful silence as the others trudged heavily through the deep Northumbrian sand.

'What happened? She was here one moment. In the next, she ceased to exist.'

The others remained deep in thought. No one knew what to say. Lief spoke first.

'She was so special,' he said, quietly. 'She possessed powers people like us only dream of. I don't think she was simply human. Freya was more. We all know that.'

Emma agreed, close to tears.

'Maybe she had no choice. She's been taken from us. We shall never see her again.'

Tall, fair-haired Astrid slipped her arm around Emma's frail shoulders.

'Freya was too good for us. She was a Chieftain's daughter but . . . '

Astrid groped for further explanation.

'Perhaps she was sent to look after us . . . and when her work was done . . . '

Her words trailed off. Now, all they could do was turn away from the beach and wind through the forest to the Saxons' settlement.

The scent of pungent wood smoke drifted through the trees. Cooking smells, too. Big Eric's famous nose told him that a hog roasted on the spit. The Saxon villagers, at first their enemies, had decided to hold a welcome feast. Once they learned the boys had built their own boat they realised the immigrants had skills to offer. And the girls would soon find work to do. Some could weave and make jewellery. Ingrid and Astrid were especially gifted at needlework. At home, they made clothes for their families and sewed dresses and tunics, traded for household goods.

'Hi!'

It was Edwin, Emma's cousin. He was so glad to have her back safely on Saxon land. Edwin had left the village to get the Vikings to come back for the feast. After all, they were honoured guests.

'Where's Freya?' he asked. 'I thought she'd gone down to the beach with you?'

It was hard to explain. And even harder to tell the story to the Saxon elders once they reached the village. Yet the reaction of Alfred, the respected Headman, was unexpected.

'I suspected your friend possessed special powers,' he told them. 'Freya stood out amongst you. No offence, mind. Remember, we Anglo-Saxons once shared our gods with the Vikings. That was when our ancestors lived over the sea. And before we became Christians, over here. My grandfather always feared Thor, the God of Thunder. When I was a child, and afraid of a storm, he would tell me that Thor was smiting his mighty anvil, in the clouds. Of course, we don't believe that now. Well, perhaps a few older folks do. Very soon we shall build our own church. You boys can help us. Your carpentry skills will be of great service.'

The young Viking party walked over to their temporary huts with heavy hearts. No one felt like celebrating. Yet not to do so would be ungrateful and discourteous to the Saxons. It was so important to make friends. Lief stepped inside the thatched hut and tore off his tunic top.

'We mustn't let this get us down,' he said to the other boys. 'Freya wouldn't want that. Let's show these Saxons what we're made of. After all, we're of Viking stock. We have to put the past behind us.'

CHAPTER 7

Lief's Big Decision

It was the banquet to end all banquets. The walls of the main hall were decorated with elaborate carvings and woven tapestries. Painted, round shields and hunting spears hung from beams. Roasted hog was served to even the lowliest villager, who normally did not enjoy such luxury. The Saxons had been looking for an excuse to celebrate, and Emma's unexpected arrival with her Viking friends provided it. It seemed as though the Saxon villagers were happy to accept their visitors as long as the Vikings paid their way with hard work. Next morning, however, with aching heads from drinking too much ale, Vimp and company learned what they had to do.

'I feel so ill.'

The inside of Vimp's head seemed to be rolling around. Eric, who had snored all night, could not be woken. And Bjorne seemed to have turned a pale shade of green.

'They got us drunk,' he groaned. 'We're not used to it. I'm going to be sick.'

Vimp looked the other way. Suddenly, the end door of their sleeping hut opened and Emma bustled in.

'Come on, Vikings!' she said cheerily. 'Up with the light. There's work to do. The sun's shining, so it's time you turned out.'

Vimp could see that one or two Saxons stood behind her. Emma, as the only person in the village who spoke both languages, acted as interpreter.

'Work?' he said. 'What work? I need rest. We've only just arrived.'

Emma took no notice.

'Building work,' she said. 'Big stuff. But first . . . breakfast. There's porridge. As much as you want then it's on with the job. You'll have to look sharp. The Benedictine brothers have arrived from their monastery and want to start work right away.'

It made no sense to Vimp. He roused his unwilling companions and told them to follow him to the communal hut. A sleepy, tousle-headed bunch of Viking boys staggered over to the large building at the centre of the village. Astrid and Ingrid were already there, stirring steaming porridge. Ingrid stared at the bleary eyed boys as they tried to hold each other up.

'Look at these scruffy Vikings,' she laughed. 'They're half drunk and half asleep. We'll have to feed them like babies!'

The boys collapsed on rough wooden stools and accepted bowls of lumpy porridge with bad grace. None of them spoke but spooned their breakfasts in silence. Lief seemed to be in the best shape.

'Tell us,' he said to Emma, blowing on the gluey grey substance in his wooden bowl, 'what do the Saxons expect us to do?'

Already, he had spotted two unusual looking men on the building site conversing seriously. They were dressed in simple brown tunics, belted at the middle with a thick rope, and the tops of their heads were clean shaven. The men held out a piece of calf-skin vellum and examined it. Being a poet, Lief knew words could be written on vellum, but had no idea how. The men pointed to the ground in front of them, then paced out distances in open sandals.

Emma had grown more confident. She was no longer the desperate slave girl of her Viking captors. She was back, now, amongst the company of her own people. Soon she hoped to return to her own village, a few miles down the coast. But for now, cousin Edwin would keep an eye on her. The village was beginning to stir. Three shepherds guided their flock through the guard gate to fields beyond the settlement. A bent old woman emerged from her hut with a basket of grain, which she scattered for her ducks and chickens.

'Come on, you lot,' Edwin said in his own language. 'You'll earn your keep, today, helping the Benedictine brothers start our church.'

The Vikings stared at him, not understanding a word. Emma did her best to interpret, but Lief kept plying her with questions.

'Why do you call those odd looking men *brothers*?' he asked. 'And why are they dressed differently from everyone else? What does your cousin mean by *church*?'

He shrugged his shoulders as the group walked slowly over to meet the strangely dressed brothers. Lief saw that each wore a wooden cross round his neck. It was all very puzzling, but they seemed friendly enough once the group got within earshot.

Edwin called out to them. The brothers smiled and stepped forward to greet the Viking party. Vimp and his friends were beginning to feel better after their filling breakfasts and found the cool morning air refreshing. The shaven-headed men spoke to Emma who listened carefully. Then she turned to her Viking friends.

'The Reverend brothers bid you welcome,' she said. 'They are men of God. The Christian God and God of the Saxons. We no longer believe in the pagan gods of our ancestors. The brothers have travelled to this village to help us build a church.'

She hesitated when she spotted the Viking boat-builders were beginning to lose her meaning.

'A church,' she explained, 'is where our people gather to worship God. These monks live in a fine, stone monastery on an island off the coast. At first light they crossed the causeway to the land because the tide was out. Their master, the Abbot, ordered them to come here and organise the first church. The people are very excited.'

Emma turned to the brothers and addressed them in her own language. Then she spoke once more to her friends.

'Brothers Caedmon and Wuffinga are pleased to learn you are shipwrights. They know you can cut and handle wood. With your skills, this little church should be up in no time!'

Vimp looked around and saw that lengths of timber had been carted in from the forest. The logs had been split and stacked in piles. He knew this was to age them to prevent cracks from opening up in the building later. An area of ground had already been dug out. It appeared rectangular, with a sunken earth floor perhaps twenty to thirty paces long and fifteen across. This important construction would demand a good deal of oak and ash. The Saxon God made big demands. Also, in the sunken floor, deep holes had been dug out. These were to take the main wooden supports of the roof columns.

'We're lucky,' Vimp told Eric, 'that the villagers have already done the tree felling. What they need now is skilful building. That's where we come in!'

Eric agreed. He was more awake now and interested in the prospect ahead. He smiled at one of the brothers and rubbed his hands. They understood. It seemed all would be well.

Back in the huts, the girls had found more domestic tasks to perform. Ingrid and Astrid were sent to a Saxon family in one of the larger huts. Like Viking dwellings back home, it was constructed of wood and thatched with straw. But the hut was smoky and dark, with a lighted tallow candle and two pottery lamps to lift the gloom inside.

A young mother and three small children bid the girls welcome. She wore a green dyed dress that scraped the earth floor. Soon they were conversing in hastily thought up sign language, although the girls swiftly picked up a few Saxon words. They learned the mother's name was Edith and her husband was a fisherman who was at sea. A charred metal cauldron simmered on the fire in the middle of a raised hearth. Edith taught the girls the names of vegetables – beans, onions, leeks, and peas. Together, they chopped them up and popped them into the cauldron. By late afternoon, on the return of her husband, the family and girls would enjoy a thick vegetable broth.

153

Over the course of the next few days, both the church builders and girls picked up phrases of the Saxons' language. They worked hard, eager to prove their worth.

The church began to take shape under the supervision of the two monks who had travelled from their monastery on nearby Lindisfarne Island. Holes in the great oak crossbeams and upright posts were drilled with iron pokers. It was simple work for boys used to skilled boat-building. Vimp and Bjorne especially enjoyed attaching long sticks of willow to the crossbeams. These wattles reached the ground and formed a network for the side walls. They were interwoven with other sticks, and once all the wattles were in place around the building the boys spent the next two days happily daubing a gooey mixture of wet clay, animal dung, and straw into the gaps. As it dried, the walls set solid and weatherproof.

All that was left to complete was the roof. Again, oak was used with ash for the rafters. Expert thatchers took over from the young Vikings to cover the roof in reeds. The young Vikings watched as the experts cut and shaped the thatch. The outside structure of the church neared completion, and the Saxon villagers were delighted with the result. Beyond that, they were impressed with the hard work and carpentry skills the boys had brought to their community.

Everyone seemed happy except Big Eric. He had never been Lief's greatest fan and suspected the young poet was not dedicated to building work. Nor did Lief show enthusiasm for cutting, sawing, and joining. Eric noticed he seemed to spend a lot of his time with the Benedictine monks. The young poet quickly grasped their language and could speak simple phrases. Brothers Caedmon and Wuffinga were impressed. They even showed Lief their prized possession – a book they had carried with them from the monastery. The young poet marvelled at the beauty of the letters he could not yet understand. And he was thunderstruck by the hand-painted decorations on the cover and some of the pages.

'Lief's not pulling his weight,' Eric told Vimp moodily. 'We have to do the daily grind whilst he spends half his time chatting away with these strange men. You should have a word. You're his friend.'

Vimp sympathised.

'I understand, Eric. But let's face it, Lief was never cut out for manual work. He's much happier working on his poems and conjuring up thoughts in his funny head. Don't be too harsh on him.'

Eric was not impressed.

'Hmmph!' he snorted. 'It wasn't Lief's poetry that carried us across the sea. It was the long boat we built. If it wasn't for that he'd still be dreaming away in our old village. He'd never earn his living. He's a waste of time.'

The last thing Vimp wanted was a row amongst the Viking community, so he promised to speak to Lief when he got a chance. But when he found an opportunity a couple of days later, Vimp was in for a big shock. Poet Lief looked embarrassed, blushing slightly.

'I know I'm useless at this building stuff, Vimp. I feel ashamed sometimes. I've been speaking to the Benedictines. As you know, I'm getting better at their Saxon language.'

He turned away and gazed at the far line of trees, beyond the outer fence of the settlement.

'There's something I must tell you,' he said. 'Don't be angry. The brothers suggested I return to their monastery with them. They said it would be a wonderful thing for a Viking to get to know their Christian God and some person they call Jesus. I'm not sure what it all means, but they'd teach me to read and write in their language. And Latin, the language of the old Romans.'

Vimp was aghast. He looked sharply at his best friend. The thought of losing Lief, who had been so brave on the hazardous sea crossing, was too much to bear. His heart already ached for the missing Freya. With these losses, how could he be expected to cope?

The young poet slipped an arm over his pal's shoulder.

'You have to let me go, Vimp. It's my destiny.'

The two boys stood in silence watching distant cattle being herded back from pastures outside the village. It was some time before Vimp spoke.

'I wouldn't stand in your way, Lief,' he said quietly. 'Sometimes we have to do what we have to do. That's how we came here in the first place.'

He looked his friend firmly in the eye.

'Promise me one thing. You mustn't disappear completely. Stay in touch. I don't think Lindisfarne's that far away. Maybe I could come and visit you?'

Lief stared at the line of purple hills on the skyline.

'I'd like that. Thanks for listening.'

Chapter 8

A Mid-Night Treasure Trove

The long walk began. Saying good-bye to his Viking friends had been hard. Perhaps Lief had not realised how close he was to them. After all, they had ventured across stormy seas and landed in a foreign country. Emma took it hardest of all. It was all she could do to hold back tears when her Viking friend left for the monastery. She tried to stay cool, but her heart was broken. Lief was the person who meant most to her.

'It will take about four and a half hours,' said Brother Wuffinga as they left the forest and headed out over the cliff path. 'The villagers were kind. They gave us food even though they have little to offer.'

Lief looked up sharply.

'They were very generous to us, too. They held a banquet as great as any Viking feast.'

Brother Caedmon, in his late thirties, strong but gentle, shook his shaven head.

'They're good people. In truth, there's little food to spare. Last year, we suffered a poor harvest. The people take it as a warning sign.'

With little understanding of the Saxon language, Lief did not understand the monk's remark. Brother Wuffinga, a younger man, lively and with a fringe of fair hair around his temples, nodded in agreement.

'The Good Lord may be angry with his flock that doesn't always follow his teachings. We Benedictines do what we can. That's why we're building a church. But the people must follow the Lord's ways. Some say he sent the famine to punish wrongdoers.'

It was difficult for Lief to understand what kind of God would starve his own worshippers.

'Only half the normal amount of grain was gathered in the autumn,' Brother Wuffinga continued. 'The people say their cows and pigs are barren. Few calves and piglets have been born during the last few months. The people must repent and mend their ways. We shall help them with our prayers.'

By now, they had reached the highest point of the sea cliff. It stretched far into the distance. The cliffs were gradually being eaten away. Only the hardest rock could withstand the buffeting of winter storms. Ahead, Lief spotted a rounded bay eaten away by fierce seas.

The three companions trudged on in silence. This gave the poet time to ponder his new life and whether he was doing the right thing. He questioned Brother Wuffinga.

'When I join your monastery, what sort of things will you teach me? Will there be much to learn?'

The two monks smiled at each other and raised their eyebrows knowingly. Brother Wuffinga slapped Lief lightly on his back.

'Learn?' he said. 'It's all we ever do. Learn about The Lord and his life and sacrifice. Then there's the running of the monastery. Our Abbot is a strict man but fair. We have land to look after and must make sure the farms are producing properly. Brother Caedmon's and my skills are in construction. Our monastery church is always in need of repair and we've just extended the younger monks' dormitories. They've got to sleep somewhere even though they're woken up every few hours to attend chapel.'

Lief gave him a sharp look. He did not fancy having his sleep disturbed in the middle of the night. Brother Caedmon chimed in.

'Some of the brothers possess wonderful skills at writing. Me, I'm a bit ham fisted, but our colleagues can produce the most beautiful work. That's as long as their eye sight lasts. Once that goes, they're given other duties. To copy out the Bible, or the Psalms of King David, is a great responsibility. And once they make a new copy of the Bible we present it to a large church. Then we get down to another one. It takes ages!'

Lief remembered the brothers had shown him a book that looked very complicated and would take a lot of reading.

'The scribes work in Latin, the old Roman tongue,' Brother Caedmon explained. 'Some folks say we should write things in our Saxon language, but I'm not too sure about that. You don't want commoners understanding too much. Besides, they're not all smart enough to take it in.'

The three walkers stopped for a rest. Beyond the next bay, and separate from a cliff headland jutting into the sea, Lief spotted a small island. It was difficult to make out detail but there seemed to be a building on its crest. He asked the brothers what it might be.

'Lief, my young friend,' Brother Wuffinga said, 'you have good eyesight. You see before you your new home. That is Lindisfarne. Can you make out the chapel, the building with the tall tower? The tide cuts us off from the land twice a day. In that way we can focus on our worship.'

Amongst the scented sea pinks they found smooth rocks to sit on and tucked into the simple picnic the villagers had provided. A gentle breeze lifted onto the cliff top. It was possible to gaze far out to sea. Lief knew his Viking lands lay opposite, but over the horizon. It all seemed so far away, and he felt a pang of loneliness. But there was no turning back. Two hours later, the three companions descended a steep cliff path and picked their way over the rocky shore.

160

'The tide will sweep in soon,' Brother Wuffinga said. 'It has a will of its own and is not to be defied, even by kings.'

He pointed to a stony causeway that was raised slightly above the beach. It ran out to the foot of a small island. Now Lief could see the monastery buildings clearly. They stood tall and stark against the sky. He had never seen anything like them. Could they be made of stone? In his young life, he had only seen wooden constructions. Stone seemed cold and forbidding.

Deep rock pools remained each side of the causeway, fringed by seaweed. Many of the sea creatures had closed themselves up to the open air. Sea anemones, small red or brown blobs of jelly, stuck to the rock. They tucked their tentacles neatly up inside, waiting for the tide to pass over once more. Tough little barnacles nestled in their conical shells. They too would open out again as water passed over them, and extend their feathery fronds to feed.

Lief stood in awe of the mighty home of the Benedictines. He marvelled at the arches and stone pillars that supported the outer walls and counted arched windows, in rows, and the highest roof imaginable. Odin, Allfather of the Viking Gods, would have been proud to own such a palace.

The three travellers approached a double set of enormous oak doors. One cranked open and they were admitted by a solemn young monk who bowed his head slightly to Caedmon and Wuffinga.

'Enter, friend Lief,' said Wuffinga. 'Welcome to the monastic way of life. We must take you to our Abbot, who, I'm sure, will welcome you. He's never met a real Viking before, so you must understand if he's a little perplexed.'

The great gaunt walls of various buildings towered over Lief. Although overcome with wonderment, he felt anxious. How would he ever find his way around such an enormous place?

'We shall introduce you to your fellow Novices,' Brother Caedmon told him. 'They're mostly boys about your age. Saxons, of course, but you're picking up our language fast.'

That night, Lief hardly slept after being handed over to the young men called Novices. They didn't seem too sure about him as one or two had heard disturbing rumours of Viking raiders. He was taken up to their dormitory, where mattresses of straw lay in a single row along the cold stone floor. High on the side of the building, the windows had no shutters and let in a cold draught. Lief longed for the warmth and comfort of wood, candles, and smoke and missed the cheery tales and conversation of his friends. Tossing and turning upon his uncomfortable bed prevented any sleep. He was just beginning to doze, however, when he was awoken by the tolling of a deep bell. Mattresses either side of him stirred. Candles were lit and the yawning boys sleepily pulled on their Novices' robes.

'You must arise,' the nearest boy hissed at him. 'It's Midnight Matins. You mustn't be late. We have to pray for our souls, our Northumbrian King, and the souls of all living men.'

Lief followed the boys down a spiral staircase. He had to grope his way as the candle up ahead was held by the lead boy. Half awake, he hardly knew what was going on, only that he was being pushed by the boy behind him. Almost in total darkness, the small troupe of novices filed through the open cloisters of the monastery. They passed through a doorway. No talking was permitted and the only sound was the slow shuffling of feet on the stone floor. A stiff breeze blew through the open cloister. Lief shivered in his prickly Novice tunic.

When he reached the door, he realised he was entering a special place. Burning candles illuminated the great pillars of the church and threw long shadows into the corners. The brothers were singing. Their song was solemn and slow, and the sounds of manly voices echoed around the bare stone walls. Lief felt insignificant as he filed into a wooden pew, where the boy ahead indicated he must kneel and place his hands together.

The brothers ceased their singing. Now, in the half-dark and half-candlelight, a senior monk rose slowly from his place and walked to a wooden lectern. A candle burned on either side and shed enough light for the monk to open a large book. In strong, carrying tones he read out a passage in a language that had Lief completely baffled. The reading seemed to go on for ages. Finally, the monk stepped away from the lectern and faced the end of the church. He bowed low.

The service droned on. Lief began to sneak little glances through the open fingers of his hands. His eyes had adjusted to the light, so now he could see much more. What he discovered set his mind on fire. At the far end appeared a table covered with an embroidered cloth. Upon it were treasures the like of which he had only heard about after raider Vikings had returned from successful expeditions. Silver plates and ornaments had been set on the table. A bejewelled golden cross stood at the centre with drinking vessels of carved ivory. They gleamed in the twinkling candlelight. Lief stared at a Saxon treasure trove. The Viking warriors would give their eye teeth to possess it.

The quiet service continued, the Abbot speaking to his monks and novices and leading prayers. Every now and again, the worshippers would break into solemn chants in a language that Lief thought must be Latin.

It was a weary and painful young Viking who, one hour later, returned to the sparse comfort of his straw mattress. He had attended his first Matins service, most of which had been a complete mystery. As he fell asleep, Lief thought about the gold, jewels, silver, and ivory that seemed so out of place in this plain place.

'Imagine,' he thought, 'what our Viking Chieftain would have made of it, back home. If raiders ever get to hear of this treasure they'll want it for themselves. They'd kill for it!'

CHAPTER 9

Ravens at Sunset

More than a week had passed since Lief's arrival at the monastery on the holy island. He had settled well and his Novice companions had been friendlier towards him. Yet they teased him over his Viking accent and struggles with their Saxon language. There was hardly a spare moment to relax. It seemed that everything revolved round attending church. Up early for a service at six o'clock, a small service at nine, followed at eleven o'clock by High Mass. And so it went on throughout the day.

Yet there was time for work. At first, Lief was placed in the kitchens, where he had to chop vegetables, knead dough, scour the cooking pots and fetch water. He was not keen on the butchering of lambs. The Abbot called him to his special lodging and spoke to him kindly.

'You have impressed your companions,' he said. 'One day, we hope to call you Brother Lief, first of our Viking converts. This afternoon, you will report to the Scriptorium, where our scribes carry out writing tasks. I am told you are a willing learner. But it won't be easy, as you have *two* new languages to pick up.'

Lief stood meekly before the Abbot and smiled.

'I'll do my best, Reverend Father,' he replied in faltering Anglo-Saxon. 'Reading and writing are my great aims. And to worship your God,' he added hurriedly.

The Abbot walked over to the window and peered out over the surrounding sea. The sun glistened on the waters racing past the rock on which the monastery was perched.

'For the rest of the morning,' the Abbot continued, 'you are excused of your duties. Of course, you must attend all services, but other than that you are free.'

He gestured towards the rocky hillside falling away to the sea.

'Explore our small island. Find time to be with yourself and your thoughts. That is how you will discover truth. Remember, we are all small creatures in God's world.'

Minutes later, Lief tasted the first moment of freedom he had been granted since coming onto the island. He scrambled down steep slopes covered in wild flowers and spiky grasses. Something was moving below. It seemed as if the rocks bordering the sea were alive with strange creatures. As he climbed down, he began to make out their plump shapes.

'Seals!' he thought. 'Just like we have back home. They don't seem afraid. Our men would have hunted them. These ones see me coming but aren't trying to escape.'

Fat, bulbous grey seals lay basking on the rocks, resting from their feeding activities in the water. The biggest, bulkiest ones possessed dark fur, mottled with blacks and browns and lighter patches. They tended to keep to themselves or flop into the sea, as the mood suited. Slightly smaller seals, lighter, greyer, and more mottled, clustered together in groups. Lief felt sure these were the females. They lolled upon their rocky places, cocking a leathery flipper in the air. He was amused by their flattened, whiskery faces and soft, dog-like eyes. It seemed as though they had gathered to pass the time of day whilst youngsters frolicked in the foaming surf. These no longer needed their mothers to give them milk and were fully-fledged fishermen – or so they thought.

Lief dared not venture too close. He sensed the relaxed females were more alert than they appeared and if provoked, the gruffer males might warn him off. He sat still on a rock to take in the scene. It was his first happy moment on Lindisfarne and he sat back in the early summer sunshine.

Climbing the steep, stone steps to the large room where the cleverest monks copied out whole Bibles or religious passages, Lief hardly knew what to expect. At the top, he opened a door and looked inside. About half a dozen brothers sat on wooden stools at high writing desks. The Scriptorium was fairly light, with windows on each side, but on every desk was perched a lighted tallow candle. Not one scribe stopped as Lief hovered at the doorway. They bent over their work as though nothing would stop them. Lief did not know what to do.

'Come in, boy!'

A grumpy voice.

'Don't stand dithering. Close the door behind you. This place is draughty enough without extra ventilation.'

Lief stepped nervously forward. A second monk rose from his writing and beckoned Lief to him.

'Take no notice of Brother Aethred. He doesn't like being disturbed. Come over here. My name is Edward and I am in charge. Our Abbot has ordered me to train you as a scribe. He has great faith in you. Come and help me mix colours.'

The patient Brother escorted Lief to the end of the long room, where various pots, plates and knives sat on a trestle table. Lief noticed small lumps of rock, eggs, dried plants, and fruits strewn over the surface. Brother Edward explained.

'This is how we obtain our colours. The pinks and purples come from the turnsole plant that grows on the mainland. Other pigments we crush from rocks. Red from red lead and green from copper. My favourite is yellow from a mineral called orpiment, but it's not the most expensive.'

He stretched out his arm and selected a small piece of the richest blue, caressing it in his long fingers.

'Ah! Lapis lazuli. Isn't it beautiful? We have to use this sparingly. It's brought to our country from the Lebanon, close to where our Lord lived.'

He placed the precious pigment back on the table.

'This red mixture,' he pointed to a small bowl of liquid paint, 'also comes from far away. It's made from the crushed bodies of insects that live on Mediterranean oak trees. Extraordinary, isn't it? Come and see what we do.'

The scribe invited Lief to return to his sloping desk. Brother Edward sat on his stool and selected a sharp quill made from the long feather of a goose's wing. He dipped it in a small pot of black dye. Then he wiped off the excess fluid, and drew the quill over a thin piece of vellum, the stretched skin of a calf.

Lief stood by the monk's elbow. He saw that marks had already been made on the vellum in strict, straight lines. He guessed these were the shapes of the letters the Saxons used for writing. Very slowly, the scribe filled in the rough marks so that they stood out in black ink. Unable to read a word, Lief was mesmerised. For the rest of the afternoon, and before the Vespers service in the church, Lief went from desk to desk as the scribes painstakingly went about their tasks. The grumpy monk took no notice of him. Lief began to understand why. This scribe was particularly skilled at colouring the most exquisite designs built into the lettering. Using thin brushes made of short animal hairs, he selected reds and blues, yellows and greens. Lief had never in his life seen anything so precise, yet beautiful. His attention was taken by Brother Edward, who had stopped for a break.

'I see you are entranced,' he said. 'Brother Aethred is our finest artist. No one here has skills to match him. He takes on the most challenging designs.'

He motioned Lief to follow him.

'As you appear to be so interested. Let me show you something to fill your eyes with wonder.'

He went over to a wooden chest at a side wall and lifted the iron bound lid. Then he bent low to lift something heavy from inside. He took it over to a table and lit a candle.

'This is our prized possession. Few people have seen it.'

Lief found himself staring at a large, bound book with a heavy cover, decorated in jewels and silver and gold leaf. Its beauty put even grumpy Aethred's fine work in the shade. Very carefully, Brother Edward lifted the cover and exposed the first page.

'The Gospels of Our Lord,' he said respectfully. 'The words of the Apostles . . . Matthew, Mark, Luke, and John. What you see before you is the life of our Lord Jesus Christ.'

Lief failed to follow what he was being told. Dazzled by the colours and the neatest handwriting, Lied could only vaguely understand what the kind scribe was trying to tell him.

'Nothing in our monastery,' said Brother Edward, 'equals the value of this precious possession. No scribe today can produce such work. Sadly it was never quite finished. None of us possesses the skill to complete these Gospels. So unfinished they remain.'

He closed the heavy book and lifted it back carefully to the chest, closing the lid with care. His young Viking companion wanted to know why the extraordinary book had not been completed. Brother Edward read his thoughts.

'Seventy years ago our finest Scribe, Eadfrith, died before he could finish his great work. No one could do the coloured lettering like him. Nevertheless, Bishop Ethewald had the pages bound and sewn together with leather cords. And a hermit called Billfrith ornamented the cover with jewels and silver and gold. I don't believe any book will ever reach the artistry of our Lindisfarne Gospels. They remain here in our safekeeping.'

Over the next few days, Lief helped the Brother scribes mix their inks and colours. He learned how to crush minerals and mix in white of egg to fix the paints. But the hardest work was stretching the skins of calves over a frame and scraping them with a curved knife. After allowing them to dry, he had to scrape away once more, until the vellum was smooth enough for writing and painting.

Returning from evening prayers, Lief slipped out of the monastery to take in the last of the sun. It was June and not far from the longest day and shortest night. He thought continually about his friends down the coast and of his family in the land of the Vikings. Yet he suffered no regrets. It seemed to him that he had made a perfect choice. He still had not got his head around the teachings of the monks. The Christian God seemed so powerful, far more so than any of the pagan gods he only half believed in.

Lief sat overlooking the shining, peaceful sea and felt at ease with the world. Nothing could disturb this peace, he thought. But he could not have been more wrong. Two shadows flashed over the ground in front of him. He looked sharply up into the sky. A pair of glistening ravens flew over the cliff top and headed towards the mainland. He watched as they soared then turned, awkwardly, to swoop over his head. As they passed, they uttered sharp, jarring calls. Lief felt the hairs on the back of his neck rise. The Viking in him knew that sighting ravens often foretold bad events. He followed their flight with increasing anxiety as they flapped their way to the top of the monastery roof. Spreading their black wings, the pair hopped along the top of the chapel, cawing and croaking. Finally, as if satisfied with their mission, the great birds set off over the sea. This puzzled Lief as he knew ravens lived on cliff faces and mountains. Why would they fly in the opposite direction and risk death over an unfriendly ocean? Something deep down in his Viking being triggered a memory of what his grandmother had once told him as a child.

'If you see a pair of ravens cavorting in the evening sun,' she said grimly, 'it spells doom!'

It made young Lief laugh. Just another of the fantastic Nordic tales he had been told with his brother and sisters.

171

'Laugh not,' his grandmother warned, 'the evening ravens foretell terrible events. They warn of catastrophe. Pray the Gods will spare you.'

The Viking boy did not take such nonsense seriously. Yet now, far more grown up and in the company of gentle Christian brothers, he felt suddenly anxious and insecure. Surely no event could upset the tranquil life of a Benedictine monastery?

CHAPTER 10

Thunder, Lightning and Fiery Dragons

Vimp, Eric Bignose and Bjorne Strawhead shared a small hut they had erected themselves. They were beginning to pick up the Saxon language, even though they spoke in a strange accent. Like the rest of the crew that had pitched up on the Saxon shore, they had made their mark and gained respect. They were learning new trades.

'It's not like me,' Eric said, 'but I really like animals . . . livestock, I mean. The sheep and cows don't argue back like human beings. And I like taking them out to the pastures once we've done the early milking. I can relax out there.'

Pretty Astrid wrinkled her nose.

'You come back stinking of cow dung. Do you ever wash? Don't dare enter our hut!'

The long June day gave over to night as darkness descended over the village. Eric left his hut to take one last look at the cows, safe in an enclosure within the village guard fence.

'Funny,' he thought, holding a flaming torch as he approached the animals. 'They're restless, tonight. Irritable with each other. What's got into them?'

He wondered if wolves had dared to come up close in the dark. But it seemed unlikely. The few wolves left in the forest were wary of men and generally kept away. As he got to his precious cows, one turned on its neighbour and lashed out with its back hooves. The victim bellowed in pain, causing panic. Eric ran back to his hut and called to his friends. They had difficulty in believing his account, preferring to settle down for the night.

As the boys hurried to the cattle enclosure, a flash of lightning lit up the blackness. Seconds later, a low rumble of thunder disturbed the quiet of the night. The air became and sticky, unusual so early in the summer.

'I know who that is,' Eric said, grinning. 'It's our old God Thor, playing tricks. He's upset. Do you remember his storms back in Viking land?'

Bjorne laughed.

'Thor's mighty hammer,' he said. 'That's what our parents taught us. The God of Thunder working late at his anvil. I guess he's in a bad temper!'

The boys smiled in the dark. The cattle, however, remained edgy. Suddenly, a flash of white sheet lightning lit up the untidy sprawl of huts. Briefly, the whole village was bathed in the brightness. The young Vikings stood rooted to the spot as a close crash of thunder erupted. It seemed as though the storm was heading their way.

Other villagers, Saxon and Viking alike, scrambled out of their huts. A second crackle of lightning illuminated the scared white faces of the crowd. A massive explosion followed. The cows panicked, trying to break down their barriers. Astrid and Ingrid came running up, followed by Emma. They sought out the three boys, terrified by noise bursting their eardrums.

A white bolt of lightning streaked out of the night sky above the village and darted down to Earth. The girls heard the fearful villagers moan. In the brief moment of light, they saw mothers feel for wooden crosses at their necks. The lightning struck a sturdy oak tree just beyond the village gates, and the stricken watchers gasped as it burst into flame. In all their lives, young or old, no one had ever witnessed such a scene.

Alfred, the respected Village Elder, called for calm.

'This storm will pass! Return to your huts. The rains will start at any moment.'

But not one villager moved, fearing the possibility of the next lightning strike on their wooden dwellings. The small gathering of Viking youngsters huddled close. Secretly, they were concerned that Thor, God of Thunder, was expressing his extreme anger but making the Saxon villagers pay. Astrid, her face pale and drawn, mumbled half-forgotten pagan prayers. Ingrid looked into the sky and pointed to a light that appeared high over the dark tops of the trees. The light gained in intensity. It glowed white then yellow, increasing by the second. All of a sudden, it exploded into a shower of red stars that danced across the heavens.

'Oh no!'

Emma watched wide eyed as the demonic lights took the shape of a gigantic creature. High in the sky, a scarlet dragon dipped and twirled, shooting plumes of orange fire from its nostrils.

'It's the gods of our ancestors,' Emma wailed. 'A terrible sign!'

Vimp summoned up the courage that had taken him across the hazards of the North Sea.

'What about your Christian God?' he shouted. 'Can't He do something?'

Emma fell to her knees, hands held out to the Heavens as the sky dragon swooped low. A second explosion of light dazzled the onlookers as a winged, green dragon sailed across the sky. The first dragon turned, bared its fangs, and swept towards the newcomer. Emma screamed, fearing a collision, but at the last split second it turned away. Angry fire raged from the flared nostrils of both beasts. Dazzling sparks fell to the Earth, starting fires in the fields.

As instantly as they had appeared, the two monsters faded into the darkness. Children cried out as their mothers comforted them. Wise Alfred, the leader, understood the signs. Like Emma, he was aware of the ancient beliefs brought by his ancestors long ago. Memories of the Saxon gods remained.

'This is a warning,' he told himself. "

Reluctantly, the stunned villagers returned to their huts but kept their candles lit. Few slept that night. They, too, knew of the warnings and could not imagine what they had done to anger their ancient gods.

Eric stayed by his cows, helping them get over the unnerving experience. When the welcome rays of first light crept over the tree tops, he was joined by Vimp and Bjorne.

'I've been thinking,' said Vimp. 'I know we don't have the magic of Freya to protect us any more but I'm not going to let last night get us down. We need an explanation.'

This puzzled Bjorne and Eric.

'The people who might come up with an answer live only a short journey away,' Vimp went on. 'I'm thinking of the Christian brothers. They're educated. Far cleverer than us and they know things from books.'

Eric brightened at the idea.

'Let's go and see them,' he said. 'See how that bookworm, Lief, is getting on!'

After all, they had promised their poet friend they would stay in touch. Vimp was delighted at his friends' reactions.

'Good! We shall. But first,' he grew more thoughtful, 'we'd better seek Chieftain Alfred's permission. I wouldn't want him worrying we were going to Lindisfarne to get out of work.'

Later that morning, Alfred listened to their plan.

'You may go,' he told them. 'I would value the views of our Benedictine friends. But I'll be honest. Last night's events fill me with anxiety. I can't rest easily until we understand the message the dragons brought.'

CHAPTER 11

Viking Raiders!

The bright June morning filled the walkers with hope. They hurried along the cliff path towards the rock island monastery. The air was salty and freshly mixed with scents of early summer flowers. Signs of the previous night's storm had vanished, cheering the boys' spirits. But deep in their minds they could not get rid of memory of the sky dragons. Vimp did not share his anxieties with Bjorne and Eric but noticed how silent they were. They foot-slogged along the rugged path. What they wanted was an explanation. Surely the Benedictine brothers would come up with something. Maybe the appearance of dragons was a good omen.

'I see it!'

Sharp as ever, Eric was first to spot the island lying close off the shore. He was impressed.

'Those sides are so steep. They've built to the top of the rock.'

As the three drew closer, the outline of the grey buildings began to take shape. Massive and arched – high, forbidding walls. Vimp stopped suddenly. A dark plume of smoke rose from the roof.

'The monks are making a bonfire,' he joked. 'Goodness knows what with. I don't see any trees on the island.'

The smoke drifted towards the land. Now the boys got wind of it, a faint scent on the breeze.

'Another fire!'

Vimp pointed to the far end of the large building he imagined to be a church.

'Flames. What's going on?'

Eric's keen eyes scouted the shoreline.

'Below the cliffs,' he pointed. 'Drawn up on the shore. Boats . . . big ones . . .'

The boys stopped in their tracks. One word passed their lips. 'Vikings!'

Vimp thrust his arm in front of Bjorne.

'Stop!' he commanded. 'Not a foot further. We must find out what's going on.'

They scrambled behind a rocky outcrop overlooking the landing bay. Black smoke belched from the centre of the monastery. The boys could hear the crackle of hungry flames. Vimp's mind raced.

'We've got to get nearer,' he whispered. 'Those raiders mustn't see us. They'd show no mercy.'

Crouching low, they hurried down the steep cliff path. One false step and they might plunge to their deaths. At the same time, they had to keep out of sight of the Vikings guarding the boats. Getting round them would be a big problem. Bjorne skidded to a halt.

'We're crazy,' he cried. 'We'll be killed!'

They clambered down to the shore. The longboats were over to their right, beached high up on the sands. With the tide running out, Vimp worked out how they could get over to the island.

'The causeway's nearly exposed. There'll be currents, but the water's not deep. We'll have to run for it.'

Bjorne looked at him as though he'd gone crazy.

'They'll see us from the boats and come after us. What can we do, even if we get there?'

His fists were clenched. There was no way Bjorne was going to cross to the great rock. Eric, bravest of Vikings, stood firm.

'Of course we've got to get over,' he said. 'Lief's there. We can't let those rogues harm him. If you're not going, Bjorne, I am!'

He got up from his crouching position.

'Stop!'

Vimp tugged Eric back by the arm then pointed to the high cliff beneath the walls of the monastery. Two helmeted Vikings pushed a young monk to the top of the wall. The monk fought back but was no match for the burly raiders. The boys watched in horror as the brutes pitched the Benedictine over the parapet. Screams echoed around the cliffs before his body hit the rocks.

'Get down!'

Out of the corner of his eye, Bjorne had spotted a party of raiders driving a group of brothers before them. The robed monks were chained together and stumbled down the monastery path towards the causeway. Their captors barked out orders, daggers in one hand; axes in the other. The wretched monks lost their footing and fell into the water. A raider splashed up to the first who had tumbled and yanked him to his feet.

'They're taking off them as slaves,' Vimp whispered. He searched desperately for Lief but failed to spot him.

'Maybe Lief's still alive,' he said. 'Let this lot get past us, then we'll make our run.'

The miserable party of enslaved brothers passed almost within touching distance. The boys laid low under the boulder, obscuring them from the Viking sailors.

'Now!'

Vimp leapt out, followed closely by Bjorne and Eric. They splashed through the shallow water of the causeway. A shout went up behind, but they did not turn round. Hearts pounding, the three youngsters sped towards the path leading up to the monastery door. Scorched roof timbers crashed down, throwing up sparks. The boys kept on running, higher and higher, until they reached the open door. Diving inside, they found they were in an enclosed courtyard.

183

'Over there!'

Eric pointed to a second oak door. He ran up and tried the handle, cautiously at first, then risking a full turn. The door creaked open. No one was behind so they crept into the outbuilding. Its curved ceiling arches supported whatever might be above it. The boys dodged behind huge wooden wine barrels to regain their breath. There was no point in rushing in. It was time to make a plan.

★★★

Earlier that day, Novice Lief and the senior scribes had left the church to enter the Scriptorium. Lief went around with ink, charcoal drawing sticks and colour pots as the brothers settled into their work. Lief wandered over to the old wooden chest, lifted the lid, and carefully picked up the treasure of the Gospels. He marvelled at its bejewelled cover. The end door burst open. A wild-eyed Novice appeared at the entrance.

'Raiders!' he screamed. 'Vikings! Flee for your lives!'

At first, the gentle brothers did not know what to do. The older ones looked up from their desks, puzzled. Brother Edward rose slowly to his feet. He smiled his slow smile, holding out his palms to calm the young man. But the smile faded swiftly when coarse laughter drifted up the stairs. Followed by shouts and hurrying footsteps.

'Arghh!'

The young monk collapsed, smote from behind by an axe blow. Blood spurted from his unprotected neck and four helmeted raiders dashed into the room. Eyes bulging with desire for destruction, the Vikings set about the monks who attempted to rise from their places. Lief gasped in horror as a second raider plunged his short dagger into Brother Edward's ribs. The kindly monk slid to the ground, crossing himself and mumbling a prayer. Two other Vikings upset every piece of furniture they could lay their hands on. The remaining monks fell on their knees and pleaded for mercy. Hand-painted bibles with beautiful patterns and scriptures cascaded over the floor. The cruel raiders snatched up paint pots and hurled them in the brothers' faces.

Lief turned and did what instinct told him. He raced for the far door, knowing if he could reach it, he might escape to the chapel. But he was not quick enough. The first, murderous raider blocked his passage and raised his axe. Desperate to save himself, Lief thrust the Gospels between himself and the attacker. The stout cover took the weight of the blow.

'Give me that!'

Lief staggered but stayed on his feet. He had no difficulty in understanding the language.

'Gold and silver. That's mine!'

The menacing Viking made a grab for the Gospels. Lief feebly fended him off as the man rained down blows with his fists. For dear life, he clung onto the treasure of Lindisfarne. His assailant cursed, wrestled with the priceless cover, and tore it off. For a fleeting moment he lost his balance. Lief, clutching the remainder of the Gospels, seized his chance, and fled for the open door. He leapt down spiral steps, three at a time.

He was not pursued. Presumably, the warrior was happy with his haul and went back to join in the slaughter. Lungs bursting, the young Novice fled towards the chapel. There he might find safety. Surely the Viking raiders would not spoil such a sacred place? But Lief was wrong. He pushed open the west door to be engulfed in choking fumes. The heat from the raging fire drove him back. With smoke stinging his eyes, Lief made out the bleeding bodies of Benedictine brothers slumped over the altar. A party of brigands stashed gold and silver ornaments. Already, they were using their weapons to dig beneath the sacred table.

'Give me a hand!' shouted one.

His companion ran up. They pushed over the heavy altar.

'There's all kinds of stuff under here,' the first man grunted. 'I got it from a monk before tipping him over the cliff. A treasure trove, he said. Noblemen store their wealth in this place of . . . safety!'

His companions laughed.

'More loot than we can imagine. A king's ransom!'

Maddened with greed, they hacked up the altar stones. It did not take Lief long to work out they had hit gold. The raiders leapt to their feet, yelping for joy, and hurled handfuls of coins into the air.

'We're rich!'

The robbers slapped each other across the shoulders and divided the booty. Lief sneaked away. He was surprised to discover he still clutched the precious Gospels, minus their decorated cover. A minute later, he fled from the burning building. Tears of rage ran down his face as he headed for the cliff top. The area was strewn with boulders. Lief's one thought was to find one big enough to crawl under and wait for the raiders to depart.

He glanced behind him, but he had not been followed. The plunderers were too intent upon theft and murder. He spotted his boulder – a dark rock perched not far from the cliff edge. Then he inched gingerly around the other side. On hands and knees he peered into a dark cavity. Was that a movement? Something underneath? A pale face peered out.

'Don't kill me! I mean no harm.'

The voice was young and Viking. Lief stepped back.

'Show mercy. I don't speak Saxon.'

Lief came to his senses.

'Get out of there,' he commanded. 'Show yourself. Leave your weapons behind.'

A boy of about his own age emerged but offered no resistance. He was shocked that the young monk spoke in his own Viking tongue.

'Who are you?' asked Lief tersely. 'Why aren't with your raiding party? Answer me.'

The boy's hands shook as he glanced around, fearing attack at any moment.

'They forced me to go on the raid,' he sobbed. 'I didn't want to go. I'm useless. Can't fight to save my life – as you can see,' he added lamely.

'You're a Viking and won't fight?' Lief said. 'Well, so am I. We're on the same side!'

He laid the damaged Lindisfarne Gospels on the ground.

'We'll have to keep out of their way,' he warned. 'Wait 'til they've gone. Their minds are on treasure. Not on people like us.'

He rummaged in his tunic and pulled out an apple he had meant to eat during the morning.

'Here,' he said gruffly. 'Try this. It might make you feel better.'

It was a kind gesture and the nervous boy responded.

'Thanks,' he said. He held the polished red apple in his hand. 'I thought I'd met my end.'

Lief grimaced.

'So did I,' he said grimly. 'Like so many of my friends.'

CHAPTER 12

Return to the Village

The Viking raiders returned to their boats full of themselves and even fuller with Saxon treasure. It was the most successful raid they had ever been on. No one could remember whose idea it was to raid a monastery, but all the warriors agreed that it was easier to attack unprotected monks than a Saxon village. As for the booty, they could not believe their good fortune. Although the Benedictine brothers led simple lives and had little wealth themselves, they offered rich noblemen a safe store for their money. It had turned out to be a big mistake.

Vimp, Eric, and Bjorne were powerless to stop the destruction by their fellow countrymen. All they could do was lie low and wait for the raiders to leave. But they had to be careful. As fire raged through the sacred building, they hid out on the cliff tops, where they had a good view of the Viking oarsmen heaving their long boats back out to sea. None of them really wanted to explore the remains of the monastery. In their hearts, they suspected what they found would sicken them – slaughtered brothers and the dead body of Lief.

'What on Earth happened in here?'

The three brave youngsters stood at the entrance to the Scriptorium. Their jaws dropped when they saw the slain monks in pools of dark blood staining the stone floor. It made them ashamed to be Vikings.

'Examine each body,' Vimp said unhappily. 'I just hope one of them isn't Lief.'

The slaughter was sickening. Most of the brothers were elderly and unable to defend themselves. Eric had examined all the bodies, young and old.

'Lief's not here. Maybe they've taken him with them. Let's get out of this place.'

The three filed down the stairs and turned into the long corridor leading to the church. Bjorne felt uneasy. He spotted smoke seeping through the entrance.

'I don't think I can go in there.'

The other two felt the same.

'We've no choice,' said Vimp. 'We've got to go back with the true story.'

The church was a scene of devastation. Charred timbers littered the floor. Even now, embers burned red.

'Take care,' Eric warned. 'The rest of the roof might come in on top of us.'

It was a scary prospect. They ventured towards the altar. Dead bodies were strewn about and no one had been spared. Venturing forward, they discovered smashed floor stones and wooden chests emptied of their treasures. In the flickering light it was possible to check each dead brother, in turn. An unhappy thought flashed through Vimp's mind.

'We haven't found Lief. Not here, or in the writing room. He wasn't with the slave party.'

It seemed to suggest only one thing and that was the worst thought of all.

'Was it Lief they threw over the top of the wall?' he wondered. It had been a long way off so he could not be sure. Eric raised his finger to his lip.

'What was that?' he whispered.

The tall Viking peered into a gloomy corner of the ruined church.

'There's someone in here. I know it. Behind the stone column.'

He wished he had a weapon.

'Something moving. Let's clear out.'

It seemed they had made a big mistake. Had the Vikings left a small party behind to mop up anything they had missed during the raid? Eric had a flash of inspiration.

'We've got all the stuff!' he spoke loudly, in his native Viking tongue. 'Nothing left in here!'

The other two had no idea what he was getting at. They stood still in the near silence, interrupted only by the occasional crackle of burning timber.

'Come on you two,' Eric commanded. 'The others will go without us. We don't want to wait around for the Saxons.'

Vimp and Bjorne feared their friend's mind had blown.

'Don't hang about, Vikings. You, Bjorne Strawhair. Move!'

Eric's scheme worked better than he dared hope. He was not jumped on by remaining pirates. Through the smoky remains of the sacred chapel came a nervous reply. At first, he failed to recognise the voice.

'Eric, is that you? Vimp? Bjorne?'

The trainee monk stepped out from the shelter of a pillar. He was dirty and dishevelled, clutching a heavy book to his chest. Vimp and Bjorne looked on in astonishment. Was their friend miraculously alive?

'I have someone with me,' Lief went on, hurriedly. 'Don't harm him. His name's Tharg. A Viking like us. No threat.'

Tharg appeared out of the shadows. It was Vimp who reacted first. He cried out and dashed through the charred embers, flinging his arms around Lief. Bjorne followed. Eric, cool as ever, strode up to the celebrating Vikings.

'Cut it!' he said. 'Let's get out of this disaster. Back to the village.'

With the tide about to sweep back in, the small party of five Vikings abandoned Lindisfarne Island and splashed over to the mainland. Curiously, the boys had almost nothing to say to each other. They could not get the shock of the day's violent events out of their minds. Lief briefly explained how he had stumbled across Tharg. They understood the runaway Viking's feelings and knew they would have to invite them to stay.

The boys had not eaten for ages. Vimp, Bjorne, and Eric had hoped to be offered food by the monks. The other two were equally hungry. They hurried along the cliff path, towards the village, aiming to beat the setting sun. Bjorne stopped suddenly and pointed ahead.

'Travellers. One's in trouble.'

They increased their pace and got to within hailing distance. Vimp had already worked out their identity. One supported the other by his arm. Both wore the habits of Benedictine monks. They stumbled on.

'Come on!'

Vimp urged his friends to hurry and gave the men a shout. The taller one turned round, his face a picture of terror.

'Don't kill us!' he pleaded. 'We've nothing to give you.'

His companion fell to the path and lay still. He appeared very weak.

'Friends!' Vimp yelled in Saxon English. 'Brother Caedmon, is it you?'

The Benedictine could not believe his eyes,

'Vimp,' he cried. 'God be praised!'

The boys gathered round the fallen figure of Brother Wuffinga. His face was pale, and from stains on his habit they knew he had lost blood.

'Eric, stay with the brothers.' Vimp commanded. 'You as well, Tharg. We'll run on and get help. Here, Eric, look after this.'

Vimp thrust the torn copy of the Lindisfarne gospels into Eric's arms. Before his friend could argue he dashed off, followed by Lief and Bjorne. Half an hour later, they reached the outskirts of the village. As they hurried through the guard gate, Astrid, and Ingrid ran out to join them. They were amazed at Lief's appearance. He was wearing the simple robes of a Benedictine novice but seemed distracted.

'Find Alfred!' Vimp called out.

The Saxons, finishing their tasks for the day, bustled round them. They sensed Vimp's urgency. A young boy sped off to find the leader and soon the young Vikings poured out their woeful tale. Alfred and his village elders listened grimly. News of the sacking of the monastery had not reached them, and they hardly knew how to take it in. Lief told them of Brother Wuffinga's plight, and Alfred made a swift decision.

'Fetch a trestle,' he instructed a group of strong farmers. 'Quick as you can. Take water and cloths!'

The Saxons, used to dealing with accidents in the fields, rushed into a nearby hut. They emerged with a stretcher made of skin, supported on two long poles.

'Show us the way,' they told Vimp, then followed him through the forest and out onto the sand dunes.

Soon, the path began to wind up the cliffs. Panting for breath, they moved with all haste. It was not long before they spotted the small figures of the boys and English monks.

The first job was to attend to Wuffinga's wounds. The rescuers tore cloths into strips and gently cleaned the damaged areas of skin. They helped the injured monk to sip water before carefully placing him on the trestle.

'Lift together!'

Four men, one at each corner, lifted the trestle and started for home. Brother Caedmon and the Viking boys followed. The Benedictine remained shocked but managed to have a quiet word with Lief on the last lap of the journey.

'My son, this has been the most awful day in all our lives. However could we imagine such things? My brothers all captured or killed. Wuffinga's injuries are grave. He is unlikely to survive. Yet there is just one good thing to have come out of this dreadful affair.'

He indicated Eric who strolled ahead, bearing the Gospels.

'The Vikings destroyed everything,' Brother Caedmon went on. 'Lives – they are the most precious – but they also burned every book they could find. Decades of work keeping our teaching alive. I thought it had gone up in smoke until I saw you with your book. The most important work of all.'

He spoke solemnly.

'Lief, you have saved something precious. I don't know where The Good Lord was in all this. But I pray He may l look down and bless you.'

Caedmon paused to wipe away a tear. Lief thanked him graciously, not revealing what was on his mind. He had no idea what had made him save the sacred book. But he was confounded by the fact that the Christian God had let good men be slain. To Lief's relief, the party had reached the edge of the forest. Soon they would be back in the safety of the Saxon huts.

Chapter 13

News of Freya

Brother Wuffinga's broken body was buried in a simple grave dug just outside the church. The Saxon villagers attended the sad ceremony and wept as Caedmon gave his final blessing. They were shocked at the violence of the Lindisfarne raid. Anger against the Vikings welled up as they listened to the tale of destruction. Alfred, the village leader, was forced to speak up for Vimp and his friends, fearing they might be picked on for revenge.

Returning to work with heavy hearts, Eric and Bjorne finished milking before setting out for the fields. They made sure the animals did not stray to the edge of the forest, keeping them within sight of the huts. Bjorne alerted Eric's attention.

'Someone's coming. Heading this way.'

Eric turned to see a party of youths bearing down on them. They were armed with wooden sticks and clubs. He rose from his sitting place on a tree stump and faced them up. Hard-eyed Saxon boys fanned out, surrounding the two Vikings. A tall youth stepped forward. He gripped a heavy stick.

'You!' he snarled at Eric. 'The big one. How many Saxons have you killed?'

Big Eric's understanding of the Saxon language was poor but he had learned enough to grasp the meaning.

'Killed?' he struggled. 'I do not kill.'

The large youth leered, puffing out his chest. He winked at his comrades, who closed in on the two Vikings. Bjorne knew there was no escape and searched for something in the pasture to defend himself. But there was nothing to hand as the leader raised his weapon.

'Stand back to back,' Eric barked. 'It's our only chance!'

Bjorne obeyed. Neither boy wanted to fight, but at heart they were Vikings. They would go down battling.

'Stop!'

A distant shout. The mob turned to see the figures of Alfred and other men racing towards them. They hung onto their weapons.

'Stop, I say! No violence. That's a command.'

Breathless, the elderly leader staggered up and demanded the stick. He broke it angrily across his thigh and hurled the pieces into the meadow.

'Return to your tasks,' he ordered.

The menacing mob stood its ground.

'Anyone who disobeys will have to fight me, too,' Alfred threatened. 'Drop those sticks and get out of my sight.'

Reluctantly, the young Saxons turned, not daring to challenge the leader. Eric felt the flash of hatred aimed at him by the main trouble-maker. The Saxons mooched off, muttering among themselves. Eric unclenched his fists.

'Thank you,' he said, in his poor English accent. 'Thank you.'

Bjorne smiled nervously.

'Come,' said Alfred. 'Stay with me. Everything will be sorted.'

Thanks to the Saxon leader and the respect Brother Caedmon commanded, the situation over the next few days quietened down. The immigrants did their best to show the villagers how sorry they were for the Viking acts. It meant working harder than ever and trying to prove they wished to settle in peace. The most difficult thing to do was persuade the villagers that Tharg, the young Viking raider, offered no threat. He was anxious he would be blamed for the raid, but Vimp and Lief worked hard to make him welcome.

That night, they lit a fire outside their hut and invited the girls over. Tharg told them about his village which was not far down the coast from their own home. Something he mentioned made them sit up.

'You're all famous,' he said. 'Well, maybe not exactly *famous*, perhaps, but everyone knows about you. Your escape, I mean. The old folks aren't too impressed but my friends thought it was a really brave thing to do. Stories went round – like you'd been sunk by pirates. And there was another story that you'd upset the God of the Sea so he destroyed your boat.'

He looked round the huddled group, their faces lit by flickering flames.

'Of course, that's nonsense,' he continued. 'Because we also heard your village elders crossed the sea to go after you. And when they found you, you refused to return. It's hard to know what to believe!'

Vimp smiled.

'Well, actually a lot of it is true. Even the stories about the pirates and Aegir the Sea God. He was furious and would have drowned us but . . . '

A quick stab of pain struck him. He swallowed hard, his eyes filling with tears. The others looked up, understanding Vimp's distress. They hoped Lief would come to the rescue.

'It's true, Tharg,' Lief said gently. 'I guess we just struck lucky. There was someone very special on board. By ourselves, we could never have survived, but with her . . . well . . . just about anything could happen.'

He stared deeply into the spluttering embers. Emma slipped in to join her friends.

'Yes,' she said. 'A special person. The best friend I ever had. She, and these others,' she turned to Astrid and Ingrid, 'saved my life. I was to be sacrificed to our Gods. With these boys, they took the boat and we escaped to sea. My friend wasn't like us. She was special and used her powers to defy a Viking God.'

A murmur of quiet agreement ran through the group.

'Then she took on the pirates,' Ingrid chipped in. 'Unbelievable! I thought it was the end but she called up the great Serpent of the World. It destroyed their boat!'

Distant memories of the great escape flooded back as the listeners sat in silence, each with his or her private thoughts. Astrid broke the dark silence.

'We miss her. If only she could be with us now. We'd all feel safer.'

Lief nodded.

'I've tried so hard to puzzle it out,' he said. 'She was on the beach with us. She'd already dealt with the Viking party that sailed over to force us to return. I've always blamed myself but there was nothing we could do. She simply stepped into the waves and disappeared.'

No one spoke. A quiet voice broke the silence. It was Tharg, the new Viking.

'Are you're talking about Freya?'

There was a stunned silence.

The wood fire died low. Even the outline of the nearest hut was difficult to make out. Tharg glanced down at his feet. It seemed he had said something wrong. Vimp jumped to his rescue.

'Freya?' he cried. 'No one mentioned her by name. We never do. We just keep Freya quiet in our thoughts. How do *you* know about her?'

Tharg wriggled with embarrassment.

'I'm sorry,' he mumbled. 'I didn't know . . . '

Vimp tried to help.

'Tell us, Tharg, how did you know we were talking about Freya? After all, you've never met her.'

The small band of young Vikings felt on tenterhooks. Tharg shrugged his shoulders.

'Oh, it's just that we have a Freya in our village. It's quite a common name, so maybe it's not the same person. She's about our age but I don't really know her. She's a slave girl, working for a nasty family. They treat her badly.'

Eric was not impressed. He stretched his long legs out and pulled a face.

'Definitely not our Freya, then,' he snorted. 'Freya was no slave. She was first daughter of the High Chief. Not only that but, like Emma and Ingrid said, she took on the gods. She really did. If I'd been Aegir I'd have been furious. Then raising the World Serpent out at sea and defeating pirates . . . that was incredible.'

He laughed.

'Slave girls don't do that.'

Tharg looked up and raised his hand, for silence. He was suddenly confident.

'I wouldn't be too sure,' he said to his spellbound audience. 'The Freya in our village was not born there. Her arrival was a mystery. The family she works for was sworn to silence, but you know how word gets out.'

Vimp glanced up.

'What are you getting at, Tharg?' he said. He hoped he did not sound too sharp. This was Tharg's big moment.

'It's difficult to explain,' he said. 'My mother heard a rumour that this Freya had been someone special, but in another life. She'd been caught playing with magical powers and upset the gods. So they sent for her and handed out punishment. They stripped her of her powers and sent her back to our world. But they didn't return her to her proper family. Instead, Freya was made lowest of the low. That's why they put her to work as a village slave.'

He paused.

'Of course, I can only tell you what my mother told me. She heard that from someone else. You know how they gossip when they're making clothes.'

He paused.

'The really weird thing was that they said Loki, the Trickster God, had fixed it up to keep in with the great Odin.'

In the near darkness, the silence was deafening. Only Lief moved. He picked up a log and tossed it into the fire.

'We need to think about this. It's a lot to take in. We'll talk about it in the morning.'

CHAPTER 14

Setting Sail

Chieftain Alfred was not amused. He had already called a meeting of village folk, in the communal hut, to calm things down. It had been rowdy with angry protests about Viking behaviour. However, he had been able to persuade his fellow Saxons that Vimp and his friends were innocent of any crimes. The villagers accepted his word.

Now, the immigrants wanted another meeting. Vimp led the party but, as he still struggled with Saxon English, he let Lief do the talking.

'Chief Alfred,' Lief said. 'We don't know how to thank you enough for sticking up for us. Now we come to you with a request. I hardly know how to put it to you, but beg you not to be angry with us.'

Alfred surveyed the Viking gathering before him and saw Emma amongst them.

'Speak up. You know I'll listen.'

Lief coughed to clear his throat. It was not going to be easy.

'I speak with respect,' he said, 'because you let us settle. We've done our best to mix in and do our work. Now I must ask something very special. We believe that some of us need to leave the village for a short time. The others will stay behind. Those that go will return – that's a promise.'

The Saxon Chief raised his eyebrows. These Vikings created one surprise after another. Lief wasted no time and explained to Alfred the details of Tharg's story. The Chieftain remembered Freya, who had run down the sand dunes on the morning a hostile raiding ship rowed into the bay. And it was Freya who had stood up to the Vikings. She defied their demands that the youngsters return home for punishment. She seemed to be the leader, even more than Vimp. When the Viking ship rowed away, Freya had not returned with the new arrivals and seemed to have disappeared. He had never discussed the matter with Vimp or Lief. Tharg's story made things clearer.

'You tell me that your friend, Freya, has been enslaved and punished?'

Lief nodded. He had deliberately missed out the parts of the story that involved the angry revenge of the Viking gods. He could not see Christian Alfred understanding these.

'Freya,' Lief continued, 'is prisoner in a remote Viking village, where she's being forced to work for a cruel family. I would let Tharg explain, but he speaks no English. We get down on our knees to you, Alfred, to permit some of us – it'll only be the boys – to return to our land and rescue our friend. Freya means the world to us and will be of great value to this village.'

Lief stopped to explain matters to the Vikings. Immediately, Alfred sensed unrest amongst the girls, Emma in particular. She had fully understood the conversation.

'I want to go,' she demanded. 'I'm Freya's best friend. How dare you suggest girls can't come?'

She turned to her friends. Ingrid and Astrid were about to burst. It was an angry Astrid who addressed Vimp and Lief.

'If you two go,' she said, 'then we go too. Girls are just as good as boys!'

She folded her slender arms defiantly across her chest. Big Eric pitched in. Pulling himself to his full height, he turned towards the girl he most admired.

'Listen, Astrid,' he said, 'girls are fine but if you, or any of the others go, then *I don't*. And I'm the one that does the steering!'

Astrid had no answer. A noisy argument broke out amongst the Vikings. Alfred shouted above the din to bring them to order.

'I haven't granted anyone permission to leave,' he said, with Lief translating as best he could. 'Boy or girl. The whole mission seems madness. I'll discuss this at our next meeting with my village elders. We'll let you know. Incidentally,' he went on, 'Eric is right. No girl leaves this village. And that's an order!'

Alfred turned and strode out of the communal hut.

'Get back to your work,' he shouted back. 'Earn your keep. That's what you're here for!'

Heated arguments started up as the young Vikings returned to the fields or the boat they were repairing.

It was after the short Sunday morning church service that Alfred gave the young Vikings the village's decision.

'The Elders failed to agree,' he told them. 'Four voted to let you go, the other four to stay. I had to decide.'

Vimp and his friends felt numb. Had their hopes been dashed?

'I may live to regret this,' the Chieftain went on, 'but I voted in your favour. So you may attempt to rescue your friend. Whether any of you come back alive is another matter. You'll be in grave danger. Have you thought of that?'

Vimp nodded gravely.

'We have,' he replied. 'I asked for volunteers amongst the boys. They all wanted to come so I had to choose.'

That evening, the prospective sailors began to plan, the girls staying in their own hut. They bitterly resented the way they had been treated. Boys could do what they liked. They felt left out.

'Our longboat is in good repair,' Bjorne reported. 'I have bunged up the leaks with tar and replaced twisted timbers. She's seaworthy. Now we need to name her. Has anyone got a suggestion?'

It's obvious,' Vimp spoke up. 'We call our boat *Freya*. That'll bring us good fortune.'

There was cheerful agreement.

'We'll wait for a good wind,' Vimp continued, 'then set sail across the sea. I've asked the Saxons to let us have supplies. We'll repay them with hard work when we set foot on their shore, again. Any questions?'

Most of the boys fell silent, already feeling the tension. The first sea crossing had been an adventure but had almost gone wrong. Now they understood what heading into storms or thick banks of fog meant. They also worried about the Gods. Would they want to take it out them as they had done with Freya? Eric, sensible as ever, suggested taking weapons on board.

'Rescuing Freya is a big risk. The Vikings holding her aren't going to let her go without a fight. We'll take daggers.'

They'd only ever undertaken two days' weapon training and learned fighting was not for them. The girls remained unfriendly and unhelpful. Only Emma kept in touch with progress, whilst Astrid and Ingrid ignored the boys altogether.

'Eric will get us across the sea,' Vimp said, on the last night before the voyage. 'From then on, we rely on memory to try and work out the coastline. Tharg knows exactly where we're heading. We'll need every bit of luck we can get. If we're spotted by a raiding boat, we've had it!'

His stomach churned. The task seemed almost impossible. Secretly, Vimp could not help wondering if the mission was really a waste of time – or life.

That morning, Alfred and several Saxons helped the young Vikings load their ship. With a Westerly wind behind them, they knew they would be off to a good start.

'You may need this,' Alfred said, at the water's edge.

The young sailors looked up to see four strong Saxon boys staggering under the weight of a small rowing boat. Its oars were stowed in the hull.

'This will help you land on beaches where you might not be expected,' Alfred told them. 'Tie it behind the *Freya* and take it with you. We've stocked it with extra provisions. Look after it. It's mine!'

The gift was a generous gesture.

Two hours later, the rowers were in place on their cross benches with Eric at the stern. His strong hand grasped the tiller, long hair blowing in the breeze. He sensed the excitement of the mission. Eric's only regret was not being able to say good-bye to Astrid. He cast a final glance in the direction of the forest village and secretly sent her his love.

Just as they were about to wave farewell to the Saxon helpers, their attention was taken by a shrill call, high up the beach. English Emma tottered towards the boat, with a heavy bundle in her arms.

'Wait!' she cried. 'It's from the girls. They've been baking for you and making cheese.'

Emma splashed into the water and thrust the bag into Vimp's outstretched arms.

'Good luck!' she whispered. 'The others are praying for you. Tell the boys.'

Vimp took the bag from Emma.

'Say we'll see them again,' he said. 'I don't know when, but Freya will be with us. Promise!'

Emma beamed, doing her level best to put on a brave face. She waded back to the shore, skirt soaked up to her middle.

'We shall say prayers for you, my sons.'

Brother Caedmon joined the farewell party. He raised his right arm and made the sign of the cross.

'God speed!'

Lief stood by the mast. It was his task to start the rowers and keep them together.

'Take up your oars,' he commanded, 'and on the count . . . *row*!'

The longboat eased through the breaking surf. The boys, out of practice on the sea, struggled to find their rhythm. They fought to control the heavy lengths of wood that would propel them through the heaviest waves.

With their backs to the curved prow and dragon head, the rowers put distance between them and the onlookers. In minutes, the figures became tiny and unrecognisable. They continued to wave, wishing the boys well.

'Break out the sail!'

The longboat was now nearly out of the sheltered bay and heading for the open sea. Lief gave out the order that would save energy, soreness, and pain. Two of the sailors unhitched strong ropes attached to the furled sail. It fell from its top spar, across the mast, and billowed out in the wind. The *Freya* surged forward, causing some of the rowers to lose their stroke.

'Stow the oars!' Lief called.

The boys pulled their heavy weights out of the water.

'Relax whilst you can. If this wind holds it may take us right across.'

He glanced back to Big Eric tussling with the tiller. He looked every bit the Viking raider like his father before him. Lief admired Eric more than any other lad on board. The two were so different but had each other's respect. As the boat thrust through the swelling waves, the steersman lifted his face to the sky and laughed out loud.

'This is what it's about!' he cried into the stiff wind. 'We'll return. Just wait and see!'

He glanced back to the small rowing boat and its load, bobbing frantically behind. It rose and tipped, as though any moment would be its last. His eyes fixed on a large bundle of clothing wrapped under a waterproof skin. It seemed to move as if it had not been properly secured. This worried him. The last thing they wanted was to lose precious cargo.

Once more, Eric glanced forward to face the wind and pushed the captive boat to the back of his mind. The far shore was now all but deserted as the Saxons finally headed home. Emma remained, watching the disappearing boat as it diminished to a tiny dot. She turned away.

'Boys aren't quite as smart as they imagine,' she smiled to herself. 'When that crew reaches the far shore it's in for a big surprise!'

CHAPTER 15

An Extra Passenger

The crew's luck held out. Unlike its first crossing the voyage was mostly uneventful, powered by a favourable wind. The rowers still had work to do when the wind shifted and were soaked by cold spray. The *Freya* bucketed up and down in heavy seas. Night-time was worst, after they had reefed in the sail and taken turns at the helm to give Eric a break. It was on the second morning that the helmsman's attention was again drawn to the small rowing skip. His eyes widened. The boat had a passenger. Gripping onto the sides, she looked wet and cold before leaning over the side to be sick.

'Lief! Stop rowing!'

Eric indicated behind the longboat. Vimp joined him at the rudder.

'You know who that is, don't you?'

Big Eric knew only too well but did not know whether to be angry or joyful. One thing was certain. Astrid could not be left alone in that hazardous little off-shore boat. It was a miracle she had not been tipped out and drowned. The *Freya* slowed nearly to a stop.

'Pull the rope in,' Eric shouted, and together the two boys hauled on the slender link between the two craft.

'Stay down, Astrid!' he commanded. 'Don't try to stand.'

Getting her on board was not going to be easy, and Lief joined in to give an extra hand. Astrid, white-faced and petrified, looked up at her rescuers. They could see she was in a bad state, but this was not the time to ask questions. Lief leant out over the stern and grabbed the pointed prow of the small boat. He took up a mooring rope, tied to a ring, and secured the other end to a projecting spar on the *Freya*.

'I'm going over!'

Before the other two could stop him, Big Eric lowered himself gingerly into the rocking craft and scrambled over to Astrid.

'You're crazy!' he shouted. 'Just wait 'til I get you on board.'

Astrid held out a trembling arm. He grasped her icy hand.

'You're freezing. Crawl forward. Steady, now.'

The frightened girl crawled up to the dipping bows on her hands and knees. The stern of the *Freya* seemed to tower over her. She felt Eric's strong grip around her middle as she reached up to take Vimp's outstretched hands. Both boats rocked up and down on the swell. Between them, the boys bundled Astrid up over the side and up into longboat. A loud cheer went up from the rowers, but Astrid was too weak to respond. Lief placed his arm gently around her shoulder.

'Fresh water,' he said, offering a leather bottle. 'Drink. Then we'll find you a cloak to wrap round. There's dry clothes stowed away – boys' stuff – they'll have to do.'

Minutes later, the boat got underway again. Vimp took over the rudder as Lief ordered the rowers to pull. Once Astrid had changed, Eric sat her down on a cross bench and rubbed her arms and back. He pummelled her hard to restore circulation and stop her teeth from chattering. His fury dimmed as she warmed.

'I still think you're mad,' he said gruffly. 'I'm only doing this to keep you alive.'

It was on the fourth morning that lookout Bjorne sighted land. This was the best news so far, although he knew this would increase the chance of running into hostile raiders. Back on the helm, Eric ran the boat parallel to the coast, never losing sight of the shoreline.

'Look out for rocks, Bjorne!' he yelled.

Bjorne waved back and scoured the water ahead for breakers. From now on, the voyage would become even more perilous. It was late in the afternoon that Tharg, who had been excused rowing duty for a while, spotted something he thought he recognised. He asked Vimp to join him, at the dragon head.

'See the cliff with that enormous cave?' he said, pointing over the starboard bow. 'Where the surf's pounding on the rocks. That's the area where my uncle comes to fish. He's always warning us to keep away from this shore. There's a drag tide and we've lost the odd boat. One of my cousins drowned around here.'

It did not sound like good news to Vimp.

'If we sail on,' Tharg continued, 'we'll reach the river mouth. My village isn't far down. That's where we're heading!'

Vimp's heart quickened. At last, they were nearing the goal of their mission.

'Well done, Tharg. Glad to have you on board!'

Vimp stumbled back between the sweating oarsmen to consult Lief.

'We've arrived! That's Tharg's home river. We'll need to hove to and plan our next move. I'll speak to Eric.'

The tall helmsman was back at the job he loved best. Astrid sat at his feet, looking stronger. He had already guessed what Vimp had to tell him.

'We've done the boring bit,' he said with a grin. 'Now for the big boys' stuff.'

He glanced down to Astrid.

'That doesn't include you!'

She smiled sweetly and stuck out her tongue.

'Lief and Bjorne will take over the *Freya*,' Vimp said. 'They'll keep her out to sea with the crew. Three of us will go in, on the rowing boat. That's you, me and Tharg. He's the one who really counts as he can lead us to Freya. When we find her, we'll have an extra passenger to get back on board. That little boat's only just up to it.'

Vimp examined the glowing western sky, where the sun was starting to sink towards the horizon.

'We'll go in at dusk. The shore boat's loaded up. I'll tell Lief to keep the *Freya* out at sea until dawn. Then he can get close in on the shore. Let's hope the tide's in our favour. We'll get back to the beach, at first light, and light a lamp. Lief will signal back from the longboat. Then we'll row out with our captive!'

He paused and stared at the calm sea. Eric gave him a funny look.

'I'm glad you think it's as easy as that, Vimp,' he said. 'You had me worried for a moment. I thought you were going to say that the Viking villagers would put up a fight and we'd be lucky to escape with our lives. With or without Freya. And rowing back out to this boat will be no problem. Four people against the tide if it's not in our favour. Are you serious?'

Vimp knew Eric talked sense. Secretly, he gave the mission little chance.

'It shouldn't take too long,' Eric joked to Astrid. 'Make sure you have a good breakfast waiting for us!'

The young Viking girl glanced up at the boy she so admired.

'You're forgetting something,' she said. 'I don't do breakfasts.'

She looked him straight between the eyes without the flicker of a smile.

'I'm coming with you!'

216

Chapter 16

Loki's Desperate Plan

For Freya, life as a slave amongst hostile Vikings was a nightmare. She had been stripped of her mystical powers. Now, Allfather Odin placed her in the Loki's keeping. The trickster God changed his form into a fine blue hawk. Then he wrapped his captive in a net. Picking it up in his talons, Loki took off, beating his powerful wings to lift her weight. He passed over the rainbow bridge, shining in the morning sunlight. Freya's heart thumped as they left the high fortress walls of Asgard and headed into the blue. The hawk's firm grip was the only thing that stopped her hurtling to death.

The air was bitterly cold and she froze hunched up, with the tight mesh of the net biting into her skin. Soon the hawk changed direction and began its descent through swirling mists of thick cloud. Freya wanted to scream but knew it would be pointless. As they dropped from the bottom layer of cloud, she spotted the grey, rolling sea. Her fear was that the hawk might loosen its grip for her to plummet like a stone into the heaving waters. It would only take seconds to drown.

Numb with terror and unable to flex her icy fingers, Freya detected the dark outline of forested mountains bordering the sea. The hawk flew at great speed, crossing the coastline before heading along the twisting course of a wide river. As it lost height, Freya made out the tall, dark silhouettes of pine trees. At last, her blood began to pulse as feeling returned to her cramped limbs. The hawk circled low over a small habitation and Freya smelt fragrant wood smoke drifting up from the roofs. Miniature animals appeared below – sheep, cows, pigs, and goats. She could see well-tended fields that had recently been ploughed.

The hawk turned into the wind and swooped down to the ground. Helpless in her net, Freya was sure she would crash land but, to her astonishment, the bird achieved a light landing on soft pasture. She rolled on, two or three times, once it had loosened its talons.

Astonished villagers ran up as the great bird took off and gained height. Freya lay trapped, surrounded by the first excited arrivals. A burly Viking blundered his way through the milling onlookers and stood over the new arrival. Pulling a short dagger from his belt, he worked swiftly, slashing at the tangled netting to release its captive. Freya lay crumpled upon the ground, unable to raise herself. It seemed that half the village had turned out to witness her unexpected appearance.

The large farmer bent down and shoved his rough hands under her armpits, heaving her to her feet. Freya wobbled, so the man grabbed her tightly by the arm. The crowd buzzed with excitement.

'She's mine!' the ruffian exclaimed. 'I saw her first and I claim her.'

The villagers, knowing his reputation, were too timid to argue.

'I need help in the home. This girl will do nicely. She'll be put to work – unless someone here wishes to challenge me?'

The man stared round and all eyes dropped.

'Clear off,' he ordered the spectators. 'Have you nothing better to do?'

The humbled Vikings turned and trudged back to their village. Few dared to glance swiftly back over their shoulders. Thorkel Gellison was not a man to make an enemy of. He was used to getting his own way.

'Follow me!' he commanded Freya. 'Don't hang behind.'

Gellison's hut was little more than a hovel. Freya detected the stench of rotting food and cooking waste in the smoky interior. Three small children, dressed almost in rags, looked up from their places on the earth floor. They were thin and grubby, gazing up at Freya with, sad eyes.

'These,' the man said, 'are mine. They're nothing special. They lost their mother a few months ago.'

Freya saw that the children were half starved. She stared blankly at them, unable to raise a smile after the terrors of her journey.

'You,' the man turned to her, 'can make something of them. That's your job.'

A small girl coughed. She was four years old and it seemed the cough lay deep in her lungs.

'Grab yourself some broth,' Gellison told Freya. 'Then start clearing this place up. It's women's work and not fit for a man.'

He lumbered over to a large jar standing in a dark corner of the grimy hut to pour himself a beer. This he gulped down noisily as the children shrank from him. Freya looked round for a broom and began to sweep the floor strewn with litter and bits of cast off clothing. The children, two sisters and a brother, stared at her from their place near the fire. Their father enjoyed two further flagons before flinging himself down on an untidy heap of furs. It was not long before the ale got to his brain and he began to snore loudly.

The days passed. Freya was relieved that her master spent most of the daylight hours attending his animals and crops. He only returned at night to complain about the state of the hut, which she had actually made quite tidy. Now the timid children had someone to wash their clothes and feed them properly. Gradually, they warmed to the gentle ways of the person who baked them small sweets. Gellison offered little threat to Freya as long as she made progress and improved things for the children. What she missed most was the company of young people. She was not permitted to mix with the village Vikings of her age. In any case, their parents were wary of Freya. Where had she come from? Was it true that a great blue hawk had appeared in the skies above the village and dropped her into a field? Mothers gossiped, fearing Freya might be a witch sent to the village by an unfriendly God.

Meanwhile, back amongst the Gods' palaces in Asgard, Loki returned in triumph. Secretly he hoped to make Freya his next wife and restore her powers. For now, he was happy to know exactly where she was. There was no chance of escape. Yet it was a puzzled Loki who, upon his return to Asgard, stood in the presence of the Allfather. Odin's fine, powerful face was set grim.

'I have grave news for you, Loki,' he said. 'The Gods have long been displeased with your children. First, your daughter, Hel. So difficult was she that we banished her below the world of mortals to look after their dead. Then that terrible sea serpent, Iormungandr. To think you have produced such an offspring. Such a fearsome creature could never live with us here. It is right that we ordered the creature to dwell at the bottom of the ocean.'

Odin lowered his voice which took on a graver tone.

'Today, we must discuss the very worst of your children. Even the great God Tyr can no longer keep him under control.'

Loki smiled although more out of embarrassment.

'Great Odin,' he cried. 'You know I have done everything in my power to civilise Fenris-Wolf. But he is beyond me. He has grown into a giant. Bigger than any wolf born. His fangs grow longer by the day. Even I can't go near him.'

Loki paused and thought about days, past, when his wolf son had been little more than a playful puppy.

'I despair,' he confessed. 'I lost control of him. He snarls at every living being. Why, even the Gods are terrified of him. They fear that he will turn on them and ruin their palaces.'

He shook his head in sadness.

'I once loved Fenris-Wolf, but now accept he can no longer live amongst us. Believe me, Allfather, I have thought long and hard about this. I can offer only one solution.'

Loki, known for his trickery, for once seemed sincere. Odin asked what he had in mind.

'He will travel with me to Midgard, the Land of Men,' Loki replied. 'There I shall find a suitable dwelling place. He will be well fed but must always be chained. I have ordered dwarves to forge me the strongest chain possible. His place of imprisonment will be remote where men rarely go. Most importantly, it will be impossible for Fenris-Wolf to escape.'

Loki tried to sound sorry for himself, but in truth he was only too willing to get rid of the problem that put him in disfavour with the other Gods.

'Trust me, Allfather. Fenris-Wolf will never return. If he breaks out of his place of imprisonment he will only attack men. That is not our concern.'

'You have my permission to carry out your plan,' Odin told him. 'As long as Fenris-Wolf is removed from Asgard we shall never ask about him again.'

Loki bowed low.

'Thank you,' said Loki. 'You have my promise that Fenris-Wolf will cause the Gods no more anxiety.'

He slunk out of the presence of Odin to find his fearsome son. Getting such a creature to Earth would be difficult, but he felt confident he could invent a cock-and-bull story that would fool the gigantic wolf monster.

CHAPTER 17

Freya Goes Missing

The *Freya* rocked on the incoming tide, anchored at the mouth of the river flowing through Tharg's village. It was a risk, but Vimp had decided to go in at sunset, when no ships would be sailing. Indeed the great orb had nearly dropped below the horizon. In the last of mauve and scarlet light, the small landing party lowered themselves into the rowing boat to pull to the shore. The craft was full to bursting. Eric and Vimp rowed whilst Tharg sat at the stern, guiding them towards a safe spot. Astrid knelt in the middle of the boat, inches from the oarsmen's feet. She stared defiantly at Eric. He tried to ignore her, still furious that she had insisted upon coming with them.

The Freya got underway, her anchor hauled safely aboard. Lief stood at the prow and waved to the tiny crew embarked upon its rescue mission.

'We'll row out to sea,' he called to his oarsmen. 'We're against the tide. So pull hard. We'll spend tonight out on the water.'

He peered through the gathering gloom, just able to make out the dark fringe of shoreline. Lief would have preferred to beach the longboat, but there was the risk of being spotted. A night on dry land seemed like luxury compared to riding out the waves.

'Steer to starboard,' he commanded Bjorne, the new helmsman. 'So far so good. They're going to land, unchallenged.'

The small craft scraped onto the beach in near darkness. Astrid was ordered over the side to help pull it in and Tharg splashed in beside her. They sank into soft mud, up to their knees.

'I'll give you a hand,' he offered, cheerfully. 'Those two have got a bit of weight between them.'

Soon, the boat was concealed under bushes, the young sailors having unloaded its goods.

'I've got flints and three torches,' Vimp said. 'I don't want to light them, but there's no way through these woods if we can't find a path. Even then, we need light. It's a risk but there's no choice.'

The others understood. They set out with Tharg in the lead. He held the flaming torch in his hand.

'We're some distance away from my village. It's round the big bend in the river. The family Freya works for live over at the far side, a bit away from the rest of the huts. That makes things easier. No one's going to be out at this time of night.'

In the feeble light it was too easy to step off the narrow, twisting path and blunder into a tree. Vimp was not convinced that Tharg knew the forest as well as he imagined. For all Vimp knew, they might be walking around in dark circles.

'Stop!'

It was Astrid.

'I heard something. Stay still.'

Tharg passed the flare to Eric, at the back, who did his best to conceal it. No one in the raiding party breathed or moved a muscle.

'There it is again,' said Astrid. 'Ahead. To the left.'

The four stood still as statues. It was not a human sound, rather the warning snarl of a wild animal. A deep growling and very near. Astrid's blood pounded and Eric moved forward to protect her. Although he had no idea where the creature was, he sensed it could see them in the poor light of the flame.

'Yellow eyes!'

The cold eyes reflected the torchlight. Eric felt sick, knowing there was only one explanation. Two more pairs of shining eyes glinted, only paces away.

Eric thrust forward. He held the flaming torch before him, gripping it like a weapon.

'Come on,' he called. 'Come on, if you're so brave!'

Two of the pairs of eyes faded into the darkness. The first pair remained steady and unmoving.

'They hate fire,' he said quickly, desperate to believe his own words. 'Stick together and we'll be all right.'

Eric took a step down the path.

'Follow me!' he commanded. Petrified, the others slid in behind him.

'Here,' he said. 'It's—'

They saw the creature at the same time. A large, grey wolf of the forest stared unblinkingly into the light of the flaming torch. It lay on its side, unable to move. Eric inched forward. The wolf turned its great head and bared its fangs. They gleamed white and cruel in the flickering torchlight. It let out another menacing snarl but made no attempt to attack. Eric probed further and spotted a wicked looking piece of rusting iron. This was chained to a stake, hammered into the ground and made of two parts, each with pointed teeth. These had closed upon the wolf's hind leg. Clots of dark, red blood thickened in its matted fur. It had lain helpless for hours.

'Keep your guard,' Eric warned. 'We saw two others. There may be more. Let's get going. This one'll be dead by morning.'

He was brushed aside by Astrid.

'That's terrible,' she said. 'Freya and I were friends with wolves. They never harmed us. Wolves were our friends.'

Eric could hardly believe what he was hearing.

'Friends?' he challenged. 'You were friends with wolves? Don't mess with us, Astrid. I said we've got to get going.'

Astrid took no notice of the young man she adored.

'I don't care,' she said. 'We can't leave it to die. I'm going to release it!'

Vimp stirred himself, as if out of a dream.

'Leave it,' he said sharply. 'That creature's not going to thank you. Put your hand anywhere near and you'll get it bitten off. Then what do we do?'

He grasped Astrid by the shoulder but she wriggled free and knelt beside the wolf. It ceased snarling.

'Well, don't just stand there, you lot' she cried. 'You're stronger than me. Get your hands on those trap jaws and pull them back.'

She touched the wolf gently on the shoulder.

'Don't stand gawping,' she commanded the speechless boys. *'Do what I tell you!'*

Tharg was first to react. He dropped to his knees and placed his hand gingerly on the evil-looking trap jaws.

'Take the other side, Vimp. Pull when I say so. Now!'

As the two boys fought back the sprung teeth, Astrid lifted the wolf's leg. For all the blood and staining, she saw it had not been broken.

'Let your part go back, slowly,' Tharg told Vimp. 'Watch your fingers. And mine.'

The trap snapped shut once more but with nothing left between its teeth. Meanwhile, to Eric's frustration, Astrid spoke comforting words to the wolf. He was keener on searching around for other pairs of yellow eyes out in the darkness.

The injured wolf tried to get up but yelped in pain. Astrid tore at her tunic, ripping thin pieces of cloth.

'Hand me a water skin,' she said. 'I'm going to clean this wound.'

She worked hard to clear the rust, blood and dirt from the injury. Then she bound it in strips, ordering Eric to make more. When Astrid finished, she found she had been joined by two solid dark shadows. They stood either side of her. She smelt their stale, meaty breath as they panted over the master wolf.

'You are kind,' one told her. 'We know who you are.'

The young wolf spoke but Astrid was not fazed. She worked cautiously on the older wolf's leg, remembering her time with Freya in their home forest. Back to the days when mystical Freya could charm birds and wild mammals.

'You're one of Freya's wolves,' she said. 'She spoke your language and taught you to speak ours. Am I correct?'

The dark shadow at her side replied.

'I speak little,' it said. 'It is our leader who speaks best. He was always Freya's favourite!'

Vimp poured water into the cup of his hand and knelt down by the big wolf.

'Drink,' he said. 'I saw Freya with the wild creatures in the forest.'

The Leader raised its weary head and licked the life-reviving water. Vimp was forced to refill his hand a number of times. The wolf struggled to its feet. Astrid supported its great weight. It flinched with pain.

'My brother is correct,' it said. 'You are friends of Freya, and you have done me great service. My wound will mend. Now, you must tell us what you are doing in our forest. Although I sense we are on the same journey.'

To relieve Astrid, Eric took over and supported the huge wolf in his strong arms.

'The wild creatures of the forest sought our aid,' the wolf continued. 'They knew only we could provide it. They said Freya had been taken from her home and forced to work in a village, by the river. We travelled swiftly to find out but had to be careful of men with dogs. Not that we are afraid of those puny house dogs, but they can alert their masters. Then we would be hunted with spears.

The Leader shifted a little on his bad leg and found he could move despite the pain.

'Freya has been taken to a farm. We have no idea why. But she is never let out. Our plan was to raid it, at night; my brothers to distract the farm dogs. That would allow me to move in for Freya. Just before we attacked, my brother caught a barn rat and was about to kill it. The creature pleaded for mercy so he let it live. Rats are intelligent creatures, so we thought to ask it questions. What it told us was dismaying news. It said that Freya had been taken *away* from the farm only days before we got there. At first, no one knew where. Then the rat came upon a valuable piece of information. It said a strange man called one day and offered the farmer a fistful of gold. In return, he demanded to take Freya away with him. She was taken to an island in the middle of a lake. A quiet lake deep in the forest. Few hunters venture there. My brothers and I knew we had seen that lake. We were certain we could find it again.'

The wolf shook himself, lifting his handsome head in the flickering light.

'We returned to the forest to make our new plan. Then this happened. Fool that I am. Agnar—the wolf who teaches our young ones to avoid man traps.'

He hung his head in shame.

'Then you came along,' he added quietly. 'We thought you were hunters seeking to kill us. You do not have to tell me why you are here. We have already guessed.'

Vimp relaxed as he realised they had struck upon great fortune.

'We shall work as a team,' Agnar continued. 'Together we can complete our mission.'

Chapter 18

Fenris-Wolf

Freya's nightmare was complete. She sat sobbing in a bleak fisherman's shelter, her new home. It had come on to rain during the night and the roof leaked. Water trickled down the walls and gathered in pools on the mud floor. In the corner where Freya had tried to make something of a bed, a draught blew through gaps in the wall timbers. She crouched in the darkness, desperate for morning. When the sun rose, Freya had finally fallen into a fitful sleep. On waking, and stretching her aching limbs, she realised her desperate situation with renewed horror.

Outside, the rain ceased. Freya raised herself and tottered over to the door. It creaked open as she lifted the crude latch. Peering out nervously, she took in her new surroundings. Having arrived the night before, she had no opportunity to work out her situation. Now, before her, she found a strip of muddy grass leading to a small lake. She was a prisoner with no hope of escape.

'So, here we are at last!'

She remembered the words from last night after the strange old man had bound her wrists, forcing her through the forest and onto a raft to cross the water. Freya was not fooled. She knew he was the god Loki.

'You will be safe here,' he said, releasing her hands. 'Do your work to my satisfaction and I shall return. That day will mark your freedom. You will marry me and live in my grand palace.'

PETER L WARD

He had left her a bundle of food and spare clothing. His final instruction sounded ominous.

'You are here for a purpose. If you succeed, I shall find favour with the Allfather once more. So far, I have carried out his command. My child Fenris-Wolf must be taught a lesson. He was an adorable puppy, but as he grew and got stronger we lost control of him.'

Loki felt Freya shudder.

'Not that he can harm you, my dear. I have chained him in his new lair, a cave under the rock at the end of this island. You will see it in the morning. I can never free him as he will devour any living creature he can catch.'

Loki sniggered at the thought.

'You would make a decent enough meal for him, but do not fear. I've made arrangements. Three times a week, men from the village will bring meat for my Fenris-Wolf. They will cross over on a raft tied up at the far side of the lake. You'll receive the meat from them – and food for yourself. Use this knife to cut it up. Fenris-Wolf should be fed only once a day, early in the morning.'

He looked up at the sun, already beginning to set.

'I must leave. Have you any questions?'

After her journey through the wilds of the forest, and the crossing on the raft, Freya was in no position to ask questions – except the obvious one.

'How do you know this Fenris-Wolf won't escape? You tell me you've chained him up, but I've heard he's enormous. With the strength of six wolves. He'll tear me to pieces. There's no one here to protect me!'

Freya fell to the floor in tears. Loki pretended not to notice and made ready to depart.

'His chains have been made by the most skilful dwarves in the deepest mines,' he answered. 'They make magical metals that not even the God Thor could break. On that you have my word.

232

If you can calm Fenris-Wolf and turn him into a decent son for me, you'll succeed in your duty. I've heard that you once possessed powers to tame wild creatures. Now is the time to rediscover your former gifts.'

It was hopeless. Loki stepped lightly onto the raft, picked up a long stick, and poled his way across the shallow water.

'Good-bye for now, my sweet,' he called. 'We'll see each other again. Look after my dear son.'

Freya picked herself up and dragged back to the hut. She thought back to her time in her own village.

'I was the eldest daughter of a great Chieftain. I loved my grandfather and grandmother. My life was without cares and my time in the forest was what I loved most.'

It seemed a lifetime away.

Butchering the meat was not to gentle Freya's taste, but it gave her time to consider the situation. Fenris-Wolf's reputation for ferocity was known by all Viking peoples. Even the Gods were terrified that one day he might turn on them. The monster spawned by Loki and his first wife had grown to six times the height of a normal wolf. Its fangs were rumoured to grow longer each day, and it was completely without fear. The Gods predicted that Fenris-Wolf would eventually devour the sun and bring about the end of the world. As a child of Viking parents, Freya listened to these stories around the fire hearth.

As she sliced through the last piece of gristle, Freya decided to face the wolf head on. It was the only way. If she showed fear, all would be lost. The monster would be in control and make her his next victim. Taking a deep breath, she gathered chunks of meat in a cloth and set out for the cave. As she approached, she heard a deep, threatening grumble. A cold shiver ran down her spine and she nearly turned to flee back to the fishing shelter. One more deep breath and Freya strode forward with the large rock some way ahead. The growling grew louder. But she kept her nerve and stopped short of the mouth of a dark cavity.

'Fenris-Wolf!' she called. He voice cracked as she tried a second time. 'Fenris-Wolf, come out of there. Your breakfast is ready for you. Come out, I say!'

She sounded bolder than she felt. The rumblings ceased inside the dark cave and Freya detected the metallic sound of a heavy chain dragged along the ground. Suddenly, she realised she had no idea how long it could be and leapt back several paces. Fenris-Wolf emerged slowly from its hideout, its huge head fringed by a shaggy mane. Freya shrank back. The creature fixed her with its blood-red eyes, glowing like coals against its dark fur. The young girl summoned up her courage To Freya's relief, Fenris-Wolf had stretched the chain to the limit. The giant pulled hard to remove its collar. It towered over the maid. Opening it jaws, Fenris-Wolf displayed fearsome fangs. It was all Freya could do not to faint. Its eyes turned even more cruel as it curled its lips and snarled. Freya stood her ground.

'Back off a few steps,' she commanded. 'I'm leaving this food where you can reach it. Don't get any ideas. I'm not for eating!'

The monster scowled, a trick it had picked up from Loki, its unpleasant father.

'Who are you, pretty earth maiden?' it snarled. 'Do you really think you make a fit meal for Fenris-Wolf? You look too skinny to me. Not enough flesh on those slender bones!'

Freya tossed the meat in front of her.

'I have brought half your breakfast and will return for the other half,' she said. 'Eat this up and you can finish what is left. If you leave any, I shall not bother to give you seconds.'

Fenris-Wolf stared at Freya through its hot red coals.

'No one has spoken to me like this before. Not even the greatest of the Gods, who fear me. I shall teach you respect. Remember, my father is a God, and even he is afraid of me.'

The wolf's monstrous jaws twisted into a wicked grin.

'Loki has no control over me. I enjoy being out of control. One day I shall wreck the Kingdom of the Gods. Indeed, I may decide to destroy the Universe. It is predicted.'

Fenris-Wolf approached its scattered breakfast on hairy legs as long as stilts. The frail human Freya regarded it with contempt.

'You're not in control whilst in my keeping,' she told him. 'You must earn your food and behave properly. Now, eat up like the wild beast you are and I'll return with the rest.'

As Freya slipped back to the hut she heard the awful sound of fangs crunching at bones. The chain clanked across the ground.

'How is Fenris-Wolf secured?' Freya wondered.

She crept back into the dark interior of her hut and sat down in the corner. She began to shake, uncontrollably.

★★★

Deep in the heart of the woods, soaked by the night's rain, Vimp and his party made slow progress. It was necessary to stop every hour or so to let Agnar, the great wolf of the forest, rest. His hind leg swelled and needed constant attention. Astrid offered to hang back with him, but the old Leader was determined to forge on. As for Hugi and Thialfi, his younger brothers, they scouted ahead. Then they run back, eager tails wagging.

'We've discovered a path that almost certainly leads to the lake,' Thialfi reported. 'Men have lit a fire. It's cold now, but we found fish bones and heads and tails tossed aside.'

'Delicious!' Hugi joined in, his long, dark tongue flickering round his wolfy lips. Vimp was impressed.

'I understand what you're saying. Fish means lake. What else? Go back and see how far off we are.'

Bouncing with energy, the youngsters turned on their tails and bounded away. In a flash, their coats merged with the dull-coloured trunks of the trees and they were out of sight. Vimp roused Agnar.

'Are you sure you need to go all the way?' he said. 'Hugi and Thialfi are more than we need. We can always pick you up on the way back.'

The wise old wolf drew himself to his impressive height. He lifted his magnificent, shaggy head and sniffed the air.

'We are closer than you think. Very close indeed. I sense something is not right.'

He sniffed once more, turning his head in the direction his brothers had taken.

'I smell evil in the air,' he announced. 'Freya is in grave danger. My young brothers are bold and brave. They will aid you. But you will need my intelligence to succeed.'

Vimp and Eric shot a sharp glance at each other. They had already learned to respect Agnar. Now they suspected the old grey wolf was going to be very important indeed.

Chapter 19

Battle of Fenris Island

It had rained for much of the night, but the party of Vikings and wolves travelled in good spirits. Only Agnar remained sombre, partly because of the pain but also because he sensed serious danger ahead. As for Hugi and Thialfi, they were proud to lead the way and inform their followers the lake had been reached.

'Over there!' Hugi said, raising his nose. 'An island.'

Some distance over the still water and shrouded in early mist, they saw the outline of a small lump of land. It had few trees, with a rocky outcrop at the far end. Hugi dived under a bush at the lakeside and emerged triumphant.

'Man boat!' he announced happily. 'Come and see.'

Eric and Vimp followed him. To their delight, they found a small raft of logs, bound together. It had been pulled out of the water.

'There must be a pole,' said Eric as he searched around in the undergrowth.

'Here it is. This must be the one the men use to ferry the raft across. We'll be over in no time.'

Agnar limped forward and surveyed the scene.

'We shall not rush. The nearer I get to this island the more cautious I feel.'

Eric was all for starting, but Vimp held him back. So far their luck had held, but it could hardly continue like this. He turned to the wise wolf.

'What do you advise, my friend?'

Agnar had been thinking.

'We must continue,' he said, 'although I and my brothers have never been on a man boat. We must keep our noses alert and eyes skinned. There is something in the air that makes me uneasy. Let us head for the far end of the island.'

The two younger wolves scampered into the water and frolicked around.

'We'll swim after you,' they laughed. 'There's no room for us.'

It was agreed. They pulled the small raft to the water and launched. Eric held it steady, gripping a nearby branch so Vimp could step gingerly aboard. Once balanced, he held out his hand to help Astrid and Tharg get on.

'Hardly worthy of a Viking!' he said. 'This thing would tip over in the sea.'

Finally, he and Eric helped the injured Agnar onto the slippery raft. The younger brothers swam out beyond, heads above the surface, paddling furiously. Captain Eric got the others to sit or kneel as he pushed the long pole into the mud, taking care not to stand too near one side. The raft slid unsteadily from the bank to begin its short crossing. The crew was halfway over when the hairs on Agnar's neck stiffened. He rose clumsily to his feet, pointing his nose at the rock. He emitted a deep, rumbling growl and bare his teeth.

'What is it?' Vimp asked. 'Tell us, Agnar.'

The brothers now swam closer to the raft but seemed to have lost some of their confidence. Agnar's yellow eyes glinted.

'Wolf!' he said. 'I smell wolf – but no ordinary wolf.'

The brothers paddled alongside. Vimp peered through the last wisps of mist rising from the surface. Now he detected something. His human nose told him nothing, but his ears picked up a truly frightening sound. Like far off thunder but more menacing. Astrid and the others heard it too.

Eric pushed even harder on the pole until the nearest stretch of bank loomed close. As the raft came to a stop in the reeds, Vimp jumped off. He helped the others onto land. Hugi and Thialfi struggled in the mud as they emerged from the lake and shook their coats. But it mattered little as humans and wolves scrambled onto the grassy slope leading up from the water. Eric grabbed Vimp by the elbow.

'On the far side. Looks like an abandoned hut. That's where Freya might be.'

He was wrong. An angry roar erupted. The wolf brothers ran to Agnar whimpering, tails between their legs. Then a high-pitched scream; the desperate cry of a human. The awful snarling broke out again.

'This way!'

Dagger in hand, Eric leapt over a boulder. He headed for the high rock with no time for fear. The others followed. Hugi and Thialfi found new courage and caught Eric up. Old Agnar limped behind as his three human companions raced across the wet grass. They heard the scream again. It echoed over the lake. Eric stopped in his tracks. The brother wolves panted beside him, hackles raised. They got ready to fight.

Before them loomed the gigantic Fenris-Wolf. In his rage, he had not spotted them as his huge head faced towards the rock. Eric swiftly took in the scene. Beyond the monster, was a girl clinging desperately to the branches of a tree growing over the cave entrance. Fenris-Wolf struggled to get at her, his fangs missing her bare toes by inches. It was then that Eric saw the wolf was attached to a heavy chain leading from the collar. The broken end trailed after him. Eric reacted at once.

'Hold on, Freya! I'm coming.'

Before the wolf giant had time to turn, the fearless Viking scaled the first ledge of rock and leapt towards the stricken girl. Hugi and Thialfi sank their teeth into Fenris-Wolf's hind legs. It was little more than pin pricks but enough to make him spin round and bare his fangs. The brothers leapt back as the huge wolf lumbered heavily towards them. The links of the chain clanked behind, enough to slow him and give the young wolves a chance to get ahead.

Eric scrambled the remaining distance to Freya. He steadied himself then put out his hand.

'Hold on!' he panted. 'Grab!'

Freya stretched out her hand. Eric gripped her by the wrist.

'Jump!' he commanded.

Freya let go of the branch and leapt into Eric's arms. But they were hardly safe. The confused Fenris-Wolf turned back to the cave knowing he stood no chance of catching the nimble wolf brothers. He launched himself at the rock outcrop. His fangs snapped at the boy and girl. Then, pushing out curved claws of his enormous front feet, he began to ascend. The snarling monster heaved his body off the ground. Little by little he squirmed up the rock. Eric pushed Freya higher then faced round with his dagger. He smelt the wolf's foul breath.

'The girl's mine!' Fenris-Wolf growled.

His yellow fangs snapped below the youngsters' feet. Eric's strength drained as he clung on but urged Freya to scramble above him. The dagger slipped from his grasp and hit the ground. Fenris-Wolf leered, knowing there was no escape for the trapped humans.

'Attack!'

Agnar, bravest of wolf leaders, led from the front. Forgetting his grave injury, he forced his way up the rock face and bit Fenris-Wolf on the flanks. His brothers joined in, sinking their sharp fangs into the tendon exposed on one leg. Fenris-Wolf lost his balance. He howled as he tumbled out of control, his mighty body thumping into the ground where he lay momentarily stunned. Then he raised himself, shook the remains of the broken chain trailing at his neck. The three wolves confronted him.

'You're no match for us,' Agnar taunted. 'Anyone can frighten a human girl. Fight us,coward!'

Vimp, Astrid, and Tharg stood powerless, knowing they could do nothing. Fenris-Wolf snarled in humiliation. Chain or no chain, he would teach the three small wolves a fatal lesson. He lowered his fearsome head and slunk forward. At first, the wolves stood their ground, but as Fenris-Wolf approached they began to back off. They had completely underestimated his size. With the monster's attention distracted, however, Eric grabbed at Freya to get her down from her high perch. They looked on with horror as their wolf friends made ready to do battle. Agnar's plan had worked, and the humans could escape. As for the wolves, they would have to take their chances.

Eric and Freya slipped out of Fenris-Wolf's sight towards the raft. Vimp and his companions stood transfixed. Eric was about to signal when he heard Agnar's call.

'Vikings,' the old wolf bayed, 'you are not like the wolf people. You are sailors, remember.'

Vimp failed to understand. What did Agnar mean? All he could do was watch as the three wolves backed away, yard by yard. Fenris-Wolf moved forward with every confident step. His plan was to trap the wolves at the water's edge, where they would drown one by one.

'I say again,' Agnar called out. 'You are Vikings. You know what to do.'

By now, Eric had reached the raft.

'Stay here,' he said sharply to Freya. 'I'm going back!'

Splashing over the boggy ground separating him from his friends, Eric arrived at Vimp's shoulder. In a flash, he understood the grey wolf's coded message. But before he could act, he saw the gallant wolves had retreated almost to the water's edge. Here they would make their last stand and sacrifice. In his fury and lust for the fight, Fenris-Wolf had forgotten about the humans. A contest with his own kind was far more attractive and would increase his reputation for ferocity. As the brothers backed into the water, Fenris-Wolf closed in for the kill.

'Come!'

Eric darted forward, followed at once by Vimp. They ran round the back of Fenris-Wolf and bent to pick up the trailing chain.

'Help me,' he called. 'We're Vikings. Do as Agnar ordered.'

Eric struggled to lift a heavy link. Half-understanding, Vimp stepped forward to help. Together they pulled the heavy metal up from the ground, but its great weight was too much for them. Watching from her vantage point, Astrid worked out what was needed.

'Help them, Tharg!' she cried, racing to her friends.

Fenris-Wolf bore down on his victims who stood their ground chest deep in water. The bully wolf stepped into the lake, stirring soft mud beneath his awesome paws. He opened his jaws ready to rip his foes into pieces.

Behind him, the Vikings strained to lift the remains of the snapped chain and staggered towards to the water. With Fenris-Wolf's concentration fixed on his opponents, they slipped round his enormous rear and threw the links in the lake. Under the chain's weight, Vimp found himself sinking up to his knees. Now, he understood Agnar's message.

'Anchors away!'

The four friends dropped the last link of chain into the water. It sank at once as the young Vikings splashed back to the bank. Just as Fenris-Wolf closed in to destroy the wolves, he felt a tightening at his neck. The collar constricted as the great chain sank into the mud. He began to choke. Agnar called to his brothers to flee. From the safety of the shore, they watched the chain disappear and pull Fenris-Wolf down. The muddied water rose nearly to his neck. He was marooned beyond rescue.

Fenris-Wolf lifted his mighty head and uttered a pathetic howl across the lake. Leaving him prisoner in his watery jail,

Freya's rescuers made their way down to the raft. By its side, they recognised someone they knew, a girl shivering in the cold morning air. Her hair was matted and her clothes filthy and torn. She had no shoes, but of one thing they were certain. They had rescued Freya from an unimaginable fate.

Chapter 20

Showdown with Loki

'We've got to be back at the beach by dawn,' said Vimp. 'That means one more night in the forest. The sooner we set off, the better.'

Astrid sat in the centre of the tiny raft, her arm around Freya's thin shoulders. Eric stripped off his top tunic and gave it to the shaken girl. Tharg donated his top to warm Freya's knees. Since being helped onto the raft she had not spoken a word. White faced and exhausted, she let others see to her whilst they prepared for the lake crossing. The mournful howling of Fenris-Wolf reverberated through the air. As Eric polled off, the crew felt no sympathy for the water-stricken monster, a dark, half-submerged object in the fading light.

To everyone's relief, the far bank of the lake drew near. Reliable Eric had succeeded in getting the friends safely across the water. Already, Hugi and Thialfi were frolicking on the grass, shaking their waterlogged coats. Just before they reached land, Vimp's attention was attracted to the lake. Not far behind the raft, a silvery burst of tiny bubbles broke the surface. He was not sure if he had imagined a quick movement in the water. As the raft touched against the bank, it was all hands on deck, the boys ensuring frail Freya stepped safely off.

Vimp jumped onto land and looked back. In the distance, the marooned Fenris-Wolf sat slumped and dejected and had ceased howling. But nearer to Vimp – very close, in fact – a second line of air bubbles disturbed the water. For a fleeting second, a small, round head emerged, then two dark eyes and long, bristling whiskers on either side of the mouth. It was an otter. Of course, Vimp had seen otters playing amongst the rock pools in his Viking village. He had always liked them, although he knew they were hunted for their valuable furs. In a flash, the otter disappeared, so Vimp busied himself with thoughts of the trek ahead – a march through the forest using flares. But would Freya – and Agnar for that matter – be up to it? Tharg had already offered his sandals to Freya. For the first time she smiled weakly, just enough to show her gratitude to the rescuers. Vimp took command.

'Hugi and Thialfi, your job is to search ahead of us. Find the track and keep a good look-out for danger. You see well in the dark.'

The brothers felt pleased and could not wait to report to their wolf pack.

'Astrid, you're in charge of Freya. Tell us if we travel too quickly. Tharg, you're in the lead. Eric will bring up the rear.'

No one argued, but all dreamt of getting home, however far, through the forest and across the sea. Once more, Vimp found himself distracted by sudden movement. A light splash at the water edge gave away the antics of the curious otter. But it did not wait around to be seen, sliding out of sight into dense undergrowth. Vimp ordered the party to begin the return journey whilst enough daylight remained.

They made good progress, so late in the afternoon Vimp suggested a break to give Agnar and Freya chance to recover. Freya seemed to be warming up a little. She turned to Astrid, slipping her arm in hers.

'I was terrified of the Fenris-Wolf,' she said. 'I tried to be brave, but once he snapped his chain I knew I didn't stand a chance. He tricked me near him with the food I carried. I had no idea he'd broken free.'

Astrid understood. Freya had been fantastically brave. It was not the time to ask questions. All that mattered was getting Freya back with her friends. The forest seemed less menacing in the company of friendly wolves. Freya stretched down to touch the tousled fur of the old wolf at her side.

'I know you. I've forgotten your name but I think we talked in the woods where I once lived.'

The injured wolf Leader raised his fine head.

'I am Agnar,' he told her. 'My brothers are Hugi and Thialfi. You were our friend in the old days.'

Freya ruffled the coarse hair on the wolf's shoulder.

'I haven't had chance to thank you.'

Agnar put her mind at rest.

'There will be plenty of time for that. First we must get you back to the coast. Then the big boat will take you away. After that, you will be safe.'

As light faded Vimp ordered a halt.

'There's still some food left,' he announced. 'Perhaps Astrid will sort it for us? We'll take a longer break but must travel through the night. The longboat will return at dawn. If we miss it we'll have to lie up until sunset.'

Vimp wandered away from the group. He was worried they might not link up with Lief and company in the rescue boat. Something rustled in the bracken close by. Its arching green fronds parted as a creature sneaked beneath them.

'I'll stand still,' he thought. 'Is it a rabbit?'

He caught the briefest glimpse of an alert, furry face squinting from the undergrowth. Bold eyes and whiskers. This was no rabbit. An otter? Surely not. He dismissed the idea. That otter would have stayed at the lake where the fishing was good.

'I suppose the mind plays tricks after a few hours surrounded by trees.'

He returned to his friends.

'Sorry, everyone. We need to move.'

Already, one or two were beginning to tire but Vimp knew he must urge them on. As energetic as ever, the brother wolves scampered on ahead. The light was fading fast, so Eric saw to the lighting of torches. In the chilled air it was hard to know whether to carry on and keep warm, or take short breaks. Once the party stopped they found it hard to get going again. At last, the jubilant pair of young wolves came tearing down the track. In the light of the flares, energy gleamed in their yellow eyes.

'The river's up ahead!' they announced. 'We've even found your man boat. Follow us!'

Springing round on their powerful paws, the two raced back into the darkness. The weary travellers soldiered on and eventually broke out of the trees. In the soft light of the quarter moon, reflected on the surface of a silvery river, Vimp gasped at the beauty of the night sky. There seemed so many stars overhead, each speaking of freedom. They lifted his weary spirits.

Vimp took the trouble to check the small rowing boat was intact. Hidden where they had left it, the boat, oars and all, was ready for the morning adventure. He ran back to his friends to find them huddled in the shelter of the trees. Tharg snored lightly, whilst the sleeping Eric looked the picture of innocence. Astrid and Freya slept soundly with Agnar nestling his great, warm body against the girl he had helped rescue. Unable to prevent a yawn, Vimp lay down on the soft earth. In no time he was dreaming of stout wooden huts and warming fires. Only a short distance away, a beady-eyed animal had found shelter under a tree root. It had pursued the rescue party all the way from the lake.

★★

Out at sea, the restless longboat crew suffered an uncomfortbale night. Lief headed the *Freya* up into waves that churned the sailors' stomachs. They slept fitfully, trying to keep out the cold with wet fleeces. As the pitch black of darkness gave way to faint morning light, the sun's first ray crept over the eastern horizon.

Sleepy and stiff, the rowers got ready, handing round lumps of rough bread. At the helm, Bjorne surveyed the water.

'The wind's dropped,' he said to Lief. 'We can row in and be off the shore before there's too much light.'

He prayed that the tide would favour their chances.

'Pull hard, lads,' Lief commanded, knowing he was asking a lot of his sleep-starved crew.

'We can't be too far off. Once we sight land, we'll get our bearings and home in on the meeting point.'

As the boat moved forward, Lief prepared a torch flare that would act as signal to the shore party. The curved surface of the rising sun appeared over the forest. They would have to find land fast, as there was always the possibility of a Viking raider slipping out on the morning tide. Bjorne hung onto the helm, steering into the sun. Then a faint dark shape appeared on the horizon, and as the *Freya* approached, the shape slowly took form. Bjorne called Lief over.

'Land ahead?' he said quietly. 'Or am I imagining things?'

Lief shielded his eyes.

'Yes. Well done. We'll go in close then work our way along the shore.'

The rowers warmed to their task. Now the *Freya* thrust through the water, creating its own bow wave.

'Steer north,' Lief suggested. 'I recognise this bit of coast. We're much closer than I dared hope.'

Looking down into the water, he saw that it was becoming increasingly muddy. It meant only one thing. A river was pouring out into the sea, but was it the correct one? Bjorne tingled with excitement. He had spotted a line of pine trees rising up a hillside and kept their image in his memory. Now he certain they were getting near.

'Light your flare, Lief. It's worth the risk.'

Bjorne continued to look out for enemy boats. Smoke streamed from the flare that Lief held high, hoping any watcher on the bank would see. Seconds later, a small, bright light shone out from the muddy spit, near to where the river entered the sea.

'They've seen us!' he cried, and his crew gave a cheer. 'Slowly now, lads. We're fighting the tide and mustn't run aground.'

He ordered one of the rowers to leave his oar and move up to the dragon prow.

'Keep a look-out for shallow water. Especially sand banks.'

★★★

On the shore, Vimp roused Astrid and Freya, who still slept. Tharg held the flare as Eric got the small boat ready for its final crossing. The wolves had been awake for some time, hunting rabbits in the forest. When they returned, they seemed wary and nervous. Old Agnar's neck hairs rose as he sniffed the air. Like his brothers, he sensed danger but knew the humans had not picked it up.

Vimp was about to order the party into the boat when he spotted a quick movement under a nearby bush. A small head appeared. He knew at once – bright eyes, whiskers, sleek furry body, and powerful tail. He saw the otter's broad feet and sharp claws. It stared at him boldly, not frightened by the presence of the wolves. Then it ran forward and approached Freya. It reared up on its legs.

'So, my dear, you choose to desert me?'

Freya felt the blood chill in her veins. The others stood rooted to the spot. Even the wolves kept back, mesmerised.

'Perhaps you thought you could escape me,' the otter went on.

As it spoke it started to grow in size. Almost to Freya's full height. Then it began to change form. The cunning little animal face took on the look of a human. A pair of cruel human-like eyes stared at their frozen victim.

'You are all fools,' Loki sneered.

He wore a robe of crimson red, bordered in gold.

'How could you think you would get away with your crazy scheme? I knew about you from the start, but I was interested to see how far you would get. How smart you must have thought yourselves, defying the might of my Fenris-Wolf. It was only a matter of time before he snapped his chain. That's why I returned.'

He grinned at Freya.

'I came to rescue you, my dear, as I would never allow Fenris-Wolf to tear you apart. But your friends made their unexpected appearance and spoiled my plan. I hoped that if I rescued you from the fangs of my young monster you would show me due gratitude.'

He paused to look round the stricken group.

'I am most displeased. Poor Fenris-Wolf still sits in his watery trap. Not that it will do him harm. He must learn from such an experience. Perhaps he's already discovered he's not as cunning as he imagined.'

Vimp held the flaming torch. His heart pounded, but he was not giving up now.

'We Vikings know you, Loki,' he said. 'You're the most despised of the Gods.'

He glanced out to sea where a bright flare was being waved frantically from the dark outline of a longboat.

'Freya's coming with us. God or no God, you can't stop us!'

Loki's evil eyes fixed on Vimp.

'You will be the first of my victims,' he snarled. 'Then I'll deal with the others. Those foolish wolves, too. Only Freya will survive so she can return with me to Asgard.'

Since her island captivity and dramatic rescue Freya had hardly uttered a word. Now, she stepped forward to confront her enemy.

'You'll not harm a hair of Vimp's head,' she told him. 'You're loathed by all. But your time has come. I, Freya, command this.'

The Viking girl stood her ground. Extending her arms, she cried out, her bold words echoing through the wood.

'Wicked Loki, you're not divine. Why should we worship you? You are nothing. You have no powers upon the Earth.'

Loki's dark eyebrows puckered. He looked bewildered and unable to answer Freya's sudden outburst. His head drooped. Then he tried to look up and speak. His voice cracked.

'Of course I'm divine,' he cried. 'I am a God. I am Loki, the outrageous adventurer. Friend of the Allfather.'

Freya regarded him with scorn.

'You're no such thing,' she said. 'Odin is not a God upon this Earth any more than you are.'

She drew herself to her full height, raising her shining face to the sky.

'Call yourself divine if you like. We say you are trash. As far as we're concerned, on Earth you don't exist!'

Vimp glanced at Loki to see his eyes grow dull. The scheming head slumped low into its shoulders and he began to crumble. His body grew paler. So pale that the young Vikings could see right through it. A wisp of smoke coiled up from the damp ground. Loki the Trickster was no more. Only a shallow hole remained where he had stood.

Birdsong broke out in the surrounding trees. Joyous calls of jays and finches rang clear to celebrate Freya's fine deed. The young Viking girl looked round shyly to her companions.

'I think it's time to leave,' she said. 'These Viking Gods are nothing on Earth. From now on, they can't possibly harm us.'

Emerging as if from a trance, Eric made the final preparations in the little boat and helped Freya and Astrid step aboard. They sat in the middle leaving little room for the boys.

'We can make two journeys,' Eric offered. 'I'll stay behind and you can return for me.'

He paused, holding a hand out to the wolves.

'And our wonderful friends.'

Agnar limped forward, close to collapse.

'No,' he said quietly. 'We cannot join you. My brothers are fit and young and must return to the pack. They will soon be leaders and keep our wolves out of danger.'

Eric saw that the younger wolves agreed. Agnar lifted his great old head and looked back, longingly, at his beloved forest.

'My time is over. I have completed my mission.'

He turned to Freya.

'I must go home. I am too old and feeble to lead the pack but will hunt on my own.'

He shifted his wounded leg. It was obvious he could not survive. Big Eric went over to Agnar. He knelt by his side and placed his strong arms beneath the ailing body.

'Make room in the boat for us all,' he said gruffly. 'It's tiny, but we can get in at a squeeze.'

With great care, Eric lifted the enfeebled wolf and staggered over to the bobbing craft. As it pulled away from the shore, two young wolves stood like sentinels on the bank. They did not move until the Viking longboat sailed out of sight.

CHAPTER 21

Storm at Sea

Bjorne stood at the tiller of the heavy side rudder that steered the *Freya* across the North Sea. Heading West, Lief took command to give Vimp a break to catch up on his sleep. Astrid sat with Big Eric, exhausted after his battle with the Fenris-Wolf. Just for once, the bold Viking teenager did not argue and Astrid had her way. She slept soundly, her fair head upon his strong shoulder, whilst in Eric's lap rested the tired head of the old wolf. Agnar had dozed off, twitching occasionally as dogs do. From his captain's position, Lief smiled at the three sleepers, although he had not yet got over the shock of taking a wild wolf onboard.

The crew, inspired by the story of the miraculous escape, were determined to get the heroes home. Fortunately, the wind picked up and they were able to raise sail. For the early part of the morning, the going was good so the rowers were given a break. It turned out that Bjorne was a natural helmsman, his only disadvantage being that he lacked Eric's strength. Lief clawed his way down the longboat and hung on at Bjorne's side.

'How's she handling?'

The helmsman grimaced at the darkening sky.

'Pretty rough! It's a strong wind. Strengthening all the time and veering round to the North. The sea's beginning to cut up and the rudder's shuddering. I'll just have to fight it.'

Bjorne was right. The fragile *Freya* was beginning to pitch and roll.

'Should we reef the sail in? It'll mean putting more crew back to work.'

Lief thought quickly, then went forward to organise a couple of lads to shorten the billowing sail. It was not easy as the longboat, filling with water, seemed unable to hold a straight course. One huge wave rose up under it as the dragon prow reared up before plunging back into the churning waters.

'One more time!' Lief called into the howling wind. 'Pull together. Keep your stroke.'

But it was hopeless. However hard the crew tried, there was no way they could conquer the turbulent waves. The *Freya* bucketed up and down, almost out of control. Cold spray broke over the backs of the sailors. Vimp and Eric were jolted out of their sleep whilst Astrid and Freya sat petrified.

'It's the Gods!' one frightened boy cried out. 'They seek revenge.'

As he spoke, a terrible shape emerged from the waters. It took the form of an old man, bearded and wild eyed. A giant rising from the depths.

'Aegir, Lord of the Sea,' Bjorne called out. 'Have mercy. We have offended you.'

The boat lurched to one side, throwing its occupants off their benches. The rowers tried to grab for their oars, torn out of their grasp by the wild sea. Rain lashed down. A white flash of lightning crackled across the sky as the *Freya* rose and dived. The boys rejected their oars, fearing their end was near. Freya roused herself, grabbed a shroud, and clung on. She faced the reluctant rowers.

'You speak nonsense!' she cried.

As she spoke, the great watery shape of the God transformed into a giant wave. Freya staggered forward to the mast.

'Grab your oars and row!'

The white-faced crew clung to their places. Not one responded.

'You're *imagining* that wave's a God!' Freya pleaded. 'It isn't. Look—it's gone!'

It was true. What had appeared to be the spectral form of a Viking deity had disappeared. The boat foundered as Lief came to his senses.

'Do what I tell you,' he shouted at his rowers. 'Grab hold of your oars!'

Spray burst over the prow. Lief clung onto the mast for dear life.

'Row! It's our only chance!'

A second dagger of electric lightning shot across the purple sky, followed by a volley of thunder. The boys rescued their oars and fought the wild sea.

'Lief! I've lost the steering!'

At the helm, Bjorne clutched a useless tiller. The leather thongs binding the side rudder to the longboat had snapped under the onslaught. Now *Freya* was truly out of control. Big Eric pulled himself off his cross bench and reached for a long length of rope. He tied it tightly round his middle. Then he grabbed another, coiled beneath the gunwhale. Before Astrid worked out what he was up to, Eric tossed the free end of the rope to Vimp.

'Catch! Hold on!'

To Astrid's dismay, he clambered over the side of the stricken vessel to disappear beneath the surface. She cried out in vain. All Vimp could do was cling on to his end of rope, hoping the other was still tied to Eric. Bjorne lurched across to help him.

Eric spluttered to the surface. He grabbed desperately at the loose rudder threatening to break off from the boat. Then he worked the rope and lashed it to a projecting spar. Once more, the sea broke over his head. Eric rose for a second time and secured a double knot, lashing the rudder to the side.

It took the combined strength of Vimp and Bjorne to heave soaking Eric back on board. He lay swamped on the shallow deck. Astrid took his wet head and hair in her hands and implored him to take deep breaths.

'Row, boys, row!'

Lief had the good sense to keep his mind on his crew. The rain ceased, and as the wind dropped the waves subsided. The *Freya* had survived. Sodden and exhausted, the tough Viking crew pulled on their boat towards Saxon England.

Astrid and Vimp concentrated all their efforts on the trembling Eric. They pumped his shaking limbs and pummelled his chest and back. Big Eric was close to death. Only his inner strength would see him through.

The return journey seemed to go on forever and the loyal crew was forced to spend two more unpleasant nights out at sea. However, with every pull of the oars, the team rowed closer to their destination. Finally, the weather cleared and they were greeted by a warming sun. The Saxon shore appeared on the horizon. All that was left to do was to navigate their way back to their home village.

Astrid clung onto feeble Eric, determined never to let him out of her sight again. He could not protest. Not one ounce of energy remained.

CHAPTER 22

The Homecoming

'Look ahead!'

In his excitement, helmsman Bjorne nearly lost control of the half-mended rudder. A thin spiral of smoke wound up to the sky, on the starboard bow.

'It might be Saxons on the alert for Viking raiders,' Lief shouted. 'You know they set fire to warning beacons.'

'We'll go in fairly close,' Vimp ordered. 'If it looks like trouble, we'll row off.'

As the *Freya* got nearer, Vimp realised that the fire had not been lit on a high headland. That would have been a sure sign of warning to nearby Saxons.

'It's on the beach,' he yelled. 'Keep heading for it. I see flames.'

The rowers pulled with mounting enthusiasm. Although they could not look round, they felt confident Vimp was guiding them to the right spot.

'People on the beach! Lief, run up to the prow and wave the white sheet. It's the signal to Emma and Ingrid.'

Lief stood by the carved dragon head and held out the sheet. Three small figures waved and danced on the beach.

'It's them!' he shouted.

A cheer rippled through the crew. On shore, Ingrid and Emma hugged each other as the leaking boat drew near. Edwin, the Saxon, watched with awe, stunned by the seamanship of his Viking friends.

'Ready with the anchor!'

Vimp's order was hardly necessary. Two of the boys had already shipped their oars and gone forward to lift the heavy weight.

'Oars up! Stow away!'

The longboat proudly slid to its anchorage, the shallow bottom crunching on sand and shells. The two girls on the beach leapt into the water and splashed out to their comrades. The anchor hit the water and the brave craft ground to a halt. Hands reached over the side to pull Ingrid and Emma on board. They tumbled into the slurping bilge water, but no matter. Radiant with joy, they hugged and kissed each member of the hard-working crew.

Finally, Emma found Freya. They gazed at each other with disbelief. Then the rescued girl stood up and took her friend's hands in hers. There were tears in her eyes.

'Is it really you?' she said. 'I never thought we'd never see each other again.'

Ingrid joined her as the crew busied themselves with the boat, checking on the sail. The only person who remained quiet was Big Eric. He sat hunched on his cross bench, slowly warming after his fearful experience in the sea. Freya released Emma's hand and turned to him.

'This is our hero,' she said. 'Without Eric no one would have survived. That's the truth.'

The big Viking smiled in embarrassment.

'It wasn't just me,' he said huskily. 'Everyone's a hero in this boat!'

Old Agnar lay at his side, barely breathing.

With the longboat anchored and moored up the beach, the wet and bedraggled Vikings made their way over to Edwin's roaring fire.

265

'We've got broth on the boil for you,' he said, in welcome, pointing to a bubbling pot filled to the brim.

'Take a bowl each, then drink. It's hot, mind. There's plenty more.'

It was the best thing he could have said. In no time, the starving sailors gained new strength.

'Well,' Edwin went on, cheerfully, 'once you've all had enough we'd better get you back to the village. Our folks are in for a big surprise. No one thought you'd survive. Except Brother Caedmon. He prayed for you night and day.'

Spirits revived, the boat party trudged through the warm sand and up into the dunes. Drifting scents of land filled their nostrils – sweet-smelling dune flowers and resinous perfume of pine. The sailors remembered the woods well. Their minds went back to the time when they had so nearly found themselves at the mercy of a hidden army of Saxons. There had been many misunderstandings that day, but finally they had been accepted as friends. Now, they looked forward to seeing their new home again and the welcome they were bound to receive.

As they trailed along the beaten forest path, excited voices sounded through the trees. Edwin had already sped on ahead to alert the people to the Vikings' homecoming. A group of village children danced along the track competing to be first to greet the arrivals.

Bjorne and Eric led the way. Bjorne laboured with the body of a large grey wolf whilst Eric gently supported its head. The children backed off, remembering fearful tales of forest wolves. Quick as ever, Lief stepped forward.

'Don't be afraid,' he cried. 'The wolf is old and unwell. When you hear how he risked his life to help us you'll want him as your friend.'

The children stopped still, unsure what to do. Leader Alfred stepped briskly past them. He extended his hand to the weary Vikings.

'We're so glad to see you. All safe and sound. It's a miracle.'

Then he noticed Freya walking side by side with Saxon Emma.

'And you have succeeded in your important mission. God be praised.'

That night, there was feasting and celebration. Even the children were allowed to sit round the communal fire to hear the new tale of Viking heroes. But two people were absent nfrom the party. Eric and Astrid remained in a hut where they laid old Agnar on a soft bearskin. They gave him water, but as time passed it seemed he wanted none. Just before midnight, Astrid slipped out of the hut to seek out Vimp, who was revelling with the villagers.

'I had to come,' she whispered. 'It's very sad news . . . Agnar. He is dead. Keep it to yourself. We won't spoil the celebrations. Wait until morning to tell the others.'

Astrid made her way quickly through the merry throng to a quiet spot. She paused for a moment to take in a long, cool breath and stare at the distant stars. From a small hut, not far away, she heard sobbing.

'Oh, Eric!'

Astrid raced over to the hut where her brave Viking remained with his dead wolf. She found him kneeling at Agnar's side, head buried deep into the soft fur. Heroic Eric, who had taken on the Fenris-Wolf and plunged into the seas, blubbered like a grieving child. Tears welled in Astrid's eyes as she joined him, slipping her arm round his heaving shoulders.

'I know you loved him so much,' she said. 'And Agnar loved you.'

CHAPTER 23

Funeral at Sea

It was a solemn procession that led down to the shore. In the fading light, young Saxons and Vikings carried flaring torches. On reaching the longboat they lined up to face each other in two rows. Eric and Bjorne appeared, carrying between them a stretcher with the lifeless body of Agnar. Freya and the girls followed behind, heads bowed. Lief strode forward and invited the stretcher bearers to place their precious load on the boat.

'All is ready. Our longboat is no longer seaworthy. We've piled it with dry brushwood. Lay our beloved Agnar on top and we shall send the *Freya* out to sea.'

A blood red sunset settled over the dunes, the burning torches appearing brighter by the minute. Vimp was already on board to receive Agnar's body. He steadied the stretcher as the two boys joined him. Then he respectfully laid the dead wolf on the brushwood. Eric touched the old Agnar's head for the last time and clambered over the side. Although his face was expressionless, Astrid understood the deep thoughts passing through his mind. The three boys moved back up the beach as Freya stepped to the side of the dragon prow. In her hand, she held a cow horn. Placing it to her lips, she blew a haunting note that carried over the darkening sea. She repeated this twice. Then stepped back and motionied to Vimp.

The young Viking took a flare from Lief and lit an arrow whose pointed tip had been smeared in fat. It took a few seconds to take light. Vimp also lit arrows for Bjorne and Eric. They burned brightly in the gathering dusk.

'Cast off the boat!'

Lief gave the order to four boys who had taken up the anchor and untied the mooring ropes. Vikings and Saxons watched as the *Freya* slipped out for her final mission.

'This is the honour Vikings give to our greatest warriors,' Lief called out. 'We do it for Agnar. Agnar bravest of wolves!'

With sail half furled and rudder lashed, the *Freya* and her precious cargo moved slowly out into the bay.

'Charge your bows!'

Vimp's strong voice rang out loud as he, Eric, and Bjorne fixed burning arrows to their bow strings and pulled back. Light danced across their faces as they held the tension and took steady aim.

'Now!'

The three arrows sped like comets. Their aim was true. They plummeted into the *Freya,* setting light to the dry tinder wood set beneath Agnar's corpse. The mound burst into flames.

On shore, the silent watchers stood motionless as the conflagration grew. The whole boat was engulfed in fire. Vivid colours danced in the rippling water. The sail took light and before long the boat's mast collapsed. Yet the stately longboat sailed slowly on, a glowing ball of fire and smoke.

Astrid stood next to Eric and looked at his steely eyes that betrayed not a glimmer of emotion. She watched as the flames failed and the boat that had carried them to safety began to break up.

'This was the best way.'

Vimp lowered his bow and rested the tip on the sand. The villagers, Saxon and Viking alike, turned to wander back to the village. Only a small party remained on the shoreline to see the last of the burning boat sink forever into the sea. Bjorne, holding a flare, walked with Ingrid along the tidemark. Lief, who had set his heart on entering a monastery, bowed his head, uncertain how to face a difficult future.

'I know what you're thinking,' Emma told him softly. 'Brother Caedmon leaves for Durham tomorrow and expects you to go with him.'

Lief turned, struck by Emma's beauty in the light of the nearest flare.

'What can I do? You know I can't let him down. He's been so good to me.'

The Saxon girl slipped her arm in his.

'You must decide,' she said. 'But I think your place lies here, with me and your friends.'

She rested her cheek upon his slender shoulder. They were joined by Eric and Astrid.

'Emma's right,' Astrid said. 'We all think you should remain with us, Lief.'

She glanced at Emma, who was close to tears.

'There's a special someone in this village who will never let you go. If you leave her now, you'll never forgive yourself.'

Lief smiled.

'I know. I guess Brother Caedmon will just have to understand.'

Big Eric smiled for the first time in days. He sounded much more like his old self.

'You were never any good at building boats, Lief,' he said. 'But you're good at writing, and now there's a big story to tell. A new Viking legend for our children and grand children!'

The four friends slowly found their way home in the torchlight whilst two other figures remained. They stared out to sea. It was Freya who broke the silence.

'I've been so ungrateful,' she said. 'I haven't thanked you. I know Lief's brainy and Eric's brave. But, above all, there's one person who's responsible for everything that's happened to us. The person who organised my rescue.'

She paused and looked at the dark figure of the apprentice shipbuilder who had taken his friends from their far away land. Vimp the Viking shrugged his shoulders.

'Don't thank me,' he said. 'We worked as a team.'

Freya was not so easily put off.

'I know why you did it. You did it for me.'

She turned and touched his face lightly. For once in his life, Vimp did not know what to say. The young Viking stood awkwardly, waves lapping at his feet. Beautiful Freya reached up and kissed him.

Epilogue

That night, far across the sea, two wolves stood on a distant shore. A cloud crossed the moon. They raised their shaggy heads to the sky and howled into the night. Turning, the brothers trotted back into their forest kingdom.

Hugi and Thialfi became joint leaders of their pack. They hunted and ruled for many successful years.

PART 3

Eric
and the
Mystical Bear

CHAPTER 1

The Dam across the Stream

In a secret spot in the Saxon forest, the faint scent of bluebells drifted on the breeze. Soft sunlight filtered through the tops of the trees. Freya, a Viking girl who no longer lived in her homeland across the sea, lingered on the grassy path.

'The foxgloves will be out soon,' she thought. 'Pink bells with white spots.'

She sighed, thinking fondly of the old village where her parents still lived. How she missed them. Would they ever forgive her? Freya and her friends had deserted their families to sail to the land of Anglo-Saxons.

Her companion, Vimp, a tall boy with knotted strands of golden hair on his shoulders, stopped short. He had caught a glimpse of deer amongst the trees. Startled, they sniffed the air, looked up, and turned. The white flashes of their rumps disappeared as they bolted for cover.

'I'd never want to harm them,' he surmised. 'They've got enough enemies.'

The deer lived in daily fear of the hounds and spears of Saxon hunters. Stopping by a low pile of stacked logs, he spoke quietly.

'We'll turn down this track. It gets steep further on, where it's boggy. The stream's just beyond.'

Freya followed him. Two cock nightingales sang noisily at each other from bushes close by. The one singing longest and loudest hoped to attract a mate.

'We're getting close,' said Vimp. 'Take care. This path's slippery. Last time, I fell into the mud!'

Freya remembered her best friend returning to the village with slime on his rough tunic.

'Boys!' she thought. 'Will they ever grow up?'

Vimp held out his hand to guide her through the swampy area. There was no path, and mud squelched under their sandals. The two youngsters clambered over damp tree roots to reach a bend in the stream.

'Be still!' warned Vimp.

In the cool air, the two young Vikings stood rigid as fragile mayflies danced over the fast current.

'Best to crouch down,' he suggested. 'The beavers mustn't spot us.'

His eyes seemed glued to the water, and Freya wondered what he had seen. Was it a fish? That was unlikely. The small stream was only good for minnows. Vimp pointed to a spot higher up.

'D'you see?'

Freya made out a higgledy-piggledy pile of branches that blocked the course of the stream.

'They've built right across. One side to the other.'

She saw at a small dam woven tightly with sticks and branches. It blocked the water flow, so the level rose. It looked as though the stream beyond might burst its banks.

'I knew you'd want to see this in daylight,' said Vimp. 'We can come back tonight. That's when the beavers come out to build.'

He smiled.

'They're never satisfied. Cutting new pieces and shoving them in to make their dam watertight.'

Freya's heart raced.

'Best keep this spot a secret,' she suggested. 'Between you and me.'

She swiftly changed her mind.

'I guess we should tell Lief and English Emma. Oh . . . and Astrid and Big Eric, of course. We mustn't leave those two out. Eric gets into huffs!'

Vimp agreed.

'He can be a bit moody,' he said. 'There'll be a full moon tonight. Why don't we all come down?'

His keen eye was caught by a thin tree stump sticking out of the swamp. It had been sawn off by something sharp, and its frayed ends showed white.

'I saw a beaver gnawing that tree. It kept on doing it until the trunk snapped. Then it backed off as the tree toppled into the stream!'

It had always been Freya's hope to see beavers. In the Viking forest near their old village, she had been able to attract wild creatures to her – song birds, deer, rabbits, even wolves. Freya felt safe in their company. However, she had never seen beavers. They had been hunted almost to extinction.

The full moon rose in the starry night sky as six youngsters made their way cautiously through the wood. Vimp led, holding a lantern glowing yellow in the dark, with Big Eric at the rear. Finding their way down the shadowy path was not easy. Twice, Vimp had to stop and turn back to find the right way. Astrid made sure she stayed near Eric, who was never afraid.

'We're getting close!'

Vimp passed his whispered message back to Lief, who sent it down the line.

'I'll have to blow out the lantern,' Vimp said. 'We'll wait for a short while so our eyes can get used to the dark.'

Emma, the Saxon girl, felt a cold shiver run down her spine. Long shadows extended like fingers through the trees. The only sound was the excited breathing of her friends. In the near silence, she reached out to clutch Lief's hand. The party moved on, nearer to the stream. They heard its busy chuckle as the waters swirled around boulders and twisted roots.

'No further!'

Vimp crouched behind a fallen trunk, rotting in the swamp. The others followed. Kneeling in cold mud was horrible, and Emma wondered why she had bothered to come. The night was colder than she had imagined. She settled down into her uncomfortable wet spot and peered over the top of the trunk. Her eyes began to adjust. It was fortunate that the moon's light fell on the swirling stream. It glistened, ever changing, as a thin ray fell on the untidy pile of branches. Emma felt a tug on her arm. Lief detected a quick movement, just above the surface.

'Straight ahead,' he whispered in her ear. 'D'you see?'

Something, dark and humpy, swam through the water. Larger than she had imagined, it carried a long branch in its teeth. The whiskered animal struck out for the dam, where it busied itself pushing the stick into the pile. Then it slid back into the water, flipping its paddle tail with a splash. A minute later, the beaver broke surface, again and clambered half out of the water. With its paws, it padded mud into the dam, sealing up gaps.

Lief tightened his grip on Emma's arm. Just beyond the growing dam sat another beaver, the tail showing beyond its wet fur. Its front paws were wrapped around a small tree. Tilting its head from side to side, the beaver slashed into the thin trunk with razor-sharp teeth. The tree started to give way, but the beaver stopped. It turned its head, hearing something on the wind. Even Emma, whose hearing was not as good as the beaver's, could hear clumsy, clumping sounds. Was a big animal approaching the stream? The beaver ceased work and headed for the safety of the water.

Emma froze. It might be a bear. She had heard that one or two survived in this deep part of the forest. A light shone, bobbing through the trees. It grew larger, followed by a second and a third. Not bothering to hide the fact they were in the wood, a gang of Saxon boys hurried down to the stream. The beaver watchers lay still, behind their fallen trunk. Flickering lights from the lanterns played over the scene, making shadows that danced into the trees.

'Right here!'

A rough voice, whose owner Emma recognised at once. It was Egeslic, an unlikeable Saxon boy from the village. He seemed to have three or four others with him. Emma saw that they carried clubs.

'Smash up the dam. Get them moving,' Egeslic laughed. 'If you get a chance, get in a good blow. We can make money on their skins.'

Emma, an English girl amongst Viking friends, felt ashamed her own people were about to kill innocent creatures. The gang ventured nearer the dam to begin probing its outer defences. Suddenly, a loud voice boomed out of the darkness. It was a Viking voice, but the language it spoke was Saxon.

'Stay where you are, Egeslic. Keep away from that dam!'

Emma stared wide eyed at the towering figure, lit in the glow of the lanterns.

Eric Bignose stood brave and defiant. The Saxon boys backed off, but Egeslic faced him up.

'Why, it's our Viking friends!' he jeered. 'Is that ugly Eric with the long nose?' He grinned at his companions. 'The big Viking thinks he can spoil our fun!'

Big Eric stepped over the trunk and strode forward. He was swiftly followed by Vimp and Lief, scrambling up on their feet. The sight of angry Eric was too much for the Saxons. They turned and fled, the lights of their lanterns disappearing with them. No one, not even Egeslic, dared face the Viking boy whose reputation for courage was legendary.

'Go on. Run!' he shouted. 'Don't ever come back here or you'll have me to answer to!'

The three girls joined the boys. Freya was impressed.

'If we hadn't come here tonight those beavers would have been destroyed,' she said. 'Well done, Eric. And Vimp and Lief!'

The small party of beaver watchers left the stream to trudge back to their adopted village, where they had been allowed to settle.

'There's going to be trouble,' Vimp told the rest grimly. 'The last thing we want is to upset the Saxons. That Egeslic will make life tricky for us!'

Chapter 2

A Blooded Nose

'We found a perfect tree in the forest,' Vimp said. 'It was just right to make the keel of the new boat. We cut it down and dragged it to the riverbank. But first you have to sink it in water for a few months.'

Lief looked puzzled. He was a hopeless carpenter and envied Vimp's skills. The other Viking boys also knew their stuff. But working with his hands was a mystery to Lief. His big aim in life was to learn to read and write in the language of the Anglo-Saxons. He thought back to the time when he and his friends had sailed across the sea from the land of the Vikings. After they had convinced the Saxons they were not raiders, they settled happily enough in the village. And it was the crew's skills in boat-building and that made them useful. Unfortunately, this did not apply to poor Lief.

'I'm hopeless,' he confessed. 'I'll stick to reading and writing this new language. It's not easy getting your head around Anglo-Saxon.'

The thought saddened him. Within weeks of landing, Lief had been taken to a monastery to live with the monks, or brothers, as they called themselves. After only a short time, the monastery had been attacked by raiders from his Viking lands. It was set on fire and valuable treasures stolen. Many of the brothers were murdered. Lief, himself a Viking, was lucky to escape with his life.

Now he was back in the Saxon village and trying to earn a living. But not at building boats. Why, for instance, had Vimp insisted that the tree trunk, the boat's future keel, should be soaked in salt water?

'It's the way the old Viking shipwrights were taught,' his friend explained. 'Soaking for months toughens the wood. We'll drag it out soon and get to work.'

The thought horrified poor Lief, who glanced at his delicate hands. Vimp laughed.

'Don't worry! We'll give you the easy jobs. Even a spot of time off to do your writing. Perhaps you'll come up with a poem about the new boat? Alfred, the village Chieftain, might read it out at the launch!'

The two boys reached the bank of the river where the craft was to be put together. Half a dozen young Vikings wielded axes and mallets. The sounds of banging and scraping hurt Lief's tender ears. Bjorne Strawhead took a break.

'Come to give us a hand, Lief?' he said, grinning. 'We've left the heavy stuff for you.'

The young poet gritted his teeth.

'I'll do my best. You know that.'

The days passed and the log was dragged from the river bottom. Ropes had been knotted round and the boys put their backs into tugging it back up the bank. Big Eric took charge.

'Pull!' he commanded.

Bjorne slipped over in the mud. The rest of the hauling party struggled to a halt. Eric encouraged Bjorne to get to his feet.

'Don't worry!' he called over cheerfully He looked around. 'Where are the Saxon boys? They said they'd help us. Why they haven't turned up?'

Bjorne knew the answer.

'They'll appear at any the moment. Just as we've finished dragging this thing into place. They always get out of the heavy work.'

Exhausted, the small party of Vikings finally positioned the trunk on the spot where the boat would be built. Lief the poet put his slender back into the task. Once they had succeeded, he slumped down in the sun to rest. Words began to form in his mind; words to honour the longboat that would one day set out to sail.

Alfred, the Saxon Chief, had asked the young Vikings to design and build a boat for battle. Vimp and his friends knew the village might be raided at any moment. Alien Vikings, thieves and plunderers, might destroy homes and carry off cattle and sheep. People ending up as slaves. By building this big boat, Vimp and his friends could prove to the Saxons whose side they were on.

Vimp got up stiffly from the churned up ground and flexed his aching limbs. He selected an axe and ran his thumb gingerly down the blade.

'Hmm. Sharp,' he thought. 'Better be careful.'

He picked up a second tool. This too had a strong handle to grip. Its metal blade had been curved over in the heat of the furnace.

'An adze,' he thought. 'Handy for shaping wood. This one's well made.'

Just then, he heard a cheery call from the nearest hut. It was a girl's voice, loud and clear.

'Lunch for hungry boat-builders!'

The boys scrambled to their feet to find Freya, Ingrid, Astrid and Emma walking towards the shore. Each girl carried a large woven basket.

'Right on time!' thought Vimp. 'Am I hungry?'

The girls struggled down to the riverbank.

'Wash your hands!' Astrid called out. 'Just look at the state of you. Disgusting! No one's having a bite to eat until they've cleaned up.' She shot a glance at Eric. 'Especially you, Eric Bignose!' she giggled, tossing her curls. Eric looked sheepish and hid his large grimy hands behind his back.

'Go on!' Astrid ordered. 'Not a bite until you've cleaned up!'

The tall Viking boy wanted to be seen at his best in Astrid's company. They had shared so many adventures together. Eric looked around at his friends as they put down their tools and sat on the grass. The tide had turned, so water streamed from the river mouth to the sea. Eric dreamt of the day the longboat would be launched, weeks from now. Hours of work were still needed to cut and shape the timbers. These would be riveted together and the gaps plugged with wool and tar. Eric especially wanted to be given the job of making the rudder. By now, he had gained respect for steering his comrades across the North Sea. Strong Eric had battled storms and mountainous waves at the helm. He also seemed to understand how to navigate, taking his bearings from the positions of the sun or stars.

The boat-builders enjoyed their short lunch break with the girls handing out hunks of cheese and lumps of bread. There was foaming beer to drink from jugs.

'Not too much,' Astrid warned. 'We don't want you all falling asleep. You haven't finished for today.'

Emma passed round juicy red apples she had picked only that morning. She sat with Lief and asked him if he had come up with any good ideas for a new poem. He shook his head unhappily.

'Not a thing!' he complained. 'Writing isn't like boat-building. With a boat, you turn up in the morning and do your job. But when I write, I need to imagine. Perhaps I need to get away from here. All this bashing and banging does my head in!'

Emma was about to say something consoling when she looked up and saw a group of Saxon teenagers approaching. They had been picking up stones in the fields, backbreaking work to help the farmers. One or two carried sharp flints in their hands but kept them out of sight. Emma sensed the young Saxons were out for trouble. She was disturbed to see Egeslic at their head. Vimp got up and faced the bully.

'What d'you want?' he asked. 'We don't want trouble.'

Egeslic, who was big for his age, took the lead.

'We didn't know you Vikings were old enough to drink beer,' he sneered. 'If you get drunk your mummies and daddies won't be able to help you. They live the other side of the sea!'

Offa, a Saxon with a hard face and mean eyes, pushed forward.

'Why don't you lot will build your little boat and go home? Good riddance! We'll be glad to see the back of you!'

His friends closed up. Some clenched small rocks in their fists. But before Vimp could respond, Lief sprang to his feet to calm things.

'Listen!' he implored. 'We can be friends. The other Saxon kids accept us. It's just you, Egeslic, and your gang.'

A large stone hit the ground inches from his foot. Lief recovered his balance and stood firm. But Offa was not finished with him.

'Listen, Viking boy,' he snarled. 'We never asked you to come here. And we don't want you to stay. You can't even speak our language properly.'

Emma strode out in front of the two warring groups. She was not taking any more insults, especially from her own people.

'You know they've never caused you any bother,' she cried. 'The ship they're building will be the best around. Some of you might even get to sail in it.'

Egeslic pulled a face and looked disdainfully at the piled timbers.

'You wouldn't catch me going out in it,' he jeered. 'It'd sink the minute a wind blows up.'

He turned his gaze on Emma.

'In any case, why are you mixing with Vikings? You're supposed to be English, like us. Everyone knows you're sweet on Poetry Boy.'

Egeslic shot a cruel glance in Lief's direction. Emma's blood rushed to her cheeks, but Lief held her back.

'Look,' he said. 'Why don't you move on? You see to your fields and we'll build our boat. Keep out of each other's way. Does that make sense?'

The small group of Saxons closed up. Offa acted as spokesman.

'Fine. No problem. But you, Lief, or whatever your name is—just keep your hands off Emma. She's English. She shouldn't be messing around with Viking scum.'

He stepped forward, raised his right hand and hurled a stone. It struck Lief on the cheek. Blood spurted out and a cruel jeer went up from the Saxons. Impulsive Eric sprang forward and grabbed Offa by the scruff of his neck. His fist sank into the young Saxon's face. The boy fell to the ground, rolling up in a ball before Eric could inflict more damage. Vimp threw himself at Eric, grasping his wrist before he could strike again. Eric's blood was up, and Vimp needed help to hold him back. Bristling with anger, the Saxons gathered round Offa to get him to his feet. Blood streamed from his injured nose.

Egeslic fixed Vimp with his steely eyes.

'You've gone too far, Vikings,' he growled. 'You'll hear more about this. Just wait 'til we get back to Chief Alfred.'

He turned to his companions and ordered them away. Offa, sobbing, stumbled back to the village. Vimp released his grip on Eric's arm and pushed him away. He ran over to Lief to find Emma caring for his flesh wound.

'I'm all right,' Lief spluttered. 'It's my fault. I should have ignored them. Let me take the blame.'

Disturbed by the sudden violence, the young Vikings reluctantly returned to their labours but found it hard to work with enthusiasm. As the afternoon wore on, they knew they would have to face the wrath of Alfred. The village Chieftain was known to be a fair man, but they could not imagine he would side with them. Far more likely, Alfred would favour the version spun by the Saxons. No one looked forward to returning to the huts. It seemed Eric had got himself, and his fellow Vikings, into serious trouble.

Chapter 3

Black Dog of the Forest

Vimp and his shipwright friends worked hard. First the keel got laid, and after that the seasoned timbers filled out the curve of the boat. Freya thought it looked like a dead giant's skeleton. She had once seen the remains of a washed up whale. Over the months, its flesh was picked by crows and wolves. Eventually, the bones of the rib cage stood out along the backbone. Flooded by tides, the skeleton took months to break up. Now, in England, she was watching something grow rather than decay.

Her mind flashed back to another time when *Freya*, the longboat her friends named after her, had been set on fire at a Viking funeral. In it lay the dead body of Agnar, Chief of Wolves. He was given a sea funeral.

'The boys never stop,' she thought. 'All that sawing and hammering. It drives me crazy.'

The vessel was built as a present to the good-hearted Saxon villagers. After the face-up with the village louts, Freya had been smart. She sought out the people's leader before they could get to him. Alfred listened, knowing the Viking girl always told the truth. He was also aware that Egeslic was a nasty bully, and it worried him.

'First, Freya, I must speak to Vimp and his friends,' said Alfred. 'Even if they feel they did not start this incident they're still here as our guests. You Vikings must learn to settle.'

Later, in his quiet way, the village Leader took Vimp and Eric aside and ordered them to keep out of further trouble.

'It's you I worry about, young Eric,' he said. 'You work hard and your heart is honest, but you have a hot temper. Try not to get into arguments. If it happens again, we shall tell you to leave. You're tall and strong so there's no need to fight. Cool heads settle fights better than fists.'

Eric stood awkwardly before the Saxon leader, shifting his weight from one foot to the other. He knew he had let his friends down.

'I promise I'll control my hot blood,' he told Alfred. 'And make up with Egeslic.'

Late in the afternoon, Eric set out for the forest. He wanted to cool off and find time to think.

'Problem is,' he thought, 'I seem to get myself into trouble without meaning to. I just don't get it.'

He despised bullies and would not be pushed around. The light began to fade but he had no thoughts of turning back. Deep in the wood, Eric suddenly came to his senses.

'It must be time to return. The others will be wondering where I am.'

Longer shadows fell across the track, but Eric was confident he could find his way home. He had been away longer than he appreciated, and his stomach told him it was suppertime. Up ahead, a young deer sprang through the dense undergrowth. Eric caught only the briefest glance as it crossed the path. He stopped to listen but the forest was silent with no birds singing. Why had the deer broken cover?

A curious sound – over to his right and hard to make out. A low rumbling; nearer now. Some creature pushing its way through dense vegetation? Eric detected the sharp snapping of twigs. Something or someone, certainly. A hunting party? Surely not at this time of day.

Eric Bignose, bravest of Vikings, stood motionless. Then, from behind him, came a deep growl. He broke out in cold sweat. The heavy crashing grew nearer. Eric looked round for escape. Which way to turn?

'Up this tree!'

Grasping a branch, he hauled himself into an ancient oak.

'I'll crawl along the main branch and hide amongst the leaves . . . '

Snaking his way along the twisted limb of the oak, Eric found cover and clung on for dear life. He peered through the leaves to see a large bear on the path. It was followed by a smaller creature. Dark, furry – a cub. But the hidden Viking sensed the parent was anxious to be on its way. The cub padded behind.

'Arghhh! Arghhh!'

A blood-chilling snarl, harsh and cruel. The mother bear turned to face the direction of the threat. Her cub hid behind her.

'Arghhh!'

The bear reared up on her hind legs, baring her teeth. Eric heard her panting. She dropped down on all fours and backed away. Her gaze remained fixed ahead. Eric, up in his refuge, squirmed round to find the reason for the bear's distress. What he saw next made the small hairs on his neck stand up. He gripped tightly onto the branch.

From out of the trees appeared an extraordinary creature. It was like nothing he had ever seen, dreamed, or imagined. Jet black; almost wolf-like. An animal every bit as large as the mother bear. Long hair; gaping mouth. Awesome fangs, dripping with saliva. The bear rumbled a deep warning. Her opponent snarled viciously.

The monster sat back on its haunches, about to spring at the mother, who stood between it and her cub. Raising her head, she prepared for battle. With a blood-curdling growl, the huge black dog flung itself on the exposed neck of the bear. They rolled over and over as each sought to find a weak spot. But as the mighty struggle continued, the bear's strength sapped and its wild attacker got on top. Its deadly jaws clamped onto the bear's neck. Slowly, the mother's life drained away.

Motionless on his high perch, Eric stared down on the saddest of scenes. The mother was mortally wounded. Of the cub there was no trace. It had fled into the surrounding forest. The black dog released its grip. Its red tongue hung from its mouth as it panted for breath. The beast seemed satisfied with its victory and stood over the bear's final twitches. It raised its head and howled into the gathering gloom. Turning on its tracks, the creature padded away.

Up in the tree, Eric found his limbs shaking. After mustering the courage to venture down, he avoided the body of the dead bear but kept a sharp lookout for the black beast. Unarmed, Eric knew he was no match.

Trees seemed to close in on all sides. Hurrying along the path, Eric became aware of a small movement in the bracken. He froze, unable to control the beating of his heart. The fronds parted and out onto the path stumbled a small bear. It was lost and bewildered, seeking its mother. Eric boy heaved a huge sigh of relief. He noticed the youngster held its ground but was not aggressive. Gingerly he approached the cub and knelt down. The little bear lifted its shaggy head and sniffed at him. Eric reached out and the bear shuffled forwards. He touched its ears and laid his hands on its furry neck. He spoke to it quietly and the cub appeared to relax.

'I can't leave you here, little one. You'll never survive on your own.'

Eric calmed the animal by stroking its back. The bear nuzzled into him.

'Will you let me lift you?'

He knew mother bears sometimes carried their young. Very carefully, he placed his hands under the chest and raised the cub to his shoulder. Its sharp claws gripped onto him.

'Better be going. Out of this forest. It can't be far.'

Eric continued down the track, but with every step he was aware of something following. It seemed to shadow his every step.

'Just my imagination,' he told himself. 'There's nothing there. If I was going to be attacked it would have happened before now.'

But there was something there. In the fading light, Eric made out the shape of a dark object blocking his path. He swallowed hard. The creature did not move. Its eyes glowed. At first, yellow, then blood red. Eyes the size of saucers. Eric gripped onto the cub. There was no escape.

As swiftly as it had appeared, the creature turned and disappeared into the darkness. The way was open and Eric ran towards the bright lights of the village fires.

'Come on, cub,' he whispered hoarsely. 'We'll get there together. You've been really brave.'

For the first time in his bold life, Eric the Brave had faced terror – far worse than when pirates had attacked them at sea. Far worse even than the time when Aegir, God of the Oceans, had raised his fist and threatened to crush his boat. He shuddered.

Eric was thankful to get back to safety. He re-entered the village with the cub dangling round his shoulder.

Chapter 4

Forest Mission

'Are you crazy?' Vimp said, unable to contain his anger.

'You've got us into all sorts of bother with the Saxons. Then you disappeared and no one knew where to look for you. Astrid was so upset. Don't you ever think about anyone except yourself?'

Eric gently lowered the bear cub from his shoulders and held it to his chest.

'Listen, Vimp, I'm sorry. I was angry. I just had to get out of the village. It drives me mad.'

Vimp was not impressed.

'You're the one person stopping us from settling. You don't see it, do you?'

Eric cast his eyes to the ground.

'I know. I got it wrong again. I'll try to do better.'

They were joined by the other boys and girls. The cub was centre of attention.

'With respect, Eric,' Leif said quietly, 'the last thing this village needs is a forest bear. You can't keep it, you know.'

Eric felt foolish.

'What was I supposed to do? Its mother's dead and it can't look after itself. I think it's still feeding on milk.'

He shuffled his feet.

302

'I look after the cows and goats. There's always a drop of milk spare. When the cub grows, I'll find it stuff in the forest.'

Astrid came to his rescue although she sounded upset.

'I'm furious with you, Eric Bignose,' she stormed. 'You're a hopeless case. You can't take the cub back. It'll have to stay here. But just one problem. What happens when it grows up?'

Eric had not had time to think about this.

'Look! What d'you expect? Should I let it starve?'

Astrid put out a hand. The cub did not appear to mind being stroked.

'I'll help you,' she offered. 'But have you seen the size of a grown bear? This one might not stay friendly.'

The others agreed. The little bear could stay for now. But the sooner it was returned to the forest, the better. And what would the Saxons think? This was one more excuse to set them against the young Vikings.

The group stood in the light of the flickering flames, illuminating the darkness.

'We'll have to make a cage for it,' Lief suggested. 'But it'll need exercise. How on earth will you stop it getting loose?'

Eric's friends were at a loss for an answer, although they were warming to the orphan. Vimp suggested getting hold of a leather collar like the ones the Saxons used for their boar hounds.

'We could ask the blacksmith to knock us up a chain. I'm sure we'll cope.'

By now the friends were in agreement. Seeing the sleepy cub nestling in Eric's strong arms made them feel happy.

'It could be our mascot,' Lief suggested. 'We need to think of a name for him—'

'Or her,' Ingrid interrupted.

They laughed. Being in charge of a bear cub suddenly seemed like fun, but in their excitement no one had seen that Eric was still shaking.

'We'd better turn in,' Vimp said. 'Our boat's nearly complete, but it's up early in the morning. And there are animals to see to. I guess your bear should sleep in our hut tonight. Only one night, mind you.'

The girls crowded round and took turns to touch the little animal on its rough neck.

'It's sweet,' said Ingrid. 'I forgive you!'

Wishing each other good night, they turned and went their separate ways. Lief, always the quick thinker, hurried off to find a spot of goat's milk for the new arrival.

'*Beowulf*', he thought to himself. 'That's the name for the bear. In Saxon English it means 'hunter of bees.'

He pulled back the leather curtain at the hut entrance he shared with Vimp and Eric. The wick of a mutton fat candle gave out a feeble flame.

'Try this.'

He offered a small wooden mug of goat's milk to Eric, who sat bolt upright with Beowulf in his lap.

'Maybe if you dip your finger in, the cub will suck,' Lief suggested.

He could not help chuckling as he watched the tough Viking boy coax the young bear to lick his milky fingers. Lief's mind went back to the time when Eric had carried the wounded body of Agnar the wolf. Agnar had fought courageously to rescue Freya from the fangs of a monster. Once more, Eric the Bold was revealing his tender side. Lief noticed the cub showed interest in the warm milk. Soon it fell asleep. Eric placed it on straw. Lief smiled and blew out the flame.

Next morning, a gathering of village leaders, young and old, met in the large, communal hut. They sat on rough benches round a fire of crackling logs. Smoke drifted up through the hole at the centre of the grimy thatch. Eric and Vimp stood before Chief Alfred. Grim Saxon faces glowered at them.

'We've called you before us because a serious story has leaked out.'

The Chief pointed at Eric.

'You! The boy who wandered into the forest.'

Alfred paused and turned to his companions.

'You returned with a bear cub. We understand its mother is dead. Our interest, however, is not in the cub. We heard you confronted another creature?'

The tall Viking ran his hand through his hair. He coughed, wood smoke catching at the back of his throat. It was hard explaining things in new Saxon words.

'It's true,' he said. 'I went alone. On my return, an adult bear and its cub crossed my path. I shinned up the nearest tree. Then . . . '

Eric's voice trailed off. He swallowed hard.

'It was horrible. A black beast. It attacked the adult bear. Killed it. Later, when I neared the village, the thing slunk out from the bushes to bar my way.'

A cold shiver ran down his spine.

'I thought it was about to go for me but it stayed still. Staring with those terrible eyes. It was getting dark. I was really scared.'

Anselm, a highly respected elder, spoke up.

'Describe the creature, young man.'

Eric hesitated but Chief Alfred insisted he went on.

'Black,' Eric stammered. 'As big as the bear. Bigger maybe. Difficult to make out in the dark . . . like a dog. A wolf, even. Terrifying teeth . . . '

'Go on,' Anselm encouraged.

'The beast fixed me with its cold eyes,' Eric told him. 'Huge. Glowing in the dark. Yellow, then red.'

'Anselm is a wise man,' Alfred said. 'We ask for his explanation.'

The elderly Saxon rose awkwardly to his feet, supported by a wooden stick. Stroking his wispy beard he addressed the assembly.

'What we've heard from this young man disturbs me. I don't blame him. This could have happened to any of us. Evil forces are at work. Forces of the devil, I suspect.'

The hut rang with anxious voices. Chief Alfred called for order and begged Anselm to continue.

'I can't be sure,' he said slowly. 'But I suggest this appearance may take us back to the times of our ancestors. The days when the first Saxons sailed to these shores and brought their beliefs. Gods of the North and spirits and devils. Today, some worship the Christian God. Few bother with the old Gods. But I know one who does. We must find him and ask for guidance.'

Anselm looked Alfred squarely in the eye.

'Don't ask me questions, Alfred. You mustn't enquire where this person lives. We seek ancient wisdom and I can't give you his name. Above all, the Christian Priest who visits should not be told of this. He'd say we are pagans, not believing in his Christian God but in the spirits of the woods. The beliefs of our ancestors. I shall need escorting.'

The old man wobbled on his stick and had to be helped to his bench. Chief Alfred thanked him.

'This conversation must not go beyond these walls. No villager should hear of it. It would create panic. We're dealing with forces few of us understand. I grant Anselm permission to seek the person he speaks of.'

Alfred looked round the small gathering.

'I ask for need volunteers. Four freemen to accompany Anselm on a dangerous mission.'

No one spoke. Men looked down at their earthen floor hoping not to be noticed. Vimp stepped forward.

'I'll go.'

'And me,' said Eric.

Two Saxon brothers leapt to their feet.

'Count us in,' one cried. 'Two Saxons and two Vikings. That's a match for anyone, mortal or spirit. And we'll look after Anselm. My name is Leofwine!'

Even Eric was impressed at the size of the broad-chested young man, straggles of hair over his craggy face.

'And this is my brother, Eadbehrt.'

A younger man strode forward. His beard and moustache hid his mouth, but the young Vikings detected a gleam in his eyes.

'Nothing frightens me,' he claimed, fingering a dagger at his belt. 'I chased wolves off my sheep last week. They haven't been back since. One black dog means nothing. I'll take on a whole pack!'

The meeting broke up, leaving Chief Alfred and Anselm with their new comrades. Alfred was grateful to the brave Saxons.

'Don't take your task lightly,' he warned. 'Listen well to Anselm and take his instructions.'

Next morning at the crowing of the cockerels, the forest party met in the first light. Despite his need for a walking stick, Anselm seemed as eager as his younger companions. Each traveller carried a bundle of bread and salted meat. Vimp and Eric had hardly slept. It had not been possible to tell their friends they were leaving. Or the reason why. The young Vikings marvelled at how relaxed the Saxon brothers appeared. Leofwine and Eadbehrt were charmed by Eric's cub. Anselm regarded it more gravely.

'It seems to have adopted you,' he said. 'I see you have a flagon of milk at your waist.'

He looked thoughtfully at the small animal.

'Bears are special creatures. No braver beast inhabits the forest. This small animal may prove helpful on our journey.'

The adventurers lifted the wooden bar securing the main gate and headed across the cow pasture. Hopping ahead of them, a scruffy black crow scavenged its first meal of the day. Crows were bad news. Saxon and Viking, they had all listened to stories passed

down by their forebears. The big bird pierced them with a sharp
look from its beady eye then lifted away over the trees.

'That's an unfortunate start,' thought Vimp. 'Was it sent to
spy on us?'

The party entered the wood, in single file. Unusually for the
time of the year, the forest was silent. Eadbehrt, guided by Anselm,
led the way with the two Viking boys following. Thoughtful
Leofwine posted himself at the rear. They plunged deeper into the
forest, occasionally resting at a stream to drink. These moments
gave Anselm time to plan the next step.

'I've made this journey only once before,' he told his
companions. 'But I'm fairly sure of my way, and I sense we're
being guided. You can be certain we're also being watched
by the Spirits of the Old Gods. This is their world, and we
human folk are not especially welcome. Treat them with due
respect.'

Big Eric was beginning to feel more himself. The shock of
the previous day had faded, and he felt confident to take on the
world. Beowulf the Bear trailed behind, never allowing his new
parent out of sight. Secretly, Eric was pleased to see it strayed
off the path to snuffle amongst old tree roots. It was learning to
feed itself.

'There is something you must know,' said Anselm as his
escorts enjoyed thirst-quenching apples. 'I'm not who you think
I am.'

He paused. A hush descended over the forest glade.

'Tomorrow a new priest comes to our village. He's found out
about my past. He may order that I leave.'

The younger Saxons and Vikings craned forward. Not one
took a bite from his apple.

'I was once respected more than I am today. Now only Alfred
seems to treat me properly. You see . . . '

He paused and looked round his friends.

'There was a time when sick people sought me out. They took my advice and drank my medicines.'

The old man closed his eyes, remembering his younger days.

'I was close to the spirits of the forest. You see the tall Ash tree over there, its branches stretching ever upwards?'

Anselm rose slowly his feet and walked over. Stretching out his hands, he felt the rough bark and bent down to pick up a twig.

'This tree is special. It connects our world with the times of ancient Gods. The Gods shared by Old Saxon folk and Viking peoples. We worshipped them before the Christian God was forced upon us.'

Holding the branch before him he made a circle in the air.

'With this wand I can fend off bad spirits. Whatever you see me do must remain secret.'

Anselm's companions stayed silent, not daring to challenge the elderly man. They watched in awe as he touched the branch on the ground. No one moved a muscle as he drew a circle in the dusty earth. He stood in the centre.

'We're now protected from serpents. The bite of the adder can no longer harm you.'

He raised the branch in front of his wrinkled face. The escorts stood transfixed as Anselm sang a tuneless chant in his creaky voice.

'I stand in this circle to guard against the venom of the serpent. We worshippers shall permit no evil to enter our souls. We fear nothing and seek and trust the trees, our friends. And the timeless rocks, blessed with goodness. Likewise, the springs of pure water.'

Even Eric kept his silence. Anselm stepped gingerly out of his sacred circle and rejoined his companions. The Ash branch remained in his hand.

'Do not be afraid. Tell no human what you have seen. Our ancestors respected these trees and creatures.'

The travellers gathered their bits and pieces. Then they plunged into the mysteries of the enchanted forest.

Chapter 5

The Stagman

The woodland explorers reached parts of the forest where only bold hunters dared venture. It was necessary to slash at brambles arching across the ancient path. Eric's hands and arms soon became scratched by the sharp thorns. He began to wonder if the old man knew where he was going.

Beowulf tagged along. He seemed happy with his new parent, never letting him out of his sight. Suddenly the cub stopped and whimpered. His master turned and knelt down at his side.

'What's wrong, little one? Are you getting tired? I can carry you, but I think your mother would have made you carry on.'

The bear uttered a feeble growl. Eric could not help laughing.

'I'm getting complaints,' he informed the group. 'An angry bear. I don't know if I can handle this!'

Anselm turned and looked at the cub with interest.

'Hush!' he advised. 'Respect your wild friend. He knows far more about these woods than we can ever know. He's trying to tell us something.'

Vimp glanced at Eric, who looked anxious.

'Up ahead,' he whispered. 'Did something move?'

Anselm held the Ash branch in front of his chest. Then he whisked it back and forth.

'Clever cub,' he said quietly. 'Pick him up. He needs comforting.'

Eric bent down and placed his strong hands under the bear's belly. He felt Beowulf tremble.

Anselm called loudly to the trees.

'Be gone, Evil Presence!'

He wafted his branch and the two Saxons joined him. They were anxious to know what was going on.

'Fear not,' Anselm replied. 'This Ash protects us. But keep your eyes open. This journey was never going to be easy.'

Leofwine remembered the wise words of Chief Alfred. Anselm had to be obeyed.

'We move on!'

Anselm was determined to continue his mission. For the next two hours, the small band plunged further into the forest. Vimp felt uneasy, as though something, or someone, was following them just out of sight. There was never anything to see. Just a hint; an occasional shaking of leaves.

'I'm being stupid,' he told himself.

Looking at Eric did not put him at his ease. He knew his fearless friend was tense. Eric clutched Beowulf to his chest. There was no way the cub would be put down again. Up ahead, Anselm raised his hand and signalled to stop.

'We're close,' he said. 'All is well. Look out now for a large grey rock. Or you may first hear the stream. It bubbles from a well in a sacred place. Only here can we be close to the spirits.'

Anselm's words failed to comfort Eric and Vimp. They agreed they should have remained in the village. It seemed so far away. Another world.

It was Eadbehrt who spotted the first signs. Hacking his way through vegetation, he stopped and pointed to a small Birch tree.

'What's that hanging on its branches?' he asked. 'Like . . . little pieces of cloth. Pale blues, reds. Looks as though they've been there for ages.' He shook his head in bewilderment. 'Who'd want to do that?'

Eadbehrt was right. Tatty pieces of torn cloth fluttered from the lower branches of the tree. He saw they had been tied on but were now bleached by sun and rain.

'Listen!'

The others fell quiet. From not far away they heard the gurgling of water rising from the earth. And as they approached they came upon a huge boulder covered in moss. Tall ferns sprang from its crevices.

'We've arrived,' Anselm announced. 'Our journey's been rewarded. Treat this spot with respect. We're with the spirits of the forest. They'll not harm us.'

Vimp remained unconvinced. He had little time for the old Viking Gods, so it was even harder to get worked up about Anglo-Saxon 'spirits' belonging to a bygone age. Cautiously he circled the rock and discovered crystal clear water springing from its source. Anselm signalled his comrades to sit.

'Rest awhile.'

He paused.

'Refresh yourselves. Wash your faces and tired limbs. Your energies will be restored. For my part, I must leave you. Have no fear. I shan't be long.'

He looked at each young adventurer in turn.

'When I come back, you must be brave. Hold your ground and don't be tempted to run away. If you do you'll get lost in the trees. Only I can find the way back.'

His wizened old face broke into a twisted smile.

'Trust me. All will be well.'

Anselm turned and hobbled past the mysterious rock. His nervous companions looked on as he prodded the uneven ground with his stick. Leofwine went over to the stream and sniffed the air.

'This is a weird place,' he thought. 'Our lives are in Anselm's hands.'

Late in the afternoon, Anselm reappeared through the trees, stick in one hand and wand in the other. He walked slowly as Vimp jumped to his feet to greet him.

'You had us worried,' he said. 'We were beginning to wonder . . . '

The old man raised one hand and waved the walking stick.

'I told you to have faith. There's much to tell you. Pack up your things.'

The final part of the journey did not take long. The air grew cooler. Gaunt trees pressed in from all sides. Eric clutched Beowulf even tighter. A snake with zigzag markings on its back slithered across the path. It made no attempt to bite.

'Stop!' Anselm raised his arm. 'Go carefully. You're now in the presence of the spirits. They see your every move. Behave with respect. Say nothing.'

He shuffled on. In front was a small clearing of wild grasses where sunlight penetrated the woodland. To one side, Vimp spotted a cave hollowed from the cliff above. Anselm lowered himself on his knees and motioned for the others to do the same. The younger travellers laid their packs on the ground and knelt. At first, Eric did not notice the breeze that caused the leaves to rustle. He felt a cold draught on his cheek. His unruly hair blew across his face. As he swept it back, the wind picked up.

Bushes and smaller trees at the edge of the clearing began to sway. The whole forest seemed alive. Windswept leaves swirled into the kneelers' faces. Vimp flung his arms up to protect his eyes. The wind ceased almost as soon as it had begun. When he opened his eyes he did not believe what he saw. From the mouth of the cave emerged a figure, taller than a man. Although it walked upright and on two legs, it appeared more animal than human. Stag's antlers protruded from its head. The face, too, was that of a deer, but it looked unreal, like a mask. The figure wore

315

deerskin tied by leather thongs. It raised two arms and lifted its head to the sun. Vimp and Eric knelt, icy shivers running down their spines. Never in their adventurous lives had they been so stricken with terror. The bear cub gave a pitiful cry and burrowed deep into his master's chest. Even Anselm did not dare look up. He cast his eyes humbly to the ground.

The half-human creature stepped towards the petrified visitors. It spoke in a sombre voice.

'You dare enter this sacred place uninvited? Except Anselm, you are not welcome. Because he has brought you here, I, Wizard of the Forest, will aid you. I do not sense you hold to our ancient beliefs. Perhaps you believe in the new God. I do not know him. My wisdom comes from the forest.'

Vimp stood rooted to the spot.

'Anselm has told me of your plight. One of you has been tempted by great evil. This may bring disaster upon him, his friends, and his family. None can escape.'

Eric raised his head. The Stagman's eyes blazed at him.

'I'm that one,' he whispered hoarsely. 'Blame me and not the rest. I'm ready to take my punishment.'

The Stagman approached Eric and touched him on the shoulder.

'You are brave,' he said. 'You are from the Norse lands.'

The Wizard reached into a large bag dangling from around his middle. One by one, he pulled out small objects and laid them in the dust. First, a buzzard's flight feather. Followed by three round pebbles, which he laid in the shape of a triangle.

'This feather was given to me by a fine bird of these woods. I place it inside the stones. Its magic works against demons possessing human souls.'

Then the Wizard took out several small bones. He held each one before Eric's face before returning them to the pouch. Eric shuddered as the Wizard placed his deerskin-covered hands on his shoulders.

'Come with me!' he commanded. 'I ask Anselm to be my witness.'

Eric rose to his feet and handed Beowulf to Vimp.

'Bring the bear cub with you,' the Wizard told him. 'He is your best protection.'

The Stagman sensed Eric's reluctance but insisted on obedience.

'The animal will not be harmed. The day may come when it will return the kindness you showed it.'

The Stagman turned and walked slowly towards his cave. Eric and Anselm followed. He invited them into the gloomy interior where a small fire smouldered in one corner. Over the fire stood a tripod from which hung an iron cauldron covered in greasy soot. The cave smelt of smoke and woodland scents.

'Take this cup!'

The Stagman handed Eric a wooden vessel, then stood by the boiling pot, turning his hands to the rising steam.

'Heal and mend this broken spirit. Drive away all poisons that have entered his poor soul.'

He bent to pick up a small bunch flowers plucked from the glade.

'This is Mugwort,' he said gravely.

Holding the slender fronds of the wayside plant in the smoke, the Stagman broke off its tiny flowers and tossed them into the pot. He picked up a large spoon.

'With this sacred instrument I stir my potion. You must drink it.'

The big Viking boy gulped.

'It smells horrible,' he protested.

'Obey,' the Stagman advised. 'No harm will befall you.'

He spooned out steaming green liquid into a cup. After a short while, he raised it to Eric's lips.

'Drink!' he commanded. 'Waste not a drop. I travelled to the Other World to learn the secrets of this potion!'

Eric submitted, swallowing the most awful drink he had ever tried. The hot liquid scorched his mouth and throat. He felt sick but fought to hold down the sacred herbal mixture. Anselm placed a comforting arm on his shoulder.

'You acted bravely, my son. Now we can return in peace and hope.'

Eric staggered out of the cave, clutching his stomach. His bear trotted behind.

'Beowulf the Bear!' the Stagman called from his cave entrance. 'I know your name. *"Bee Wolf." He who attacks bees.* Guard your friend with your life.'

Eric struggled back to his friends. Anselm spoke to calm them.

'What you have seen today, you have not seen. Neither have you heard what you have heard. Tell no one of these events.'

He bowed gravely towards the cave before turning towards the path.

'Follow me,' he commanded. 'And forget!'

The comrades did as they were told. Vimp glanced back, but the cave had vanished. Like its strange inhabitant, it was no longer to be seen.

CHAPTER 6

Black Shuck

'You people are pagan fools! You continue to worship spirits that never existed. There is only one God. Only He may be worshipped. No other.'

The wooden church in the Saxon village rang with the strong words of Wilfred, the new priest. Sent from the nearby Abbey, he thundered at the gathering of humble folks before him.

'None of you are worthy of God's love. Yet Our Lord is forgiving.'

The young man in the brown robe stood before the altar. Turning his shaven head to heaven, he asked for God's blessing upon the people who knelt with bowed heads.

'Show mercy to these simple sheep. They have lost their way.'

Wilfrid looked grimly at his new flock.

'Little did I realise,' he said, 'that when I came to your village I would be amongst heathens.'

A feeling of dread passed through the packed congregation. It was the first time Eric had attended the church he and his Viking friends had helped build. Now they knelt with the Saxons. The priest fingered the white rope tied around his middle.

'Do you seriously believe trees and animals can be worshipped? That a rock is sacred and your forest full of demons? I understand that a young man amongst you claims to have confronted a creature of great evil. What rubbish!'

319

Wilfrid faced his humbled audience.

'I hear he's a Viking. You've shown him and friends great kindness. See how he repays you.'

Eric began to feel uneasy. Why was the priest was turning the village against him? A wild feeling of panic welled up. He rose to his feet and pointed an accusing finger at the priest.

'What do you know? You weren't there. I know what I saw. That black dog was a demon. It killed a grown bear!'

The Saxons shook their heads, in dismay. The Viking boy was insulting their priest. Brother Wilfrid stood in front of Eric.

'How dare you speak like this in God's house? We've been told you and some others entered a forbidden part of the forest. You consulted a Wizard who hides in a cave.'

A murmur of outrage swept through the gathering.

'And,' the priest stormed on, 'a *senior* member of our community led you there!'

All eyes turned on the kneeling Anselm, who kept his eyes down.

'This man misled you. Anselm consulted with spirits that don't exist. *A world that has passed.* Only the Christian God can conquer evil. It was to Him you should have turned.'

'I'm not a Christian, so I wouldn't know!' Eric announced.

His outburst shocked the worshippers.

'Brother Wilfrid is right!' one called out. 'That Viking's a heathen We should be rid of him. He's a curse upon us. Ban Vikings from our village!'

Anselm struggled to his feet. He raised his stick to the noisy congregation.

'These young people are not to blame,' he shouted over the noise. 'It's true I led them to the forest, but I did it for a reason. Eric speaks the truth. The Demon Dog of Saxon legend is amongst us. It stalks our village by night. What does the Christian God know of this? Only by consulting the ancient spirits can we rid ourselves of this demon.'

321

A farmer leapt to his feet and struck Anselm on the head. The blow toppled the old man. His stick crashed to the floor. Anselm collapsed and lay lifeless. Vimp and Bjorne hurried to him but knew he was dead.

'God have mercy on us all!'

The priest raised his voice to the wooden rafters as the congregation shrank back. The farmer stood transfixed, horrified at his own action. His friends moved away and women wept. Astrid and Ingrid hurried to Eric.

'Come away,' Astrid said, clamping his arms. 'It's not safe . . . '

She did not finish her sentence. A piercing cry went up from the back of the church. The door burst open and a gust of wind howled through the building. The figure of a hideous wolf-monster filled the entrance. Parents clutched their children. The beast exposed its yellow fangs, evil eyes glowing with menace. In a single bound, it leapt at the throat of the priest. Women screamed. Then the creature turned and glared at the worshippers cringing behind the altar.

The assailant sprang at the open church door, its awful claws scoring marks into the ancient oak. The villagers fell on the knees, seeking God's protection. The Demon Dog howled then fled the building.

A small group gathered round the frail body of Anselm whilst others ran over to the priest. But it was hopeless. The young man lay where he died without a mark on his throat. An Elder, shaking as he spoke, called for silence.

'Anselm was right. Our community is haunted. We have seen The Black Shuck!'

CHAPTER 7

Eric's Departure

The people departed the church clutching their near ones for comfort. The Saxons were horrified at the slaughter of the new priest. Some felt guilt, expecting their new God to send down punishment. They hurried home, avoiding the Vikings. Meanwhile, Vimp and company trudged back to their shelters. Astrid held onto Eric, offering support, but she knew he felt responsible for the dramatic events. Beowulf got up to greet his new friends and Astrid fondled his ears.

Eric collapsed onto his mattress. Nothing made sense. The situation was out of control. Vimp offered him a drink but he refused.

'I can't stay here,' he said 'I bring bad luck. Far better for me to leave so you can settle down with the Saxons.'

'If you go, we all go,' Vimp replied. 'It isn't fair you should take the blame.'

Lief agreed.

'Somehow we've to get the Saxons back on side. There must be something we can do.'

No one came up with any suggestions. They sat silently in the semi-darkness with their own thoughts. It was not long before a small party of Saxon leaders stood at the curtained entrance.

'Eric Bignose,' one called out sharply, 'you're summoned before the Village Court. You're to come alone.'

The tall young Viking rose to his feet.

'Look after Beowulf,' he said. 'I must face my fate.'

He pulled back the curtain, blinking against the bright afternoon light. Leofwine and Eadbehrt were amongst the group. He shot Astrid a parting glance.

In the community hut, he was dismayed to see that Chief Alfred and the Elders had assembled. Alfred spoke immediately.

'We're sorry to have to call for you,' he said. 'You've done much since your arrival. But now you place us in a difficult situation.'

Eric stood upright, holding his head high.

'Leofwine and Eadbehrt have spoken up for you,' Alfred went on. 'They told us of the journey into the forest. Perhaps poor Anselm was mistaken. We understand he sought a certain person in contact with the forest spirits?'

Eric nodded, his head low. Alfred looked grave.

'Even though Anselm did us no favours, I blame myself for this. I let him go. The evil remains with us and haunts the village.'

Leofwine stepped forward.

'With your permission, my brother and I are equally guilty. We all ended up at the cave and saw what went on.'

The Chieftain looked round at the small group of Elders.

'It was not you, Leofwine, who first encountered The Black Shuck. We also understand Eric drank a magic potion prepared by the Wizard. That was foolish, and certainly did no good. The Demon Dog attacked our village. A holy priest lies dead.'

It was true. The Saxon brothers could not argue. Alfred drew himself up to his full height.

'Unless there's anyone here to challenge me, I order Eric Bignose to leave our village at dawn. We'll help him with a parcel of food and he may take anything that belongs to him. He must never approach this community again.'

A murmur of assent sounded from the Elders. Leofwine and Eadbehrt looked on with sadness, knowing there was nothing they could do. Eric's mind spun. He hardly grasped the Chief's stern words.

'You must go,' Alfred said. 'May God protect you.'

The Saxon brothers took Eric gently by the arm and led him back to the hut. Invited inside, they explained what they had heard.

'We promise,' they said, 'to see Eric through the dangerous part of the forest.'

Turning to the shocked Vikings – Vimp, Astrid, and Lief – they smiled sadly and left.

No one slept that night. Eric tossed and turned on his straw, fearing what might befall him. No friends. No Astrid. Only his bear. He stretched out and fondled the cub.

'At least we'll stay together, Beowulf,' he whispered.

The boys were dismayed. Their hero, Eric, was being sent away. Yet he was innocent; it was hardly his fault The Black Shuck had chanced upon him. In her own hut, Ingrid held a sobbing Astrid in her arms. Neither could sleep. Astrid dreaded the dawn, for it would be the last day she would see her brave warrior.

A cockerel crowed and a second answered as the Saxon village began to wake. Barely able to speak, Vimp and Lief helped Eric put together a shoulder pack. It contained enough food and spare clothes to get him started.

'I've collected your carpentry kit,' said Vimp. 'Your hand axe, a scraper, chisel, two hammers and the saw. You'll need them to build a shelter. We know you'll survive.'

He sounded more confident than he felt. Vimp had been thinking, too.

'Your best bet is to head for the coast. You're from a fishing family, so you don't need any lessons.'

Miserably, they stepped into the grey stillness of the morning. Leofwine and Eadbehrt were waiting for them.

'We don't break promises,' Eadbehrt said. 'We'll set Eric on his way.'

The small group, Beowulf padding along behind, reached the village gate and gazed into the meadow. A thin mist rose from the damp ground, blotting out the distant trees.

'Eric!'

Astrid's cry reached their ears. She ran towards him, holding out a small bundle.

'Apples,' she cried. 'They're all I could find.'

It was clear from her tear-stained face she had wept long into the night. Ingrid came running up behind her, followed by Freya and Emma.

'We can't believe you're being sent from us!'

The girls hugged the boy as he prepared to leave. Lifting the gate bar, Eric bent and kissed Astrid on her soft cheek.

'I'll never forget you,' he told her. 'You're my world.'

Eric turned to follow the Saxon brothers and did not look back. Astrid watched the party disappear into the mist.

'He's gone!' she sobbed. 'I'll never see him again.'

The sad youngsters trudged back to the huts. But Vimp's mind was buzzing, partly in anger and partly in despair.

'Let me tell you, Astrid,' he said firmly. 'If you think I'm letting our Eric go this easily, you're wrong. I make a vow to find him. Even if I have to track him to the ends of the Earth!'

Lief agreed.

'Count me in. Vikings don't let their friends down.'

He slipped a comforting arm round Astrid and escorted her back.

'Look after her,' he told the other girls. 'There's serious thinking to do.'

The rising sun dispelled the mist as the village awoke. The tempting scent of freshly baked bread spread through the huts. For the Viking boys, it was yet another busy day, building their sea going boat. It would not take long to finish and would soon be handed over to the Saxons.

Meanwhile, deep into the trees, a gloomy Eric and his Saxon guides headed North. They spoke little, stopping at streams for breaks.

The brothers stayed with the outcast for the rest of the morning. As the trees thinned out, more light penetrated the forest floor. The earth became sandier and the travellers scuffed up clouds of dust. Leofwine stopped to sniff the air.

'I smell the sea,' he said. 'We're near dunes.'

They looked out over the very bay where the crew of Viking escapers had first landed. Seeing it again brought memories flooding back. Eric recalled how they had heaved the longboat onto the beach. It was in these dunes where an armed bunch of Saxon villagers lay hidden, ready to do battle. Yet these had been the same folks who finally agreed to let the invaders settle. Now it seemed that his whole world was turned upside down.

Brave Eric Bignose flexed his aching shoulders and fondled Beowulf's fuzzy head. He turned to his companions.

'I'm on my own now. I'm grateful. You did your best for me.'

He held out his hand.

'Don't waste any more time. Return to the village.'

'If you run into trouble with people along here,' Leofwine said, 'remember to mention my name. Leofwine, brother of Eadbehrt; son of Cuichelm.'

His brother agreed.

'And mine: Eadbehrt, son of Cuichelm, brother of Leofwine. Our names will grant you protection.'

Thanking them, Eric called to the bear cub who toyed with a piece of driftwood.

'We may meet again,' he said. 'Look after my friends.'

CRISP 2010

Eric sighed and stepped into the shingle. The Saxon brothers turned and made their way back to the tree line. From there they looked back, but the outcast and his bear cub had already disappeared. They slowly plied their way to the village. Few words passed between them.

CHAPTER 8

Beowulf's Big Moment

Hardly knowing where he was going, Eric Bignose headed along the coastal path. He looked a sad and forlorn figure, his long hair blowing in the stiff breeze. Over his shoulder he carried his stick and bundle. Beowulf held back his progress, hurrying off the track to investigate anything new. Any log washed up on the beach had to be turned over, or clumps of smelly seaweed turned inside out raising clouds of flies. For the hundredth time, his master called for him to come, but Beowulf was not a dog seeking to please. He had the mind of a bear that was not meant to serve man. In the end, Eric gave up and saw the funny side.

'We'll never get anywhere at this speed,' he pretended to scold the cub.

He realised they were not heading anywhere. The light was going and Eric knew he had to hole up for his first night. His thoughts flickered back to the village, where his friends would be tucking into hot broth. He imagined them sitting huddled round a crackling fire. And how was the longboat progressing? His great hope had been to sail it, standing at the helm in a strong, following wind, but the craft always holding steady. It had been put together with all the Viking skill he and his friends could muster.

'It's weird talking to myself,' he said out loud. 'And chatting to a bear.'

Eric reckoned the night would be dry with only a gentle breeze lifting from the sea.

'I'll sleep under the stars and accept what tomorrow brings.'

Unpacking his things, he tore a lump out of a hard loaf.

'Here, Beowulf, try this. I've got a piece of pork wrapped up somewhere. We'll need to find a stream. Maybe there's one amongst the trees.'

The cub was happy with his supper. When they had finished, boy and bear set out to search for water. It did not take long. A small river flowed from the wood and Eric decided to track it.

'It'll be salty as the tide's bound to run up. If I get up far enough the water may be fresher.'

This took longer than he imagined and it was not easy pushing his way through the undergrowth. Suddenly, he noticed the cub was not with him.

'Beowulf!'

He called several times. Eric thrashed around, desperate that the small animal had lost its way. A quick movement in bushes caught the corner of his eye. A frantic Beowulf burst out pursued by a swarm of angry bees. They attacked on all sides, burrowing into his thick fur. In his mouth, he carried the remains of a dripping honeycomb. No matter how hard the bees tried to sting, Beowulf held onto his prized trophy. He pawed at the boldest bees. In no time, he devoured what remained of their winter stores. Eric hid behind a tree and waited for the storm to die down. Backing under a mossy rock, Beowulf managed to survive until the bees lost interest and flew back to the remains of their nest. When he emerged, there was a sticky grin on his face. The bear was extremely pleased with himself.

'You didn't leave any for me,' Eric complained. 'I could have done with a spot of wild honey!'

Secretly, he was delighted. Beowulf had shown he was able to look after himself, bees or no bees. Eric had no need to worry about feeding him, and the clever bear knew when to return.

Bending over a stream, the Viking boy cupped his hands together and sipped gratefully. The cool water restored his spirits.

Night closed in and he made his way down to the shore. He took out his flints and struck a flame to light a pile of dry sticks. Adding larger branches, he made a warming fire. There was plenty of driftwood around. Sitting under the starry night sky, Eric felt bolder to face next day's challenges. His bear cub was not so keen on the dancing flames. But he grew brave and nestled close to his master.

'Good night, little one.'

Eric stretched out on the thin covering of grass but could not stop his mind tracking back to his friends. He wondered about Astrid. Did she miss him?

The next day, with a freshening wind, Eric and Beowulf set out early. As they walked, the lone Viking planned ahead.

I must find a place to settle,' he thought. 'I can't just go on tramping up this coast. Building a shelter's number one. That'll be easy since I've got tools. It'll have to be on the edge of a wood. Then I must start fishing. There's plenty of bait in the mud.'

He was thinking of fat sea worms his father used to dig up.

'I've got fish hooks and lines, so it shouldn't be a problem. And maybe I could knock up a raft and try river fishing.'

A blinding thought flashed into his mind.

'River!' he cried out loud. 'That's what I need. A tidal estuary where the sea moves in and out. Just right for fishing.'

Packing his bits and pieces, Eric called Beowulf over. To his surprise, the cub obeyed. The outcasts were starting to work as a team. Eric reached the target he had in mind. Early in the afternoon, he came up against a broad river estuary where water from the land met the sea. As the tide moved out, a huge area of mud flats was left exposed. Divided by winding channels, it smelt salty and rotten, and Eric was careful not to get too close. The mud lay thick and treacherous. One slip and he would be up to his waist. It was harder keeping Beowulf off the tidal flats. He enjoyed getting covered in mud and came back with a prize, a wriggling eel clamped between his jaws. After a couple of chews the eel disappeared. Beowulf had discovered fish!

Eric gazed out over the dark expanse of liquid mud where crowds of wading birds fed by the water's edge. A pair of black and white oyster catchers scudded low over the waves. Eric turned and walked towards the trees.

'This is where I put up our first shelter.'

By nightfall, the skilled carpenter had selected branches and cut them to size. He bound them with twinings found in the wood. The tall branches met at the top to be tied together. His rough, round home would do for one night, but more work would be needed. The shelter could never keep out wind or rain. Eric was fortunate. The night stayed dry, with only a light breeze blowing off the land. With his food stock dwindling, he knew he would soon have to start fishing.

'I can put a raft together and shape a paddle. Or maybe use a long pole and push up and down on the tide.'

He made a fire outside his primitive shack and enjoyed its cheering glow. Beowulf managed to catch a second eel but also explored the wood for tasty roots and fallen fruits. His master was delighted at the young bear's independence. After dousing the flames, just in case the wind got up during the night, Eric lay out on the soft turf. The bear preferred to sleep outside, disturbing his master with snorts and snuffles. Was the bear keeping guard? Eric was not sure, but it was good to think he had a watchdog.

That night, Eric dreamt of sea journeys. Impossible battles with mountainous waves. The longboat pitched up and down. An exhausted Astrid huddled against the side.

The Viking outcast awoke with a start. Dawn had not yet broken, yet he knew where he lay—in a makeshift shelter, alone and far from his friends. The thought depressed him. How could he fend for himself with no one to help? It was at this very moment Beowulf chose to visit his master. The cub ambled into the shelter and pushed his black snout into Eric's face. It smelt of fish and honey. Eric stretched out an arm and fondled the bear's forehead.

'I love you, bear,' the Viking boy told him. 'What would I do without you?'

He drifted off to sleep, again, to be woken by the sharp calls of feeding birds on the estuary. The air smelt salty and fresh. There was lots to do. First, he would need to find some sturdy young trees to build a raft. It took time to bind them together.

'I suppose we call this a raft, Beowulf. It'll make do to catch our first fish supper.'

The cub too had been busy. It seemed he had already found food and joined Eric by the fire.

'Not afraid of flames anymore?'

The cub settled by Eric's side as the sun rose over the sea. The rest of the morning was spent at the edge of the wood, selecting raft timbers. He worked hard on a tall ash pole that would propel the craft forward. Back at the hut, he lashed the timbers together and the skilful boat-builder soon made a workable raft. He gathered his fishing lines and hooks.

Unfortunately, Beowulf refused to join him on board. As Eric pushed off, the cub hurried along the bank side, worried his master might desert him. With the tide running out, Eric tethered his raft in a clump of reeds and let out his lines. He kept a sharp look-out for the bear, but need not have worried. Beowulf was busy turning over clumps of seaweed and catching crabs. Not only did they taste good, but they amused him. Meanwhile, his master achieved success when a couple of flatfish took his bait. The tide ran strong so Eric secured the raft. He could come back for it later when the waters ran back in.

Pleased with his haul, he headed for the rickety shelter where he was joined by a happy bear.

'I know this is like an adventure for you, Beowulf,' Eric said. 'But it's not quite the same for me.'

Minutes later, he kindled a fire and fixed up a spit of branches from which he could hang the fish. They were delicious smoked, the finest meal he had ever tasted. Handing scraps to Beowulf, Eric chuckled at the young bear's enthusiasm. It seemed the two had formed a growing bond. Revived by his outdoor lunch, Eric felt his spirits rise. He went down to the bank of the estuary and scooped up huge handfuls of runny mud. Some of it ran through his fingers as he hurried back. His idea was to daub the disgusting goo in gaps where it might harden and keep out the rain. What he had not banked on was how long the work would take. He must have trudged back to the mud flats a hundred times before the shelter seemed likely to hold up in bad weather.

'I'm exhausted,' he thought. 'I can't do anymore.'

Eric crashed out on the marsh grass as the sun sank over the trees. Nothing could wake him, not even the cub's whimpers. Beowulf turned his nose into the breeze and sniffed. He smelled danger and padded up and down. Alarmed by sounds beyond the trees, he pushed his black muzzle into his master's face. The drowsy boy came to life.

'What is it?' Eric asked. 'What's up?'

He soon found out. Two bearded strangers stepped out from the cover of the trees. They gripped long bows and each carried a quiver of arrows over his shoulder. They were dressed in dull, dirt-stained tunics and leggings. Daggers projected from sheaths at their belts.

Eric rose slowly. He lifted his hands to it make clear he had no weapons. The rougher looking of the two men approached.

'Cover me,' he ordered the other, who slipped an arrow into his bow. He stared suspiciously at the stranger.

'Who are you? We don't take to newcomers in these parts.'

His companion trained his bow on the visitor. Eric had been taken by surprise. The first man dropped his bow and placed a hand on the handle of his dagger.

'We don't know you,' he said menacingly. 'But let me guess.'

He looked sharply at Eric's fair hair.

'A Viking if ever I saw one!' the man growled. 'Go on. Deny it. I bet you don't even understand what I'm saying.'

His companion snorted.

'We've seen his sort before. Viking raiders who lose their ship, then get washed up on shore.' He grinned menacingly. 'They don't last long around these parts. Saxons don't like Vikings!'

Eric's heart pounded. He remained silent, not knowing where to turn.

'Say something,' the first men sneered. 'I bet he can't speak a word of our language.'

Eric bridled.

'I'm on my own. I'm doing no harm.'

The Saxon hunters were stunned.

'He speaks!' said one. 'But not like we do. He's from the North.'

'That's right,' Eric answered, seizing his chance. 'From beyond the hills. We were fishing and a storm blew up. The boat ran onto the rocks. I think I'm the only survivor.'

The two men looked at each other. They did not believe him.

'Strange accent,' said one. 'I never heard anyone talk like that before. If you'd been fishing out at sea why did you have a bear cub on board?'

This stumped Eric.

'I came across it in the forest yesterday, while I was cutting branches for my shelter. The cub seemed lost,' he added lamely.

The bowman narrowed his eyes. A mean smile spread across his face.

'That bear would make nice little fur coats for my children. Keep them warm in winter!'

He trained his arrow on Beowulf and pulled back the string.

'One shot should do it!'

Eric leapt forward.

'Stop!' he cried. 'Leave the cub alone!'

338

He was too late. The arrow flew straight and true towards the defenceless bear. Eric screamed and hurled himself at the hunter. They hit the ground and rolled over in the dirt. The man struck out, landing a heavy blow on the side of the boy's head. Eric lay gasping as the man got up to check his shot. He cursed.

'Missed!'

Beowulf snarled as the fellow pulled a second arrow from his quiver.

'How could I fail from close range?'

Eric shook his bruised head. The bear was alive.

'You didn't miss,' said the second Saxon. 'The arrow went straight and didn't leave a mark. I saw it with my own eyes.'

An angry Beowulf advanced on the man who had tried to murder him.

'It's magic!' shouted his companion. 'The boy's a wizard. Run!'

The two cowards turned. Eric struggled to his feet as they escaped through the trees.

'Are you all right, bear?'

Beowulf stopped growling and settled down. His master ran his hands over his fur searching for a wound. But there was no sign of injury.

'The arrow passed through you?' Eric mused. 'That makes you very special.'

The cub nosed his master before wandering away to explore the estuary. Swirls of muddy water streamed into the channels as the tide crept in. Eric was content to watch from a distance. Beowulf splashed about, poking under floating strands of seaweed.

'I'd better start a fire,' Eric thought. 'Those men aren't likely to come back in a hurry. I'll do a little fishing, then try to think out my future. Do I hang on here, or move?'

In truth, he had no idea. But he need not have worried about fishing. Beowulf charged back with a big, live catch in his mouth. It struggled for freedom, thrashing its silver tail. The bear deposited his prize at Eric's feet.

'A salmon? Thanks, Beowulf. We'll go halves!' He picked up a sturdy stick and struck the fish's head. 'Now it's out of its misery.' The salmon lay still and Eric got out his knife to gut it. 'These are the bits you like!' He tossed the fish's guts over to Beowulf. 'And you can have the head and tail!'

Fixing the remains of the salmon on the spit, Eric looked forward to a fine supper. When he came to taste the fish it was smoked to perfection. Beowulf hung around expecting more. He was just as interested as Eric in the tasty, pink flesh. The two travellers settled back to enjoy the night. Beowulf made a final trip to the forest, where he rooted for bulbs and beetles. His young master lay back on the ground, seemingly without a care in the world. But it was not so. As darkness fell, he remembered the friends he would not see again.

The flames leapt as Eric tossed on a couple of dead branches, the heat buoying up his spirits. He gazed into the night sky, where the pinpoints of light shone.

'I'll imagine the brightest are my friends. With Astrid brightest of all!'

His eyelids felt heavy. An owl screeched in the trees.

A rapid movement brought Eric to his senses. He sat up straight, peering into the near blackness. A fleeting shadow. A rumbling snarl. It was certainly not Beowulf.

'Who's that?' the boy cried out.

His heart raced and he grabbed a burning branch from the fire. Something was out there, dark and menacing. A flicker of movement, but no more. First in front; then behind. Eric whirled around with the flaming torch. It was the only weapon to hand. Again, the threatening snarl. He began to panic, turning one way, then the other. Shadows played tricks in the flames, conjuring up shapes of devils and demons.

'Grrrrrr! Grrrrrrr!'

An enormous beast leapt into the space between Eric and the fire, a black silhouette standing out against the light. Glistening fangs, eyes glowing like hot coals. The boy stepped back in terror.

'Oh no!' he moaned. 'The Shuck!'

The beast widened its jaws, dripping with saliva. Eric stared down its throat, the long tongue lolling out of the side of the mouth. Rooted to the spot, he felt weak and helpless. The Shuck raised its head and howled into the night. The outcast froze, dropping the torch, which broke into pieces on the ground. The Shuck inched forward. No amount of Wizard's potion could save its next victim. The boy gulped. He smelt its evil breath.

The next moment, Eric was bowled off his feet as something heavy and powerful cannoned into him. The Shuck stopped in its tracks. Beowulf the bear raised himself onto his hind legs. Unbelievably, he towered over Eric. With one mighty swipe of his paw, he cuffed The Shuck across the head. With the other paw, claws outstretched, he struck out and sent the Demon Dog sprawling into the fire. Its anguished howls echoed across the estuary.

As Eric regained his senses, he made out the burning shape of The Shuck in the flames, which sparked and crackled with a new intensity. He covered his eyes. When he dared open them, The Shuck was no more than a pile of ashes. A giant of a bear stood at Eric's side. It dropped down onto all fours before growing smaller by the second.

Beowulf looked up at his master seeking to be petted. Eric knelt and buried his face in the fur. The young Viking rocked back and forth, circling the bear cub with his arms.

'I knew you were special,' he sobbed. 'What kind of bear are you?'

The cub wriggled out of his master's grip and pounced on a chunk of leftover salmon.

'You deserve that,' Eric said, laughing happily. 'You can have all the salmon in the world!'

He wiped his tears and fondled the cub's muzzle.

'You're small again,' he said. 'But you weren't when you took on The Shuck. You were enormous. The Wizard of the Forest promised you would protect me!'

CHAPTER 9

Lief's Smart Plan

Life in the Saxon village went on. Blacksmiths slaved over hot furnaces, shaping melted iron into tools or weapons. The freeman tended their animals on small strips of land. And women of all ages worked hard in their homes as the children ran in and out. Some women fashioned jewellery, sewed, or wove cloth. From dawn to dusk, the community pulled together to make the village a good place to live.

Beyond, where the river flowed towards the sea, boat-builders repaired their craft. Hammering and sawing. In only a few weeks, the young Vikings produced two sleek vessels to rise to the sea's challenge. Chief Alfred was pleased with the progress, but had little idea how unhappy the immigrants were. The girls were especially down. They were concerned about Astrid, who hardly ever smiled. She rarely ate, and some mornings she refused to leave her hut. Freya fretted for her friend.

'She can't carry on like this. Of course Astrid misses Eric. We all do. But he'll survive.'

Emma was not so sure.

'I'd hate to be kicked out on my own. I wouldn't last a day.'

Deep down, the two girls were worried sick for big Eric. It was Ingrid who understood Astrid best.

'She can't get him out of her mind,' she said. 'I've tried talking to her, but I can't get through.'

As time passed, Lief sensed things were not improving. Sitting with Vimp in their hut, the two boys got into deep conversation.

'D'you know?' Lief said, 'We'll never settle here. We don't really belong. It's not that the Saxons are unreasonable. Maybe we should go back home.'

The idea shocked Vimp.

'You can't be serious. This is our big chance. We deserted our own land. This is all we have.'

His friend bowed his head in thought.

'I think we should return,' he said firmly. 'One or two of the others are thinking this way. I miss my family and the girls miss theirs. Why don't we build a new boat and leave?'

Vimp had no answer. He longed for his family too, especially his younger brothers. His mind was in turmoil.

'We should talk it out,' he suggested. 'Have a word with Bjorne. He's sensible. And Freya. If anyone knows what's right, it'll be her.'

But as the days went by the Viking youngsters grew sadder. One evening, after supper, they met up by the river. The air was still, with clouds of insects hovering over the surface. Freya spoke first.

'The girls got together. It won't be easy to return our old village. The leaders might still be furious with us. But we agree it's a risk we have to take.'

The group sat down in a circle. Astrid's thoughts turned to Eric. If they left Saxon England, he would be abandoned forever. After the meeting, Lief did not say a word. His mind worked feverishly. Next morning, he and Vimp met up with Freya.

'You're on your own, Vimp,' said Lief. 'Everyone's for packing up and going home. I have a plan. It involves Eric, but I'm only telling you two. It might just work. Tonight we should talk to Chief Alfred.'

Lief explained his idea. His friends listened carefully, but Vimp still had doubts.

'If you want to get Alfred on side,' he said, 'you've got to tell him everything. You're suggesting we only reveal *part* of your plan. The rest we keep secret – even to Alfred. Surely that can't be right?'

But Freya sided with Lief.

'I understand,' she said. 'It's a really smart idea. *Why* should we tell Alfred everything?'

Vimp remained dubious.

'I need to think about this. It's a risk. If the plan goes wrong, things could get tricky. The Saxons will go mad!'

It drizzled that day. Boat-building was not much fun, but it did give Vimp time to ponder. After supper, he, Lief, and Freya visited the Chieftain's hut. Alfred made his Viking visitors welcome.

'I think I know why you're here. I'm just as unhappy about Eric's punishment as you are. But the villagers are afraid of the brooding forest and its threats. You do understand?'

Vimp nodded.

'Thank you for seeing us. It's not just what's happened to Eric. We've all tried hard to settle and fit in, but . . . '

Alfred invited the young Vikings to sit down.

'Lief's come up with a scheme,' Vimp continued. 'He can explain.'

Lief rose from his bench.

'With your permission, Alfred, we'd like to construct our own boat. Make it seaworthy and test it out. Then, when wind and weather are set fair, we'll sail back home. Return to our families. We'd have to beg them to forgive us. We'll always be thankful to you for giving us a chance to settle.'

He paused.

'I'm sorry,' he went on. 'Things simply haven't worked out as we hoped.'

Chief Alfred looked solemn.

'We gave you a home. You were welcomed and earned respect with hard work. What you say does come as a bit of a shock. Yet,' he paused, stroking his greying beard, 'perhaps not. Last week, I had people on my back complaining about the barley in the fields. It hasn't grown high and the yield will be down. There'll be barely enough grain for winter. Only yesterday, I had to deal with an angry farmer whose cattle have gone lame. He blamed it on Eric and the curse of The Black Shuck. Now the whole village seethes with rumour. It could get ugly. The people are turning against you Vikings. Blaming your arrival for our misfortunes. The death of the priest was terrible.'

Freya felt scared.

'That was horrible. We were just as upset. Even though it wasn't his fault, poor Eric was found guilty. You say the villagers are turning against us?'

The Chieftain nodded grimly.

'I fear so. Some haven't forgotten the old beliefs. When they can't explain events, they look for easy victims to pick on.'

He paused and looked them in the eye.

'For your own safety, it might be better if you did leave. I can't say more now. I shall speak to the Council.'

He rose and showed the youngsters to the door. They returned to their huts, deep in thought. At least Alfred had been good enough to listen. It seemed he understood the Vikings' desire to return. And that would suit the village.

Over the next few days, Vimp and company went about their tasks with heavy hearts. Now and again, they caught a hostile glance from a passing Saxon. The girls reported that the families they worked for did not seem to trust them any more. Chief Alfred called the Viking group to see him and warned he had serious news. He did not waste time. It had been decided by a Council vote that the new settlers were to leave at once.

So keen was the village to rid itself of The Shuck's curse, it was agreed the Vikings could take the new boat they had just completed.

'I'm very sorry,' he told them finally. 'I've no quarrel with you. But it's for the best. We'll see you're stocked for the voyage. You leave by the end of the week.'

Vimp and his friends stood dejected. They left the meeting and shuffled back to their huts. Bjorne and Vimp would have to be the leaders, organising the expedition and testing the seaworthiness of the boat. Freya would take charge of food and clothing and support the girls. She wondered how Emma would react. What would she decide? To stay with her own people or leave with her Viking companions?

Meanwhile, Vimp and Bjorne saw that Lief was not around. The gentle Viking who had only ever wanted to write poetry had gone missing. So too had Eadbehrt and Leofwine, the brave Saxon lads who had helped old Anselm find the Wizard. The villagers were not too worried, as they assumed the brothers had gone hunting. But for the Vikings, losing Lief was a worry. A complete mystery. Vimp sought out Freya but was surprised by her cool manner.

'Lief's a clever fellow,' she said. 'We'll see him again – mark my word. And remember, *he didn't tell Alfred the whole of our plan.* There's that special little bit he left out. Trust him. He's never let us down.'

Freya's words puzzled Vimp. He trusted Lief and knew he would come up with something different.

The day arrived. Many Saxon villagers were sad to see the Vikings go. Few believed in the tales of forest spirits. With Chieftain Alfred, they lined up on the river bank to wave the youngsters off. The person they most regretted seeing depart was Emma. She had gone in with her friends, who had rescued her from Viking slavery. Now she bid farewell to her own land to

347

set out on a new voyage. But Emma was more concerned about Lief. Why had he not returned? Was he hurt, or lost, somewhere deep in the forest?

Chief Alfred prepared to give the signal to push the longboat into the water. But as he did so, two strong Saxons appeared on the riverbank. Leofwine and Eadbehrt splashed up to their waists to have urgent words with Vimp.

'Go in peace,' they told him. 'Sail north along the coast and keep a good lookout. A lighted fire will be your sign.'

The new vessel slid into the river on the turn of the tide. Bjorne stood at the helm, with Vimp giving orders to the rowers. Huddled against the side, Astrid refused to look up and wave good-bye. Freya spoke softly to her.

'You've got to trust. I can't say more. All will be well.'

Soon, the longboat rocked on the turbulent waters where river met ocean. The craft cleared the sandbanks, and Vimp struck out for the open sea.

'There's not much wind, boys,' he cried. 'You'll have to dig in and row hard.'

The longboat ran along the coast. Freya arranged for the girls to go round with water and bites to eat. Only a light breeze blew, which relieved Vimp. He needed an easy start knowing that bad weather was bound to follow. The afternoon sun blazed down on the unprotected rowers. As evening approached, Emma moved forward and stood at the prow. Its mighty dragon head carved through the swell. Something attracted her attention. Was that smoke? Emma raised her hand and squinted into the light.

'Vimp!' she cried. 'Fire! A beacon.'

The young captain pushed his way forward to join her.

'Where? I don't see it.'

Emma pointed. A puff of grey-blue smoke snaked into the sky. Vimp stumbled back through his oarsmen.

'Steer to port!' he ordered Bjorne. 'Steady now. We're entering shallow waters.'

The longboat glided into a bay protected by two low headlands. A bonfire blazed on the shore.

'Steady now! We're about to land.'

Emma stared ahead. Two boys raced down the beach. They jumped up and down, arms beating the air. Behind them trundled a small bear. Emma could no longer contain herself.

'Lief! Eric!'

She waved wildly. Further back in the boat, Freya helped Astrid to her feet.

'This is for you,' she cried. 'Look ahead!'

Astrid held on to the mast as the boat's hull ground onto the sand. She recognised the dancing figure of the boy she so admired. Ragged and sun-burned Eric, bravest of Vikings, punched the air. Lief, standing by his side, grinned from ear to ear. His master plan had worked. Using Leofwine's and Eadbehrt's forest skills, Lief had managed to track down the outcast.

Beowulf, on the other hand, was unimpressed. He had found a crab, but it scuttled off to a hiding place. He padded around impatiently, hoping it would come out.

Chapter 10

Freya Goes Home

With all the friends joined up again, it was time to celebrate. The boys went fishing and returned with mackerel and herrings. English Emma took over the cooking, helped by happy Astrid. Eric took everyone to see his shelter.

'It wouldn't win prizes,' he confessed, 'but it just about keeps out the wind and rain. Beowulf lies outside most nights. I think he likes the heat of the fire once the embers die down.'

The voyagers were thrilled to see the bear cub had stayed with Eric. They petted him and offered pieces of smoked fish. Out of sight of the others, Lief and Vimp drew Eric to one side.

'It's great to have you with us. You're the one to get us across the sea,' they told him. 'We've thought about it hard. We're returning to our old village to try and make it up with our parents. It won't be easy. Once the fuss dies down, we can prove we're good boat-builders. They'll back down.'

Eric came slowly on side. He took one final look at the strange construction he called home then went down to the boat. Bjorne took the helm, insisting Eric deserved a break. It meant he could sit with Astrid. Beowulf sat with them both, making little sense of boats. It was not long before Eric wanted to take his turn at an oar.

With a change in wind direction, it was possible to put up the square sail. This gave the rowers a rest. The longboat picked up speed and powered on. Vimp could not believe his luck. At this rate, the sea crossing might only take a couple of days. Up at the dragon head prow, Lief clung to a rope holding up the mast. He relished the spray breaking into his face. Suddenly, his attention was drawn to something ahead. It was a large object. A rock, perhaps? Sticking out of the sea with waves breaking over it. Yet it appeared to be moving. Vimp came forward.

'I see it now. Dead ahead. Steer to starboard. Reef in the sail and get ready with the oars.'

He caught Bjorne's attention and signalled. Bjorne leaned on the tiller. The boat creaked, taking on the waves at a new angle. Hand over eyes, Vimp squinted into the distance.

'It can't be a rock,' he speculated. 'Not this far out.'

Lief agreed.

Suddenly the object disappeared.

'Am I imagining things? Now you see it, now you don't!'

The ship's skipper did not argue. He felt uneasy. The thought of colliding with something just under the surface worried him. The two lookouts scanned the horizon.

'We're going to hit it!'

The thing was back on the surface. Vimp shouted at his helmsman to change course. A plume of spray burst from the mysterious object. Bjorne fought the tiller. Now even he could see what the fuss was about. A grey lump, lined and wrinkled, and nearly as long as the boat, slipped across the bow. Another spout of vapour exploded from the object. Up front, Lief and Vimp had the best view. It moved across their course. Tharg scrambled up to join them.

'It's a whale,' he cried. 'Seriously big!'

He stood up on his toes.

'Did you see that? A second spout! Smaller. There! Over to the left.'

The others followed his finger. Emma could not contain her excitement.

'It's a baby. The far side of the big one. Will they attack us?'

Tharg laughed.

'I don't think so. Can we get nearer?'

Vimp was not too sure. With a few more pulls on the oars, the longboat was about to cross the whales' path. But he gave no orders to alter course. When they got close, he told the rowers to turn and take a quick look. The boat slowed and the sailors gazed at a pair of sperm whales ploughing through the sea.

'Huge head!' Vimp cried. 'Takes up about a third of its size.'

At that moment, the mother humped close to the surface and let out a thunderous, watery gasp. The calf kept to her far side, bravely keeping up with its parent.

'I heard whales were all smooth and sloping at the front,' Emma said. 'This one's got a head like a big chunk of rock. Where's the eye?'

'There!' Lief pointed. 'She's seen us!'

For a fleeting moment, the gentle giant appeared to fix the boat with a look that was neither unfriendly nor afraid. She swam majestically through the waves making sure her calf was on the side furthest from the onlookers. The rowers rested their oars and watched the ocean giants swim off. The mother dived, lifting her gigantic tail before thrashing it down onto the surface. Both she and the calf disappeared from view, only to re-emerge and continue their long journey. Vimp wasted no time.

'Start the rowing!'

The boys got back into their stroke and pulled to a rhythm. The weather held fair and the boat made progress. Lief concocted a cunning plan. He called Vimp and Freya over and asked Tharg to join them.

'With any luck, we may spot the coastline tomorrow. Then we'll have to work out which way to turn to find our home river. But I'm still worried about our welcome. We had to escape from the village to save Emma's life. Also, because none of the boys wanted to fight. There'll still be people who are mad at us.' He paused. 'So here's my idea.'

Lief reminded them that Tharg was not from their village. He was just a stranger they had stumbled across. This meant that no one in the village could get angry with him. Lief suggested the boy from a different community might be very useful.

'I can't force you, Tharg,' he said, 'but if we land a bit down river and out of sight, you could make first contact with the Chieftain. Find out what kind of reception we might get. Ask if he'd be pleased to see us again. Or be really angry. If the village refuses to forgive, you could slip away and return to the boat. At least we'd know where we stand.'

It was a lot to ask of Tharg, but he saw sense in the idea.

'You were good to me when I needed you,' he said. 'I haven't forgotten. Lief saved my life. So it's time to return the favour.'

Tharg felt proud he had been given a special task to do. Freya and Vimp suggested he should think it over first, but his mind was made up.

'You could be running into danger,' he told them. 'That would be terrible after what you've been through. So I'm pleased to help.'

Lief slapped him over the shoulder.

'We shan't let you go alone, Tharg. Three of us will accompany you most of the way. We can lie up at the forest edge until you make contact. Then, one way or the other, we'll know what to do.'

Two long nights spent in a rocking boat at sea was no fun. But the young crew stuck to their task. Early in the afternoon of the third day they sighted land. It was a fantastic moment. Although few admitted it, they had all missed their Viking homes. When they left the village they had defied their parents. Now their return was giving them problems. They would have to admit their bold adventure had failed.

'I know the coastline well,' Tharg told Vimp. 'My family fished up and down it. So I should spot a familiar landmark.'

Eric was back at the helm.

'We'll head south,' Vimp commanded. 'Keep an eye out for sandbanks. The look-outs will shout if they spot rocks ahead.'

Still the weather held, and by early evening Tharg guided them to the river outlet they sought. As the sun began to sink over the western horizon, he called Vimp over.

'Those blue hills in the distance – and the mountains beyond – that's where the stream that flows past your village starts.'

Vimp looked up into the dark tree slopes. Three hills, two humped and rounded and a higher one rising nearly to a point. His heart beat faster. Vimp remembered this view from his earliest days. He could not thank Tharg enough.

'You recognised them before I did. And you're not even from our village.'

Tharg smiled. His father and uncle were skilled fishermen and had taught him well. Vimp made up his mind. Summoning Freya and Bjorne, he discussed pulling into the shore, where they could anchor for the night. The rowers brought the longboat in close, shipping their oars. The vessel ground into the muddy sand as four or five of the boys leapt overboard with ropes. Wading waist deep in the gentle swell, they hauled the boat as high up the shore as it would go.

Lief and Freya jumped off next. It was their task to collect wood and start a fire to make a camp for the night. Being on dry land was magical, but they felt happy just to be home. It was amusing watching Eric and Freya coaxing Beowulf off the boat. At first, the cub did not seem to catch on. But once he scented the distant trees and felt the sand under his paws, he got on message.

Keeping his master in sight, he snuffled around, searching for tasty delicacies under rocks or seaweed.

After supper, the Vikings sat round the fire to enjoy the red glow of the smouldering timbers. The hunched figures of Lief, Vimp, Freya, and Tharg sat some way off. As the half-moon rose in the night sky, they planned next day's expedition.

'I'll explain everything to the others before we set out tomorrow morning,' Vimp said. 'We'll talk it out between ourselves for now. The village isn't too far down river. In daylight, we'll find a forest track. Get as near as we can without being spotted. Remember, there'll be guard dogs out with the sheep. I think you know what to do, Tharg?'

The Viking, who did not belong to the village, nodded gravely.

'I'll go in on my own. That won't frighten anyone. And I'll ask to be taken to Chieftain Harald saying I have news of his daughter, Freya. Also the rest of her friends.'

'I'm coming with you,' Freya stated plainly.

Lief raised his eyebrows, but Freya was not to be argued with.

'I want to talk to my father. He'll listen to me.'

Tharg felt more confident. Going in on his own was not easy. Lief and Vimp gave way.

'We'll tell Freya's father that our longboat's landed some distance away,' said Tharg. 'And that everyone wants to return to the village. But only if none of the crew, Vimp especially, isn't punished for deserting.'

Vimp smiled ruefully.

The Chieftain's daughter tried to hide her excitement. She loved her parents and wondered about her grandmother. Was she even alive? And what about her brothers and sisters? Freya could not wait to see them again.

'My father will be fine. I can twist him round my little finger!'

357

Lief was not so sure.

'Listen. I don't want to be a spoiler. Things could go wrong. So what happens then?'

Tharg had given the matter some thought.

'That's the tricky bit,' he agreed. 'If things don't work out, Freya and I will have to get back to you to give the warning. We'll make a run for it. They won't know which way. We'll know the route but it'll take them time to work out where our boat is. We can push off before they launch a raider.'

Vimp felt concerned as he knew how good the raider rowers were.

'We might get a head start but they have much faster boats. We'll have to row for our lives!'

Freya protested.

'It's not going to be like that! It'll work out. Trust me!'

They got up and rejoined the others before settling down beneath the stars to grab a few hours' sleep.

The day dawned bright and clear. First, there were boat repairs to carry out. Some of the planking had leaked so gaps were stuffed with coarse hair. A fishing party put out lines, with Bjorne and Eric taking command on the shore. Late in the afternoon, Vimp, Lief, Freya, and Tharg set out on their crucial mission.

'Good luck!' Eric wished them. 'We'll have the longboat ready to sail the moment you need it. But it shouldn't come to that.'

He too was thinking of his family and longed to see them. The small party set off and waved back when they reached the trees. It was not long before they discovered a hunting track that led to their birth village. The path was overgrown, so they selected stout branches and beat down the brambles.

The pungent scent of wood fires told the adventurers they were getting close. They hid in the trees to spy on the huts, clustered by the river. Vimp could hardly contain himself. He spotted his family home and thought of the folks inside. Nearer, were the fields where farmers grazed their animals. Cows munched at the lush grass and pigs snuffled under the trees. Vimp knew there was no time to waste.

'We'll watch you all the way,' he said. 'Be brave. Don't let anyone push you around. We'll make a deal with our people. We mustn't fail.'

He and Lief stood in the shadows as Tharg and Freya set out across the open meadow. The livestock took little notice as they approached the wooden defence gate. A villager stepped forward to challenge them. If Tharg was nervous, Freya's pulse was racing. Everything was so familiar. It was almost as if she had never been away.

'Halt, strangers! Show yourselves.'

A rough voice demanded to know who they were. Tharg took a deep breath.

'We come in peace. My name is Tharg. I live along the coast. Our Chieftain sends you his greetings.'

A fair-bearded man stood in their way. He showed no hint of friendliness.

'That may be so. But we don't welcome newcomers.'

He looked curiously at Freya.

'Do I know you? Have I seen you before?'

The young girl smiled shyly and looked him in the eye.

'You should know me,' she told the man. 'I'm Freya, eldest daughter of Chieftain Harald. Take me to him. I've not seen my father for some time.'

The guard called over to two other men, repairing a nearby hut. They put down their tools and strolled across. Neither smiled, and Freya did not recognise them. The first man winked at his companions.

'Young lady says she's the former Chieftain's daughter. A likely story. If it's true she wouldn't bother coming here. *Not after what happened!*'

He leered at her.

'Well,' said the man. 'We've got news for you, miss. Your so-called father is no longer around. He got captured by us Norsemen. We stuffed half your people into boats. One was lost at sea. No survivors. This village is in our hands now. There aren't too many old inhabitants left.'

Freya stood dumbfounded. Had her family been drowned? One of the men stepped forward.

'We need new slaves to rebuild the village,' he sneered. 'These two will do nicely.'

He lunged forward and grabbed Tharg by his tunic.

'Take them along to the new Chief,' the first man commanded. 'This way!'

He shoved them forward. There was no point in struggling. Freya and Tharg were marched to a small hut and forced inside. They groped in the dark as a bar clamped across the door. As far as they could make out the hut was bare. No furniture, with nothing to sit on except the earth floor. Outside, the men discussed what to do next. It was a total disaster. Lief's plan for the young Vikings to return safely to their families had been ripped into pieces.

Chapter 11

Hugi and Thialfi

On the edge of the wood, Lief and Vimp felt nervous. Had something gone wrong? Perhaps Freya and Tharg had been asked to stay the night. But then why had no message been sent to them? As daylight faded they began to fear the worst. They could not stay in the forest, but were afraid to move down to the village. It was now too late to get back to the longboat. In the deepening shadows, Vimp thought he detected a slight movement. Something, or someone, ghosted past.

'Lief,' he whispered. 'We're not alone!'

His friend needed no telling. He too had spotted something stir. Were they were being surrounded? Vimp peered across the meadow in the gathering gloom. A grey shadow slipped past. Then another. His heart missed a beat.

'Not people,' he hissed. 'Wolves!'

Lief shuddered. He had heard tales of children being taken from villages at night. It hardly seemed possible. Now he was not so sure.

'Where are they going?' he whispered.

The wolves did not seem to be interested in the human intruders. The boys watched as a hunting pack sneaked across the field; heads lowered, shoulders hunched. The grey predators slunk towards the animal stockade.

'They're going for the sheep pens,' said Vimp. 'But the walls are too high.'

'Not if those wolves are hungry,' Lief replied. 'They'll create chaos in there.'

Unaware of the threat, the villagers prepared for bed. Freya, imprisoned in her hut, was startled when the door suddenly opened. Men with flaming torches crowded round. A fierce looking ruffian spoke in an accent not easy to understand.

'Chief Einar sends us,' he told the frightened pair. 'He expects answers and it's our job to get them.'

He took a step forward.

'Don't try anything clever. Especially that one!'

The brute pointed at Freya.

'We know about you.'

His companions followed him in.

'Tell us,' he went on, 'where you're from. Where's your boat? How many fighting men do you have?'

His eyes smouldered in the light of the flickering flames. Tharg struggled to his feet to protect Freya.

'We come in peace,' he stuttered. 'You can see we're no threat. Since you know about Freya, you'll know she escaped from this village. We're just kids. Not fighters.'

The man coughed with scorn.

'A likely story! You've been sent to report on us. Check out our defences. It's a trick but we're not falling for it.'

Freya got up, anger rising.

'Tharg speaks the truth,' she told the alien men. 'We're just a boatload of boys and girls. That's all.'

She folded her arms and tried to look defiant. One of the men spoke up from the back.

'Boys and girls, eh? This place needs new slaves. We could sell them on. Young slaves are worth their weight in gold!'

Immediately, Freya realised her mistake. The leading man seized the advantage.

'A boatload of kids? As Sigurd rightly points out, you could be worth a fortune if we trade you on.'

He lunged at Tharg, grabbing him by the throat.

'Tell us where your boat is. If you don't, we'll take your little friend away. She'll soon cough up.'

Tharg felt the cold point of steel beneath his chin. He had to tell. There was no choice. But before he had the chance there was a commotion at the door. A hysterical woman ran in.

'Wolves!' she screamed. 'Amongst the sheep. Hurry!'

The leader hesitated then ordered the men out.

'Don't dare move!' he called back to his prisoners.

Freya heard raised shouts above the bleating of panicking sheep. People rushed to the scene with weapons and fire torches. She and Tharg stood rooted to the spot. A sinister shadow fell across the open door, followed by another. Two large wolves stood framed at the entrance. Tharg shrank back, pulling Freya with him.

'Fear not, my friends! We're not here to harm you. Freya knows who we are.'

Tharg thought he was losing his senses.

'Follow us,' the leading wolf demanded. 'Don't delay.'

Freya shook herself free of Tharg's iron grip.

'Hugi! Thialfi!'

She threw herself forward and buried her arms in the wolves' thick fur.

Tharg stood open mouthed. Freya laughed with joy.

'They saved my life! Hugi and Thialfi, brothers of Agnar, the great grey wolf.'

She turned back to the wolves.

'What are you doing here? How did you know?'

Thialfi wasted no time on explanations.

'Come!' he ordered. 'We must hurry!'

He sprang out of the hut with the two escapers, close behind. Brother Hugi brought up the rear as they raced for the outer fence. Thialfi scrambled over whilst Freya and Tharg clambered over the top. Freya fell heavily. Tharg dragged her to her feet.

'Run!' he implored.

Hugi padded alongside to keep her going.

Out at the tree line, Vimp and Lief watched in bewilderment. Bright flames lit up the scene and angry voices rang across the meadow. Swift wolfine shadows snaked back to the wood. Two human figures followed, one struggling to keep up. Vimp ran out of his hiding place to aid Freya. He was astonished to find two fine wolves at her side.

'Hugi . . . is it you? And Thialfi?'

Tharg interrupted, 'Don't delay! They're after us. To the boat!'

It was easier said than done. The deeper they headed into the wood, the greater the gloom.

Hugi and Thialfi took the lead, using their excellent night vision. As they fled, Vimp was aware of quiet footsteps padding behind. The whole pack of wolves had joined them.

'Torches!'

Dancing lights threaded between the trees. By now, Freya limped badly, but Tharg urged her on.

'Vimp! Get ahead with Thialfi. Tell Eric to make ready. Half the village is after us!'

The Viking boy and wolf increased their pace. It seemed as though Thialfi knew exactly where the longboat had landed. Reaching the edge of the wood, they saw its dark silhouette in the moonlight. Vimp raced to the beach and alerted the waiting crew. Bjorne immediately organised the rowers, ordering the girls to climb on board.

'We're not leaving without Freya!' Ingrid shouted.

She lit a torch and ran towards trees. Eric and Astrid chased after her to discover Freya hobbling towards them.

'I can't go any further!'

She crumpled into a heap. Eric saw her ankle was black and swollen. He bent down and lifted her in his arms.

'We'll make it!' he promised and tottered back to the beach with his precious burden.

Angry shouts went up and he spotted the leading torches through the trees. As Eric broke out of the woods, the longboat was already half afloat. The oarsmen crouched at their benches. The big Viking boy splashed into the water and pushed Freya into the waiting arms of Vimp and Bjorne.

'Jump aboard, Eric,' Vimp yelled. You're last!' They heaved their friend over the gunwale.

The longboat slid across the silvery surface of the estuary. Two proud wolves stood at the water's edge and howled their farewells into the night. Freya struggled to her feet, tears spilling down her cheeks. The rescuers saluted the wolf brothers until a dark cloud passed over the moon.

Hugi and Thialfi could not hang about. They turned away, satisfied with their evening's work. The pack followed, keen to escape the men with torches. Morning would bring its revenge when hunters would set out with hounds and weapons. Curiously, not one sheep or lamb had been harmed.

CHAPTER 12

An Odd Fish

'Loosen the sail!'

Two of the oarsmen leapt forward to open the great square sheet. The sail flapped loudly in the rising wind. Eric watched from the helm where he had taken over. He was anxious that the alien Vikings were in pursuit.

'Are we doing the right thing?' he called. 'They'll see the sail in the moonlight and run us down. We can't outpace them.'

Vimp insisted it was best.

'We've got time to get clear before they can set off. And they'll have to navigate the river. Tricky in the dark. If we use this wind we'll get away with it.'

Meanwhile, the rowers put their backs into the work. The craft cut through the waves in the freshening breeze. Black clouds obscured the moon, making both longboat and sail harder to see. Back at the helm, Eric was more worried about the rise in the wind. It was great for escaping but would prove troublesome if it increased. He looked at the fleecy clouds racing across the sky. The further the vessel sailed out, the more powerful the waves.

The crew rowed in near darkness. Only now and again did Eric glimpse the Pole Star, which was necessary to stay on course. Glancing over his shoulder, he hoped the Norsemen had not risked setting out. Vimp made his way aft.

'I think we're safe.'

His helmsman was more concerned about the wind.

'We should furl the sail,' Eric urged. 'Hoist it back up and make secure. There's a stiff breeze blowing behind us. And I don't know what the tide's doing. If it's moving in the opposite direction, things could get tricky.'

The ship rolled.

'We're losing control,' he went on, fighting the sea with the rudder. 'It's cutting up rough. We'll have to ride out the storm.'

Vimp knew Eric spoke sense.

'I'll order the sail up,' he shouted, grasping onto a stay as the longboat pitched and rolled.

'Sooner the better!'

Vimp lurched forward to organise the urgent task. Now, only the rowers powered the boat. Dimly, in brief moments of moonlight, Vimp saw the longboat's dragonhead rise and fall. Ahead, he spotted an enormous swell. The creaking boat climbed it, trembled at the crest, and crashed down the other side. A cloud of chilling spray burst over the prow. Two of the rowers tumbled from their benches and lost their oars. Wind whistled through the rigging. Eric was right; a storm was brewing.

As the craft rose to the top of the next wave, it shuddered and pitched sideways. The tiller tore out of Eric's hand. Lief spotted the danger and grabbed it to force the boat back on course. Huddled against the sides, the girls clung on to each other. In previous times, Freya might have used her strange powers to summon aid from the Gods. Now she was no more than a frightened human being. Up at the mast, Vimp saw the dragon rise to take on the next wave. The boat perched on top of the crest for a split second, before plunging down. The dragon's neck snapped off to be whisked away in the angry waters.

'Slow the boat down!' Eric yelled into the wailing wind. 'Get forward and bundle up the spare oars. Tie them together. Secure the rope then cast them over the stern. The weight will help drag us back.'

Lief splashed forward. He was astonished at the amount of water the boat had shipped. Vimp put all hands to work, baling over the gunwales. With Bjorne and Tharg's help, he tied up the spare oars and hitched the end of the rope to a spar. Then they dropped it over the stern.

'The spare sail!' Lief shouted at Bjorne. 'Chuck it overboard. Secure the rope first!'

They pulled the emergency sail bundled under the rowing benches.

'Make it tight!'

With an enormous heave, the boys pushed the massive weight over the back. The sail sank like an anchor and the boat responded. The two weights prevented it from tipping over the top of one wave to smash down into the next.

With the dawn, the awful storm showed signs of blowing out. Virtually everyone had been seasick, but they had ridden out the gale. As the sky cleared, calmer waters lay ahead. The crew was dismayed to discover the loss of the dragon head. A jagged spar stuck up where it had once braved the waves. The ship was waterlogged, oars broken or lost, but they recovered the spares thrown overboard. As for the second sail, it had to be abandoned. No one had the strength to pull it in.

The longboat wallowed on the calmer swell, and Lief roused his rowers for a final effort. Eric was released from the helm, to be replaced by Bjorne. He collapsed over a rowing bench and dropped into a deep sleep. Once more, the helmsman's courage had matched whatever had been thrown at him. Astrid stayed at his side whilst the soaked bear cub nuzzled his master's back.

Lief slapped Vimp over the shoulder.

'We made it!' he said. 'You saved your ship.'

Vimp was too exhausted to smile but his spirits were suddenly raised by a call from the lookout.

'Land ahead!'

What lay before them was not especially inviting. The longboat approached a line of low sea cliffs. The beach was narrow, and the sailors feared hazardous rocks might guard the shoreline. They were in luck, however, as the craft beached safely. Some of the boys leapt overboard to pull it in.

'I've an idea where we are,' Vimp told Lief.

'I can't be sure,' he went on, 'but that gale was a southeasterly. You're not going to believe this. I think we're back on the island of the Saxons. Just a lot further North.'

He ran his hands through his dripping hair.

'We've been blown way off course.'

He studied the forbidding cliffs.

'I think we've been carried far up the coast. Maybe to the land of the Picts.'

Lief gave him a funny look.

'Picts?' he asked. 'They're supposed to be really fierce. We'll have to keep watch.'

Bjorne struggled to light a fire on the beach. He had managed to keep his flints, but it was hard to find tinder wood. With help from the girls, he found bits and pieces and made a cheering blaze. Water and rations were shared. Bread and hard cheese had never tasted better. As for Beowulf, he nosed around, scratching under piles of seaweed for anything to satisfy his ravenous hunger.

Over the next two days, the crew repaired the boat that had sprung numerous leaks. But they could not replace the dragon. Vimp, Lief, and Freya planned what to do next. Fortunately, the weather improved, allowing for a bit of exploration. Bjorne and Tharg struggled along shore tugging something behind them.

'We found a shipwreck!' they cried. 'A fighting boat packed full of stuff. Except it's got soaked. Tools, weapons, bales of cloth. All the food's perished, but there's gold and jewellery on board. The raiders must have stolen it. We think all the crew drowned.'

Bjorne spread out a net discovered in the wreck.

'See this!' he said, as his friends crowded around. 'For fishing, just what we need. Trail it behind the boat and we can catch mackerel!'

Vimp jumped for joy.

'Show us!' he commanded.

The others needed no bidding and ran along the shore after Bjorne and Tharg. Rounding a small clump of rocks, they discovered the broken hull of a Viking raider. They waded out to explore every inch. The washed-up goods were no longer any use to the dead crew. Eric was impressed by an array of axes, mallets, and other building tools. It seemed as though the raiders might have been searching for somewhere to settle.

It was time again to go to sea. Vimp and Freya decided the group had to find a gently sloping coastline with a sheltered landing beach – and hopefully trees to provide timbers for buildings.

Lief still had his doubts.

'The farther North we travel, the fewer trees we see. The ones that do manage are half-sized and battered by the winds. My guess is we'll have to learn to build huts from stone. There are plenty of rocks scattered around. I expect winter up here is really fierce. The winds would blow wooden buildings down.'

Vimp listened carefully. No one knew how to erect stone dwellings. Two days later, the boat was ready to put out, and the sea was calmer. The rowers kept close to the shore, fearing they might get lost in a vast ocean. Each night, the longboat headed back to the land so the crew could find harbour and make a fire. Smoked fish all round. The happiest eater was the young bear. Beowulf had adjusted to life at sea, as long as he was with Eric or Astrid. With the others he was slightly grumpy, behaving more like a bear normally would.

The longboat cruised up the coast giving Bjorne a chance to try his fishing skills. With Tharg's help, he thrust the new net over the stern. To delight of both boys, they netted their first catch.

'Throw the little ones back,' Bjorne urged. 'We'll never eat them, so let them live.'

When he hauled the next load aboard, he was in for an almighty surprise. Captured with the sleek, shining mackerel was the oddest fish he had ever seen. It lay gasping at the bottom of the net. The head was large and bulbous and enormous eyes looked up mournfully from the deck. Bjorne pointed it out to Tharg. Although Tharg's family were all fishermen, he had never encountered such a sea creature. He glanced at Bjorne, who appeared just as puzzled. Tharg broke the silence and asked the obvious question.

'Is that a fish or a human? I've heard folks tell of mermaids after they've returned from voyages. But this one's different!'

Bjorne bent low and slipped his hands beneath the scaly catch and lifted it. His eyes nearly popped out. This was no mermaid. It certainly did not have the face of a beautiful young maiden, nor the flowing hair. Further, the creature possessed no tail, yet, with head and fins, it looked extremely fishy.

'Am I imagining things?' Tharg asked Bjorne. 'It has a fish head . . . '

His voice trailed off, and Bjorne attempted to finish his sentence.

'And sort of . . . '

Bjorne blinked and looked again. The fish, if that was what it was, possessed spindly looking arms and legs. Bjorne held the unhappy creature in his hands as everyone crowded round. No one spoke. It was the fish creature that broke the long silence.

'Please don't harm me. I need water. I can't breathe without it. Don't throw me back in the sea. My left leg's in agony. It got caught in your net. I'll never be able to swim again – not that my pitiful legs were ever any use. At least that's what my wife says. She calls me a good-for-nothing waste of time. It's hardly my fault I'm hopeless!'

373

A big salty tear rolled out from one eye. Recovering from its shock, the creature looked round pleadingly at its captors. By now, Freya, and Vimp had joined the interested crowd. The girl who had once possessed extraordinary powers over wild animals spoke gently to the little fish person.

'I think I know what you are. Don't be afraid. We'll look after you.'

Freya stood up and asked Bjorne to lift over an empty water barrel.

'Fill it with sea water as quickly as you can!'

With Tharg's help, the barrel was soon half full. Bjorne carried the fish-man and dipped it in. It dived for a few seconds before breaking the surface.

'So kind,' it murmured. 'So very kind. I can't tell you how grateful I am.'

Freya tried hard not to laugh at the curious politeness of her fishy guest.

'I don't breathe air, you know. I use gills. Not like my wife. She breathes too much and never stops talking. You'll excuse me?'

It dived back down into the water before struggling back to the surface. It was an extraordinary sight, holding its head above water and flapping its tiny arms. Freya saw that Beowulf was showing sudden interest. The bear's eagerness for a tasty bite of fish was well known.

'No you don't, Beowulf!' Freya scolded the cub, who was about to dip his paw into the barrel.

The fish-man dived out of harm's way as Freya pushed Beowulf off and ordered him back to his place. The next time the fish-man appeared, it stuck only half his head out, looking anxious.

'Don't worry,' Freya said. 'We'll keep an eye on the bear. Beowulf won't harm you!'

The fish-man popped his head out a little further.

'Most grateful. You must call me Murrough,' he said. 'That's what all we mermen are called. A foolish bunch. No good for anything. Excuse me!'

Again, Murrough disappeared before re-emerging. Dripping and spluttering, he fixed Freya with one big eye.

'You wouldn't have a nice strand of seaweed, by any chance? So tasty. I can never get enough of it!'

Freya searched through the net and retrieved a few bits and pieces. She fished them out and offered them to Murrough. But he had dived deep in his barrel to gain oxygen for his gills. He splashed up.

'Ah! There you are.'

By now, half a dozen curious faces were staring into his new watery world. Murrough was proving excellent entertainment. He grasped the slimy seaweed in his tiny hands and crammed it into his mouth.

'Mmm . . . lovely! Any more?'

As the crew fed him with delicious morsels, he grew even more talkative. It seemed he had swum out from a rock pool he shared with his wife. Carried off by a strong current, Murrough had found it impossible to turn back.

'I panicked at first,' he told his enchanted audience. 'Then I had a marvellous thought. I was out of range of my wife. You wouldn't want to meet her. She's dreadful!'

He dived to replenish his gills then returned to the surface.

'Now, where was I? Oh, yes! Mrs Murrough. My wife. All sweet looks and wet smiles. But don't believe it. She'd have you under the sea in the twinkling!'

Granting Murrough a few more seconds for his next dive, Lief questioned him even closer.

'You mean your wife's a mermaid? They're legends. Relaxing in the sun. Gazing into mirrors and combing their long hair. I've heard they sing to lure sailors to run their boats onto rocks. Is that true?'

Murrough sighed.

'Mermaids look all innocent. But they're not to be trusted, believe me. Don't go near them. That's where I went wrong. A big mistake. If you take my advice, steer clear of mermaids. Now, if you'll excuse me, I need a rest. See you in the morning!'

With a final splash, the little merman upended. His admirers caught a glimpse of his pathetically frail human legs. Beowulf was fascinated by the new arrival and understood every word. The cub had decided to make a friend of Murrough. He would guard the barrel against all intruders, especially mermaid wives!

CHAPTER 13

Morag's Song

'Hello!'

Beowulf stared over the top of the barrel as Murrough broke surface. The merman gulped, wide eyed, before realising the bear meant no harm.

'Oh, hello!'

The two creatures looked each other with curiosity.

'I thought you were a fish,' said Beowulf. 'You certainly look like one.'

Murrough paused for thought.

'I suppose I do. But only half a fish, actually. You promise you won't eat me?'

Before the bear had time to reply, Murrough dipped under the surface. He returned for more conversation.

'I don't suppose these humans take me seriously. Who does?'

Beowulf thought hard.

'We're in the same boat.'

It was quite a good joke for a bear.

'They're a good lot. Eric Bignose rescued me. They think I'm simple but don't know I'm intelligent. I keep it to myself, of course. I understand every word they speak.'

Murrough looked serious in his fish-like way.

'Very wise! You never know when that can come in handy.'

For the rest of the morning, as the craft sailed along the coast of the Picts, Beowulf and Murrough enjoyed each other's company. The bear got used to the fact of his new friend's underwater plunges.

'I can swim a bit,' the bear said. 'I like splashing in pools and diving. It's dark deep down, isn't it?'

'Hard to port!'

A shout went up from Vimp standing at the prow with no dragon.

'The coast's turning west. We should follow!'

Back at the helm, Eric did as ordered. The longboat hit a rough patch of water. Eric was glad Astrid had joined him.

'What's Beowulf up to?' he asked.

Astrid tossed her hair and laughed.

'He's best friends with that incredible Murrough. Which is nice. After all, bears can't communicate with us.'

Eric felt strong vibrations run up the rudder, making his hands shake.

'What's this tide doing?' he wondered, peering over the side. 'It's racing past. The wind's one way and tide the other. I don't understand.'

The craft began to bucket up and down. Although the waves were not large, they were choppy. Eric clung on to the tiller.

'I can't control it,' he shouted. 'Call Vimp!'

But Vimp needed little telling. He had already seen the rushing waters up ahead. It seemed the currents were running in different directions. He turned and waved to his helmsman.

'Go left!' he yelled. 'Steer away from this rough water.'

Try as he might, Eric kept fighting the rudder. Vimp pleaded with the oarsmen to pull harder, one side. But the boat failed to respond. It rocked precariously in waters that swirled in all directions. Dead ahead, there seemed to be a deep hole in the sea.

'Keep steering left!'

There was not time to look back and watch Eric losing the battle. The vessel was being sucked towards the forbidding hole of circling black water. Vimp had heard about whirlpools. Now he stared one in the face. As he did so, a hideous figure emerged from the centre where the water spiralled down. It had the head of a wild woman, long strands of untidy hair dripping over her bony shoulders. She grinned wickedly, showing large gaps between blackened teeth. The sea witch cackled over the roar of the waters, threatening to engulf the boat.

'I have you in my power. No one escapes the clutches of Old Morag!'

Vimp looked helplessly on as the craft circled to its doom. The witch sang in a grating voice.

'Sweery, sweery, linkum-loo! Do to them as I now do.'

With a supreme effort, little Murrough leapt out of his barrel and flopped on the deck. Half stunned, he crawled between the legs of the shaken rowers. Then he wriggled his way up to the prow. Vimp glanced down. Murrough waved his puny hands.

'Throw things into her pool,' he urged. 'Barrels, oars, crates – Morag loves possessions.'

As the sea witch sang her song, again, Vimp came to his senses. The boat was about to drawn into her lair.

'Chuck anything in,' Vimp shouted. 'Barrels, oars, weapons! You others, row for your lives!'

A barrage of goods and belongings cascaded over the gunwale. Old Morag broke off her song.

'Thank you! Thank you!' she screeched. 'All for me. Where's my net?'

She busied herself collecting new trophies as the longboat broke away from the pool's magnetic pull. Soon, the waters calmed allowing the rowers to pick up a steadier rhythm. Vimp looked down at Murrough, who had saved them. He lay gasping on the deck, eyes clouding over. The young captain saw the little merman was close to death. He knelt and picked him up. Then he hurried back to the water barrel. He dipped Murrough in the brine, holding his gills just under the surface. Very slowly, signs of life returned. The merman's head twitched and he rolled one eye. Freya joined Vimp at the barrel. She touched Murrough's scaly face and spoke lovingly to him.

'You said you were useless. I didn't believe that that at the time. Now I know for certain. Murrough, you're a hero!'

Vimp smiled and let Murrough slide into the water. The two friends stayed by the barrel to see the merman recover. Beowulf lumbered up to join them, raising himself on hind legs and peering in. His new friend swam slowly around the bottom, preferring to keep himself to himself.

Vimp shuddered. He had been the one who stared into the treacherous depths of the whirlpool. The voyage was becoming a nightmare – disaster following disaster. How long would it go on like this? The crew had lost over half its goods and provisions. Everyone was exhausted and losing heart. What would happen next?

He kept the question to himself although he knew Freya read his mind. He thrust his head in his hands and began to cry. His brave shoulders shook as he sobbed. Freya took Vimp in her arms. She threw Lief a knowing look as he made sure the rowers kept their stroke. And Eric, who had also seen what was happening, made way at the helm for Bjorne. He moved forward to kneel by his friend's side.

'Cry as much as you want, Vimp. Let it go. You're the one who got us this far. We're not finished yet. We'll reach our destination – wherever it may be.'

He ruffled his pal's hair and moved off to join Astrid, who organised the next round of rations. Freya gave Vimp a hug and rocked him softly.

'Eric's right,' she whispered hoarsely. 'Don't despair. Without you we'd have perished long ago. There's a big inlet ahead, where we'll find shelter for the night. Remember, Vimp, tomorrow's another day. The sun will rise and warm us with its rays.'

Freya knew she needed to take more care of the boy who had rescued her. The young longboat captain was at the end of his tether and needed a break. But Freya was confident the others would rally round and do their duty; Eric, Bjorne, Tharg, Astrid, Ingrid, and English Emma. She sensed they were nearing the end of the long journey, and something deep inside hoped all would be well. But the voyage was not finished. There was a long way to go yet.

Chapter 14

Battle of the Giants

The crew rallied round to give Vimp his well-earned rest. Lief took over and Bjorne felt good standing at the great side rudder feeling the power trembling in his hands. A fresh breeze blew in his face. Sunshine streamed on him down from a cloudless sky. He was stunned at the height of the black cliffs along the coast. Hard, defiant rock jutted out as though it been there forever. And perched high up on narrow ledges, rows of seabirds guarded their eggs, or their young. Above the towering cliffs circled brown skuas that snatched slower victims. Skuas had young to feed too. Ingrid stood at the helm with Bjorne. She tried to count the army of seabirds camped on the ledges of the nearest rock face.

'I give up,' she shouted over the piercing cries from the cliffs. 'There must be more than all the Vikings on Middle Earth! I wish I could fly as free as a bird!'

It certainly seemed better than voyaging by longboat. But at that moment, a stubby looking black and white bird crossed the bows. Ingrid marvelled at the radiant colours of its striped beak. Two small fish dangled over the lower part. A skua darted down to ambush the puffin. The helpless bird flopped dead in the air, and its attacker flew back to its nest. Bjorne had been watching the spectacle.

'I'll stay human. I wouldn't want to be up on those ledges in a storm. How do the birds survive in winter?'

The two friends remained silent for a while. Then Ingrid spotted the opening of a large inlet. It was guarded by two high, rocky headlands. The waters between the sentinels looked reasonably calm and easy to navigate.

'Is there a landing place?' she asked Bjorne. 'The beaches are sandy and look easy to pull up on.'

The longboat rounded the first headland.

'I can see low land behind the shore,' Ingrid continued. 'And grass, I think. Almost like pasture. I don't see any signs of life. No flocks or grazing animals.'

Lief came to join them. His oarsmen were in a rhythm and did not need his direction. He too had a good feeling about the sheltered inlet.

'We've got to stop, somewhere. Our rowers need to rest. If we pitch up here we could spend a few days exploring. We can feed on fish and other sea creatures. What we now need is to find a spot where we can live off the land.'

He gazed ahead.

'Not too many trees,' he pointed out glumly. 'Just a few scraggy ones growing out of the wind. Following the lines of streams.'

The three agreed this was the place to beach. As Lief went forward to tell the crew, Bjorne turned to Ingrid. He needed to tell her what was on his mind.

'It's some time since we saw mainland. In the last two days, we've pushed farther north and passed a few strung-out islands. My concern is that we've left the land of Saxons. If we push on, we may never find another island!'

Ingrid thought she understood.

'You mean we could run out of land and end up lost at sea?'

Bjorne nodded, unruly hair flying in his face.

'Winter isn't that that far away. We're way up North. But never mind the seabirds – what about us? If we don't find the right spot to settle before the icy winds blow, we'll perish. At least these islands are rocky. We can work out how to put up rough shelters.'

He steered the boat between massive headlands guarding the inlet entrance. The wind dropped.

'This'll do!'

The bay looked sheltered although the surrounding land was uninhabited. Lief and Freya stood at the mast as the boat approached the shore. Before they made their final move, they had a quiet word with Vimp, who was feeling stronger.

'We're going in to land,' Lief called to the oarsmen. 'Vimp's happy with this place. It looks like a safe haven.'

But Lief and Vimp were in for a big shock. A huge boulder hurtled through the air and plummeted into the nearby sand. On top of the higher headland strode an enormous figure – bearded, long haired, and wild. He towered over the inlet as the adventurers crouched in their boat. A voice of thunder echoed from the cliff top.

'Come out, Herman, you coward! It is I, Saxie, who calls. I invite you to take up my challenge.'

Lief jumped up and commanded the oars.

'Pull!' he cried. 'Pull with every muscle!'

Another missile sped through the air, this time hitting the water. The longboat rocked on the powerful wave it created. It pitched up and down as the swell passed underneath. At the point where the cliffs met the sea, a noisy bubbling and boiling of water forced itself through a rocky hole. Bjorne steered away. He heard the tide fizzing and hissing in the basin that steamed like a cauldron over a fire.

'D'you hear me, Herman?' repeated the booming voice. 'You owe me half an ox!'

To the despair of the Viking crew, a third lump of rock whistled over the boat. It crashed into the cliff face across the inlet. The giant shook his fist as a second figure appeared on the opposite headland.

'You won't get anything out of me!' the new titan roared. 'I've eaten my ox, bones and all. There's nothing left for you except the tail. You can use that to tie up your tunic!'

A rumbling growl echoed from over the water. Saxie was getting angrier by the minute.

'You asked me for the loan of my boiling sea kettle,' he thundered. 'You promised to give me half of that ox when it was cooked. And you've gone back on your word.'

He bent down, broke off an enormous chunk of earth, and prepared to toss it over. Meanwhile, giant Herman wobbled precariously on his own headland. He held a heavy boulder, ripped out of the cliff top.

'You insult me,' he shouted. 'Take this!'

The projectile sailed from one headland to the other and crashed in front of Saxie's feet. Part of the cliff crumbled and thundered down, dust and debris rising in the air. When the cowering Vikings looked up they saw a tidal wave heading for them.

'Stow the oars!'

Lief's command saved the day. The rowers lifted their oars seconds before the water monster lifted the longboat. The craft pitched and rolled but remained upright. High on the headlands, the giants continued their barrage of insults.

'You couldn't hit an island in front of your fat nose!'

'Pebbles don't frighten me, beetle legs!'

'Your ugly wife can do better than you, frog spawn!'

Rocks, bellows and bad language flew to and fro. The sailors had to protect themselves as chunks of cliff rained down. Vimp issued immediate orders.

'Get on that helm, Eric. We've got to get of here. Bjorne, help the rowers!'

Despite massive boulders exploding into the sea, the oarsmen rowed furiously out of the bay. The titanic row, created by Herman's broken promise, stormed on. Saxie's kettle was the boiling cauldron of sea water. Herman had used it to boil his ox but refused to hand over the promised half. The battle had raged for hundreds of years. As the longboat rowed away, Saxie and Herman stood on their headlands shaking fists and swapping insults.

Once the excitement died down, Lief had a quiet word with Freya.

'I don't know where we're heading. We lost contact with the mainland and escaped the sea witch. We've nearly been sunk by rocks flying through the air. What next? These are crazy islands. We must find somewhere calmer to settle. No whirlpools or mad giants!'

Freya agreed.

'We'll find somewhere. Didn't you hear what the argument was about? They were going on about an ox. That can only mean one thing . . . '

Lief got the message. Freya was suggesting the chance of some of the islands being grazed. But which ones? If only they could find a settlement. Even if it was inhabited by fierce Picts.

'One thing's certain,' Freya concluded. 'It can't go on like this. No one can stay at sea, forever. How long is our search going to take?'

Under Vimp's command, the longboat headed further West. But that risked losing sight of land altogether. If they sailed too far, they might get lost in a vast ocean. It was essential to find the mainland once more.

The longboat ploughed on. But the crew had to be wary of tiny islands and jagged rocks on which they could founder. They entered a treacherous looking stretch of water with racing tides and swift currents. Eric took over the tiller, with Bjorne standing by. He gazed out over the churning, white-topped waves.

'The perfect landing place doesn't exist,' he told himself. He cast a glance at Astrid and the sleeping Beowulf. 'Perhaps it never did!'

CHAPTER 15

The Mermaid's Cage

The weather held as the battered longboat struggled along the coast. It was about the only piece of fortune the young Vikings had enjoyed since setting out. They were navigating the turbulent waters of the Western Isles. Threading their way between one island and the next meant fighting opposing tides. These swept in from the Atlantic Ocean. The biggest problem was finding a place to land. Freya and the girls acted as lookouts. Their job was to try and detect signs of life. Just now and again, a curl of smoke rose into the sky. Was a human settlement nearby? But the crew had no idea how they would be welcomed if they landed. They suspected Viking longboats had prowled these islands before. If their crews were brutes, Vimp and company feared the worst. The girls had also been instructed to look out for dangerous rocks. Some were easy to see, whilst others got covered at high tide, close to the surface. The longboat needed only about a metre of water beneath it to sail. Most of the time, it managed to stay clear of hazards. Ingrid and Emma stood at the shattered prow of their tattered vessel. Strong waves beat on the rocky coast of the nearest island. Thundering spumes of spray burst into clouds before collapsing into the sea. As they passed a rocky spit projecting from the shore, they heard a new sound. A low moaning; almost musical. They had heard it before, and it made Emma happy.

'Seals!' she said simply. 'I love them. Their calls are so gentle. But they're very nosey. They might swim out to look at the boat.'

Ingrid was a seal fan too.

'D'you remember when they surrounded us? Staring up from the water. Those big eyes and side whiskers. They don't see many humans so they're curious. At home, our boats used to hunt them. Their blubber was used for candles and the skins kept sailors warm. Why are humans so cruel to wild creatures?'

The eyrie sounds continued. It was almost like singing. From their vantage point, the girls saw the seals lolling on nearby rocks. They looked so human. Emma could hear no other sound. It was both beautiful and mesmerising across the water. For the first time in ages, she felt at peace. The singing seemed to blot out all anxieties. She relaxed to enjoy the gentle motion of the boat.

It was the same for the rowers. Even with their backs to the music, the oarsmen grew enchanted. Rowing no longer seemed to require effort. They smiled as they pulled the next stroke, drawn happily towards the choir of seals. Even bold Eric relaxed into a trance at the helm. He had never heard such sweet sounds and steered the craft towards them.

Only Emma kept her head. As the longboat drew closer to the rocks, she saw the singers were not seals. She tried to open her mouth to speak, but words refused to come out. The creatures draped over the rocks looked human. But as one slipped into the sea, she saw it possessed a scaly tail. They drew close. Three pretty maidens smiled serenely from their rocky perches, golden ringlets of tumbling to their shoulders. Ingrid was right; they did possess tails. She had heard about these beings in stories her seafaring grandfather told. They were mermaids beckoning the crew to join them on their rocks. Ingrid sensed the danger and tried to call to Eric. Again, no words came as the enthralled helmsman set his course for collision.

The choir of mermaids sang sweetly as the Viking longboat crunched on top of a jagged outcrop. It rose out of the water, timbers splitting, and rolled over. Ingrid was dragged under the surface, water filling her lungs. She coughed, spluttered and struck out wildly, grabbing a wooden spar torn from the boat. The tide dashed her against the rocks before sweeping her out again. Ingrid's frail body bobbed on the surf like a floundering fish.

A pair of arms wrapped gently around her waist. She rolled over to find a beautiful maiden supporting her. The girl smiled before twisting round with a flap of her tail to bear Ingrid to the depths. The Viking girl blacked out. It was several hours before she became conscious. Her head swam with confused images. When she opened her eyes, she imagined she was in the middle of a nightmare.

'Where am I?'

Her frightened voice echoed round a damp cave. Only a trace of green-blue light penetrated. The deep rumble of tide filled the cavern. She lay on a rock bed of seaweed. Stunned, Ingrid peered into the dim light. A pretty face looked into her misty eyes.

'I don't know your name.'

The mermaid hauled herself out of the water and slid up to her.

'You're one of the fortunate ones. You survived. Now your troubles are over. You will remain with us for always. One day you may become like we are.'

Ingrid shivered in the bleak gloom. It was so hard to see even a small distance. The sea continued to thunder into the cavern.

'Your friends are here,' the maid continued. 'Not all, of course. We did our best to rescue, but many are lost. In any case, how could we keep you all? The cavern isn't large.'

She smiled sweetly.

'I'm sure we can be friends.'

Ingrid's eyes were getting used to the dark. She could just make out the female half-human, half-fish who sat close by. The mermaid's hair fell almost to her waist, where it met the fishy scales of her tail. Her face and arms were pale. She smiled serenely. Yet Ingrid suspected coldness in her green eyes. She understood she was held a prisoner with no way out.

Cold drops of water dripped from the roof. They hit the hard floor, echoing around the walls. The young captive was aware of other people trapped close by. In the dim light, she saw prone bodies lying over the floor. One person groaned and rolled over. Another called out feebly. Ingrid recognised the timid voice.

'Is anyone there?'

Ingrid dragged herself up onto her knees and peered into the blackness.

'Astrid, is that you?'

The mermaid edged closer. She wished to keep the two friends apart.

'Don't distress yourself. Your friends must rest.'

Ingrid slumped onto her bed of damp seaweed, wondering who might be sharing her ordeal. The mermaid tried to comfort her.

'No harm will befall you. Regard yourself as our guest. We will bring you news of your old world. Occasionally, we spot a boat like yours passing by. That's when we sing. Other sailors have visited this cavern before you. It's so sad. They pine for sunshine and fresh air. In the end, they lose heart and die. We have to replace them. This is why you are here.'

Ingrid could not have felt more miserable. How could she survive in this gloom? Escape was impossible. With the sea roaring in at the entrance she would be dashed to pieces on the rocks. Another figure stirred on a ledge close by.

'Ingrid, it's me . . . Lief! I've swallowed so much water, I feel sick. How many of us are here?'

The young prisoner's heart leapt.

'I can see you,' she cried. 'It's just you, me, and Astrid.'

She crawled across the hard rock floor and felt for Lief's chilled hand. He grasped it weakly.

'It was the singing. It was spellbinding. I tried calling to Eric, but he'd been taken. Our beautiful boat broke in half. Most of the rowers drowned. We're the lucky ones.'

He paused and shivered in the oppressive blackness.

'If you call this luck,' he added.

The long hours passed slowly, but neither captive had much idea of the time. Mermaids slipped in and out of the cavern to view their new captives.

'We've brought you shellfish,' they said. 'Mussels from the rocks and cockles from the sand.'

As time wore on, the survivors linked up. Vimp remained half-conscious, hardly knowing what was going on. Emma lay bruised and sore, whilst Eric sat huddled in a sad hump, refusing to communicate. Bjorne too had managed to stay alive, but he was distressed to discover his friend Tharg had drowned. To Ingrid's relief, Freya had survived. So now it was just the eight; all the others had perished. Lief tried to raise their low spirits after the mermaids slipped out.

'We can't stay here,' he said. 'I've no idea how we got here. But if there's a way in, there's a way out. The mermaids know the secret.'

Lief had already worked out the escape route had to be under water.

'Bjorne and I are up for exploring,' he said. 'When we're on our own, we can dive and find out. It'll be dangerous when the tide floods in. But when it's at its lowest we might discover a way out.'

He sounded more confident than he felt. Diving in pitch blackness was just about the most perilous activity he could think of. But there was no choice. Remaining in the underwater dungeon meant certain death.

Days went by, although the captives could not calculate how many. Lief had worked out the mermaids returned for longer periods at night. During the day, they preferred to sun themselves on the rocks.

Eric was miserable at this time, remaining in his dark corner, refusing to speak. Vimp crawled up to him.

'Why are you taking it out on yourself? It wasn't your fault we ended up on the rocks. We were all under the mermaids' trance. No one could resist their singing. You're not to blame.'

He slipped a damp arm round Eric's shoulder. The longboat helmsman tried to speak through his tears.

'Of course it was my fault. I was weak and let the music get to me. I tried to resist, but my mind went blank. It's a terrible thing to lose a boat and half your crew.'

Gentle Astrid joined the two boys. She felt for Eric's cold hand.

'Vimp's right. You know that. It would have happened to anyone steering.'

But Astrid knew the real reason for the deep sadness at the bottom of Eric's heart.

'You're missing your beloved Beowulf,' she whispered. 'That's the bit that really hurts.'

Eric's head slumped. Suddenly he let out a howl of anguish. It echoed around the cavern. Astrid and Vimp held him tight. The big, brave Viking boy who had been in so many scrapes could not stand the pain of his terrible loss.

There was a sudden flurry at the water edge and two mermaids appeared with handfuls of shellfish.

'Time to eat!' they trilled merrily. 'We hope you're settling in. It's lovely having your company. Please stay as long as you wish!'

Few of the captives found they could face another meal of uncooked seafood.

'We're just popping out to the rocks!'

The mermaids, unaware of the distress of their guests, dived deep and swam out of the cavern. The survivors moved together to keep each other warm. Moments later, a familiar voice sounded from the swirling water.

'Hello, folks! I've been searching all over. Got talking to the mermaids. You know what they're like. Chitter chatter, chitter chatter! Never stop. Bad as my wife, I can tell you.'

It was Murrough, cheerful as ever. There was a short pause whilst he dived to fill his gills before popping up again.

'I've been sniffing around,' he went on. 'Found a secret way in. Same way out, of course. Just one problem . . . '

He dived again.

'You're too large to squeeze through. One of you needs to take a look. Who's the best swimmer?'

The captives were dumbstruck. Vimp recovered first as Murrough turned and dived. He waited impatiently for his return.

'Bjorne's the strongest swimmer,' he said. 'He can hold his breath for ages.'

Vimp could just make out Bjorne's figure crouching in the dark. The deputy helmsman was up for it.

'I'll do anything to escape, Murrough. I can't get any wetter. Tell me what I have to do.'

Murrough invited Bjorne to join him but requested that he stay close. It involved a short underwater swim. After that, Murrough explained, they would find a side cavern which led to the light. But there was an obstacle, which was what Murrough wanted Bjorne to examine. Without further discussion, Bjorne slipped into the water.

'Take care,' called Ingrid. 'Don't take any risks!'

Murrough advised taking a deep breath. When they emerged, Bjorne found what the merman had said was true. They were in a second, narrower cavern. He blinked in the welcome light streaming through the entrance. However, as he approached it, he saw the problem Murrough could not solve. Thick iron bars reached down from the ceiling to below water level. The spaces between were little wider than Bjorne's clenched fist. It was a cruel blow. However hard he wrenched at the bars they would not to shift. Freedom and light were within his grasp yet he remained a prisoner.

'See the problem?' said Murrough. 'I can squeeze through, but not even Freya or Astrid could do that. You'll have to come up with a brilliant idea! *Think away*, my friend!'

With that, he took his customary dive, leaving Bjorne alone with the problem.

Chapter 16

A Place to Settle?

Bjorne's return to the main cavern did not raise the captives' spirits.

'I'm sorry,' he told them. 'Murrough expected too much. He's found an escape route, but it's cut off by thick iron bars. I couldn't shift them. He suggested I reported back as one of you might come up with a bright idea. But what we really need are hammers and saws. They went down with the boat. Murrough doesn't have the strength to fetch them. He's too spindly. But give him credit; he means well.'

Freya listened carefully.

'If I've got it right, we've got to break those bars. Now, we have four strong boys. You could find lumps of rock and beat them 'til they bend.'

Vimp and Lief were willing to give it a go, although not keen on the underwater swim. Eric sat apart, showing no interest. His spirit was broken and he wanted to be left alone. Vimp crawled up to him and did not mince his words.

'You're not helping, Eric. No one's a strong as you, yet you're doing nothing. What about Astrid? D'you want her to be locked up for the rest of her life?'

Vimp grew angry.

'I think you're pathetic. You've blown!' he snorted angrily. 'Eric Bignose, the brave, bold Viking? I don't think so!'

The former helmsman swung round and punched Vimp on the chin. He scrambled to his feet to do more damage, but Astrid moved over in the bleak light and begged Eric to stop. She grabbed his arm just as he was about to deliver his next blow. He slipped on a strand of seaweed and tumbled over.

'Don't try me!' he cried. 'I'm stressed.'

His friends backed off. Eric swallowed his pride and offered Vimp his hand.

'I'm sorry. I blew. I'm with you. Show me the way!'

This lifted the captives' spirits. With Eric on board, anything was possible. Minutes later, the three boys led by Bjorne, braved the underwater channel to surface in the secret cavern. They examined the bars but were disappointed to find they refused to budge. Eric went in search of a stray lump of rock. He staggered towards the cage and brought the rock down hard. It shattered in pieces, making no impact on the bars. The boys took turns trying to bend the iron, but the bars remained in place.

Vimp called for a rest. He could not face going back to the girls with the bad news. A sudden disturbance in the water caught his eye. Illuminated by a thin beam of sunlight was the little Murrough. He was surprised to see all four boys.

'I heard the racket you're putting up. Be careful. Sound travels. We don't want those mermaids interfering. That would put an end to your escape plans.'

He plunged back under for a breather, but it was not long before he splashed up again.

'As I was saying, no noise or brute force. We need to think this one out!'

Eric, who had performed much of the hard work, was in no mood for lectures from a half-fish.

'If you're so smart, Murrough, why don't you come up with the answer? You should have warned us about mermaids. Even I've heard tales about their singing. Except I thought it was all rubbish.'

CRISP 2010

Murrough cocked his big fishy eye at Eric. He almost seemed to smile.

'Well, perhaps I *can* come up with the answer. If you get nearer to the bars, I'll show you.'

The boys crowded round as Murrough swam out.

'I'll be back!'

Vimp had no idea of what he was up to. Was he just 'talk'? But it was not long before the merman re-appeared and asked the boys to look into the light. As they did so, a dark shadow fell across the cavern. A large, hairy paw reached in, from outside, and closed round the nearest bar. Vimp noticed curved, black claws gripping the metal. A second paw grasped the next bar. It was not long before both began to give way. Little by little, they were being pulled apart. Just enough for a slim human to slip through.

Eric watched in disbelief as the gap widened. Was he imagining things? A furry muzzle poked through the damage, followed by the familiar face of a very wet bear. Its little black eyes scoured the dim interior. Eric groped forward and touched the bear he knew so well. Beowulf grunted delightedly. It was a triumphant moment for Murrough.

'Don't ever tell me fish have no brains,' he said sparkily. 'Get back to those girls and bring them here right now. The mermaids may return at any time. You've not a moment to lose.'

Vimp came alive and issued instructions.

'Eric, stay with Beowulf. If it's possible, make the gap wider. We might get two out at a time.'

Back in the major cavern, the girls plucked up courage to face the underwater dive. When they came up for air, in the new cavern, they were stunned by the light. Astrid thought she was dreaming. Silhouetted behind the bars was the bulky figure of a large bear. Vimp was in no mood for happy reunions.

'Look sharp!' he ordered. 'Ingrid, you go first.'

One after the other, the girls squeezed through to escape. Vimp chose to leave last. They were out!

'Keep down,' he urged. 'Crawl along that ledge covered in seaweed. Not a word from anyone.'

Little Murrough swam gamely alongside, worrying about the punishment he would suffer if the mermaids discovered his treachery. The thought of facing fearsome Mrs Murrough made him kick faster.

Eric was amazed at the size of Beowulf. The bear seemed to have grown nearly into an adult in the short time since the wrecking. It was inexplicable. The escapers struggled on, splashing through rock pools and keeping a wary lookout. To their dismay, they stumbled across bits and pieces of the longboat. Shattered timbers lay scattered along the shoreline. Yet the party was in for a spot of luck.

'Over there!'

Bjorne drew Lief's attention to a pile of debris, washed up on the shore.

'Is that a water barrel? A couple of crates – food, maybe?'

The mermaids were not to be seen, so Bjorne led the escapers to the booty. Whilst they sifted through, Vimp and Eric stood guard. The sooner they got away from the rocks, the better. Vimp noticed a winding stream running down from the hill above.

'We'll strike inland,' he ordered. 'Pick up what you can and follow me.'

He took the first step only to be called back by Lief.

'What should we do about Murrough?

Lief sensed the little merman wanted to stay with his new companions. But how would the fragile fish-man cope out of water? He would never make it up the slope. Bjorne knew what to do.

'We left an empty barrel back on the rocks. Someone come with me. We'll half-fill it with water and drag it up between us.'

Eric volunteered. With Beowulf padding after him, he helped Bjorne dip the barrel into the sea. After all, it was Murrough who had rescued the young voyagers. Stocked with a plentiful supply of seaweed, the merman settled down as his two slaves dragged it along. The short episode had given Lief and Vimp time to consider the next step. They had no idea of the size of the island, but they knew they had to explore. The sun sank in the early evening. Reaching the brow of the hill, Freya stopped everyone in their tracks.

'Look' she hissed. 'Over the next hill – smoke!'

Her pulse quickened.

'We're not alone.'

The hungry escapers did not know what to think. Their spirits were still low after the shock of the shipwreck. Now they had little fight left. Bjorne and Eric plonked down Murrough's water barrel. The others gathered round to discuss what to do. There was little choice. In their Viking hearts, they knew their only chance was to make contact. Freya took up the challenge.

'It's a risk,' she said. 'Massive. We must find out.'

It was agreed they would reach the crest of the hill, where they would make their final decision. Climbing proved tough. The youngsters were weak with hunger, whilst Bjorne and Eric had to drag Murrough's heavy load. Vimp was first to reach the brow and crouched in the heather. The others slid alongside to peer over the top. They looked down on a small cluster of primitive stone dwellings. Rough, low thatches acted as roofs to keep out the rain. They were tied down by ropes, fixed to the ground by heavy stones. Small, bent figures cut slabs of brown peat from a nearby bog. Once dried, it would act as fuel to heat the huts. Hardy looking sheep nibbled at grass covering the hillside. And beyond the simple homes, other folks worked on the thin soil, digging and picking vegetables. Vimp turned to Freya and Lief.

'I suggest the three of us go down to speak to them. We're only going to perish up here on the hill. If we can make ourselves understood, these people might not be hostile.'

Freya thought back to the time when she and Tharg had tried to contact the hostile Vikings in her old village. They had ended up prisoners. Vimp's plan was just as risky.

'We'll go down as a group,' she advised. 'Then they'll know how many we are. We're hardly a threat!'

The scheme appealed to Lief.

'She's right. Let's face it. We don't look very fierce!'

Vimp got everyone to their feet. He agreed that the starving group did not appear menacing. They were a band of unarmed teenagers, helpless and lost. Nevertheless, their hearts were in their mouths as they set off.

Two sheep turned and scattered, setting off another pair. The movement caught the attention of the peat-diggers, who glanced up from their work. A child sped back to the huts to raise the alarm. Moments later, dogs barked and people streamed out. Men hurried from hut to hut or ran in from the fields. The youngsters stopped halfway as the settlers came out, brandishing weapons. They held stout shields and lined up, ready to do battle.

'Keep going!' Vimp ordered, although doubting they were doing the right thing. 'They can see we're not armed.'

This was easier said than done. The men at the foot of the hill moved up. Women held their children back. One thickset fellow strode in front of his comrades, long hair tumbling over his shoulders. He raised his sword and called out.

'He's telling us to come no further,' Lief said. 'What are we supposed to do?'

It was the trickiest decision Vimp ever had to make.

'We go on. Eric and Bjorne, put Murrough's barrel down. Everybody raise their hands above their shoulders. Show these people we mean no harm.'

The opposing forces moved suspiciously towards each other. Now, the hard faces of the men could be seen, stern and forbidding. As they advanced, they held the wooden shields across their chests.

Their intentions were obvious. Freya dashed forward a few paces. She did not know what language the people spoke, but it hardly mattered.

'We are friends,' she called out in her native Norse. 'We have no weapons.'

She turned and gestured towards the defenceless party.

'We come in peace!'

The leader stopped the advance of his men whilst the youngsters stayed routed to the spot. Frey, however, continued down the hillside. As the ground levelled, she broke into a run, blond hair flying in the wind. Only paces away, the leading man dropped his sword and shield. She flung herself into his outstretched arms. A cheer went up from the men, who put down their weapons before ploughing up the hill.

'Freya? Is that you?'

Chieftain Harald and his beloved daughter clung to each other. Tears of joy rolled down the Viking leader's cheeks. Women gathered round, thrilled at the unexpected reunion. Then they ran up the slope to greet their long lost children. Lief's mother flung her arms round the son. She believed she would never see again. Bjorne was nearly bowled off his feet as his father cannoned into him. A wild-looking woman singled out Eric. She eyed him up and gave him a loud telling off.

'Where've you been, you naughty boy? Your father has had to do all the fishing by himself. You always were a difficult lad. Oh, I could . . . I could . . .'

She enveloped her son in her arms and smothered him with kisses.

'Eric Bignose,' she wept, 'it's a good thing I love you!'

The tall Viking lifted his mother off her feet and swung her round.

'I'm so sorry, mother!' he said, laughing. 'It just seemed like a good idea at the time.'

When his mother's feet touched earth, she was horrified to find herself confronted by a large brown bear. Eric plonked her on Beowulf's back. She demanded to be put down.

'I'm not having this bear in my hut,' she protested. 'Whoever heard of such a thing? It would be uncivilised!'

Eric lifted her down.

'He's too good for that. Beowulf will have his own hut. And if he's willing, I'll share it with him!'

Sadly, the joy of all the youngsters was not shared. Vimp soon realised his parents were not amongst the happy throng. What had happened to them? His younger brother explained.

'Our mother and father were lost at sea,' he said. 'In a storm. We're orphans, Vimp. You and me.'

Emma stood quietly to one side. She was the only young survivor who had no one to greet her. Her Saxon family were back in England. Lief sensed her sadness and asked her over to meet his mother and father.

'You remember the Chieftain's slave, Emma? The Saxon girl who was going to be sacrificed?'

He looked his parents in the eye.

'From now on, you have a new daughter.'

Lief's mother looked fondly at Emma and welcomed her in her arms.

'You're family now, Emma. Live with us!'

Ingrid and Astrid hung onto their parents' arms. The delighted party made their way down the hillside. Soon they reached the heart of the hamlet, where other Vikings gathered round. Freya walked hand in hand with Vimp. Chieftain Harald kept with them.

'Vimp's been a brother to me,' said Freya. 'Far more than that. He saved my life.'

Her father beamed down on them both.

'We'd be proud if you will share our humble dwelling, young Vimp.'

He took his daughter's arm and led her away.

'Freya, there's someone you haven't seen yet. Since landing here, your mother's not been well. Go in and talk to her. You're the very best thing that could have happened. Be gentle,' he urged. 'Seeing you will come as a great surprise.'

He turned to Vimp.

'We'll let the young lass handle this,' he said. 'Her mother's frail, but she'll mend.'

Vimp and the Chieftain strode past the stone huts cowering under the hill.

'You must tell me everything, young man. From start to finish. Your friends were never far from our thinking.'

Vimp understood.

'We missed you too, you know.'

The Chieftain looked at the boy kindly.

'Maybe you taught us all a lesson. Later, we learned to respect the wishes of boys who didn't want to become warriors. Vikings have been responsible for so much slaughter over the years. From now, it must cease.'

Vimp asked what had become of Olaf Skullcrusher, the warrior trainer the boys feared most.

'The coward's not with us,' Chieftain Harald scoffed. 'When the village was attacked by wild Norsemen, Olaf Skullcrusher was the first to flee. He escaped to the forest. We think the wolves might have taken him.'

They walked on.

'I shall never forgive myself,' Harald continued. 'I was Chief when our village was overrun. The Norsemen meant to trade us with primitive people, even further North. We were to be swapped as slaves for seal and bear skins.'

Harald and Vimp wound slowly out of the hamlet to circle the fields. The Chieftain explained how a frightful storm had separated the boats of their captors. After battling with tides and winds, their own longboat foundered on rocks. They had no choice but to settle on this wild, windswept island.

'We were fortunate,' Harald went on. 'We stumbled upon a colony of Vikings already settled here with animals – sheep, pigs, geese. They made us welcome. We lead a hard life. In winter, there are only a few hours of light in the day. The long nights can be very dreary. That's when we sing and tell tales around the fire.'

He smiled and gazed up the hill.

'Of course, this will never be like our old homeland. But we're alive and free. Home is what you make of it.'

Vimp did his best to fill in the Chieftain on the adventures he and his friends had experienced. He told him of the return to the old village, occupied by hostile warriors. And the shock at not finding their families.

'There's a lot to catch up on,' Harald agreed as they approached the huts. 'I don't think we'll be short for time. You and your pals can entertain us on those winter evenings.'

A small crowd had formed at the centre of the settlement. Young children buzzed with excitement at the sight of little Murrough swimming in his water butt. They were equally enchanted by the large brown bear keeping strict guard on his friend. Already, preparations for celebrations were underway. Men gathered wood to light a fire and roast two sheep for the feast. And women prepared chopped vegetables for the steaming cauldron. Eric drew Vimp to one side.

'Having a fire's a great idea. It's the best thing we've seen for ages. But is it sensible? There's not much wood about. They're even using planks from the boats that ran onto the rocks.'

Vimp did not see what his great friend was getting at.

'Tomorrow morning,' Eric told him, 'the bear and I will search the shore for timbers. We might even find the odd box of tools washed up. I reckon we owe it to these folks to build a boat before they burn all their wood! Then we can explore the local islands and maybe sail across to the mainland.'

Setting out on another adventure was the last thing Vimp planned. All he now wanted to do was settle, and learn about farming.

'The sea's in my blood,' Eric went on. 'I can't help it. Whatever it throws at me, I'll be out there battling. It's what I'm meant to do!'

Vimp slung an arm round the proud Viking's shoulders.

'We'll see what Astrid has to say about that,' he grinned. 'Although I don't suppose even she could stop you.'

Eric burst out laughing.

'Exactly! And when I finish my first boat I'll name it *Beowulf*!'

The brave voyagers enjoyed that night's celebration around the fire. They told their tall tales like good Vikings. Except, in their case, they were all true.

Next morning, bear and master set out for the beach. Eric tugged a barrel of sea water behind him. At a suitable rock pool, he lifted out Murrough.

'This one's perfect, Murrough,' he told the small merman. 'We'll watch out for the tide so you don't get swept away. And when we've finished we'll carry you back to the huts.'

The merman dived towards the nearest strand of olive seaweed to find his breakfast. As Eric searched the shore for washed-up timbers, the bear snuffled noisily around for shellfish. But Beowulf's black eyes kept a close watch on the sea. He was ready to act if a bossy mermaid turned up, demanding her husband's return. One quick snap of the bear's jaws would drive the unpleasant creature away!

Epilogue

Many years later, a small party of settler Vikings climbed the hill. At the crest, some of the older children raced over to two stacks of rocks. These had been erected by the villagers, one higher than the other. Freya cradled her new baby in her arms and watched her older daughter run round the back of the smaller pile. Her husband looked on. Vimp was the new Chieftain of the community. Next to him, Lief and Emma linked arms. A toddler perched on Lief's shoulders.

'Be careful, Asvald,' Emma called as one of the children tumbled over.

He scrambled to his feet with a cheeky grin. Lief smiled at Bjorne and Ingrid who stood close by. Only Astrid lacked a strong man by her side. She gripped the hand of a sturdy eight-year-old boy.

'You see the larger stack, young Eric? We built that to honour your father. It's from him you take your name. But his body doesn't lie beneath it.'

She gazed thoughtfully out to sea.

'It was never found.'

Tall and serious for his age, the boy glanced up.

'I'm proud of my father,' he said. 'People say he was brave. He rescued sailors stranded in a storm. Then he swam out a second time.

The boy's expression clouded.

'He was swept away by a big wave.'

Astrid slipped her arm around the child and held him tight. They walked over to the smaller mound.

'Under that one is buried Beowulf, your father's bear. He lost the will to live after his master failed to return. Now their memorials lie side by side.'

She looked over the bay and pointed to an elegant longboat beached on the shore. The man she adored had been its designer, builder and helmsman.

'D'you see the prow? The carved figure of a handsome bear?'

The boy nodded, gravely.

A dark shadow flitted briefly across the gathering. Astrid turned her beautiful face to the sky where a mighty sea eagle circled beneath the clouds. The bird spread its wings and swept low over the heads of the settlers. The young mother watched the eagle lift high over the cliffs. She raised her arm and waved.

Astrid needed no telling. She knew.

Also by Peter Ward
The Adventures of Charles Darwin
ISBN 978-1-4251-4253-7
Cambridge University Press
Re-printed in paperback 2008
(Illustrated; age range 9-12)

'Children's writing at its best'
Nature Magazine
'An excellent introduction for young readers'
Times Literary Supplement
'If Darwin sounds a bit heavy for children, think again'
The Sun, Australia
'A minor classic'
Junior Librarian

Musical for Stage

'The Viking's Song'
By Michael Fields and Peter Ward
(Adapted from the first book in this Trilogy)

Details on author web site: www.peter-ward.net
including youTube demonstration video

An eclectic mix of music. Early instruments such as gemshorns,
cow horn, kantele (zither) and six-stringed lyre. Lyrical songs –
solos, duets etc. Heavy Rock numbers and a Viking calypso!
For Upper Secondary (High School) or University/College performance.
Also adaptable to main stage Theatre Repertory Companies.

Enquiries for score via author web site

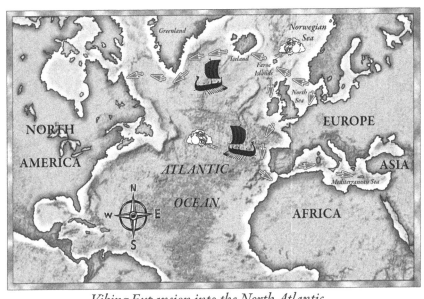

Viking Expansion into the North Atlantic